Bach Again
Copyright © 2013 Joseph W. Bebo
Published by Joseph W. Bebo
(An imprint of JWB Books Publishing)

Joseph W. Bebo
PO Box 762
Hudson, MA, 01749
Email: joewbebobooks@gmail.com
Editor: James Oliveri
Interior and Cover Design: Elyse Zielinski

Library of Congress Cataloging in –Publication Data
Joseph W. Bebo
Bach Again /Joseph Bebo – First Edition

ISBN: 978-0-9819724-8-0
1.   Techo-Thriller; Science-Fiction
Printed and bound in the United States of America

Bach Again

Joseph W. Bebo

Prologue

Dear Brother

    Finally, the great wind-bag is gone. He who has caused our family so much grief and misery will humiliate us no more. The curse has ended. Though the world mourns his passing we rejoice, for it is we who made it so. The arrogant effrontery to tradition, to the ways of our forefathers and the holy church, could be no longer borne. The overly complicated sounds of the devil have been silenced, we pray forever. And so we pledge to erase his name from the annals of history and his music from the halls of time. Never again will it pollute the air. Never again will it disturb our tranquility. Wherever a piece of manuscript of his exists we will scrape it up and hide it for all time in the bowels of the earth. Where his body lies, we will steal it and hide it so that no one well ever find him. His family will go without our aid, his music made light of by our teachers. And so it will be, from now to the end of time, as long as one of our blood may live to carry on.

JAE

Leipzig University, August 1750

Chapter 1

David Reid was at the peak of his career, the top of his profession, all at the tender age of twenty-six. He was not only the most renowned of the current crop of international maestros, conductors, and composers. Thanks to the adulation of the media and fans he was world famous, his services demanded by the most prestigious orchestras and studios in the US and Europe. Although known as a child prodigy on the keyboard, no one could have foreseen the heights he was to achieve and the revolutionary impact he was to have on music itself, no one that is except for his father, John Reid. John was not the least bit surprised by his son's achievements. Although never one to brag, he knew something about his son that no one else did, and swore to take his secret with him to the grave.

David made his way into the city through the busy midday traffic. He was having difficulty keeping his mind on the road and his Roadster under the speed limit, as he'd had trouble sleeping the night before. Today was the first in a progression of days leading to what would be the most important day of his life, which was saying a lot, for David's young life had been nothing if not eventful.

One could just as easily say the day he was appointed director of the New York Philharmonic, the youngest ever, at the age of twenty-three, was a great day; or the debut of his groundbreaking series of string quartets at eighteen, which stunned the music world; or his hit Broadway musical that launched him on the road to fame and fortune. Those too were the greatest of days, but they were only preludes, mere hints at what was to come. It would all reach a crescendo in the next two weeks, as he rehearsed the orchestra for his newest creation.

He tried to calm his nerves as he came up too fast behind a slower moving driver, dawdling in the left lane when they should have been moving speedily to their destination. He wasn't sure why he was so nervous. This was only a rehearsal, the first of many. Only the musicians and a few assistants would be there, not one critic within miles. Still, it felt to David like a first night debut. Perhaps it was because this was the first time his new piece would actually be played by an orchestra. It was like the birth of something he had labored at far longer than a mere nine months. It felt like he had been working on it all his life. He rubbed his eyes with fatigue.

Consciously relaxing, he pulled over to the right-most lane, where he'd be lucky to reach fifty mph. Let them wait. There was no rushing the birth of creation. It took its own sweet time. It came when it was ready and went just as fast. It was one thing to write music for fun, to pass the time when inspiration happened to touch you. It's entirely another matter to create something on commission, when someone's paying for your time and wants it performed at a specific date, with professional singers and players waiting on the clock as well. Then that blank piece of manuscript looks like an endless pit that you have no hope of filling, let alone with something good. Then the pressure mounts and creativity, especially the refined kind David was dealing with, is throttled like a skinny-necked chicken. At least for some, but David Gordon Reid was not the usual type of composer.

It all came so naturally to him that it was like someone had made a pact with the devil. He had such a facility, such a gift for composition that music flowed out of him almost as fast as he could pen it on the staff. He never had to search for a melody or harmonic progression. Whenever he needed something musical it was there. The harmonies and melodies flowed from him like lava, and what music, the music of the ages. It was as if he heard it fully composed and orchestrated, heard it whole in his head, which was in fact what he did.

You'd think David would have been at the top of the world, enjoying his success and fame, glorying in the joy his gifts spread to those who heard his music or saw him perform, but David was far from happy. At times he was downright despondent. It wasn't that he didn't enjoy what he did. He loved his work and was thankful for his gifts, but there was something missing from his life. Perhaps it was the failed marriages and the loneliness they brought in their wake, or maybe it was something deeper. How could he have a normal relationship when his life had never been normal?

There was no one since perhaps Lenny Bernstein, who combined musical talents together like he did, conducting, performing, composing, serious music and popular, but even Bernstein didn't reach the levels achieved by David Gordon Reid, an acknowledged master of each discipline and a truly revolutionary composer.

His personality certainly didn't help his peace of mind. Combative and self-assertive, he was often considered rude and arrogant by those who didn't know him, and even some who did. His inability to take an insult or suffer fools didn't help win him friends, and the pressure he was under much of the time just made it worse, as his countless failed personal relationships would attest.

David was now between marriages, just finishing up the less than friendly divorce of his third wife. It had started out well enough. Sue had been the most promising of them all. Understanding and loving, she had done everything she could to make him happy and give him a home. They even talked about having a family, but she too soon became a widow to his music and his fame. He saw her on weekends and between concert dates and world tours, when work and his hectic schedule would allow, which didn't leave much time for her and the other half-dozen scattered women he was seeing. Only David's immense salary and royalty fees from his conducting and recordings could bear the vast cost of supporting the three neglected ex-wives he left in his wake. He had added many regrets to the baggage of his success and it was starting to wear him down.

He pulled into the garage beneath the concert hall and into his reserved space. He could have hired a chauffer-driven limousine like just about every other conductor of his stature but he preferred to be behind the wheel, in control, like he felt in front of an orchestra.

There was nothing like the power of a hundred musicians of the best caliber playing a piece of one of the masters, like Beethoven or the more modern Mahler, someone who really understood the orchestra and knew how to make it soar. The surge of sound could carry you away and was downright intoxicating. He had finished pieces so emotionally drained and enraptured that he could not move when the music ended, he was so transfixed by the beauty of it. It could transcend time and place, and bring tears of joy to a grown man's eyes. At times like these you were beyond yourself, as if sitting in the audience listening with the others, and just as astounded.

Today would be nothing like that. A first rehearsal is rough and ready, a coming to know the piece for the first time, getting acquainted and making new friends – or enemies - as the case may be. David knew it would be a love affair, but only after the pangs and tribulations of birth. His eyes felt heavy from lack of sleep. He rubbed them again and gulped down the rest of his coffee.

Grabbing his bag, he jumped out of the car, slammed the door, and headed for the elevator. He was late and his mood was improving with the anticipation of hearing his creation come to life. He was moving at a good pace when he was suddenly overcome with dizziness and a sharp pain over his eyes. He stopped dead in his tracks and held his head, opening his eyes wide in the attempt to steady himself. Grabbing the hood of the vehicle he was passing, he held on for dear life, waiting for the attack to pass. This had never happened to him before.

The vertigo was intense, the pain in his eyes severe. He fought down the urge to vomit. Where had this come from? He was already late, so he tried to move on, but almost fell over, as if he had just stepped off a revolving platform. Finding the nearest pillar, he leaned against it for support. What could be happening to him?

He thought back to the previous evening. He had eaten in after an early date and a rather annoying conversation on the phone with his lawyer. Ralph was giving him a damage report, the results of his most recent matrimonial meltdown. He was so upset after the call that he had taken a pill to help him sleep. Never one of the soundest sleepers, he had usually been able to get eight hours more or less, but lately, some time near the completion of his last piece, he had begun waking up in the middle of the night and not be able to fall back to sleep. Sometimes four am, sometimes three, sometimes even earlier, it was beginning to worry him. Now on top of everything he was having dizzy spells and eye pain. He wondered if it might be the strain of work, just what he needed at a time like this. He'd have to talk to his doctor about those pills. Perhaps they were the problem.

He was starting to get his equilibrium back and made his way unsteadily to the elevator. He speculated on whether someone was trying to poison him, with a half smile, an inside joke he had with himself due to his penchant for making enemies. It wasn't because he was trying to. He genuinely liked people. At least he gave them the benefit of the doubt. It was just that he expected them to act in a rational way and give him all they had when they worked with him. It wasn't his fault many couldn't stand the pressure, or weren't up to his standards, or were envious of him. It wasn't his fault things came so easily.

As soon as he stepped out of the elevator he was mobbed by news cameras and the press, all greedy for a piece of him, for a sixty second shot on one early evening news journal or another.

"How do you like working with this new orchestra, Mister Reid?" asked one of them.

"How does it feel to have your own philharmonic?" asked another, alluding to the unprecedented power he had in selecting the personnel and the material performed, making it virtually his own personal orchestra to do with as he wished. Not even Toscanini had had such power.

"How come you're not allowing any music critics or the media into the rehearsals, Mister Reid? Isn't that a bit unusual?"

"Not at all, just the opposite," he answered, stopping to continue. "You've all been spoiled by the extravagances and habits of some my colleagues, who just can't get enough publicity. They have to open rehearsals to attract attention. This isn't just another replaying of Mozart or Beethoven, as wonderful as those things are, but the debut of a new twenty-first century symphony. It is to be simulcast worldwide, something never before done with a work of this kind. It is a highly complicated and ambitious piece that requires a double-orchestra and two choruses, and it will require a great deal of practice, repetition, and possibly some serious sweat and blood. It is like a birth, gentlemen, and who wants to watch something like that, unless maybe the proud father and even they have been known to pale and pass out at the sight. So you can understand my reluctance to subject the music public to that. I promise you, however, that on opening night it will all be worth the wait. I want it to be a surprise."

"Thank you gentlemen and ladies," said his manager, Mark Burns, with his tough Scottish accent, which reminded David of his childhood in Edinburgh. Mark took his boss's arm and directed him through the maze of cameras and lights. "The maestro is late and has a lot of work to do. I'll give you all a statement later in the day, if you just let us through here. Thank you, please…"

The men with microphones and questions reluctantly gave way as David and Mark made their way to the rehearsal hall.

"Where the hell have you been?" asked Mark, once they had passed the media, as if he were a stage manager talking to an errant stagehand. "You've got 100 highly paid musicians in there who've been waiting almost an hour. This is the first rehearsal. You really don't want to piss them off."

"Sometimes they play their best when they're pissed off. We'll see what it's going to be today," said David with an enigmatic smile. "Sometimes you have to give them a little tough love."

"You OK?" asked his business manager and the closest thing to a friend David Gordon Reid ever had. "You don't look so great."

"I'm fine, just a little headache, eye-strain perhaps. It will pass. Just get me a can of ginger-ale and some of those peanut-butter crackers I like."

"OK, David. I'll have them on the podium before you unfurl your mighty baton."

"Thanks Mark, and Mark…"

"Yes?"

"Make sure no one gets in here, no one."

"Don't worry. I'll make sure security's tight."

"Thanks. Wish me luck as I go into the lion's den."

"Good luck, but you have nothing to worry about. It's the lions who should be afraid. You'll do fine as always. They'll love you and the piece."

"Yeah, I wish I could be so sure."

He made his way into the concert hall by the central double front doors where the audience would enter, and walked down the long, sloping center aisle to the brightly lit stage. A few of his assistants and students were in the audience near the stage, while the musicians mingled on the platform where they had been waiting since one. The rest of the large auditorium was empty.

When they saw him approach, they all stopped what they were doing and clapped, as a sign of respect and admiration. Not a little of it was motivated by the hope he would be gentle with them and forgive them their failings. He could tell from their reception, however, that they were ready to give him their all. He hoped it would not be too painful.

His assistants scurried about, handing out parts and answering questions. One of them handed him the score, while the musicians all returned to their places. As promised, one of the students put a can of soda and a glass on the podium, with a couple packages of his favorite crackers. He had already forgotten the bout of dizziness with the anticipation of making music.

He greeted the orchestra, yelling hellos to many of the players, joking with others, waving and smiling. It was a love-fest, but that would be over as soon as the battle began. It was always a fight, wrestling the truth out of an orchestra, that subtle quality that determines an inspirational performance from an ordinary one. Problem was there was nothing new in music. It had all been done before - tonal, atonal, exotic scales, polyrhythmic, and polyphonic. It didn't matter. The number and variety of musical combinations is immense, but it isn't infinite. That is until David Gordon Reid came along.

He placed his satchel on the stool and took out a long leather case, from which he removed his baton. He tapped it on his music stand and instantly the large stage became quiet.

"I want to start in the middle," he said. "The eightieth bar of the third movement just before the stanza. There is some pretty difficult bowing for the strings in this section and I want to make sure we're all on the same page. This is the backbone of the movement."

He waited while the players found the spot he had in mind, the strings already nervous that they were being singled out for the conductor's attention. The rest of the orchestra sat relieved but somewhat miffed that they would be waiting even longer to get a chance to play as the string section rehearsed alone. It was going be a long afternoon for all of them.

"Notice the time change at the tenth measure, and the pizzicato. Pay attention to the bowing. It's everything. If we get it right it will be acoustically stunning. If we don't it will be a disaster. It's your choice. Ready?"

There were a few questions and clarifications, at one point David even taking one of the fiddles and demonstrating what he had in mind. They had all been given several weeks to go over the parts, alone and in ensemble, and the bowing instructions were very clear and explicit. But this was the first time they would be doing it all together in front of the composer, who was also the conductor, which just made everything more intense.

After another pause, David stood on the podium with both arms raised, the whole orchestra gazing at him expectantly. He looked directly at the string section, counted two measures with slight wrist movements of the baton, and gave them a solid down stroke with both arms to start them off. The tempo was moderate, slightly slower than he intended to perform it, but close enough to the real pace to capture the feel of the phrasing, while allowing them to learn the complex bowing. A good composer knows how to write for the different instruments of the orchestra. They are taught to understand what phrases and series of notes are more natural to play for which instrument. Some things are easier to perform on a particular apparatus and some things are just plain awkward to execute. What might be easy on a clarinet may be extremely difficult on a violin or trumpet. David's piece rewrote some of these rules.

The strings played the first four measures before David stopped them abruptly, as if he had been offended by the attempt.

"No, no, what are you doing?" he shouted. "That's not it at all. Can't you read simple instructions? You, second chair, third row," he said pointing to an unfortunate second viola player, a young female who quaked before him. "You're not even playing the right notes. Didn't you practice?"

David had intended to let them play it through, but he was surprised at how bad it sounded. What was being played was so far from what he should have heard that he could not let it go on one measure more without fixing it. Some would have to learn to play their instruments all over again.

The young woman tried to stammer something in defense, but David would have none of it, cutting her off rudely.

"Violas, alone, from the top of bar eighty," he yelled.

"Now, one, two, three," he counted off. They weren't all ready and started with a jagged screech. He stopped them before the second bar. "Again!" he shouted. "Together!"

"No, no, no," he stopped them again after four measures. "That's not even close. What are you doing?" He stared at them angrily. Some of the more seasoned of the musicians raised an eyebrow. They had seen a conductor meltdown during a rehearsal before, but usually not this quickly.

"Again, one at a time, starting with you there," he said pointing at his first unlucky victim. It only got worse from there. No one could do anything right. It was like he was out to break the orchestra's spirit, which can be the kiss of death for a conductor.

After he finished humiliating each and every one of the string players in turn, he started in on the brass section. It went like that all afternoon and into the evening, past the usual late afternoon break. Again and again, he'd have them play the same sections repeatedly, criticizing every attempt they made to play the piece. Like a martinet, he couldn't be pleased. He never gave them a chance to become acquainted with the overall work, but hammered them with details. Like he had predicted, it wasn't a very nice thing to watch, and several of the students left after the first hour.

When the musicians began to grumble he only worked them harder. Even David himself was surprised at how hard he was being on them, but like everything he did, he did it on instinct and for a reason. He had an inner conviction that this was how it had to be, because what he was attempting here was a musical revolution. It was a synthesis of techniques and styles of everything that had gone before but at the same time different, a new approach to the art that required retraining all these master musicians in the very art they were masters of, making them forget everything they knew. The music in them had to die before the music in him could be born.

Finally, at exactly 6:00 pm, in the middle of a very difficult passage where he had the whole orchestra endlessly repeat the same eight-bar phrase ad infinitum, he abruptly dismissed them and walked off the stage, leaving his assistants to deal with the perplexed, angry, and humiliated - not to mention hungry - musicians.

"Well that went well," said Mark Burns as he met David near the front of the auditorium. "What am I supposed to tell the press?"

"Tell them whatever you like," answered David. "I told you what it would be like."

"But when you played it for me on the piano it sounded so beautiful. You didn't give them a chance to hear it, to fall in love with it like I did."

"There's plenty of time for that," replied David, taking a towel and wiping his face. "Anyway, that was just the opening movement I played for you. That's the easy part. Now they have to relearn a few things. Why don't you have Ernie give everyone another hundred for the extra hour. Take it out of my account."

"That's mighty nice of you boss. That will smooth some feathers, I'm sure. I knew there was a method to your madness. Don't worry about the press boys, old Markey the spin doctor will take care of them." He walked off whistling as if he was the one getting a bonus instead of giving it out.

In his own mind, David wasn't so sure now if he had done the right thing, but when he thought again and realized that he was just being sentimental. He knew that playing his new music would take courage, some intestinal fortitude on the part of his musicians. It wasn't so much fear of what the critics or public would think, but something deeper, something more profound. His music required approaching the instruments in a new way. Not like someone who had played the thing for years, but like a child taking it up for the first time, although with the facility of all the actual years of practice. He was standing there thinking of this when one of his female assistants approached.

"You forgot this," she said, looking up at him and smiling. "You seemed to be driven this afternoon." She handed him his baton and case.

13

"Oh, thank you," he said taking both from her hands. Most of the musicians were still on the stage packing up their instruments. A few looked his way and muttered silent obscenities. He knew he had left his baton up there when he made his dramatic exit. He had wanted to make a statement. That it would no longer be business as usual. He knew they could play. He knew they were the best at what they did. That's why he had handpicked them. This wasn't the first time, after all, many of them had worked together, but this was different. This was something they'd never done before. This was a test, which if they could pass would make them into an orchestra of a truly different kind. However, now that he had made his point, he didn't want to go back to get his baton like a forgetful child. And here this wonderful young woman was bringing it to him. She couldn't have been a day over eighteen or nineteen.

"I would have noticed I'd forgotten it eventually," he laughed, "probably on the freeway halfway home. How can I thank you? Want to grab a bite to eat?"

Even as he heard himself go into his habitual banter with the comely student as he took his stick and put it back into its case, he was transported back in time to his early childhood, when he would stand in front of the radio conducting the music with a pencil. This is how it all began, he realized, and wondered if his life could ever have been different, if it could have ever been normal.

Chapter 2

David Gordon Reid was born in Edinburgh, Scotland in 1988, the son of an English biologist and his pious Scottish wife. The first thing he remembered - he must have been two or three at the time - was sitting on his father's lap being bounced in time to the music. He didn't know what piece it was, but later came to speculate that it must have been Johann Sebastian Bach, because that's practically all his father listened to. He was a regular aficionado of the great seventeenth century composer. That is when he wasn't at the institute doing research in the latest advances in biotechnology with his colleagues.

His father was also a talented amateur musician, playing the piano and organ, so his son picked up the instrument at a very early age, becoming a child prodigy by five. Those who heard him were amazed, but for some reason his father didn't want him to perform in public and did his best to avoid publicity. He was no elder Mozart wanting to exploit his son. It was almost as if he wanted to keep the boy's gift a secret.

It soon became obvious that David had more than keyboard talent, for he soon began writing his own piano pieces, playing the melody and counter melodies, jumping back and forth between parts, even adding the base lines, while every so often playing a chord for accompaniment. David was not yet eight years old. The music had an unusually beautiful and complex quality, which was stunning for someone so young. But again, he father did more to hide these talents than promote them.

David never knew why his father left Scotland, but one day, when he was ten years old, his dad came home and informed them he had gotten a position teaching in Boston, Massachusetts. They were leaving for the States in a week. David was thrilled. His mother was devastated, for she had a big, close family and the thought of leaving them distressed her greatly.

David left for Boston with his father on schedule. His mother was supposed to follow later, but never did. His parents got divorced over the mail. He later supposed they had probably agreed to do that all along, but just didn't want to upset to boy with too many changes at once.

David was snapped back to the present moment by an angry bus driver who almost sideswiped him as he sped past on the right, beeping. He looked at the comely, young assistant sitting next to him in the bucket seat of his sports coup. Part Oriental and part Caucasian, with an exotic look he found alluring, she filled out her tight sweater and short skirt to perfection. David wondered what she looked like underneath.

He had been so preoccupied with his daydreams of the past that he hardly remembered getting in the car with her. The more work and pressure he faced in the present, the more he seemed to dwell in the past.

"What do you say we skip the restaurant and go to my place," he suggested. "It's getting late. It'll be a mob scene wherever we go with the press and paparazzi. I'll cook us a couple steaks with mushrooms and onions. We'll sit by the fire and eat by candlelight. How does that sound?"

"Great," she said, wiggling closer to him and flashing him a smile that curled his toes.

David leased a good-sized penthouse in Manhattan overlooking Central Park, with a view of the city skyline. It had plenty of space and light, and provided the privacy he needed when writing, or pursuing other activities like tonight.

A few hours later, he was caressing her smooth backside as she slept. She was naked, lying on her stomach next to him in bed. He hadn't planned spending the night with her, but she was intoxicating. They had made love several times. She was certainly worth the trouble she was more than likely going to cause. One more notch in a string of one-night stands and affairs. He loved and hated women all at the same time, much like his relationship with his father. They got in the way, but also provided the intimacy and distraction he needed to get through his high-pressure life. He couldn't live without them.

He hoped today's rehearsal would go better than yesterday's. He made a mental note to lighten up a little and let them slosh their way through the piece before he started picking things apart. His bedmate began to respond to his caresses and turned over moaning.

"What time is it?" she purred.

"Quarter to seven, time to go," he answered. "I have a busy day. Want me to drop you off someplace?"

"No, I have a few things to do in town." She looked at him shyly. "Do you want to hook up later?"

"I don't know," he said, panicking and thinking fast. "I have to see my business manager tonight and go over some things for the concert. About last night, I…"

"You don't have to explain," said the young woman. He didn't even remember her name. "No big thing. Stuff happens."

He was grateful for her nonchalant attitude. Thank God for that. She certainly didn't strike him as the shy type.

"Are you sure I can't drive you somewhere? It's cold out there."

"No, the walk will do me good."

"Well, I'll see you around. You coming to rehearsal?"

"We'll see. Thanks for the wonderful evening."

Pulling on her sweater and skirt, and slipping on an expensive pair of shoes, Tina Fong was out the door before David had even pulled on his pants.

He looked at himself in the bathroom mirror and shook his head disapprovingly, feeling guilty and used at the same time. He wondered where his life was headed and why he felt so rootless, like he didn't' belong any place even though he had the city at his feet. The youngest, most powerful conductor in the Philharmonic's history; a world famous pianist, renowned composer; one Broadway hit still running and the music public waiting with baited breath for his new symphony; what more could he ask for? Suddenly, a serious classical composer was being followed like a rock star, his music playing on all the radio stations like Michael Jackson back in the eighties. If fame and fortune were what you longed for, David had it, but there is more to life than that. Exactly what that was, David Gordon Reid didn't have a clue.

He thought about his failed marriages and felt more guilty and caged than ever. Not a good way to face a difficult day. He had so much to do, so much to look forward to, but all he could do was think about the past. Perhaps all he ever really wanted was to be normal like everybody else, to fit in, but with his talent and gifts he was almost destined to be exceptional.

He had just finished putting on his sweater when there was a knock on the door. Two men in suits faced him when he opened it.

"Hello, Mister Reid. We're with the New York police department. We'd like to ask you a few questions regarding a missing person we've been looking for. Do you a Miss Donna Fredericks?"

"Yes," replied David, in alarm. "I know her casually. We've gone out a few times. You say she's missing?"

"Yes. She hasn't been seen in over a week and her family is very concerned. When was the last time you saw Miss Fredericks?"

"Last Saturday evening. We had dinner together at Gallaghers, around nine. Why?"

"Oh, just a routine question. She told her mother she was going out that evening. That was the last anyone heard from her before she disappeared. It appears you were the last person to see her."

"What did you do after dinner?" asked the second detective, silent until this point.

"We went to my apartment," David said with a sinking feeling.

"Did she stay overnight?" the man inquired.

David was tempted to ask them what business was it of theirs, but realized they were only doing their job.

"Yes," he replied slowly, "but she left the next morning. The door man can verify that, I'm sure."

"We'll check," the first cop assured him.

"You don't think anything has happened to her?" David asked with concern. "She's a sweet girl."

"How well did you know her?" continued the first man.

"Not well. A mutual friend introduced us. We met at a house party. Saturday was only our second date. I was just getting to know her. I hope she's all right."

"So do we. Her family says it's unusual for her not to call them every few days. She doesn't answer her phone and has never disappeared like this before. How did she seem to you when you last saw her? Did she act upset or scared?"

"No, she seemed perfectly normal. She did not appear to be the type of person who would take off like that, or get in trouble. She seemed quite intelligent and down to earth. She was a literary agent, I believe, and was looking forward to her next project."

"Do you know what that was?"

"She was working with a new author. She thought the manuscript was especially good, something about a man coming home after many years to care for his dying brother, real life stuff."

"Do you remember the author's name?" asked the first detective.

"No, but you should be able to find that out easy enough from the publisher."

They took notes and asked a few more standard questions before thanking him and leaving, handing him their cards on the way out.

"Call us if you think of anything else."

"Of course, I'll do anything I can to help," replied David. "I hope you find her. This is very distressing news."

As he drove to the concert hall David tried to focus his mind on the upcoming rehearsal and all he wanted to accomplish that day with the orchestra, but try as he may, his mind kept going back to the missing woman. What could have happened to her? He hoped it wasn't foul play, and began to wonder if the police suspected him of somehow being involved. That thought obliterated any hope he had of concentrating on the rehearsal. This was the last thing he needed on the threshold of his new symphony.

Chapter 3

He was met at the concert hall by his manager, Mark Burns.

"You look terrible. Didn't you get any sleep last night?" asked the wiry Scotsman. "You think it's wise to mess around with your assistants with this big divorce you've just been through? The news hounds will have a field day if they find out. You already have enough publicity."

"What do you want me to do, crawl into a hole? It's not my fault women throw themselves at me."

"Yeah, you're a regular rock star."

"The police were at the apartment this morning," David informed him. "You remember Don's friend, the one he introduced me to at his party."

"Not really. I can hardly keep track of all your flames. You're getting quite a reputation as a playboy."

"Well, she's missing. They were asking a lot of questions. It appears I'm the last person to see her."

"What did you tell them?"

"The truth. That we went out last Saturday, she stayed the night and left the next morning."

"Great, that's all we need."

Mark was David's only link with his childhood and his only friend. Hearing his thick Scottish accent always transported David back to the streets of Edinburgh where he grew up.

Despite all the activities he participated in as a kid – the full calendar of lessons and recitals; the long hours of practice and study - the thing he remembered most about his boyhood was the loneliness. His mother was too preoccupied with church activities and social crusades to spend any time with the boy, while his father, when not seeing to his musical training and education, was busy with his research at the institute. If it wasn't for his music, which he had a passion for, and his friend Mark, David would have been totally alone.

Mark's dad was the only person his rather eccentric and private father associated with, at least until they stopped talking over some disagreement shortly before David moved to the States. When their fathers were friends, Mark and his family would come over quite often.

The two boys, both the same age, became best friends, although they were complete opposites in most respects.

David was stout and on the heavy side, while Mark was small and wiry. Where John Reid's son was intellectual, a star student, Mark was physical and failed grades like wimps fail the Marine Corps. But they were suited to each other, each providing the right kind of stimulus and companionship the other needed.

Although David could take care of himself in a fight, he had the kind of arrogance and temper that frequently got him into more trouble than he could handle. It was then that he was happy to have Mark on his side. Sometimes he wouldn't even know he was there. Mark was like his guardian angel, watching out for him, always around when David needed him.

The first time he saw him in action, David was amazed. Mark could do things with his fists on an opponent like he could do with his hands on the piano. It was a thing of beauty, and just as much an art as his music, thought David with admiration. Mark in turn admired David as well, especially the fact that he could play so many different instruments. It was a deep shock to them both when their fathers stopped talking, and John Reid and his son moved away. Mark was the only person to come see David off at the airport. His mother, who almost seemed happy to see them go, hardly said good-bye when he left.

They had lost touch over the years, David being too preoccupied with his own fast-paced life to give his old friend much thought, until Mark turned up unexpectedly just when David needed him the most. He assigned it to serendipity and thanked his lucky stars, never giving a second thought to Mark's motive for showing up at his doorstep.

"I hope Donna's OK," remarked David. "Hearing about her disappearance really bothered me."

"Well, try not to worry about it. Try to forget all that and concentrate on the rehearsal. You have a lot a work to do. Are you at least going to give them a chance to play the first movement today?" They talked as they walked toward the auditorium. "I'd really like to hear that opening part."

"Yeah, don't worry," answered David looking around the room, happy there were no autograph hounds or newsmen about. "I just didn't want them to get complacent. That can happen when you work together too long. You start to take things for granted."

"No chance of that happening with you, 'eh boss? You jumped on them like a terrier on a field rat."

They both laughed.

"By the way," said Mark. "Have you heard from your dad recently?"

"No, why?" asked David, a little surprised at the turn of the conversation. His dad had returned to Scotland soon after David left college and moved to New York. They hadn't talked to each other much since. As a matter of fact, David hadn't heard from his father in over a year.

"Oh, just wondering how he's doing. Have you heard from any of the boys?"

"The boys? Unlike you, Markey, I was just ten when I left, remember. Anyway, I was pretty much a loner. I didn't know any of the boys except the ones who used to beat me up. You hear from any of the boys or are they all in prison?"

"No, the boys all turned out pretty well. All except me, that is, I work for a soddy prick."

"Thank you, I resemble that remark," said David, doing his Groucho impression, and starting to feel a little better after bantering with his friend.

They entered rehearsal hall together. It was a little after 10:00 am. Mark sat about halfway down in the middle of the auditorium, while David made his way to the stage. Most of the musicians were already there. There was little banter and no applause this time, as the conductor jumped up onto the stage.

"I want to take it from the top," he announced without preamble, as everyone got into their places. "No stopping, a straight run through. We'll take it like this." He counted off several measures with the baton. "A little slower than we'll play it, I want to give us all a chance to hear the first movement together. The rest of the piece hinges on it, and if we get it right it will suck the audience in for what's to come. It's the simplest part of the symphony and we'll spend the least amount of time on it, but well, let's just play it down come what may, OK?"

Everyone nodded expectantly.

"I just want to say," he went on after a moment. "I have nothing but the deepest respect for everyone here. I know you are the very best at what you do and bring years of dedication and hard work, love even, to your profession. I've worked with some of you for a number of years. But I want to instill in you all a feeling that it's not business as

22

usual. I'm about to lead us where few have gone. Not to seem overly dramatic, but this work is intended to challenge you all to the utmost, not only musically, but emotionally and physically as well. This piece is to be played like you were conquering a great height, with an air of élan. You may think I'm being melodramatic, but before we're though you'll understand what I'm talking about."

They all looked at him with perplexed expressions.

"I want a sustained legato in the strings here, before you take on the main theme, one by one, then the woodwinds, and then the horns with the counter melody. Any questions? Good then, let's begin."

He was silent for a moment with his eyes closed. When he opened them again, he looked straight at the section of the orchestra that would start things off and began to count softly. "One, two, three, four."

They did not stop playing for twenty-minutes, although David had ceased to conduct halfway though the piece. The lack of sleep had hit him even before he got to the stage, and he had been rubbing his eyes frequently. Suddenly, while conducting, he felt a sharp pain over his eyes that made him close them tightly. When he opened them again and looked at the score, the notes on the staves swirled and danced before him as if they were flies on a greasy counter. Clutching the podium for support, he closed his eyes again and almost swooned because of the pain. The room started spinning. His eyes began to tear-up and burn as if hot ash had blown into them. He hugged his arms around him and put his elbows on the stand for support as he tried to get his equilibrium back. A few of the musicians noticed his discomfort and stopped playing.

"Don't stop!" he yelled, moving his arms again strenuously to get everyone back on track, before he stopped and held his head. "Keep playing," he commanded.

He wondered what could be happening to him. Was it something serious, or just a result of burning the candle at both ends? He promised himself he would get a check-up.

While he stood listening with his arms wrapped around him and his head bowed, the orchestra played on. It was rough in parts, and the errant second chair violist from the day before stopped playing altogether, but he let it go on, mistakes and miscues and wrong notes and all. Even for a first run through it was wonderful.

Just before the end of the movement, David took up his baton again to conduct the last few measures, just prior to the ending coda.

Then he stood silent with his head bowed, as if the silence was a continuation of the music that had just disappeared

Everyone sat silent, looking at him expectantly.

"That was beautiful," yelled his agent, clapping alone in the audience. Some of the players clapped as well.

Is something wrong?" asked one of his assistants, who noticed his discomfort and approached him. David had finally been able to open his eyes without the searing pain.

"No, just got something in my eye, have a bit of a headache. Could you get me a couple aspirin and a bowl of cool water to splash on my eyes?

He didn't know if he'd be able to continue the rehearsal. He felt awful. He took a pull of ginger-ale, swallowed the pills his assistant brought, and tried to carry on.

"There were a few rough spots, which we'll smooth out," said David. "But I want to move on to the tougher sections before we come back to it. It will all make more sense after you see how some of these themes are developed."

There was a warm hum from the musicians, most of who were smiling and going over the parts they'd just executed.

"Good job," Mark yelled from the base of the stage. "I'll see you tonight." He shouted this over his shoulder before he dashed off and out of the auditorium. It was a good thing he left.

The rest of the afternoon was a disaster. David tried to soldier on, but his bout of pain and dizziness, together with the lack of sleep, had left him drained. They were rehearsing the same section of music that caused the consternation on the previous day. This time the whole orchestra got lambasted as they repeated the phrase over and over again. Halfway through the battle, David gave the baton over to his assistant conductor, looked at the musicians disapprovingly, and walked off the stage.

"I want you to go over that section for the rest of the day," he said, as he conferred with the backup conductor in a huddle off too the side. "Keep repeating it until I return. I don't feel well and they're not helping much with their playing. If I come back and you're playing anything but bars 80 through 360 of that movement, this will be the last orchestra you ever conduct. Repeat it until they dream it in their sleep. Don't talk about it. Don't explain. Don't do anything except repeat that section. Got it?"

"Yes, David," said his conducting assistant feeling slightly ill himself. "When will you be back?"

"I don't know," he answered, putting his baton in its case and walking off a little unsteadily, rubbing his eyes.

They were all glad when he left and wondering if David Gordon Reid had turned into David Gordon Hyde.

Chapter 4

Despite the weather forecasters' predictions it was still raining hard when he jumped into his sports coup and sped off to his apartment on the other side of town. His wipers worked overtime to clear the windshields, and he was squinting intently to see the speeding vehicles and plodding pedestrians who were everywhere, amid the swirl of lights.

Suddenly, he was struck with a blinding pain in his eyes. It was so sharp and abrupt he momentarily grabbed them with both hands, almost swerving off the road. He looked up just in time to avoid rear ending the car in front of him, slamming on his brakes at the last moment. Straining to open his eyes wide enough to see, he was almost blinded with tears of pain.

Somehow he managed to move slowly through traffic, as cars honked their horns and whizzed passed him. Hardly able to open his eyes to see, he jammed the wheel from left to right, just squeezing by barely seen obstacles. On he went, unable to stop or pull over, only able to follow the taillights of the cars in front of him. Just when he could stand it no longer, every peek out of his damaged orbs an agony, he glimpsed an empty spot under a large overpass and steered for it.

It was dark and deserted under the bridge. Somehow he pulled to a stop without crashing. All the cars and pedestrians had disappeared. He was alone with the pigeons and piles of trash. Rain pelted the streets and sidewalks, and pounded on the thin metal hood of his car. He sat with his head down, both hands over his eyes, rocking back and forth.

Someone rapped on his window.

"You OK, buddy?" asked the stranger, a heavy set black man in his mid-forties, about his own size, with a couple days' grey stubble covering his craggy cheeks and chin. His eyes were bloodshot and his voice was thick, but he looked intelligent and concerned.

"No, I just had an eye spasm and had to pull over. I'm OK now," David said, blinking out at the man.

"Well, you looked like you were in some kind of trouble the way you pulled in here. This isn't a good place to be stuck in, even at this time of day. Things can get kind of rough down here if you're not careful, just junkies and drunks."

"What does that make you?" asked David, looking at the man more closely.

The man laughed and then coughed.

David was getting nervous. The car was still running, but when he looked up at the road he was blinded by searing pain, even in the half-light underneath the bridge.

"You don't look in any shape to drive," observed the stranger. "Hey, I know you. Ain't you that conductor fellow, Gordon Reeves, or something?"

David didn't know whether to admit who he was or not. He was still unable to see the man or the road clearly.

"I used to play in the pit band for your show. I toured with them when they went on the road. The name's Lenny Zeigler, they call me Zeiggie. I play the cello. Not every Broadway musical has a cello part like you wrote."

David suddenly felt a little better on hearing the stranger was a fellow musician, even though he looked one step up from the street.

"Hi, Mister Zeigler, nice to meet you. David Gordon Reid. You were close. I appear to be having a bit of a problem. I've never had anything like this happen to me before but I can't see a thing. If you could just help me dial my manager." He grabbed for his cell phone, but there was nothing there. "Damn it, I left it on the podium with all my other stuff. I was going to return." He seemed confused and disoriented.

"Lucky you didn't have an accident," said the stranger. "I don't have a phone, but I live a little ways down the block, over that liquor store down the street there. You want to come in and rest? Maybe we can call from the store, though they ain't too fond of me in there. I owe them a little money."

Hearing there was a phone and a place to sit out of the rain, David accepted the stranger's offer and let him drive them the half block to his apartment.

"Your car will be safer in front of the liquor store than back there under the bridge," he assured David, as he made a wide U-turn and drove them back down the street.

Once inside Zeiggie's tiny but tidy one room apartment, sitting at a small table, David asked something that had been bothering him since the stranger introduced himself.

"I don't mean to seem rude, but if you were touring with the show, how'd you end up here?"

"Ah, you want to hear my hard luck story?" said Zeiggie. "You got a little while? It's a long one, but I'll make it short and sweet for you. You want a drink?"

He went to the pantry and pulled out a half-empty bottle of Wild Turkey. "This calls for a celebration. It's not every day I have such a illustrious celebrity in my home. This just might be the thing to make you feel better."

"I only drink beer," David said, but took a glass of tap water to help him swallow the aspirin his host gave him for his pain.

"I could tell them at the liquor store that we've got a medical emergency," offered Zeigler. "But I doubt it would make any difference, unless I could pay them the seventy-five bucks I owe them. Not that I'm asking *you* for it, mind you. The owner's OK, but his son's a real prick. I hate asking that guy for anything."

"No, that's all right, don't worry about it. I'll feel better soon." Despite his optimistic words he was still having trouble looking up without squinting and blinking so his eyes watered.

"Here, try these," said his host. "It's already kind of dark in here, but these should help." He handed David a thick, dark pair of wraparound sunglasses. He put them on and instantly felt some relief.

"I know what might help," offered Ziegler. "My mother used to do this when I had eyestrain as a kid from practicing my fiddle too much."

He went over to the stove and began boiling a pan of water. "We'll try putting some warm tea bags on your eyes, something about the tannic acid in the tea that helps sooth them."

"Anything that will stop the burning would be great," replied David, putting his head back and closing his eyes.

"I studied in Boston, at New England Conservatory," began his host, standing by the stove as they waited for the water to boil. "Did well enough when I finished to find work in the City here. Hooked up with your show through Stanley Morrison."

"Yeah, I know Stanley. We've done some work."

"Well, he got me the job when the show went on the road, back in '09. Lot of fun, one of the best gigs I've ever had. I loved the music, great cello part. I dig your stuff. I was hoping you'd do more of that kind of thing, although I think your string quartets are great too. Though I have to admit, they're a little out of my league, all those double-stops and crazy fingerings. That's not really my thing. I made most of my living playing electric base around town."

28

"I'm glad you like my music, the show I mean," said David.

"Why didn't you do another one?" asked the ex-cellist.

"I only did it as a lark with a playwright friend of mine. It's really not my genre. I was hearing different things. I guess I don't like to repeat myself."

"Well, there's nothing wrong with repeating success, I say," replied Zeiggie, shutting off the burner and dipping a few tea bags in the boiling water.

"So what happened?" asked David, interested in hearing the rest of the stranger's story.

"A woman is what happened. I'd been married for fourteen years. Not the best of marriages, kind of bumpy really, but things were starting to go better. We had a kid. We were finally getting the hang of it. I was working steady, doing club gigs and concert dates, and shows here and there. I was even starting to get some studio work. I never should have gone on the road, but it was such a great opportunity, to play in a show like that. I figured it would really help my career, you know, be good to have on my resume."

He took the two tea bags that had been steaming in boiling hot water and strained them on a spoon.

"Here, put these on your eyes for awhile. The warmth will sooth them, even if the tea does nothing."

David placed the two, still hot, wet tea bags on his eyes, and leaned back with them closed. The warm, damp bags full of tannic acid instantly made them feel better. The aspirin was also starting to take effect.

"Anyway," Zeiggie continued. "I went, despite my wife's objections. I should have known better, but hindsight doesn't help much. I thought she'd get over it when she saw the money I was making and what it did for our situation, but she didn't get over it. She got over me's what she did. I should have known something was wrong when she didn't answer any of my letters. I tried to call once a night at first, then once every other night, then once a week. The conversations were short and sweet, that is when she was there to answer the phone, which wasn't very often. She wouldn't join me when I asked. Pretty soon I stopped calling altogether."

"I started drinking more. It gets lonely on the road, so I was messing with women and partying and having a good old time. By the time I got back to New York, she had taken the kid, all the money in the bank account, and left, served me with divorce papers the very next day. She even got custody of our boy, everything. She must have found out about my infidelity. I'm not into drugs, but, you know, I fooled around with some coke and pot once in awhile. It came with the partying and the women, but nothing serious. She used it to take my son from me. Told them I was an addict and an unfit father, even though I paid all the bills and took good care of them both. Of course, she being white and me being a black man didn't help. I was drinking pretty heavy by the end. That didn't help matters either I suppose. That was my downfall, the same old story. I'm sure you've heard it a hundred times. How you feeling, a little better? Here, let me warm those up for you."

He got up from the table, where he had been sitting while he told his story, and took the tea bags from the conductor's eyes. David sat up and actually opened them without pain for the first time since his incident in the car.

"That's great. I feel much better. Thank you so much for your kindness."

"Don't mention it. I'm glad I could help."

"I don't know, but after what you told me, I'd of thought you'd have a grudge on account of what happened because of my show."

Zeiggie laughed. "Naw, I don't blame you. It's my own fault. I took her for granted practically our whole marriage, her and the kid. Now that they're gone I realize my mistake, but it's too late."

"Well, you shouldn't let that ruin your life," said David speaking from experience. "You've still got a chance to turn things around, Mister Ziegler. Maybe I can help."

"That's generous of you, Mister Reid, but…"

"Call me David. Can I call you Zeiggie? And I'm not being generous. If you can really play the cello well enough to work in my show, then perhaps you can help me. I'm always on the lookout for good musicians. Do you still have your instrument?"

His host looked embarrassed. "No," he said, sadly. "I had to pawn it. Things are kind of tough right now. Not much demand for washed-out forty year old cellists. I still got my bass guitar. I can always get a gig here and there playing bass. It's in the closet, although I have to double up on someone else's amp. Like I said, things are tough. I had to hock that too."

"I'm sorry," said David, disappointed but not that surprised.

"I've actually been trying to get things back together."

David looked at the bottle and the inch of golden liquid in the glass, which the stranger hadn't actually touched yet.

"Oh this?" Ziegler replied, noticing the direction of his guest's stare. "That's just moral support. I've been straight for twelve weeks. I figured if I have it around and know I can always have some whenever I want, I don't get that anxious feeling. Then it's not so hard to go without it. I just tell myself I'll have a little nip later, but just never get around to it. I thought you might want some. Just keep it for special occasions."

With that he brought David the re-warmed tea bags and slowly poured his glass back into the bottle, putting the bottle back in the cupboard. David didn't know what to believe.

"I'm glad to hear that," he said, placing the warm tea bags back on his eyes and tilting his head back. "I mean about you quitting and all. Sorry about your cello. That's too bad you had to sell it. Maybe now that you're straight, things will get better."

"Oh, things can always get better as long as you're sucking air," replied Zeiggie. "The secret to life is knowing how to enjoy the simple things. That's what I've learned in all this. How to appreciate and be thankful for what you have, 'cause it can always get worse."

They sat in silence for a while. Finally, David sat up, removed the now cold tea bags from his eyes, and opened them wide.

"I feel much better," he said, running his hand over his eyes several times lightly. "I think I may be able to take off soon."

"Well, you better be careful. It's getting late. It'll be dark soon. It may be hard to drive at night with the lights and all. It's still raining. Maybe you should stay until you're sure you're OK."

His host seemed a little hurt David was in such a hurry to leave, as if he was offended somehow. In an attempt to mollify him, David looked around the room and noticed the stack of CDs.

"That's a nice collection of Bach you've got there."

"Bach's my favorite composer," said Zeiggie. "His Cello Sonata in B-flat is my all time favorite piece."

"Yeah, Bach wrote some nice cello music. My dad loved Bach. That's about all he listened to when I was a kid. I remember being bounced on his knee to the Brandenburg Concertos."

"Bach was killed you know," said Zeiggie suddenly, "murdered by his adversary, the rector of Leipzig University."

"What?" replied David, a little taken aback. "What are you talking about?"

"I said Bach was murdered by his enemy, Johan August Ernesti."

"Bach died of complications stemming from eye disease," insisted David, remembering his music history.

"That's what everyone thought, but I know differently," replied the ex-cellist.

"That's crazy," answered David, starting to get angry. He wasn't an aficionado like his father, but he knew a little about the great seventeenth century composer. He had read both volumes of Spitta's great classic, as well as modern biographies, and knew the cause of Bach's death was eye disease brought about by working for decades in poor light. What was his host talking about? Maybe he was a nut after all.

"There was a great deal of speculation at the time of his death about what really happened," said Zeigler. "Especially among some of Bach's assistants and copyists, as well as his son Phillip Emmanuel, but they couldn't prove anything. The rector was a very powerful and vindictive man."

"I recall reading about Bach's run in with the rector over his teaching duties, but nothing to the extent you're talking about. There certainly was no murder."

"That little 'run in' lasted over ten years," replied Ziegler. "And in the end Bach got the last word. He never did get disciplined like Ernesti wanted. In practical terms, Bach thumbed his nose at him. Ernesti hated Bach and everything he stood for. He thought Bach was a prima donna. That he was so taken with himself and his music that he considered himself above the canon of the university, using the church and sacred music to gain glory and fame for himself instead of giving glory to God. When Bach outmaneuvered him one too many times, he decided to put an end to the great composer once and for all and poisoned him."

"How do you know all this?" asked David, unable to hide his annoyance. "Where did you hear such nonsense?"

"I didn't hear it," said Ziegler, pouring himself a cup of boiling water, which he had just heated up again, and hanging a tea-bag in it. "You want a cup?"

"Sure," said David, no longer in a hurry to leave.

"Bach had a copyist. No one knows his name. He had a lot of them, his second wife, his sons and some of his pupils, all of whom are known by their work, all being very distinctive. As a matter of fact, all of Bach's copyists are known except this one. It's one of the great mysteries of his life. I've been trying to figure out who he was all my life, since I was a kid.

I spent a lot of time in Boston, in the University and city libraries. I must have read Spitta fifty times and all his appendixes. I read everything I could get my hands on about Bach and the rector. Then one day, in the Library of Congress, in the foreign language building, I came across an obscure letter that purported to disclose the whereabouts of some of Bach's missing music. It was to Bach's second son, Frederick, the ne'er-do-well, who sold and squandered most of his father's inheritance, some of his most famous masterpieces. I believe the letter was from this unknown copyist. In it he told Bach's son of something he had seen with his own eyes, a letter purported to be from the Rector Ernesti. In it Ernesti gloated over Bach's recent death and threatened to destroy his works. The unknown copyist was trying to warn Frederick to beware of the man.

It took me years, but I tracked this letter down. I found it in a small library archive outside Vienna when I was stationed in Germany in the army in1986. It was the smoking gun I had been looking for. It took me a while to decipher it as I did not speak German. It was in Ernesti's own hand with his moniker, practically admitting to the crime and gloating at his final victory over his famous adversary."

"That's crazy," David said before he could stop himself. Zeiggly looked at him with a hurt expression that turned angry.

"That's what everyone says."

"Do you have the letter?" asked David, thinking that would clear everything up.

"No, my wife threw it out with all my stuff when she left. She thought the whole thing was a stupid waste of time, an obsession of mine that could lead nowhere. She wanted me to sell the letter to a collector and be done with it, but I was going to use it in a chain of evidence to prove what really happened to Bach. I had quite a case going. She threw it all in the incinerator."

David looked out the window. It had stopped raining and grown dark.

"How do I get out of here?" he asked, standing up. "I think I can drive now."

"I can go with you if you want, get you going in the right direction."

"That's very kind, but you've already done enough. Can I, er, can I reimburse you for your trouble?" he said, fumbling for his wallet.

"No, please, don't insult me more than you already have."

"Well, you have to admit that's a pretty far out theory. You already said no one else believes it."

"If I had that letter and all the other evidence they would. I was going to write a book. That fool wife of mine didn't know it but she probably burned a fortune when she burned that letter."

Another dreamer, thought David, with one more farfetched idea of how to make a million instead of thinking steady enough to get and hold a job.

"If Bach was poisoned like you say, how come he died of eye disease? What's that, some kind of cover-up?"

"Something like that. It was ingenious. First they got him to go to an eye specialist when he had simple eyestrain, a specialist in league with the rector. The doctor operated, twice, and then prescribed some eye medicine, which they adulterated with arsenic and other toxins that would make him sick after prolonged use. It was the perfect crime. It would have been hard enough to detect now with modern pathology, let alone four hundred years ago, when such things were barely being discussed in the universities."

"Well, maybe you have a point there. Too bad you lost all your evidence. It would have made a good book. I don't know about making a fortune, but it would have made interesting reading. I would have bought it."

"Who knows, I may still write it someday, but I have more pressing needs at the moment."

"You sure I can't help you out with a few dollars? Let me at least pay your bar tab downstairs. You might be on better terms with your neighbor."

"Naw, I couldn't let you do that. Really, thanks, but it's not necessary. I'm glad I could help you out. I really admire your work. I'm honored to meet you."

"Now look at who's being rude," laughed David. "I'll tell you what. I'm not quite sure of myself driving at night in a strange neighborhood. If you take me back to my place on East 57th street, I'll pay you $300 for your trouble. That will pay for a place to stay for the night and a cab ride home in the morning."

Zeiggie, deep in thought for a moment, said nothing.

"OK, that's fair," he said finally. "But that's way too much. I don't need to stay in a hotel for the night and I can make my way home a lot cheaper than that. How about $150?"

"Two," said David, handing him ten twenties.

"One-eighty," said Zeiggie, handing David back a twenty.

"A deal," he said laughing and taking the bill. Lenny Zeigler was a man of honor.

"Now let's have that cup of tea," said David. "And drink to our new friendship."

Chapter 5

No one had seen David Reid since he left the rehearsal around one the previous afternoon. He had missed his dinner date with his manager, Mark Burns, and had not returned to his apartment. Although he had not turned up on the evening's police reports, which was a good thing, his associates were concerned nonetheless. There was some comment on his mental condition. Some thought he had been preoccupied and bothered by something. He'd had several angry outbursts during rehearsals.

"Does he take drugs," the detective taking the call asked. "Does he gamble? Does he mess around with women? Does he have a history of mental illness?" No one really knew, except maybe Mark Burns, and he was highly offended at the questions.

"No, he doesn't bloody take drugs," said Mark. "And his behavior is perfectly normal. You try rehearsing for a world debut of a new symphony with only two weeks notice and see how calm you are. He didn't go home last night. He's been missing for almost twenty-four hours. Don't sit there asking stupid questions. He's a normal guy with no bad habits who's gone missing for no apparent reason."

"Hardly normal," observed the detective. "Anybody have a reason to want to harm Mister Reid?"

"Not really. Oh, he has enemies, if that's what you're asking, ex-wives, competitors, crazy fans and colleagues he might have pissed off along the way, but no one who would want to actually harm him. No, something's happened to him. This isn't like him."

In the middle of the conversation, David walked into the auditorium.

"Eh, officer, he's just walked in. Yes, he's here now. Yes, thank you, sir. Yes, I'll let you know. Sorry to bother you. Thank you, bye."

"Where the hell have you been?" Mark demanded, hanging up the phone, as David walked toward him across the wide, carpeted lobby. There was a strange black man with him, walking a few feet behind.

"See, I told you what his reaction would be," David confided, looking over his shoulder at the stranger. "He hasn't even said hi or asked me if I'm OK."

"Are you OK, you freaking jerk? You had us all freaking worried about you. Where have you been, you a-hole? This isn't freaking funny!"

"Don't ever get a Scotsman mad," observed David, looking back at Zeiggie again and laughing.

"I'm sorry," he said, taking Mark by the arm. "I didn't think you'd be this worried. I had car trouble on the way home yesterday and didn't have my phone."

"I know. We found it on the stage with all your other stuff."

"I was a bit indisposed. Zeiggie here was kind enough to give me a hand and let me stay with him until I could get my car back this morning. I don't know what I would have done if it wasn't for him. Mark Burns, meet Leonard Ziegler. Zeiggie here played on 'Dreams' when it toured. He's a cellist."

"Nice to meet you," said the business manager, eyeing the stocky black man suspiciously. "Where'd you say you two met?"

"He was down near the garment district, underneath the 113th street overpass heading for the bridge," said Zeiggie.

"That's a rough area," said Mark, even more suspicious now that he had heard where David encountered the man.

"That's what I told him," replied Zeiggie.

"What the hell were you doing down there?" Mark asked, looking at David.

"I needed to blow off some steam. Things were going bad at rehearsal. I was having some eye trouble."

"Eye trouble? Since when have you been having trouble with your eyes?"

"Since the day before yesterday. Since rehearsals started."

"Must be eye strain," observed Mark. "Maybe we can postpone the opening for a few weeks."

"No way. I'll be fine."

"Well, I'll make an appointment with Dr. Tuttle for later in the week. Thanks for helping, Mister Ziegler," said the business manager, looking at Zeiggie as if to say, you can disappear now, back to the gutter you crawled from.

"Zeiggie's going to work with me for awhile," announced David, as if reading his manager's mind. "As my personal assistant. I have a few things I want him to do. We had a great night listening to his Bach collection. He's doing some research on the old master for me. He knows a lot about him."

37

Mark became even more suspicious and took his boss aside so he could speak to him in private.

"I know this guy helped you, David, but do you really know anything about him? Why has he latched on to you all of a sudden? He looks kind of down and out. Why don't I give him some money and send him on his way. You don't know who he is or what his agenda is. Can he be trusted? Does he know who you are?"

"Yes, he recognized me immediately. I told you, he played cello in the show. He knows Stanley Morrison. He's just a little down on his luck, that's all. He's a nice guy."

"I don't care who he knows. He can't be trusted. He knew who you were. He's up to something. He wants something."

"He doesn't want anything. I never had to negotiate with anyone so hard to give them money."

"That's because he's holding out for the big score. He's playing you."

"You're such a cynic, Mark. You wouldn't trust your own brother."

"You're my bleeding brother. I don't trust him," said Mark.

"Well, trust me then. I know what I'm doing. Zeiggie's all right. He's going to watch my back for me."

"What do you mean by that?" Mark asked, now offended. "That's what I do. That's what you pay me for."

As they were talking, Ziegler came up looking a little sheepish. "I guess I should be going. I don't want to cause any trouble."

"No, don't be silly. You're not causing any trouble," replied David. "We just had some business to discuss. Mark here's a little over-protective at times. He used to take care of me when we were kids, sort of kept the bullies away."

"Don't let this dandy here fool you," said Mark, smiling and holding out his hand to the stranger. "He didn't need any help with the bullies. I had to protect the bullies from him. Thanks again for helping. I didn't mean to be rude. We have a killer schedule and there are a million details to attend to, which unfortunately only David here can do. When he goes missing like this without telling anyone, well, it's just hell to pay. I'm the one who's got to get us back on track."

"They ready?" David inquired, nodding his head toward the concert hall.

"Yeah, they've been here since nine. Everyone's concerned about you. You want me to go in and tell them you're here or do you want to make a grand entrance as usual."

"Why don't we just walk in normally and go to work."

"Sounds good to me," replied Mark. "I'm not leaving your side, so you can do anything you want. I'll be there."

"Coming, Zeiggie?" said David, motioning toward the auditorium door. "I think I'm going to need more than one person watching my back today."

David flung open the double doors to the auditorium and strode down the center aisle purposefully with Mark at his side, while Zeiggie slid into a back seat all but unnoticed in the darkened hall, feeling out of place and vaguely uncomfortable. He was having second thoughts about coming, though the hundred-fifty dollars a week was a blessing he hadn't counted on. Maybe with this guy's help he would get his life back together. Hearing the string players tuning up made him think about playing his cello again.

As the musicians noticed David, the room became quiet. The sound of the instruments stopped one by one into a jagged silence, each note dying with a cry. He seemed even more preoccupied and self-absorbed than usual to the stunned musicians, who looked at him with a rainbow of expressions - some questioning, some concerned, some sullen or angry. There was a hushed whisper in the hall as band members conversed quietly with each other concerning his tardiness and appearance.

Instead of addressing the orchestra, David studied the score, shuffling the pages back and forth as he looked at one section or another. When he looked up the whole orchestra was sitting there silently, staring at him. His business manager and Zeiggie both sat in the audience holding their breath waiting for David to start.

"Sorry," he said. "I wanted to make a few notations."

David felt invigorated being back on the podium with the orchestra poised before him. It was as if the events of the previous day had never occurred. Spending time with his new friend had relaxed him. He had never met anyone who knew more about Johan Sebastian Bach, not even his father. He felt better than he had in days, after a good night's rest on his new friend's couch.

"OK, everyone," he said finally, addressing the orchestra. "I want to hear bars 80 through 360, the section you rehearsed yesterday, each section alone then with the whole orchestra."

There was an audible groan from the entire band, like you'd hear from a third grade class being told they were having a surprise quiz. The last thing they wanted was more torture like the previous two days. If anyone had expected an explanation for his disappearance, they were sorely disappointed. Granted, he had only been missing since the previous afternoon, and it wasn't unusual for a conductor to hand the orchestra over to his second now and then as need demanded. But they all knew that he'd been missing twenty-four hours and the police had been called – news travels fast on the stage – and they were curious as to what had happened.

An assistant brought a can of ginger-ale and a glass, along with a couple packages of his favorite crackers. He had stopped with Zeiggie at a greasy diner near the ex-cello player's apartment in the 'hood' and had a simple breakfast of grits with gravy and briskets. The place reminded him of the diners he'd seen down south when he played the concert halls in Biloxi or Memphis. There was little likelihood of someone tampering with his food here, unless it was the vermin that infested the place. David was willing to take that chance. He might be paranoid, but that didn't mean someone wasn't trying to poison him. He wasn't going to make it easy for them by eating in the same place every morning.

There on the podium was his baton and cell phone. He picked up the latter, made sure it was off, and hung it on his belt, leaving the former on the stand. He wasn't going to use it today. Today he was going to direct the orchestra with his hands.

When he was a kid he had always connected conducting with waving a stick. As a small child he had instinctively picked up a pencil or one of his mother's darning needles to conduct in front of the radio or CD player. It was only years later that he realized how much better his hands were for expressing himself than a stick of wood. The hands can convey dynamics better than anything, and the long sweep of a melodic phase almost as well as singing it. Of course, when you want to get a hundred musicians to all play the downbeat together, there's nothing like a big baton. He had learned that while studying with the great Kaminski at Julliard.

Kaminski, a visiting maestro from Eastern Europe, was there as an emeritus professor of conducting. Internationally famous, he only took a few students out of the hundreds from all over the world who applied. As he stood there in front of the orchestra, waiting for everyone to finish tuning up, he thought about the first time he had met the great man.

When he arrived at his audition, the maestro was standing next to the piano where a wide score was laid out.

"Do you know this piece?" he asked, as soon as David entered the room.

"I don't know," said David, staring at the pages of staves covered with hundreds of little black dots. It didn't look familiar. It appeared to be an original manuscript. There was no title.

He sat down at the keyboard but didn't play. It was a full score for a large orchestra. All the parts were written out on the various staves one over the other, the strings at the top, woodwinds and brass underneath. Some, like the violins and trumpets, were written in the familiar treble-clef. Others, like tubas and bassoons, were in the bass-clef. While the violas and oboes were in the strange-looking alto-clef. He perused the music silently, sight-reading it, hearing the notes in his head. It sounded familiar as he went over it in his mind. Finally, he started playing it on the piano, a little slower than it was actually performed, covering each major line - winds, strings, brass, high notes and low, melody and counter lines, cords and accompaniment - all together.

"Oh, yes," he said, over the music as he played it on the keyboard. "It's a Stravinsky piece, La Sacre du Printempts, the Right of Spring."

"Yes," said the maestro, impressed. It was a ferociously difficult orchestra piece. David was playing it flawlessly on sight, giving it the correct interpretation, having no trouble with the time changes and relentless dissonances. "You will do fine. Tell the dean." And that was that, David was in and thus began his great love affair with conducting.

"OK, strings, ready?" he said, coming back to the present moment as if from a dream. "Together now."

He counted off the beat. They played it down in a few minutes and were done, expecting to be asked to repeat it for the rest of the day. Instead, David said nothing, and went on to the next section of the band, and then the next. Finally, the whole orchestra played it together.

"Good," said David, without further comment. "I think we've got the idea. We'll come back to it later. Now, let's work on the last movement. We'll do it without the chorus for now. There're some major dynamic changes here, but I don't want to stress them today. We'll work on the bowing and phrasing with the strings and the entrance points for the woodwinds and brass. Let's just get familiar with it for now. We'll do it a little slow. Like this…" he counted a few measures in 7/4 time, the starting rhythm.

It was a good rehearsal. The musicians enjoyed their parts and how it all fit together, as well as the interesting way the different rhythms were woven together to form a rich tapestry of color and sound. It was a stunningly expressive use of the orchestra, a thrill to play. Instead of the bad, impossible to please David, they got the helpful teacher, the David that instructed and coached and explained as only someone who knew the music and instruments intimately could. It was one of those experiences that make all the hard work and effort worthwhile, and by the end of the day the conductor and orchestra were in love again. Mark was pleased as punch. This boded well for the premier. Zeiggie was also impressed, and wished more than ever that he had kept his cello, although he doubted he could have played the demanding part.

Later that day David met Mark for dinner, the meeting David had missed the previous evening. He hadn't had a dizzy spell or blinding attack all day. Whatever it was that had plagued him seemed to have gone away.

"Orchestra sounded good today," Mark observed enthusiastically. "I think this is going to be a great success. Wait until they hear this music. It'll knock their socks off!"

"We have a long way to go yet. It's still pretty rough and there are a lot of things we have to improve. No, we have a long way to go."

"Well, things went well. If it keeps going like it did today, there should be no problem. You were starting to worry me."

"Oh, I'm sure I'll have you worried again before we're through," said David. "You seem to thrive on worrying."

"I only worry when I have to. You hold the fate of my hairline and blood-pressure in those valuable hands of yours. Say, how come you didn't use your baton today? I don't remember seeing you conduct without it. That is when you bother to conduct at all."

"I use it most of the time, but sometimes you can express more with your hands, without holding the stick. I wanted to show them the phrasing and timing in a more subtle way, I wanted to make it more personal for them. The stick was getting in the way."

"You're going to use it during the concert though, right?" said the business manager.

"See, now you're worried about that. You certainly are a worry-wart, my friend."

Zeiggie, who had joined them for dinner listened quietly, feeling even more out of place in the expensive restaurant than he had in the concert hall. Here, there was no way he would be unnoticed and invisible, sitting in the middle of the room with his distinguished employer. Luckily, David had bought him a new suit to go with his new job. Mister Leonard Ziegler was moving up in the world. Unfortunately, in Zeiggie's experience that only meant the fall would be greater.

"How about you, Mister Ziegler," asked Mark. "What did you think of today's rehearsal?"

"For one thing, that's about the best orchestra I've ever heard. Even the third and fourth chairs are better than the first chairs in most other orchestras. And the music, well it's downright beautiful. I've never experienced anything like it. I only heard a small part of it, but what I did hear makes me think it's going to shake up the musical world."

"See, only here a few hours and already he knows how to suck up to the maestro," joked Mark. "No, I'm only kidding Zeiggie. I've been telling him that for months. Wait until you hear the first movement. It's one of the most beautiful things ever written. There's nothing like it."

"OK, you two, that's enough brownnosing for one evening. I've just finished eating and don't want to lose my dinner."

They laughed.

"Speaking of that, David," said Mark. "How have you been feeling? Having any more of those spells you mentioned?"

"No, I felt fine all day. I think I may be over that. It was probably just eye strain."

Zeiggie was silent, thinking of how he found the conductor the previous day, half blind and in agony, helpless and disoriented.

"Maybe you should see a doctor anyway," suggested Mark. "I'll make an appointment first thing tomorrow."

"I don't have time for a doctor right now," insisted David. "We have a tight schedule and a lot of work to do. One good rehearsal doesn't make a successful concert. If I have any more spells I'll call the doctor myself, how's that?"

"OK I guess, but..."

"Good then," said David, cutting his friend off. "We'll hear no more talk of doctors."

Three hours later David woke from a sound sleep shivering with the chills so bad he had all he could do to pull the blankets tight around him and curl in a ball. Every time he tried to move he was overcome with violent shaking spasms. It seemed to him he had lost all his body heat, despite the thick blankets about him. Then just as suddenly, he was overcome with nausea and sweating profusely. When he finally stood up to change his wet T-shirt, he was overcome with dizziness. Staggering around the bedroom, he fell against the dresser, then back across the bed. He tried sitting up, but it seemed the room was spinning around him so wildly he clung to the bed for fear of falling off. Finally, he made a mad dash to the small bath off his bedroom, making it just in time to throw up the half-digested remains of his expensive dinner in four heaving spasms. Then just as suddenly, he was seized with the chills again, and wrapped the blankets around him, shivering so much that he could hardly move. He spent the rest of the night like this, oscillating back and forth between the chills and sweats until around six am, when he fell into a fitful sleep only to be woken by the phone a short while later.

When he woke up he felt un-rested but well. The fever, or whatever it was, had passed. David wondered vaguely if he'd had food poisoning, but if so, it was a kind he had never experienced before. Other than lack of sleep, he felt fine.

"Hello," he said.

"David, it's half-past ten," said his business manager. "Remember, you called an early session today. You've got the chorus rehearsing."

"Yeah, I'm sorry, had a bad night, running a little late."

"You OK?" asked Mark with concern.

"Sure, just didn't sleep that well, that's all. Don't worry, and for God's sake don't call the doctor."

"OK, but you'd let me know if something was wrong, right? Nothing's worth ruining your health over, not even your big debut."

"No, things are fine. I'll pick Zeiggie up and be right over."

"Why are you going to pick *him* up?" objected Mark. "What do you need him for? You're already a half hour late. By the time you pick him up it will be after eleven."

"You're right, Mark. I'll tell you what. You pick him up and bring him to the auditorium."

44

Mark tried to object, but David said he was taking up valuable time and hung up after giving him the address. He knew his manager would do whatever he asked.

Chapter 6

Despite his lack of sleep, the rehearsal was going well. By the time Mark arrived with Zeiggie around noon, David was already well into his session with the singers in the choral group, who were rehearsing for the first time that morning. They worked a cappella, familiarizing themselves with the text, which was written in several languages, French, Italian, German, and English. Later that afternoon, after a quick lunch, the musicians arrived and the orchestra rehearsal continued until seven that evening.

David was exhausted. In spite of the good rehearsal with the singers and band, he felt nervous and on edge, although he hid it well with smiles and banter. Behind it all he was deathly afraid he'd have another spell or attack in front of everybody. That evening after rehearsal he invited Zeiggie over to his penthouse for dinner. His new friend had been bragging about how good he could cook a chicken and David took him up at his boast.

"I'll do the buying and you do the cooking," he suggested.

After his first bite, he looked up at Zeiggie, who was sitting across from him, and said, "Zeiggie, this could be the beginning of a long friendship."

David had a beer with dinner. Zeiggie had ginger-ale. After eating they relaxed in the living room listening to Bach's Solo for Cello in E-flat.

David's eyes had been feeling tired since that afternoon. Now they were so heavy he could hardly keep them open. He needed a good night's sleep.

"I should be going," said Zeiggie, around ten. "I'll catch a cab on the street."

"I'll call you one or you can stay if you like. I have a spare room."

"Naw, thanks, but I should be going," his friend replied heading for the door. "I want to hit the library tomorrow and do some research. I have some ideas where I might find the evidence I'm looking for. Bach was poisoned, purposely murdered, and I know who did it. See you tomorrow."

David thought his friend's quest to find Bach's supposed killer a little odd, but there were many mysteries surrounding the famous composer, so why not another, as farfetched as it sounded. It would make an interesting book if he could ever prove his theory.

After Zieggie left, David was overwhelmed with exhaustion, and crashed in his bed not even bothering to remove his clothes. Although he fell asleep almost instantly, by midnight he was wide awake, and despite his heavy eyelids could not fall back to sleep. His mind was racing, rummaging through all the failed relationships. The loneliness seemed to creep out of the floor and walls to engulf him. He ended up sitting in front of the TV for company, watching an all-night movie, barely keeping the immense solitude at bay. It didn't help his eyes much. He ended up dozing off sometime after five am and woke up again a little after six-thirty, still feeling dead tired.

After trying to get a few more hours of shut-eye, he called his chief assistant and asked him to take over rehearsal. David had an ambitious program planned for that day's practice, combining the three sections he had rehearsed separately on the preceding days. It was something he should have done himself, but he just wasn't up to it. He spent a half hour explaining what he wanted done.

"Call me if you have any questions. I'm going to try and get some sleep," he said, hanging up.

Mark called a short while later.

"What wrong?" he asked as soon as David picked up the phone. "Why aren't you coming to rehearsal? Did you have another attack? Was that Zeiggie character there last night? What was he doing there?"

"You sound like a jealous lover," replied David, laughing despite his lack of sleep.

"I don't trust that guy. He's up to something," said Mark.

"He left early. I had a bad night, that's all."

"Kind of a coincidence he's always around when you're having trouble."

"Don't be ridiculous," replied David. "Zeiggie's all right. You're being crazy."

"What happened? Be specific. Should I call your doctor?"

"I couldn't sleep," David explained. "I was dead tired, but woke-up around midnight and never got back to sleep."

"Did you take a pill?"

"No, I was afraid to after what happened last time. I just want to rest my eyes for a few hours. I'll be in by noon."

He promised his manager he would see a doctor, and almost made the call, but decided against it. After all, all he needed was a little sleep.

While his benefactor rested, Zeiggie arrived at the library, where he toiled through some of the more obscure appendixes of Spitta's and other arcane texts looking for that elusive clue to what really happened to J.S. Bach. In the meantime, his new employer rested in his darkened room.

Zeiggie was convinced that someone had murdered Bach and he was determined to find the proof and uncover the killer. It was as if he had been assigned the post of public prosecutor for the state.

Bach's enemies had every reason to want him dead. He was becoming too powerful. He was instituting too many revolutionary changes in the church music of the day. He was influencing too many young people with his newfangled ideas. All the youthful musicians flocked to him. He was making those who were already prone to disobedience flaunt the rules, none of which applied to the great master. He was too full of himself, treating others - his superiors in fact - with unconcealed scorn. Hadn't he once been imprisoned for almost a year for his cavalier attitude to one of his betters? Granted he had written the first part of the Well-Tempered Clavier while incarcerated, but he had worked hard to expunge the shame and hide the truth of what really happened. He had many enemies, some of them very powerful. He had offended many more with his arrogant ways and belligerent attitude through the years.

Of course, Bach had even more friends and admirers, a multitude of fans and followers for every one gainsayer, but that only made his opponent, surreptitious as he was, more angry and vindictive. It was the very fact of Bach's fame and great popularity that made the approach his opponent took so secretive, and made it so hard to uncover. Like any good detective, however, Zeiggie had put himself into the murderer's shoes, and thought he had found the motive.

Bach had paid the ultimate price for his fame and notoriety, the final penalty for his amazing gifts. It's understandable that he'd have eye trouble after a lifetime of writing and reading music by candlelight at night, or in early morning or dark, cloud-covered days. There wasn't that much light filtering into a house in those times even in the brightest of days, at least not for more than a few hours or so, until the sun moved on. It was rare enough that a room even had windows, although Bach's dwelling while in Leipzig was spacious and well lit.

Even the great composer Hayden had eye trouble, much the same as his older colleague. He was even treated by the same specialist from England, and he recovered nicely. His successful treatment was part of the reason Bach agreed to the frightening operation in the first place, twice! Admittedly, everyone is unique and reacts to things differently, and who's to say the surgeon didn't mess up in Bach's case, although he seemed to be recovering at first. Then he took a turn for the worst, some kind of complications, most likely from the post-operative treatment he underwent. Or was he poisoned? Information on the details of what happened had been difficult to come by, just like the location of Bach's final resting place.

It was while Zeiggie was in Leipzig on leave from the army, doing his initial research into Bach's death, that it was rumored that the great composer's burial site had been rediscovered. At some point, the location where Bach was buried had been lost. There were so many renovations, demolitions, and re-buildings over the intervening four centuries that his exact resting place remained unknown. There were several cities in widely diverse areas of Germany at one time or another that claimed to house his remains. However, it had always been believed by scholars, including Spitta, to be somewhere in the courtyard of Leipzig University, the city he died in and where he spent the last twenty-seven years of his life. Recently, so the reports had said, the exact location had been unearthed and DNA samples taken that proved it was Bach. He was never able to verify the rumor, but it all seemed to indicate that he was on the right track, so he spent the next thirty years of his life trying to prove it. Now he had met another master, this one in the twenty-first century, with a similar problem.

It was funny. David was like Bach in a lot of ways, world famous keyboard player and composer, director and teacher. He even had eye trouble. Zeiggie closed the book and looked up, thinking.

"I wonder..." he said out loud to himself. Was someone trying to poison Reid like they did old Bach, subtly, with some non-detectable poison, somehow administered without his knowing?

Bach could have easily been poisoned through the eye medicine he was taking, either by someone inside who had been paid off or one of the doctors, who were all from the university. Some were even recommended by the rector. No, that was no mystery, but what about David's case? If someone were trying to poison him, how would they do it? And Why? No, it was all too farfetched. His obsession with Bach was starting to seep into his normal life, blurring fact and fantasy. It was all just a coincidence. Or was it?

After leaving the library, Ziegler took a cab to the Philharmonic building to get a few things for David, who contrary to his promises, hadn't showed up for rehearsal. When he had left the auditorium the day before, he had expected to be back the next day. Now he wasn't sure when he'd return and asked his new assistant to get his bag for him, along with his baton and case.

The baton wasn't like a violin, costing thousands to replace, but it was of sentimental value, given to him by his teacher, Roger Kaminski, who had since passed away. It was one of the few things of the great conductor's he had given away, and a sign of high prestige. David had always felt it gave him a special power when he held it in his hand in front of an orchestra, to inspire the players to new heights. He was getting careless. He should have taken it home with him, but it was late and he figured it would be OK in the highly secured area. Now he was having second thoughts and had asked Zeiggie to get it for him.

It was dark and mostly empty when the ex-cello player arrived at the concert hall. Rehearsal had ended hours ago. There were only a few assistants around, cleaning things up and putting away music sheets. The backup conductor had left for the day. David's baton was in the drawer beneath the podium along with a few other items he had asked Zeiggie to get.

Zeiggie picked up the stick and began playing with it, as if he were the maestro, waving it in the air, pointing to the make-believe musicians, beating time to some imaginary piece. He had always enjoyed watching the great conductors like Bernstein and Ozawa. David was obviously as good as any of them, and here he was using the man's baton. Who would have thought? It was just like his mother always told him. You just never know what life's going to spring on you next. Good luck, bad luck, who knows.

He had been fooling around like this for awhile when one of the assistants came by with an armful of parts, which she piled on a table next to the podium.

"What are you doing?" she asked. "You shouldn't be here. What are you doing with David's baton?"

"I'm his assistant, Leonard Zeigler," he replied, putting the stick down abruptly. "He asked me to pick up his things for him since he was not able to come in today."

"No one informed me. I manage all David's assistants. I don't know you. You have no business here. You better go or I'll call security."

"Call Mister Reid if you don't believe me," he answered.

"I will," she assured him, leaving the stage.

"Wait," he called after her, not wanting to cause trouble, and taking out his cell phone. "I didn't mean to be rude. I'll get David. He'll explain everything." But the girl ignored him and disappeared through the stage door.

He was about to leave the hall when he was suddenly overwhelmed with a searing pain. His eyes began to water. He was having trouble keeping them open. The slightest light made them burn. He tried to rub them, but that only made it worse.

"Whoa," he said out loud, as he almost fell off the stage, grabbing the back of a metal chair and sitting down. He rubbed his eyes with the sleeve of his jacket, trying to clear them. He was having an episode just like David.

This is too much to be coincidental he thought, as he groped his way to an off-stage wash basin and ran the cold water. Finally, after several minutes of washing his eyes out, he began to feel better.

Taking the baton from the case, he examined it carefully, holding it up to his nose for a long time. Finally, he broke the stick in two and threw it in a trashcan next to the table with the music sheets piled on it. He was about to leave the stage, thinking of what he was going to tell David, when he had a second thought. Going back to the wastebasket, he retrieved the thick end of the baton, the end held by the conductor, and wrapped it in a paper towel. He was sticking it in his pocket when someone yelled out.

"Hey, you! What are you doing there?" It was the security guard, coming from the wing of the stage where he had been standing with the young female assistant Zeiggie had talked to earlier. "You're not supposed to be in here."

"He broke Mister Reid's baton," said the girl. "He just snapped it in two. He told me he was David's assistant, but I've never seen him before. He made lewd remarks to me."

"OK, mister," said the guard, coming toward Zeiggie angrily. "Hold it right there. What have you got there?"

Zeiggie tried to explained, but without much success. He had been in this situation before, a poor black man trying to proclaim his innocence to a white cop with an attitude. The security guard called Mark Burns who ordered the intruder arrested, which was done without further ado. Zeiggie was charged with trespassing, attempted theft, and destruction of private property. He waited quietly in the back of the squad car while passers-by stared at him through the windows. He knew everything would be OK once he had his one phone call.

51

Once at the station, Leonard Ziegler was fingerprinted, photographed, and put in a holding cell to await his day in court. Since it was late by the time he was booked, he had to wait until the next day for his phone call as well. Mark, finally glad for the excuse to get rid of the unwanted newcomer, wasn't about to tell David what had happened. He could always say he didn't know for sure who they had arrested and locked up that night. For all he knew, it could have been anyone. It wasn't his business to get involved with every trespasser and thief they caught trying to steal something of David's.

David had been waiting for his friend, Zeigie, for quite some time, and wondered where he was. He had expected him hours ago, and it was almost ten pm. He had tried to call him on his cell, but there was no answer. He wondered where his new assistant had gone off to. Had he made a mistake about Leonard? Had he fallen off the wagon and gone on an all night binge? David gave up around eleven and called Mark, but his business manager said he hadn't heard anything and gave him an earful.

"You better get some sleep tonight. Take a pill if you have to. You can't miss any more rehearsals or we'll have to postpone the concert."

David assured his worried manager and got off the phone as quickly as possible.

He had all intentions of running the rehearsal the next day. There was a tremendous amount of work to do and no more time to be lost. He wanted to work the chorus and orchestra together on the grand final movement of the symphony. He decided to take a sleeping pill and slept right through the night. He was up early the next morning and felt fine after his first restful sleep in days.

He arrived at the concert hall to find everyone ready, musicians and singers all in their designated places, warming up their voices or tuning their instruments. After searching for his baton for awhile, he called over one of his assistants.

"Have you seen my stick?" he asked.

There was no reply for a moment.

"I'm not sure. You'll have to ask Mister Burns," the young man said.

Slightly perturbed, David left the stage to find his business manager. Mark was in the lobby talking on the phone.

"What's up?" he inquired, seeing David's expression. "Oh," he said a second later, figuring it out for himself. "Can I call you back?" he asked over the phone. "Thanks."

"Your baton," Mark said to David. "I was meaning to speak to you about that, but didn't get the chance."

"What happened? Did someone steal it? I thought we had airtight security in this place. I'm certainly paying enough."

"The security is great," said Mark. "They did their job. Unfortunately, it was too late to stop the damage."

"What damage? What happened?" asked David losing his patience.

"I didn't know until just a short time ago," lied Mark. "Your new assistant, Lenny Ziegler, came in drunk last night, made lewd and insinuating remarks to Tina Fong, and broke your baton in a fit of rage when she turned down his advances. They had him arrested."

"Zeiggie! Arrested?" yelled David, beside himself. "I asked him to come down and pick up a few things for me."

"Did you ask him to make rude remarks to Tina and break your baton in two? I'll get you a new one this morning."

"I don't need a new one. That was from my teacher. It had personal value to me. It was irreplaceable." He felt saddened that the man he had tried to help had turned on him in such a hurtful way. "So much for human nature."

"I tried to warn you about that guy," Mark told him. "He was no good."

"I don't need to hear I-told-you-so from you," replied David, storming off angrily.

Mark watched him walk off with a look of satisfaction. "Don't worry, David," he said to no one in particular. "I'm watching your back."

Chapter 7

Zeiggie got his one call the next morning after a breakfast of stale toast and soggy cereal, brought to him in his cell by the same female cop who had given him a blanket the night before. She must have left soon after that, because he was escorted to the phone by another officer who stood a short distance away while he made his call. He contacted David and left a message explaining what happened and telling him it was vitally important they talk. That he had found out something about his spells, but didn't want to say any more over the phone. Then he went back to his cell from where he was taken to the courthouse to be arraigned a short time later. He pleaded not guilty, and was assigned a court appointed lawyer who immediately tried to get him released on bail. It was harder than expected.

"Bail denied," said the judge, after hearing the lawyer's request.

"But your honor," the man began. "My client didn't steal anything and he wasn't trespassing. He was getting Mister Reid's things as he was asked to do by Mister Reid himself. I'm sure as soon as we can contact him, he will clear things up."

"Mister Ziegler here made unwanted advances to a young woman and vandalized property of the said Mister Reid," said the female district attorney. "I'm not sure Mister Ziegler is not a danger to public safety."

The judge continued to consult with the two attorneys, while Zeiggie stood watching from the docks.

"Bail set at $5000," the judge announced finally.

"I can't afford that," said Zeiggie, when his court appointed lawyer walked up smiling smugly.

"Don't worry. A bail bondsman will be by. He'll get you out for five hundred bucks. You got that?"

"Just," said Zeiggie looking haggard and scared. This was just about the worst thing that could have happened to him. He had only been arrested once before, for a stupid college prank he and a few of his buddies pulled after a Red Sox game, but nothing serious like this. It was hard enough to get your life back together without having a criminal record.

A few hours later he was back in his tiny apartment, not sure what to do.

He was almost positive someone was trying to poison David. It was just too much of a coincidence that he had eye spasms after touching the baton and then rubbing his eyes. David had touched it too and look what was happening to him.

Suddenly, everything made sense, the dizzy spells, the eye pain. Someone was poisoning him just like they did Bach. The similarity seemed too much to be happenstance. Someone else knew about Bach's murder and was using the same method to incapacitate David. As farfetched as it sounded, there was no other explanation, at least none that presented itself to Zeiggie as he sat alone in his apartment. He had to tell David, had to convince him, but how? Even with what he knew and suspected, it still seemed hardly possible to believe let alone prove, but that was what he had to do.

Then again, if they did find out the baton had been poisoned they just might blame the whole thing on him. The way things were going, he wouldn't be surprised if they did.

He had had the presence of mind to stick the other end of the broken baton into the cuffs of his trousers before the police came and took him away. It was still there, a hardly noticeable bulge in the right bottom leg, which he barely felt when he reached to pull it out. He placed it on the coffee table in front of him. He'd have to have someone analyze it to find out what, if anything, had been put on it. He started thumbing through the phone book, then remembered a friend of his who worked in a lab. He hadn't talked to the man since his divorce, but he still had his phone number in an old address book at the bottom of a kitchen drawer.

He wondered why David hadn't returned his calls. The cell phone he had bought him was dead and no longer working. He hoped David didn't believe what they were saying about him, but then how well did the man really know him. He thought about the half-bottle of Old Turkey sitting in his cabinet. Knowing it was there if he needed it, like an old buddy, somehow helped. Maybe later, he told himself, as he called the number of his friend, hoping he still worked in a lab.

"I can't believe Zeiggie would do a thing like that," David said for the tenth time that day. "He seemed like such a good guy."

"Well, you just never know," said the young assistant who was sharing his bed.

They had hooked up again after rehearsal. The practice had gone exceptionally well. The orchestra was fully inspired now with the heat of creative passion after hearing the moving climax of the piece with the full orchestra and chorus. Everyone had been struck with the magnitude of what they were doing, and dedicated themselves to being the best they could be. David was thrilled, so pleased in fact, that he celebrated by inviting the comely assistant who was helping him clean up the stage after rehearsal to dinner. From the supper table they moved to the bedroom, much like last time.

"What exactly did he say to you again?" he asked her a second time.

"I really don't want to talk about it," she insisted, leaving the bed and grabbing a pack of cigarettes from her purse.

"Please don't smoke in here, Tina," David asked politely.

"Oh, crap," she said losing her temper.

"I'm sorry, but you know how I feel. Go out to the den and open a window if you want to smoke."

She put the cigarettes back in her purse.

"You should have heard him, David," she said. "It was horrible, the way he leered at me and asked me if I wanted to have sex. When I said no, he grabbed your stick. I thought he was going to stab me with it, but he broke it into pieces instead. I was so scared I ran out to get the security guys and they had him arrested. He was acting crazy, like he was on drugs or something."

"Did you smell anything on his breath, pot or alcohol?" asked David, trying to put it all together, surprised at how wrong he could have been about the man.

"I don't know. I didn't want to get that close to him. His eyes seemed bloodshot though."

David remembered how Zeiggie's eyes looked the day he first met him, bloodshot and glassy like he had been drinking or smoking pot. At least that's the way it seemed to him now, after he had found out the truth about him.

"Well, it's a good thing we have security," David observed. "We won't have to worry about Mister Ziegler any more."

"I sure hope not," replied Tina, snuggling back under David's arm.

She had her reasons for lying, just like she had her reasons for seducing the love-sick divorcée and poisoning him with small doses of a toxin she sprinkled on his baton, where it was sure to get into his eyes. She was being paid handsomely to do it and she was having fun at the same time. They had sex again. Yes, Tina was enjoying herself while she earned her pay.

Sunday was a short day. Rehearsal didn't start until one and ended at five. They spent the morning together and then went back to the concert hall. There were several messages from Zeiggie on his cell phone, which he deleted without listening to. He had canceled the account on the phone he had given the ex-cello player, but not before another half-dozen messages had been sent from it. The phone would be useless now, just like their friendship. His resentment against the man grew. He had no intention of dropping the charges, and was thinking of hiring a detective to help the DA develop a profile on Mr. Zeigler, if that's who he really was.

Mark had gotten him another baton, but David hadn't used it. He was crestfallen at the loss of his great heirloom and couldn't conceive picking up another, not now when his latest creation was just coming to birth. He needed time to reconcile himself to the loss. He'd conduct with his hands in the meantime.

As the days flew by, the music grew and was perfected by the singers and players. The buzz on the street and in the media grew as well. Word had naturally leaked out, a lot of it from the musicians themselves, of the revolutionary nature and beauty of the piece. It was being heralded as something the likes of which had never been heard before. David tried to downplay all the hoopla.

"It's just a piece of music," he told them when interviewed. "I hope people enjoy it."

When asked the reason for the secrecy, he merely replied that it was a difficult piece to play. He wanted to forestall any premature criticisms from the media until they were ready to perform it. Unfortunately, starved for the truth, they had fabricated a pure fiction, making it out to be more than it really was. He hoped people wouldn't be taken in by any of the hype.

"Just go with an open mind and enjoy an evening of new music," he requested.

He started alternating full run-throughs of the piece with sessions concentrating on specific areas needing work, sometimes with just a section or subgroup of the band, sometimes with the whole orchestra and chorus. Now that they were familiar with the composition, he built up the confidence and élan they would need to pull it off and make the impossible look easy. Everything was coming to fruition.

He had not had an attack of dizziness or eye pain since the last bout almost a week before. There were only four days to go before the big premier. The publicity and the pressure were building to a climax.

Things had been hectic and he hadn't seen Tina in a few days, mostly of his own choosing. He was busy and wanted to stay focused. He was equally anxious to keep things casual and at a distance. The last thing he needed right now was a serious relationship, especially after the debacle of his recent divorce. But a little fling with a young, hard body now and then was just what the doctor ordered, so he had invited her over for dinner. She arrived ten minutes early, just before seven.

"Hi," he said, answering the door and taking her coat. "You're early."

"I can go and come back," she teased.

"No, I just haven't changed yet," he replied, removing an apron. "I was just tidying up."

"Why don't you hire some help? You're rich enough. This is a big place."

"I do OK. I don't like a lot of strange people around."

"I have to admit, it's spotless."

"Thanks. I like things clean."

"Sounds like you'd be a hard person to live with," she observed. "I like to eat in bed."

"No eating in bed," he scolding, laughing. "I've prepared linguine in lobster sauce with chunks of fresh lobster."

"Hmm, sounds delicious. You bought wine I hope?" she asked.

"Yes, a bottle of red."

"I suppose you're having beer."

"How'd you guess?" he laughed again. David was in a buoyant mood. They had dinner and bantered good-naturedly over coffee and desert, and were soon necking on the couch, when there was a knock on the door.

"You expecting somebody?" Tina asked, annoyed.

"No," replied David, getting up from the couch and straightening his clothes. "Who is it?" he called out. "If it's Mark, I'll get rid of him," he whispered to Tina.

There was no answer. He looked out the peephole It was Zeiggie. David opened the door. His old friend's eyes were bloodshot and his breath smelled like he'd been drinking.

"David," he said as soon as the door was opened. "I have to talk to you. It's..."

"Who is it?" asked Tina coming up behind David.

"Zeiggie, what do you want?" said David to the ex-cello player and friend.

"I need to talk to you," replied Zeiggie hurriedly, looking over David's shoulder to see who else was in the room. "They're trying to poison you like they did Bach," he blurted out, not able to hold in all the thoughts that had been building up over the past few days. They now came tumbling out like jumbled building blocks. "They were using your baton. I'm having it analyzed."

"It's not him, is it?" screamed Tina from behind David when she realized who was at the door. "Keep that man away from me."

"Zeiggie, I don't think you should be here," said David through the crack in the door, after all but closing it in Zeiggie's face. "You're upsetting Tina. I really don't want you around here. You better go. I don't want any trouble."

"Damn it, listen to me!" shouted Zeiggie, frustrated after days of silence. "They're trying to poison you. You've got to listen to me."

"You're not well. Please go before I call the police," pleaded David. Tina was already doing so.

"Tina!" shouted David annoyed. "Put down the phone. Zeiggie's leaving. He doesn't want to cause any trouble. Stop by later. I'll call," he whispered to his ex-friend conspiratorially through the narrowing crack in the door.

"Wait!" said Zeiggie forcibly, pushing his way into the room drunkenly. "You've got to listen to me."

Tina screamed like someone was being murdered and yelled into the phone. "He just broke into the room. You've got to send help. Help, help!" she screamed.

David tried to quiet her while he attempted to push Zeiggie out of the apartment. They were both about the same size and girth, and were soon tussling back and forth in the hallway. No one wanted to throw a punch and no one was gaining the upper hand as they grappled. Soon the doorman came rushing up and tackled Zeiggie around the arms, taking him to the floor hard.

"Easy," said David, worried about the way Zeiggie's head bounced off the thin carpet. The doorman outweighed the shorter and older black man by at least fifty pounds and was about twenty years younger. "You're going to hurt him."

"That's the idea," said the doorman, jamming his fist into Zeiggie's mouth several times, cutting his lip and breaking a tooth. The ex-cello player sat back dazed and hurt.

"Stop it," David yelled, as the police rushed up the stairs. They bullied Zeiggie onto his stomach, pulled his hands roughly behind him, and for the second time in as many weeks, cuffed him. David watched, queasy with anxiety, as they dragged his ex-friend away.

"You didn't have to do that," he said to Tina after things quieted down.

"He was crazy. Who knows what he would have done," she responded calmly, as if nothing had occurred.

"He may be a little disturbed, but he wasn't going to hurt anyone. He just wanted to talk."

"Well, he shouldn't be coming up here at night, unannounced. He should never have gotten by the doorman."

"They probably recognized him from before. I never alerted them to stop him from coming up. It won't happen again, I'm sure."

"I was so scared," she said, snuggling up to him and putting her arms around his shoulders. She kissed him on the lips, leaning her whole long, voluptuous body against his, but David had lost his appetite.

"You'd better go," he said, moving away. "I don't feel much like company right now. The whole evening's ruined. The next few days are going to be very busy. I'll give you a call."

She didn't protest, having done what she had come there to do, and left a few minutes later. David cleaned up the kitchen and retired to his room, but couldn't sleep.

He kept going over in his mind what Zeiggie had said. Of course, the thought that someone was trying to poison him had popped into his head more than once, but he had just as quickly dismissed it as being too absurd to take seriously. Zeiggie had looked like a man on the edge. There was a desperate, almost insane look in his eyes as he tried to enunciate his neurotic fears. No, it was just too bizarre. He was taking every precaution. If someone was trying to poison him, it would be next to impossible. He was paranoid enough, he didn't need this. Desperate for sleep, he took a sleeping pill, but it had no effect as his mind raced and sprinted here and there like a runaway pet. He was exhausted and still no closer to resolving his dilemma when he got up with the first glimpse of light. He called Mark at six.

"Why are you calling me at this ungodly hour?" Mark asked on recognizing who it was. "It's bloody six am."

"Sorry, Mark, I had to talk to you. I had to have Zeiggie arrested last night. He was drunk. He tried to break in. We had a little tussle that the doorman got in on and they had to cart him away. He was babbling

60

on about someone trying to poison me. I'm afraid he's a very sick man."

"Well, I told you. Poison?" he asked. "Who in hell would want to poison you? That's crazy."

"That's what I thought. The poor guy must be delirious. This whole obsession he has with proving Bach was murdered has addled his brain. Now he's transferred it to me."

"Ah, I see. It all makes sense then, he *is* crazy."

"Yeah, that's what I wanted to talk to you about. I feel sorry for the guy. I want to help him get all the assistance he needs."

"Yeah, that's all well and good, but I'm going to make sure he doesn't bother you again. I'll get a restraining order on the son-of-a-bitch so that he doesn't come within a hundred yards of you."

"Do you really think that's necessary?" asked David, not wanting to make any more trouble for the unfortunate man.

"Yes it's necessary, but don't worry, I'll see he gets all the help possible."

"Good. I didn't get much sleep last night. I'm going to lie back down for a couple hours, but I'll be there at ten."

"OK, David, I'll see you later."

David snapped shut the phone feeling better he had talked to Mark and things were in his capable hands. He lay back down and was pleased when he woke up with the alarm at 8:30. He had managed to get a couple hours of sleep. That would have to do.

Driving himself to the concert hall, he arrived ten minutes past ten and got right down to business. For the next rehearsals, the last few before the final concert, he intended to work the whole piece beginning to end with the entire ensemble, musicians and singers, only stopping when there was an overriding reason to do so. Today was the beginning of the exercise and it was not going well.

He was nervous and on edge. Every little miscue or wrong note jarred his senses, irritating him even more. For some reason, his agitation was rubbing off on the musicians, who seemed to be getting worse the more they practiced.

"No, no, no!" he yelled at one point, looking at the string section. "What are you doing? That's not the way we rehearsed it. Again," he bellowed, hardly giving them time to pick up their instruments. It was much the same as it had been that first horrible day. He stopped them after a few notes and looked at the errant players, the second violins specifically.

"Are you afraid to play?" he demanded to know. They all sat there meekly looking at him. No one answered. "You play like you're afraid of the music, instead of the other way around. I want you to own it. Play with some balls!" he yelled. "Again, with me."

He yelled while they played.

"Louder basses....fortissimo....now build....watch the bowing....horns...OK, build...louder...build..." he swept both hands across his body and in the air.

It was at that moment the dizziness overtook him. It came on suddenly and took him completely by surprise. One minute he was directing and commanding the orchestra to play, listening intently to the notes and pitch, the next he was fighting to keep his balance.

He wheeled clumsily off the podium, almost knocking it down as he grabbed it and tried to catch himself. Hitting the stage floor like a man leaving a merry-go-round, he lurched across the space between the podium and the first row of woodwind players directly in front of him. He tried to catch himself on their metal music stands, as they suddenly stopped playing and held out their arms to help. Knocking over stands and chairs, he reeled backward into the first violin section, where he completely lost balance, crashing through the row of music sheets and falling into the laps of the musicians. Women screamed and men stood up. The whole place was in pandemonium, as some ran to the stage and others scurried off it. David had lost consciousness for a moment, his eyes fluttering white. He lay sprawled on the floor, his head cradled in the lap of the second violinist he had just been berating.

Someone yelled to get an ambulance, while another brought a glass of water to the already recovering conductor.

He felt more embarrassed than anything. His one big fear of having a spell in public had come true in spades. Now it was over, he tried to perform damage control.

"I'm all right," he protested weakly, as several hands tried to restrain him from getting back up. "Really, I'm fine, just lost my balance for a moment. I'm afraid I haven't been getting much sleep. I think I have a little bug. I'll be fine."

"No you won't," said Mark who had made it from his seat in the audience to his boss's side in less than ten seconds. "You're going to bloody lie there until the ambulance arrives. I'm not taking any chances. That was a nasty fall you took. You looked like a fighter out for the count after a right hook from the champ."

David had to undergo the further embarrassment of being strapped to a stretcher with his neck in a brace while the entire band looked on with concern and not a little curiosity. They were all wondering if there would be a concert or not. It didn't look good. Luckily, Mark was able to decoy the press to the front of the building where he gave an impromptu news conference, while David was carried out the rear to a waiting ambulance.

He spent the rest of the day getting every kind of ultra-sound, brain-scan, body probe, and test they could think of, with Mark Burns directing the investigation from the patient's room. They could find nothing wrong. Other than the usual high cholesterol and minor ailments, David was in the best of health, or so the hospital staff affirmed on discharging him. Mark drove him home that evening. It was hours after supper time, but David didn't want to stop and eat. Instead, he insisted on being taken directly home. He didn't invite Mark in and hardly spoke, but that didn't stop Mark from speaking his mind.

"David, I'd be the last person to tell you this, but I think you should take a break, postpone the concert, at least until you feel better."

"Are you crazy?" David said, drawn out of his silence quickly. "After all the work we've put in, now when we're so close. I just had a little fainting spell. I didn't sleep well last night and was upset after what happened with Zeiggie."

"I don't care what you say. It could be something serious. You've been working too hard. I think we should have more tests, just to rule out the scary stuff."

"They just conducted every scan and test known to man. That's one of the biggest hospitals in the country. They certainly know how to check for the scary stuff, if that's what you're worried about."

"I think we should have a specialist look at you."

"What kind of specialist?" asked David, wondering what his friend was getting at.

Mark hesitated, as if afraid to answer.

"A brain specialist," he said finally.

Chapter 8

Zeiggie was surprised he hadn't been arraigned yet. He refused his phone call this time around, having no one to talk to and nothing more to say. He had given up trying to help the great David Gordon Reid. Look where that had gotten him. Still, it was strange they hadn't brought him to court. It wasn't long before a Hispanic woman came to the door of his cell with two men in white.

"Hello, Mister Ziegler," said the woman. "My name is Anita Cortez. The court has ordered you to undergo a psychological evaluation. You are to be taken to the state facility for observation."

"Wait a minute," objected the surprised ex-cello player. "I want my day in court."

"You'll have your day in court, Mister Ziegler, but first you'll have to go with these men. It's for your own good."

There were two beefy guards behind the men in white who looked as if they'd like nothing better than for Zeiggie to resist. He was still hurting from the excesses of the overly exuberant doorman of the night before, and didn't feel like another beating, so went along in spite of his reservations. Sometimes it was a lot easier getting into these places than getting out.

Despite the vigorous objections of his business manager and the backup conductor, David insisted on conducting the rehearsal the following day, much to everyone's surprise. Several had taken odds he would not return and the concert would be scratched. They were wrong. To their dismay, David took up right where he had left off the previous day, yelling instructions, encouragement, and corrections over the music.

"That's it," he exclaimed when they had played the passage. "That's what I'm talking about."

Everyone relaxed. It was a turning point, like conquering the highest peak, surmounting those overwhelming odds and returning triumphant. It was as if someone had hit them with a wand. The stage seemed to glow with inspiration. They all sat congratulating one another.

"OK, from the top now," David announced, not giving them time to rest on their laurels. He felt good and had almost forgotten about the previous day's attack of dizziness, overcome with the music and what they were accomplishing. Before they could begin, Mark ran onto the stage, grabbed David's arm, and whispered something into his ear.

"I just got a call from the police," he said. "They found something. They want you to go down to the station immediately."

"Why, what's wrong?" asked David in alarm.

"I don't know. They wouldn't say over the phone."

After making arrangements for the backup conductor to continue the rehearsal, David left with Mark for the station. On arriving he was directed to the detective in charge.

"What this all about?" Mark asked on being introduced.

"Tina Fang was found hanging in her apartment this morning. She works with Mister Reid, right?"

"Tina! Hung herself?" blurted David.

"Yes, I'm afraid so. Of course, we will have to determine if it was suicide or murder."

"Murder!" both David and Mark said simultaneously.

"You think she was murdered?" asked the conductor.

"We don't know, but we have to assume the worse, until we can show otherwise. It appears to be a suicide, but that will have to be confirmed. The body's being examined now."

David recognized the detective as one of the men who had come to his apartment concerning the missing Donna Fredericks.

"How well did you know Miss Fong?" asked the detective, who was sitting behind a desk.

"Pretty well," replied David, sitting down opposite him. "She was a student at the Conservatory. She was working as an assistant for the Philharmonic. We dated a few times. She was at my place a couple of nights ago."

"Did she seem depressed?"

"No, not that I could tell."

"Can you think of any reason she would want to kill herself?"

David thought for a moment, wondering if his recent rejection of her had anything to do with it, though she hadn't seemed to mind

"No, I don't think so. There was an incident at my apartment last time she was there, and I asked her to leave, but she didn't seem bothered about it. I haven't seen her since."

"What happened?" asked the detective. "What kind of incident?"

"It's really nothing, I'm sure," answered David. "I don't think it has anything to do with this."

"Let me be the judge of that," advised the detective. "What happened?"

David was reluctant to involve Zeiggie, but the police had a job to do and needed all the information they could get. They would probably find out about him anyway. Before he was able to reply, Mark chimed in.

"There was an incident at the concert hall. Miss Fong had a confrontation with one of David's new assistants, Leonard Zeigler. He's only been working for us a few weeks. Apparently he was being lewd, and came on to her. When she turned down his advances he got mad and broke David's baton. It was an irreplaceable heirloom. We had to let him go."

"We don't know for sure that's what happened," interjected David.

"That's what Tina said," replied Mark. "You can confirm that. It must be on the police report. He was taken to the local precinct near the concert hall. Then the night before last he came barging in on David while the girl was there. He was drunk and disorderly and had to be arrested again."

"Was Mister Zeigler trying to harm Tina Fong?" asked the detective looking at David.

"No," he replied, giving Mark a look to shut him up. "It had nothing to do with Tina, although she became a bit hysterical. He was trying to warn me about something."

"Warn you about what?"

"He was doing some research for me on J.S. Bach. He has this theory about Bach being murdered, poisoned, and said someone was trying to do the same thing to me. It sounded crazy. He'd been drinking. There was a ruckus and he ended up being arrested. His preoccupation with Bach is getting to him, I'm afraid."

"Sounds like this guy could be dangerous," observed the inspector.

"The DA thought so at the bail hearing," interjected Mark.

"This happened last night at your apartment when the young girl was there?" the detective asked the conductor.

"No, the night before," David corrected him. He gave the officer the address of his apartment.

"And you say you fired this guy?" inquired the detective as he wrote down the information. "Sounds like he could have held a grudge against you and Miss Fong."

"He was trying to warn me about something," insisted David.

"Could be a ruse. Maybe he used it as an excuse to gain entrance. We'll have to check him out."

"Well, that should be easy enough. He's probably still locked up," David informed him.

"Donna Fredericks was a friend of yours too, wasn't she?" the detective asked casually.

David had been expecting the question.

"Yes," he answered. "I already told you that when you came to my place a few weeks ago. Have you found her?"

"No, not yet, but we have reason to suspect foul play." He looked hard at David. "Women have a way of disappearing around you, don't they?"

"Now wait a bleeding minute," objected Mark. "Mister Reid was very gracious to leave his rehearsal and come down here. He's a very important man, at the threshold of an unprecedented international achievement. I doubt the police commissioner would like to learn you've been harassing the country's premier composer and director. You have no right to talk to him like that."

"I'm sorry, Mister Burns. Mister Reid, I didn't mean to imply you had anything to do with this. As far as I know Miss Fong took her own life. Your work must be very stressful. I certainly don't want to add to it. That's probably what happened to Miss Fong - stress. Do you know if she was seeing anyone else?"

"I think we've been here long enough," insisted Mark. "We should be going. It's getting late and David hasn't eaten."

"That's all right, Mark," said David. "I don't know who Tina was seeing. We didn't talk about it, although she could have been dating other people. It was only a casual relationship."

"Was she the promiscuous type?"

"I really couldn't say," replied David standing up.

"OK, thank you for coming down, Mister Reid."

"Glad I could help," replied David. "This is just terrible, poor Tina."

They left the station a short time later.

"Poor Tina," David repeated as Mark drove them back to the concert hall. "This is terrible. I don't feel so well. I don't think I'll be able to eat."

"There's nothing more we can do tonight. Try to relax and eat something. You need to concentrate on the concert. You've only got a couple days left."

"This is all I need, just before the debut."

"I'll take care of everything," Mark assured him. "You just focus on your music. Don't worry about anything else. The poor girl must have been very unbalanced. You know how some of these young, artistic women can be."

"I feel just terrible. She seemed to be normal, that is until the night Zeiggie showed up. Then she became downright hysterical. After Zeiggie was arrested she acted as if nothing had happened. I hope it wasn't something I said."

"Exactly what did you say?"

"I was upset after they hauled Zeiggie off. She wanted to carry on as if nothing had happened. I asked her to leave."

"What'd she say?"

"Nothing, she seemed fine, like she could have cared less."

"Maybe she just didn't want you to see her upset. You never know with these types. She was probably one of those manic-depressives, or on drugs or something."

"Well, Zieggie had nothing to do with it. You shouldn't have gone on like you did. After all, we really don't know what happened. It's just her word against his. He was trying to warn me about something and I got him thrown in jail for his trouble. We've got to help him."

"Don't worry about him. You have more important things to worry about. I'll go down to the courthouse in the morning and see he's taken care of."

"Thanks, Mark. I knew I could count on you," said David. "Tell them I'm not pressing charges."

"You want to grab a bite to eat?" asked Mark, dropping David off at the auditorium where his car was still parked.

"No, thanks, I'm not really very hungry. I just want to get home and crash."

"Ok, but try to eat something. You've got to keep you strength up."

"Thanks, Mark. See you tomorrow," he said closing the car door.

As he drove back to his flat on base-brain, the thoughts swirled around the rest of his mind like rapid sixteenth notes in 2/4 time. Three divorces and one suicide; he wasn't having very good luck with women. Maybe he should go gay like old Lenny Bernstein. It would probably be a lot cheaper and a lot less trouble.

He was totally depressed by the time he reached his apartment. He knew he'd have trouble sleeping despite how tired he was. The one person that could have given him some solace and relaxation had killed herself. Every time thought about Tina nestled under his arm, he saw her hanging from a shower stall. He knew there was no way he would be able to eat. He was in despair. He needed rest, but knew a sleeping pill wouldn't help.

Was this the price of fame and success? Was this the pound of flesh he had to pay for creating divine music, for his pact with the devil? He was starting to think the price was too high. Perhaps he was looking for happiness in great achievements and world fame when all the time it lay in just being loved. He couldn't think of a worse thing to have happened. All his acclaim, all the great music seemed trivial somehow. Someone, a human being he had grown close to, hated life so much that she had committed suicide. Why? Why had she done it? He searched his soul for solace, but all he found was guilt. He shouldn't have kicked her out, rejected her when she was in such a state. Maybe if he had been more sensitive and understanding she'd still be alive. He might have been able to help her. He shouldn't have been in such a hurry to get rid of her. These thoughts plagued him as he lied in the darkened room.

Much to his surprise, when he regained consciousness it was 7:00 am. He had slept straight through the night without taking anything. He woke feeling rested but un-refreshed. If he'd had any dreams, he didn't remember them.

The phone was ringing.

"Hello," he said reaching for his cell.

"Have you seen today's papers?" asked Mark on the other end.

"No," replied David. "I suppose this is your way of getting back at me for calling you at 6:00 am.

"It's all over the morning news."

"What is?" asked David, still not sure what his friend and manager was talking about.

"Somehow the papers got hold of the fact that one of your assistants committed suicide. 'Late yesterday, twenty year old Miss Tina Fong of 127 Oak Drive, was found hanging in her apartment. The police believe it was suicide. An autopsy is being conducted today. The dead girl was an assistant at the Philharmonic for world famous conductor and composer, David Gordon Reid. Miss Fong, who was known to be dating the world renowned maestro, is survived by her mother and sister who live in Mystic, Connecticut. The famous conductor, preparing for the world premier of his newest symphony, was questioned by the police.'

"That's not the best part," Mark continued. "'Sources speculate that the young woman may have been depressed after her break-up with the composer, who has recently gone through his third divorce.'"

"Great, what did they have to bring that up for? It's bad enough Tina killed herself."

"This is the worst possible publicity," observed the business manager.

"I thought all publicity was good."

"Not this kind of scandal, not when half your audience is the crème of New York society. Your music will be drowned out by the chorus of people screaming about your love affairs."

"I think you're exaggerating. Anyway, isn't that what I hired you for, to take care of this kind of thing?"

"Well, with the way things are going, I'm going to need a raise or an assistant. I was up half the night trying to squelch this thing."

"How'd they find out?" asked David, not feeling overly concerned. His life had been a glasshouse ever since his first slide into fame with the musical hit show on Broadway. He had long since given up his privacy. Each divorce had been a national event. Why should this be any different?

"Somebody at the precinct must have blabbed it. Mac Davis at the Times picked it up. He actually went to try and interview your doorman but he didn't get far."

"I'd like to know why she killed herself," said David, still mystified by the whole affair. "It doesn't make sense."

"She's probably one of those crazy women obsessed with famous men and angered by rejection. I can plant some kind of counter story that she's an angry, rejected, psychotic woman who you tried to help and who ended up committing suicide. By the time I'm through with her, she'll really have a reason to kill herself."

"I don't know, Mark. Why would you want to do that? What happened is bad enough. Don't make it worse by throwing dirt on the poor dead girl. Better to not say anything. Have you had a chance to find out what happened to Zeiggie?"

"No, not yet. I've been a bit preoccupied of late with all your other problems. I'll make some calls today, as soon as I hang up with you."

"Good, I'd like to talk to him. Maybe he knows something. He did talk to her, you know."

"I'll check it out, don't worry. In the meantime, concentrate on the rehearsals. You don't have much time left. The concert's in two days."

"I know, don't remind me."

Traffic was light and David made good time, arriving at the Philharmonic parking garage and pulling into his reserved VIP parking spot. Despite the eight hours of sleep, he felt drained. Even the anticipation of hearing his creation come to life couldn't make him forget Tina's untimely death.

Chapter 9

David bumped into Mark in the lobby. There were a mob of reporters at the front of the building waiting for a scoop.

"Don't let this distract you, David," said his manager. "I'll take care of everything. You just get in there and rehearse."

"I don't know, Mark. I don't feel much like conducting. It all seems so trivial after this."

"Well that's where you're wrong, my friend. Your music's more important than the random death of someone you hardly knew, who for some insane reason killed herself. Who knows why. Maybe she has a past. You can bring something special to the world, something that can change the way people think about music. Don't let this incident spoil that."

David's resolve to flee to the private confines of his bedroom began to dissolve in the light of his business manager's encouragement. That's why David hired him, and that's why he trusted and listened to him. What could he do about this poor unfortunate creature's inner nightmares and demons? He was lucky he hadn't been engulfed in them. No, he should treat it as a learning experience, thank his lucky stars, and go on with his life. No sense dwelling on things he couldn't control. So he took Mark's advice and entered the auditorium, while Mark jumped back in his car and sped off to do damage control.

David greeted the orchestra a little uncomfortably. There were a few odd looks, as everyone had read the newspapers and knew the person in question. A few of the musicians consoled him and showed their support. After the triumphant practice of the day before, which was interrupted by the phone call from the police, no one knew exactly what to expect. David tried to keep everything to business as usual.

"Today we're going to play the entire symphony from beginning to end. Andre's going to wander about and listen. No stops," he said. "I want it played right through as if it's the concert. It is a concert. You are all going to play for Andre. I want him to hear it whole as the audience will."

He took a small tape recorder and handed it to his second, telling him to go into the audience and record the orchestra from specific areas in the auditorium. Andre found a seat approximately in the middle of the hall, while David brought everyone to attention and started the piece. After a short time Andrea got up and moved to another location, where he sat and taped as before. Then he moved again, first to one side of the hall, then the other, at one point close to the stage, at another as far away as possible. He even stood in the balcony and recorded, as well as in the wings offstage, taking notes the whole time.

Again, the music drove all but the miracle of sound out of David's mind. Even though it wasn't perfect and he had noted many areas he wanted to work on and improve, it was an inspiring performance. Once more the musicians and singers were moved. Some had tears of triumph in their eyes. There was spontaneous applause as David put down his baton, which he was using for the first time since his old one had been broken.

"That wasn't bad," he said, clapping in return. "Strings, you've really got that bowing pattern down at bar eighty. That was so smooth you sound like you could do it in your sleep."

"We can," one of them replied, eliciting much laughter and good natured ribbing.

"The horn passage in the third movement was really nicely done," continued David, giving out praise as well as good-natured criticism. "You people are so expressive.".

Just as he was about to begin working on the first of his improvements, one of his assistants tapped him on the shoulder.

"Sir, the police are here to see you."

David turned to see the same two plain-clothed detectives that had visited his apartment two-weeks before, standing at the foot of the stage. He beckoned the backup conductor, who once again took the reigns after a few instructions from David.

"Hello," he said, walking down the short steps from the stage to the two policemen who were standing in the center isle. "What can I do for you?"

"Hello, Mister Reid. Sorry to disturb you again," announced Detective Reilly, the man he had talked to at the station. "This is my partner, Inspector Hendricks. Is there somewhere we can talk?"

"Yes," said David, pointing toward the wing of the stage. "We can talk in my office. Do you have information on Donna Fredericks?"

"No, this is about Tina Fong."

David said nothing and led them to a small room in back of the stage, cluttered with music scores, scattered books, and assorted instruments. He removed some sheets of music from two plastic chairs to make room for the officers.

"We believe Tina Fong was murdered," said Hendricks, who was short and stocky like David, "The physical examination was not consistent with suicide. Someone strangled her."

"What?" said David in shock. "How do you know that?"

"Suicide victims don't usually have bruises. There was a struggle. The ligature marks on the front of her neck don't match the knot in the rope, which was tied in the back."

David was stunned to silence as he digested this disturbing information.

"Do you know anyone who would have wanted to harm Miss Fong?" asked Reilly, "anyone with a grudge or who was bothering her?"

"No," replied David.

"What about this Leonard Zeigler, the one who tried to pick her up?" inquired Hendricks. "It sounds like she was quite afraid of the man."

"What gives you that idea?"

"We've talked to your manager, Mark Burns," Reilly told him. "He said Zeigler threatened her. You said yourself that she became hysterical when he came to your apartment."

David was conscious of how they made him divide his attention between them, his head going back and forth in slow denial.

"That's hearsay. Mark gets a little carried away sometimes. It was nothing like that. He's exaggerating. Anyway, last I heard Zeiggie was in jail. That sounds like a good alibi if you ask me.

The two detectives looked at each other.

"The coroner says the time of death was between one and four, the day before last," Reilly informed him. "Leonard Zeigler was released from jail on his own recognizance at eleven-thirty that morning. We haven't been able to locate him. He seems to have disappeared."

"You don't think he has anything to do with this?" David asked.

"How well do you know him?" continued Reilly.

"I thought I knew him, but after what happened at the concert hall that night, I'm not so sure. I don't know what to believe. He seemed like such a nice guy, and Tina's story didn't make sense. I just can't imagine him trying to pick her up."

"You think she was lying?" suggested Reilly.

"Why would she do that?" countered David.

"Maybe he was drunk," said Hendricks. "Did he have a drinking problem?"

"I've never seen him take a drink or under the influence. He might have had a problem in the past, but he was on the wagon."

"Maybe he fell off," said Reilly. "You said he was drunk that night he came to your apartment."

"Yes, but that's the first time I'd seen him that way."

"Did he try to assault the girl?" asked Hendricks. "Was he mad at her for reporting him, trying to get back at her?"

"No, like I told your partner here," replied David. "He hardly looked at her. He wasn't interested in her at all. He thought someone was trying to poison me. He was trying to warn me about something."

"Sounds crazy if you ask me," said Hendricks. "Crazy people can do crazy things."

"He thought someone was trying to poison you," repeated Reilly, "like they did Bach."

Hendricks snorted.

"Sounds like a nut case to me. How long did you say you knew this guy?"

"We met a couple of weeks ago when he helped me after I got lost in town. He worked in one of my shows. He played the cello. He seemed nice enough. He was a peaceable kind of guy. He never showed any signs of violence, or of being disturbed in any way."

"Sometimes these guys seem normal until one of their buttons is pushed, then they go off," Hendricks observed.

"Where were you Thursday afternoon?" asked Reilly.

"I was at the Mount Sinai Hospital getting examined. I had a dizzy spell during rehearsal. I guess I must have passed out for a second and took a bad fall. I was getting checked out. Mark was there as well."

"Have you been having feinting spells?" asked Hendricks.

"No, the doctor told me I was just a little run down. It's been a stressful, busy two weeks. I haven't been sleeping that well. They did a number of tests but didn't find anything wrong."

"Sounds like it could be serious," Reilly inquired.

"Maybe you were poisoned," suggested Hendricks. "Maybe Tina Fong was poisoning you."

"Don't be absurd," replied David indignantly.

"Well, that could be a motive for killing her."

75

"Wait a minute," said David loudly, standing up "I haven't got anything to do with this. You're out of your mind. I'm trying to get ready for the debut of my new Symphony, which took me nine months to write and prepare. I don't have time for this. You'd better talk to my lawyer. This interview is over."

"I'm sorry," said Reilly. "Ted here is just hypothesizing, thinking out loud. I apologize. No one here is trying to suggest you murdered Tina Fong. As you say, you were at Mount Sinai all afternoon, which is easy enough to verify. We're just trying to get to the bottom of this and can't leave any stones unturned. We don't want to have to take you down to the station to question you, not with all those news hounds standing out there. We just want to ask you a few more questions. Ted will refrain from any more hypothesizing."

"What did you hire Mister Zeigler for?" Hendricks asked, not sounded a bit apologetic.

"To help me with rehearsals," replied David. "He's a trained musician."

"You have a lot of other people for that," the detective continued. "What did you need him for?"

"He is an amateur historian of J.S. Bach. I was having him do some research on him, for a book I was thinking of writing."

"How much were you paying him?" asked Hendricks.

"I don't see what that's got to do with anything," replied David.

"He wasn't working under the table, was he?" Reilly inquired.

"No, he was on the books."

"Then you can tell us what you were paying him," he continued.

"I was paying him twenty-five dollars an hour on a W2, and we were picking up his medical and dental. He took home around $150 a week."

"You have quite a reputation," observed Hendricks out of the blue.

"What's that supposed to mean?" replied David, offended.

"Well, you date a lot of women. Like that Fredrick girl. A lot of casual sex, eh?"

"You have a lot of nerve," said David, beginning to get annoyed. He was sure that's what they were trying to do, so he resolved to keep his cool. "I'm no longer married. I'm trying to get on with my life. She seemed nice enough. I had no indication that she was troubled. She brought me my baton after rehearsal that first day. I had left it on the podium. We got to talking. One thing led to another and I invited her out to dinner. I was working hard, under a lot of pressure. I needed the companionship. Fame and money doesn't keep a person from getting lonely. I'm only human. Anyway, we hit it off and went out a couple of times"

Hendricks opened a large manila envelope he had been holding and took out an 11x8 black and white photo, placing it on the table in front of David.

It was a full-length morgue shot of a nude Tina Fong. She looked small and vulnerable, her eyes only partly opened. David froze, his gaze riveted on the photo.

"Someone tried to make us think this woman committed suicide to cover up their heinous crime," said Reilly. "Anything you can do to help us capture her killer would be greatly appreciated."

"Oh, God," muttered the shocked conductor. "How horrible. Poor Tina."

"Right now, Mister Zeigler is our number one suspect," said Hendricks again. "Maybe this Zeiggie was getting back at her. Maybe she was lying for some reason and he got enraged at what she was trying to do to him."

"I think there are more likely suspects," replied David

"Like who?" queried Reilly, leaning his tall, lanky frame forward. "Can you think of anyone else who might have wanted to harm Miss Fong?"

"No," answered David slowly.

"Are you sure?" Reilly asked. "No jealous boyfriends? No dirty looks from across the room? No arguments with colleagues? No leering stagehands lurking in the wings?"

"Not that I noticed. I'm focused on trying to put this concert together."

He wondered where Mark was, and why he wasn't here now when he needed him. His old neighborhood protector would have put these two cops in their place.

"What about your manager?" said Reilly as if reading his thoughts. "Mark Burns? He was with you yesterday when you were at the station."

"Yes, that's right."

"How long have you known this gentleman?" asked Hendricks, working with his partner like an expert musician in a Mozart duet.

"All my life, we grew up together. He came over here a short time after I moved to New York."

"Did he know the young lady?" Reilly inquired.

"Only in passing. He really wasn't interested in my social life, only running my business, which is a full time job."

"OK, Mister Reid," said Reilly. "Thank you for your time. You've been very helpful. We'll get to the bottom of this, don't worry."

The two detectives ended the interview. Neither seemed interested in his upcoming concert.

After they left, David didn't feel much like working. Again, the premier of his great symphony seemed trivial next to the death of another person, a woman he had been intimate with. Now he'd never get a date, he thought without amusement.

He was disturbed to hear Zeiggie had disappeared. Even the police didn't know where he was. He tried calling Mark but only got an answering machine. He left a message and went back to the auditorium where the sounds of his symphony came to him, but his heart just wasn't in it. He said a few words to his backup and hurriedly left the hall, his head bowed, completely absorbed in his thoughts. Rehearsal was almost over anyway, but his long absence and sudden departure left a pall that even the astounding music and amazing musicianship couldn't overcome. It didn't bode well.

Zeiggie was not having a good day either. As a matter of fact, he hadn't had a decent day since he arrived at the maximum security mental facility in Trenton, New Jersey, thirty-two hours ago. His agitation had increased the further they drove him from the city, until he had no idea where he was. By the time they arrived at the psychiatric hospital he had to be medicated. Whatever they gave him completely unhinged his mind. Any thread of sanity was lost in the jumble of thoughts, images, and memories that flooded his brain.

During his initial evaluation he babbled on about Bach and how he had to save him from his murderers, explaining how the great master was writing a cello sonata for him, which demanded all his time.

He spent his days alone in the common area or in his room, practicing his imaginary cello, the fingers of his left hand moving up and down a long cardboard strip he had made himself with black lines penciled on it for strings. Lenny Ziegler was fitting right in at the prison for the criminally insane.

With minimal background investigation and a scant twenty-minute interview, Zeiggie was diagnosed as having acute schizophrenia, with paranoid delusion, and immediately pronounced a danger to the public.

The prognosis was poor. No, the doctors didn't know when the patient would be well enough to leave.

Chapter 10

"That's bloody unbelievable!" Mark swore after hearing about David's interrogation. They were having dinner at the club. Luckily only members were allowed, and the few that were there respected each other's privacy. Still, Mark's outburst elicited stares. "They believe you were involved?"

"I don't think so, but they asked me a lot of personal questions. They said Zeiggie was their number one suspect."

"That figures," replied David's manager. "I never did trust that guy."

"This is all we need. Her murder will be in all the morning papers," said David, thinking about the effect this was going to have on the concert and the dark cloud it would cast over the orchestra and audience.

"You just have to put it out of your mind," counseled his friend.

"What do think happened to Zeiggie?" asked David.

"I don't know. There's no record of an arraignment. He was logged out, but the paperwork wasn't filled out properly and no one knows where he is. So far a search has turned up nothing."

"That's strange," said David. "Maybe it is a conspiracy."

"That's even more ridiculous. Who would want to poison you like Zeigler said?"

"I guess you're right," agreed David. "It's just all so crazy."

"Forget about all this and concentrate on the music. Keep focused on what you started out to do and finish it like you've done everything else in your life. It's all been too easy. Now you have to fight a little to succeed. Don't let us down. What you've done is special. It only comes along once in a century. It happened a few hundred years ago with Bach and Mozart and Beethoven, and again at the turn of the twentieth century with Stravinsky and Bartok. Now it's about to happen again. Don't deny the world your creation just because of this nonsense. It's all over. Don't dwell on it."

Mark could be very convincing at times, but it was hard not to notice the curious, sometimes hostile looks of the other diners. Fame was one thing but notoriety that comes with lurid headlines and mysterious death was another matter entirely.

Lenny Ziegler lay awake in his bed watching the shadows of the moon float across the ceiling of his darkened room. The sounds of the night and his ward wafted to his ears like voices from the past.

Zeiggie had taken control of his situation, finally realizing in a moment of lucidity that it was the drugs they were giving him that were causing all his problems. Gradually, through trial and error, he learned how to fake swallowing the pills by holding them under his tongue. When they checked for that, he'd regurgitate them before they fully dissolved in this stomach. He only ate food that medication couldn't be meshed up in and drank only sealed cans of soda or bottled water. By such means he was able, at least for the most part, to clean his system of the medication - a combination of Thorazine and other psychotropic drugs - and regain his sanity.

Zeiggie had been in the system before, but he had never seen anything like this. He knew there must be a reason for it. Someone with a lot of power was trying to make him disappear. Whoever it was must have perceived him as a threat of some sort. Zeiggie had to walk a fine line between paranoia and the truth considering his situation, but it seemed to him that it must have something to do with David Reid.

He didn't think Reid was responsible. He remembered the look of concern on his face when the doorman was beating him up. No, David wouldn't have done this. Maybe his business manager, that a-hole didn't like him from the get-go, but would he have had the power to pull this off? Zeiggie didn't know, nor could he rule out the possibility. That little oriental bitch, the one with the big tits and bigger mouth, the one who got him in trouble in the first place, what was she up to? Was she the one who was trying to poison David? Could she have done this? No, it just didn't add up.

Despite Zeiggie's new found sanity, his mind was far from stable. He kept slipping into thoughts of Bach and his suspected murder by his rival the Rector Ernesti. He let his mind stray. Was something like that happening again? He wondered. Whatever the case, he had to figure a way out of his current predicament.

In the wee hours of the morning when the faint light hinted at the coming of dawn, Zeiggie fell into a light sleep, where he had a dream he was playing the cello in a large orchestra. It was the debut of David Gordon Reid's great symphony, being played before a live audience of millions. The orchestra itself was so large it filled the floor of an immense coliseum. He was in the cello section, 3000 strong, and could barely see the conductor on his raised, seventy foot podium in the center of the massive stage, a tiny spec in the distance. Wanting to get a little closer so he could see his cues better, he picked up his chair, his cello, and his music stand, and taking his bow, started awkwardly toward the podium. Of course, it was very tough going, like climbing Mount Everest in a blizzard, as he struggled through the tightly-packed crowd of musicians. No one wanted to let him pass, everyone jealous of their positions. His chair kept bumping into people who complained bitterly, while his cello was in constant danger of being smashed. His bow almost broke several times as he tried to protect it from the crush. The music was falling off the stand, so he was constantly obliged to stop and pick it up. It was a long, disheartening trek, but finally, sweating and bleary-eyed, he made it to the base of the great marble podium at the center of the stage. The concert was about to begin.

He tried to place his music on the stand, but it kept falling over. Everyone was waiting, all eyes on him, but he could barely keep his own from closing they were so heavy. His bow and cello weighed a100 pounds. He could barely hold them. His music was in complete disarray. He realized that everyone, including the conductor, was waiting for him, but he had completely forgotten how to play. It was as if he never knew.

Finally, able to delay no longer, he took a deep breath, closed his eyes, and slid the bow across the strings to produce the most hideous screeching sound imaginable. Everyone threw their hands to their ears and cringed. Just as the stage crew was rushing toward him to drag him back where he belonged, he noticed the baton in David's hand was covered with a black, creeping sludge. It seemed to be seeping from the end of the stick and spreading downward, unseen by the conductor. Forgetting everything, Zeiggie started running up the great flight of stairs that ran back and forth across the broad, black face of the seventy-foot granite podium to warn David of the danger. But he could hardly move. His feet felt as if they were weighed down by chains. His eyes burned as if filled with hot ash. He fought to keep them open. Finally, almost at the top, he collapsed and fell over the edge down into what seemed like an endless pit, falling and falling until he woke up being roused by an orderly.

"Wake up, Zeiggie," said the attendant, "time to take your Meds."

So far everything was going perfectly, better than could have been expected considering all the things that stood in his way. His employer would be pleased. Too bad Tina Fong had to take the fall. It was unfortunate, but probably necessary once she started to get greedy. He tried to warn her. Evidently his employer wasn't fooling around. He would have to tread lightly or the same thing might happen to him. The meddling of Reid's new friend, who stumbled upon the poisoned baton by accident after talking to Tina, had threatened the whole scheme and forced his employer's hand. She had said too much, knew too much. It was a risk he had advised against, but the huge amount of money involved made it all essential. So far so good, now for the coup de maitre.

There would be plenty of opportunities to finish the task, but timing was critical. Too soon and it would all be for nothing. Too late and they would lose what they most sought. His instructions had been clear and explicit. He knew what he had to do, but the window of opportunity would be narrow.

Tomorrow would be the last day of rehearsals before the concert the next evening. A final dress rehearsal was scheduled for 7:00 pm, the same time as the actual performance. There would be no practice on the day of the concert so everyone could rest and relax before the big event, and what an event it promised to be.

There would be concerts all around the city that day to celebrate the grand premiere. Music from the early Baroque and Classical through the Romantic and Impressionistic periods, would be played, right up to the twentieth century greats, all conducted by some of the most renowned directors in the world, to climax with David's new symphony that evening. The concert itself was being simulcast live around the world to an estimated audience of 100 million people, and was being hailed as the international cultural event of the century. It was imperative to Mark and his employer that it go as planned and that it be a great success. It was the aftermath of that success that had to be controlled.

He still didn't know how he was going to pull it off, but he knew he would, he had to. If only David would cooperate.

The next day Mark went to the final rehearsal and sat in the back of the auditorium unobserved, listening as David conducted and worked with the band. He stopped them several times, but it was all done with good-natured humor. Everyone was in high spirits, even though the pressure on them was extreme. Mark watched and waited.

Toward the end of the practice period, just prior to the two hour break before dress rehearsal that evening, David took up his baton and conducted the entire piece from beginning to end, only stopping a few times to have them repeat something until he was satisfied with it. Mark was also satisfied. As usual, David rubbed his tired eyes often. Yes, his plan would work.

Even in its still unfinished form, the music was astounding. What David had created was truly miraculous. Mark wondered if he ever considered why it all came so easy to him. Why he heard things no other composer, except maybe one, had heard before. They had tried to renege on the deal, take it over for their own, but it wasn't going to happen that way, not if his employer had anything to say about it.

In spite of himself, Mark was excited at the anticipation of his coup. If he had any pangs of conscience he squashed them as quickly as they came with thoughts of how he was getting rich beyond his wildest dreams.

"Sounded kind of rough for a last rehearsal," he observed as David left the stage, trying to add to the pressure.

"It will be fine," replied David. "It was really quite good today. One walk through tonight at dress and we'll be all set for tomorrow, trust me."

"I hope so."

"Now look who's worrying," said David. "Any news on Zeiggie?"

"No, but it's just a matter of time. I've got my own people working on it."

"Good," said David. "Have the police learned anything more about Tina's murder?"

"I don't know," answered Mark. "Just what the papers are saying, but it's all speculation. Some of them are saying she was raped. Maybe it was a sex crime. The police are under a lot of pressure and are being pretty tight-lipped about it. I think it's over as far as you're concerned, though. We were lucky they didn't bring you in for questioning. The papers would have had a field day."

"What a mess," David observed.

"You want to get something to eat?"

"I was going to grab a bite with Andre. He's been carrying a big load with me being preoccupied with all this other stuff. I promised him we'd go over some of his notes before dress rehearsal."

"Do you mind if I join you? I have to attend a fund raiser for the Civic Center tonight. A lot of your audience will be there and I want to make sure they're kept happy. I wanted to talk to you before then."

"Actually, I'd like to concentrate on the music tonight. I promised Andre. It's really a work session. I know you, you'll want to talk business."

"No I won't. I just don't want to eat alone. I'm part of this you know."

David was surprised at his friend's petulant tone.

"But if you don't want me around, that's bloody fine. I'll just collect my paycheck like a good flunky and thank my great benefactor for the job."

"Mark, don't be like that. I'm surprised at you."

"Well, I'm surprised at you. I'd of thought you'd want to spend time with a friend after all that's happened. Who can you trust if not someone from your own neighborhood? Who's going to watch your back better than me? Who's going to take care of you when all the hand-grabbers and ass-kissers have left town? Who's stood by you through three divorces?"

"I didn't think you cared," said David laughing. "Of course you can join us if it means that much to you, just don't talk business. I'll tell Andre your date stood you up. After all, I need someone to watch my back tonight."

Chapter 11

The day of the concert arrived with little fanfare, much like any other late autumn day in New York. Dress rehearsal the previous night had been a stupendous success, like nothing any of them had experienced before. It was a good thing there was no audience, not because the performance wasn't good, but because the musicians and singers were so overwhelmed by what they played that tears streamed down their faces. At the end some became so overcome with joy they jumped up from their seats and hugged each other. They played so hard it seemed that smoke would rise from their instruments. After the last note echoed to silence in the vast empty hall, David leaped straight up in the air with a burst of excitement, as if he had just hit the game-winning home run in the last inning of the World Series.

"Now that's what I'm talking about!" he yelled, giving the whole front row a high-five. He had conducted like he never had before, with an energy surpassing even his usual expressive intensity. "If we play like this tomorrow night, the world will be at our feet. You will all make history. Now forget about it until then."

The post rehearsal love-fest lasted late into the night, as everyone congratulated one another on the superb job they did, recalling especially moving or challenging passages as they nibbled pastries and guzzled wine.

David had trouble sleeping that night, and suspected many of the players and singers were having the same problem, with the excitement of opening night approaching and the exhilaration of playing one of the greatest pieces of music ever written. They would have the whole next day to rest and relax. Even if they only played it half as well as they did during the dress rehearsal, it would be a stunning success.

Mark had kept his promise the previous night and sat quietly as David and Andre discussed last minute details and compared notes before the practice. He didn't mention business once, except to say that the house would be packed and royalties for the initial worldwide simulcast would be unprecedented.

David slept late, and spent the morning listening to some of the other concerts being given that day over the radio. He read and sent emails to his various friends, teachers, and associates around the world, telling them how the rehearsals had gone and how he wished they could all be there in New York in person. He had a light lunch, took a short nap in the afternoon, and drove himself to the concert hall two hours before the scheduled performance.

Even at that early hour, the place was a beehive of activity. Musicians were tuning up and running through their practice drills, some still in their street clothes. There were dozens of TV crews and news vans surrounding the facility, the ground a maze of thick cables and bundles of wire, satellite dishes everywhere. Inside the hall were armies of stagehands, electricians, soundmen, and light crews, making ready for the live broadcast and taping. Columbia Records was there, setting up their equipment for the recording, which alone would net David over a million dollars.

In his intense focus on the music, it was easy for David to forget the huge amounts of money involved in this one concert. With movie rights, publishing rights, broadcasting rights, and advertising rights, he and his company stood to make millions, and that was just the beginning. None of this mattered to the composer, only the music, only the sublime sounds that flowed out of him to the rest of the world.

David didn't go to church or read the bible but that didn't mean he wasn't religious in his own way. Brought up in the Anglican Church by his pious mother, he had always thought of his talents and abilities as a gift, something he had been blessed with. He didn't do anything but let it out. Sure, he had studied and worked hard to learn and perfect his art, and he had practiced and applied himself prodigiously. That was part of his gift, the ability to work longer and harder and smarter than others, but that didn't make it any less of a gift, any less miraculous, any less of a responsibility.

Instead of feeling proud and self-satisfied after hearing his creation being played perfectly for the first time, he felt humbled by it, as if he himself were only the messenger, just as amazed and moved by it as the next listener. He realized that the masterpiece of sound was greater than himself and was thankful for it.

His baton was on the podium when he arrived on the stage, as he had left it the night before. It felt good to have the stick in his hand even though it wasn't his old one, the heirloom Zeiggie had broken. Why had he done it? Where was he now? He wished the ex-cello player was in the audience this evening. He was a musician, and would have appreciated the music. He felt the urge to dedicate the

87

performance to the deceased, Tina Fong, but thought better of it. There would be no extemporizing tonight.

The audience wouldn't be arriving for another hour yet, but there were already several music critics and newsmen sitting in their seats, trying to get a leg-up on the competition with some advanced scouting. David's attempt to keep the music secret had been successful, despite all the other publicity. In spite of this, however, some of the announcers hosting the pre-concert show had already proclaimed that this new symphony promised to change music forever.

David worked his way through the musicians and singers, greeting this one, joking with that one, waving and blowing kisses as is normal with show business people of all persuasions, even serious musicians. There was a festive atmosphere in the air, and even more important, an intense feeling of confidence. The orchestra felt they owned the piece, a work they loved. They were more than anxious to show it off and astound the world. The anticipation on and off the stage was enormous.

There were no last minute instructions or exhortations, no practicing of hard passages. That had all been done in the previous two weeks, ending the prior evening. Now all he had to do was let it happen and get out of the way.

David's conducting style mirrored the music itself. In spots where the passage was soft and melodic, his arms moved gently with the phrasing, often only his hands in motion at the wrists. In other places, he would conduct passionately and with intensity, his whole body swaying and bouncing with the rhythm, his head shaking, his arms waving. Sometimes he would throw them out as if striking the air to punctuate the accents. Often criticized for being undisciplined and distracting from the music itself, he was just as often praised for his exuberant performances and exquisite interpretation. To David it was a natural expression of the joy and passion he felt for his art.

About an hour before curtain, the musicians disappeared to their dressing rooms to put on their suits for the performance, men in black tuxes, women with black skirts and white blouses, singers in red and blue robes.

David went to his own dressing room and put on his tux. As he dressed he felt like a matador going out to meet the bull, with either death or triumph awaiting him. He conducted various parts of the piece, as if shadow boxing before the fight to warm up, hearing the music in his head as he wanted to hear it performed. He used the baton, getting the feel of it in his hand, as if it were a rapier he was about to use in a duel.

Then he walked the short distance to the wing of the stage, and peeked through the curtain at the gathering audience. The auditorium, which was well lit, was slowly filling up. Everyone was in tuxes and evening gowns, diamonds sparkling on fingers and around necks and wrists. In the lull before the big moment, David felt the lack of sleep from the night before and rubbed his eyes.

"Break a leg," said Mark from behind him. David turned around.

"Oh, hi Mark. I guess this is it. Enjoy the show."

"I will and you do the same. Don't let us down, old boy. Jesus, you look terrible. Did you get any sleep last night?"

"A few hours. I took a nap this afternoon. I'll be fine."

"Well, we need to do something about those bags under your eyes."

"Don't worry, I'll be facing away from the audience, remember."

Mark called back stage for makeup.

Out of habit, David held out his hand to his friend to shake.

"Well, wish me luck," he said.

"Good luck, mate," said Mark, seeming not to notice the extended hand. "But you won't need it. You'll knock them dead as always."

Then he dashed off, as if he had someplace to be other than a seat a few yards away. David was just as happy. He didn't feel like talking.

His mouth was dry. He grabbed a bottle of water off the tray where they were kept for the orchestra. His eyes felt heavy. He consciously tried to keep from rubbing them, but every now and then he'd find his hands automatically going there. He hoped the makeup people would be able to cover the bags under his eyes. Then he went back to his dressing room to wait, the proverbial butterflies starting to build in his stomach.

The stage manager soon knocked on his door and told him they had ten minutes to go, at which point the makeup team came in, two young girls and a gay male who did all the work and all the talking. When they had finished it was hard to tell David only had a few hours sleep the previous night.

"Don't rub your eyes," the gay man said. "It will smudge your makeup."

Like the star pitcher in a big game, everyone left David alone. No one approached him with questions or well wishes, as if afraid to jinx the enterprise. Everyone was concentrating on their own parts and private hopes and dreams, the fulfillment of which would write their names in music history and bring them fame and fortune.

As he waited in the wings for his introduction, the chorus and orchestra already in their places, he tried to clear his mind of everything except what he was about to do. He slowed his breathing and pinched his nose between his palms, closing his eyes. He heard his name to a thunderous ovation, which stunned him for a moment. They hadn't even heard the piece yet and they were clapping and cheering. They had been revved up with all the advanced publicity. It didn't sound like the scandal had affected their receptivity. If anything, it may have increased it with sympathy. Mark was definitely an expert spin doctor. He had done his job well and was indispensible. David decided to give him a raise as he smiled and walked on stage.

The lights were dazzling, although the auditorium itself was darkened. Only the vague outline of faces was visible as David peered out at the crowd. He planned to give a short introduction, which he had practiced all day.

"Ladies and gentlemen, and music critics." There was a polite laugh. "Thank you for coming to our concert tonight. This is an unusual venue as we are going to play only a single piece of music, my new Symphony in Four Movements, for double orchestra and chorus. Note there is no key signature even though it is a tonal piece, at least for the most part, which stresses the linear and polyphonic nature of the composition. And while the movements follow a traditional ABCA structure, it extends these in a number of ways as the various themes are developed, but I won't bore you with the details of it here."

A few half-hearted pleas for him to do so elicited more laughs and a chuckle from the conductor.

"I apologize for all the secrecy surrounding the rehearsals," he continued. "This was done mostly to protect the players while they were learning this very difficult piece, made harder by the many unusual fingering and bowing patterns required from the various instruments. In a sense, the musicians had to relearn how to play their instruments. The final result should be an enjoyable, exciting experience. Please sit back and relax, and join us in a little musical excursion."

With that he turned to the orchestra, made a few light remarks to those in the first row, picked up his baton, and silently counted off two bars for the first movement. The rest of the evening was pure magic. It lasted for an hour and twenty-minutes. In the brief pauses between movements not a sound was heard, no applause, no talking, not even a cough. It was as if everyone was holding their breath, not believing what they had just heard, and waiting for the next note, afraid of missing a single sound. The musicians were moved as well, but since they had already experienced the effect, they were ready for it and played with dry eyes and controlled exuberance.

It was as if they were gods, not humans, for no mortal man or woman could have played like they did that night, let alone a whole orchestra. They were making history, and like those who make history, they were reveling in the admiration and astonishment of those who watched. Not an orchestra in five hundred years of trying had played anything like this.

The lyrical lines and counter lines sang, soaring over the intricate polyphonic background until they broke the heart. Women fainted from the sheer beauty of it, while men cried like babies. The rhythmic, dancelike movements made one want to jump out of their seat, rising to a climax that carried the audience away to an unimaginable height, building even when you thought it could build no more, to end with a crescendo that took the breath away and left one clutching their seat.

It was a complete success, more than anyone could have dreamt of, except for one thing, halfway though the performance, David Gordon Reid went totally blind. It happened suddenly, almost taking him unaware. He was so carried away with the power of the orchestra and how it reacted to his every subtle move - the incredible sound engulfing him - that he almost didn't notice. He had his eyes closed at one point, and when he opened them the room remained black. For a second, he thought they were still closed.

Amazingly, although in a state of shock, his heart pounding so hard he could hear it over the 100 piece orchestra, he managed to keep his arms moving in time to the music, while he tried to ride out whatever was happening to him. Fighting the mounting terror, he somehow continued to conduct. Luckily, there was only one more movement to play, but it was the most difficult of all and contained the climax of the whole symphony. He prayed that he would get through it.

The third movement ended in a stuttering pattern, the audible rendering of a fractal equation, continuously repeating itself at many levels that got softer and softer the more interesting it became, until finally it stopped.

David stood motionless, both hands poised above his shoulders, his head bowed, his features hidden from the musicians who watched him intently for their cues. He stood there for some time, as millions of people around the world waited with bated breath for what would come next. Counting off two silent bars, with a slight upbeat, he brought the entire orchestra and chorus in with a strong down stroke. They hit the opening bar like an explosion, making some in the audience jump in their seats. The music grabbed them by the throat and never let them go, taking them on an excursion through the realm of musical tonality never heard in combination before. It was as if someone had learned the secret of how to put the notes together that composers had only been groping for all this time. One had to remind one's self to breathe while listening to it, it was so overwhelming.

All the while, as he conducted, the world remained black, a darkened void, but in the darkness he could see the notes, the entire score before him in his mind's eye, moving forward with no need to turn the pages. The whole time, he kept the orchestra in reign, exhorting them to play harder and faster, even as he was totally incapacitated with blindness. It sounded like the entire universe was exploding before him, as if it would blow him off the stage.

Unable to see, knowing the score by heart, he closed his eyes and gave himself to the music, which overcame the panic and fear surging in his breast and made even his blindness seem trivial. What was blindness when one could hear the music of the universe? He almost felt like throwing his arms wide and letting the music splash over him, but somehow he kept conducting, moving his hands, pointing and gesticulating for more volume, more feeling, more timbre, until finally it ended. One minute the music soared and the next silence reigned.

The audience sat as if in a daze, transfixed. To some only moments had elapsed. To others it seemed to have lasted an eternity. They were all transported to another place, a place where time stood still. All knew they had experienced something extraordinary.

Suddenly, spontaneously, all at once, the room exploded with a thunderous ovation that kept going until one wondered how it was possible to keep up such noise. Some screamed, some fainted, others cried and stood on their chairs, while a few tried to break their chairs they were so overcome. No musical work in history had had such an effect, and that was only the beginning, only the immediate, spontaneous reaction. It was nothing compared to the years of intellectual, artistic, emotional, and social impact it was to have. It revolutionized the art.

None of this mattered to David, however, who stood through the whole thing blind as a baby mole, with his back to the audience. He was afraid to move, not sure how he would look, or even if he would end up facing in the right direction. He wanted to run off the stage and hide but that was impossible in his helplessness. Finally, able to avoid it no longer, he turned toward the audience with a grateful smile and fell flat on his face, right off the podium. To make matters worse, when he hit the floor, he continued rolling over the lip of the stage into the first row of the audience, turning applause and cheers to screams of pandemonium.

Even in his confinement, Zeiggie was aware of the upcoming performance of David Reid's symphony. Although there were no newspapers or radios, and the TV was tightly controlled, he had overheard one of the orderlies talking about it.

Still pretending to be taking the heavy doses of medication they were giving him and in a semi-comatose state, Zeiggie had been busy, collecting a number of items that would help his escape, various keys, cans of food, medicine and warm clothes, along with a rope, though he still had not gotten up the nerve to try it. As much as he hated to admit it, in a way, it was more comfortable in here than on the street with no means of support. At least the food was good and the bed was warm. He knew, however, that it was only a matter of time before he'd have to leave, if for nothing else than for his own sanity.

A common area, which was normally locked, was separated from the rooms of the patients by a long hallway. A guard station stood on the opposite side of the common space, separated from it by a wide plate-glass, mesh-reinforced window that gave a clear view of the entire area.

A couple of the night staff, a few nurses and orderlies, were music lovers and had the TV on in the guard office to hear the concert. Zeiggie, who had long since been able to leave his supposedly locked room at night, snuck out this evening to make use of the dark common space to hear the concert. Crawling across the floor to avoid the light filtering through the large window from the brightly lit office, he crouched against the wall listening. He had learned there was an acoustical oddity caused by the structure of the building and the location of the various air vents that made it possible to hear everything said in the guard room even if whispered. It was an invaluable ability from which he had learned much.

It was less than ideal, but Zeiggie was determined to hear the concert as best he could, if only the people watching the TV would let him. One nurse talked so incessantly and loudly that he almost stood up from his hiding place and shouted for her to shut up. Finally, she grew silent of her own accord like everyone else, taken with the music. And what music!

"Oh, my God," he said, on hearing the first movement in full, played as it should be for the first time. "Oh, my God."

He had never heard anything so beautiful in his life. The constantly shifting melodies and the counter lines of such wondrous quality left him spellbound. He had never wanted to play the cello more than he did this night. When he heard the rich sonorous sounds of the string section as they played their long, sweeping phrases, he would have given anything to be part of it. Note after note, measure after measure, movement after movement it continued, as if sprouting spontaneously from the ground. "Yes!" he said, on hearing the third movement end, almost giving himself away. The fourth was simply incredible, and he started to cry at the realization that this music had been composed by another human. Where had he heard this, in heaven?

Then something happened that he didn't quite understand. The concert had ended to a thunderous ovation, like the cheering of an out of control political convention, then nothing, a dead, stunned silence.

There were a few exclamations from the small group watching the TV in the guard room, as they all reacted to what was happening on the tube. Zeiggie strained to hear what was going on.

"That was just terrible," he heard an announcer say. "If you somehow missed it, ladies and gentlemen, the conductor, David Gordon Reid, has just fallen off the stage into the audience."

"It looks like he took a bad fall," said his co-announcer, a well-known music expert.

"He seemed to stumble blindly as he turned, and fell right off the stage," said the first man again.

"There's still quite a bit of commotion down there. It's hard to see what's happening," said the music expert.

"It looks like he's still down and not moving. He appears to be unconscious," said the first announcer again. "This is just terrible. Right on the debut of his great masterpiece the composer appears to have fallen off the stage and may be hurt."

"It certainly was an incredible piece of music, but it has all been upstaged by the tragic accident."

"Yes, Bill, he seems to be unconscious."

"Can we play that clip again, Fred? OK, there's the thunderous applause as he's facing the orchestra. Now he's turning around."

"He appears to be a bit unsure of himself."

"There he goes off the podium. He's rolling forward. Oh, my God, right off the stage. Oh, he landed right on his face!"

"This is terrible," said the first announcer again.

Zeiggie heard it all in a state of suspended animation, like he had just been informed the president had been shot and his name given as the assassin. He knew whoever was after him had finally gotten to David. For a while, he was starting to doubt himself, but now he knew it for certain. He had broken one baton, but they had gotten another and did the same thing to it. He knew what he had to do.

Collecting his meager belongings and cache of supplies, he let himself out of a second story window off the common room, and using the rope, shimmied to the ground. Leaving the premises he had only two things in mind – talking to his lab friend, who still had the broken end of the baton, and helping David, the greatest composer since J.S. Bach.

Chapter 12

The whole city, not to mention the nation and the world, was in shock at what had happened. It was on the front page of every newspaper in every major city on earth. The combination of historical musical event and accident, together with the tragic blindness of the composer right at his moment of triumph, had caused a sensation the likes of which are rarely seen.

Speculation as to the cause of the accident and affliction were rampant due to a lack of real facts. Some thought it had been brought on by stress and overwork - too much reading of tiny scores in bad light; too many late hours and long days with little or no sleep. Some pointed to more sinister causes, suggesting a possible conspiracy to sabotage the great work out of jealousy, spite, or some supposed offense. Others remarked on the parallels between David's sudden blindness and the deafness that overtook Beethoven in his later years.

Mark had been the first one to his fallen boss's side, directing activity and helping the paramedics who soon arrived on the scene. He took complete control of the situation and subsequent affairs, including what hospital David was taken to and what doctors he would see. He also controlled all access to David by the media, which meant there was none. All news regarding the patient came directly from him, which was not unusual in such cases.

Except for a dozen stitches beneath his nose and across the top of his lip, and the fact that he could not see a thing, David was fine. The doctors, through Mark, told the public that more tests were needed to determine exactly what had happened, but that it could be one of a number of degenerative diseases of the eye. David would remain under doctors' care until further notice. All his public appearances, including encore performances of the groundbreaking symphony had been canceled.

The musical fallout from the concert was just as sensational as the accident and blindness. Several critics called David the first great composer of the twenty-first century and perhaps the greatest composer of all time. It wasn't just a few writers who may have felt sorry for him. It was everyone, even hardnosed critics who could not have cared less if it was their mother who had fallen off the stage. The music reviewer for the New York Times summed it up the best when he tried to put into words what made this composer's music so revolutionary and at the same time, so popular.

'Dave Reid has a unique gift for making something entirely new out of what people have been doing for over five hundred years. Through the use of a continuous and highly inventive counter-punctual or polyphonic style where melody upon melody intertwine each other; where rhythm and time change like the wind; where instruments are stretched and probed like never before; and where orchestration and scoring build texture upon texture to create such a rich tapestry of sound it carries the soul away. This is but to hint at the experience of hearing this music for the first time. And it only gets better after that, for upon each hearing one discovers things one missed before. It is as if the music transforms itself each time it's heard, as the brain takes in another aspect of the piece that it had completely overlooked previously.'

Such triumph meant nothing to David, who sat enclosed in blackness, as much of the soul as of the eyes. David had never actually lost consciousness during the ordeal, though he wished he had, especially when the anesthesia wore off and the nurse was only partly done stitching up his nose. He was seriously dazed and hurt, however, and bled profusely from his cut. But he was awake the whole time, lying still with his eyes closed, nodding to those close to him in answer to their concerned questions.

The blindness was the main concern. No one could answer his queries as to where it came from, but he didn't like the things that they were telling him it might be, like cancer. More tests were needed. In the meantime, he would stay with Mark in his luxury flat near the hospital.

"Don't worry about it," Mark assured David, who would rather have gone home to his own apartment. He wasn't sure being at Mark's place was such a good idea.

"What are friends for?" replied Mark when he tried to object. "You can't manage alone right now. We need to let the doctors find out what's wrong and take care of you. In the meantime, you can rest at my place where we can keep an eye on you. You've had quite an ordeal. You've also had a fantastic debut. Have you seen these reviews?" He stopped in embarrassment.

"No, but it doesn't matter," said David. "None of it matters."

"Don't say that," replied Mark. "You're going through a lot right now, but things will be OK, don't worry. Enjoy your success. You've earned it."

"I wish I could. For a moment there I almost forgot my blindness, hearing the music so close like that, with such an incredible orchestra. It was so overwhelming. But when it was over and I stepped off that stand into the blackness, I knew the worst thing in the world was happening to me. It makes all the so called success seem worthless."

"It may only be temporary. And if not, you can still work."

"How?" yelled David. "I'm blind! How am I supposed to write music when I can't see the score?"

"They have computer programs that can practically write the score themselves. You could play it and have others transcribe it for you. Look at Beethoven. He was stone deaf and wrote music, the most beautiful music ever written until you came along."

"Beethoven, Beethoven, I'm sick of hearing about Beethoven, and all the others. We're all a bunch of self-centered, self-indulgent, egotistical hacks, just as dubious and deceitful as any other show business people."

"I know you're bitter now," said Mark. "I understand. It's OK to feel that way after what's happened to you. Just don't give up entirely. I know things well get better. The world needs you. I need you."

"Thank you, Mark," said David. "I don't know what I'd do without you."

While David struggled to recover his eyesight and his will to live, the fruits of his creation, all controlled by Mark, his business manager, flowed in. It came in the form of commissions for new works, and orchestras that wanted him to conduct his new music, performance contracts, and recording deals. Not to mention the immense royalties and publishing fees that poured in as orchestras and music publishers vied to be the first to perform or print the piece. Then there were the immense fees from the re-televising and performance rights – including his fall at the end – on DVD, cable television, and your local movie theater. When the world found out that he had conducted the last movement completely blind, he became an instant icon, fanatically loved by millions, hallowed like a saint. People sat transfixed just hearing his name.

None of this meant much to David, who left it all in the capable hands of his manager. He couldn't even count out change for a ten. He was totally helpless, and had no thought of helping himself. He had lost all hope and determination. David Gordon Reid had not only fallen from the stage, he had fallen into a deep depression.

After the tests, in the weeks and months following his blindness, he never left his friend's flat - that's what Mark called the luxury, 2400 square foot, split-level penthouse apartment two blocks from the hospital. He became a recluse. He saw only his manager, and then only when Mark stopped by occasionally on his way to the house in the suburbs he was sharing with another man's wife. David's only companion was a live-in male nurse employed by Mark. He preferred things this way. He wanted to be alone. He didn't want to be pestered about joining the human race, let alone trying to write again. Look where that had gotten him.

Much to his dismay, after a battery of tests, the doctors could find nothing physically wrong with him. One by one, the normal possibilities had been eliminated, leaving only uncertainty and medical curiosity. The human body was still a mystery, they explained, especially the mind. Perhaps it was a psychosomatic illness. They suggested a number of specialists that might help, the last thing David wanted to hear.

The darkness of his days and nights was nothing compared to the blackness of his soul. He dreaded waking up in the morning and going to sleep at night. Each breath was an agony of despair, though he resolutely refused all drugs and medication. He barely ate, and the more helpless he became, the more paranoid he grew.

"David, you've got to try to eat more," pleaded Mark, on one of his weekly visits. "Ben tells me you're not taking your medicine. How do you expect to get better?"

"Who cares," was David's habitual response.

While things were going stupendously as far as the business was concerned with the recent phenomenal success of his new work and David's notoriety - if not worldwide public adoration - Mark was concerned. They wanted David helpless but productive. In his present state he would be no use to anyone. He would have to be careful or his employer might decide it better to eliminate the composer. Mark, however, argued there was much more to come, so why cut down the tree prematurely. Still, if David's health and mental condition didn't improve soon, it would be a moot point. He just didn't think he'd have to play nursemaid.

"Here, try some of this," he said, spooning David a mouthful of thick, beef stew he knew his friend loved from his childhood. "Your mom taught me this recipe."

"You're the only one I can trust, Mark," confided David, taking the spoon in his mouth gratefully, like an invalid. "I don't know who's feeding me, or what half the time. Do you know what that's like?"

"I know, I know, but Ben is the only one here most of the time. You know him, and you've met Hilda who comes in on the weekends."

"I don't trust either of them," said David petulantly. "Why can't you stay here with me? Why do you have to spend all your time with that woman?"

"I told you, David. I have to work and watch over your business. I can't take care of you all the time. That's why I've hired the best people I could find, people I know and can count on. So you have to trust me on this. You know what I'd do if I thought someone was hurting you. Don't worry. I'm not going to let anything happen to you." He gave David another mouthful of the rich tomatoey broth and wiped his chin with a napkin.

Zeiggie had no idea where he was or what he was going to do when he left the mental facility, but he had made up his mind to try. Using a second rope and a strip from a large cardboard box, he scrambled over a twelve-foot high chain-link fence topped with razor-wire. He was not an athletic man, though he had played street hoops in his youth. He had certainly never done anything like this before, except maybe in basic training and that had been twenty years ago, but weeks of rest and good food, and sheer determination fueled his will and gave him the strength he needed.

Once outside he made good time in the bright, moonlit night, loping along the deserted highway between empty buildings and fields. He could dimly see the direction he needed to go from the vague, hazy light in the eastern sky that signaled the false dawn of the city.

He knew it was only a matter of time, a few hours at most, before they realized he had escaped and would send out the alarm, with photographs and news bulletins across ten states. He would easily be recognized, so time was of the essence, though he had no plan. Maybe if he could somehow get to the city before daylight he'd be able to blend in easier. But how?

It was then that he noticed the dairy. It was still dark and unlit at this hour, but he reasoned they would be moving produce into the city before dawn. Climbing into the building's lot the same way he climbed out of the prison, he cautiously wandered between the rows of milk trucks, keeping to the shadows, looking for an open one. It wasn't long before found a van with an unlocked door. He quickly slid it open and slipped inside.

Once inside the milk truck he took a quick look around. Edging into the passenger seat, he tried to think things through. What if he hid in the back? Would they find him in the morning when they started filling the truck? Could he remain hidden and hitch a ride to the city without being discovered? There were too many unknowns. If he was found, he would be like a badger in a trap. Then he spotted a pair of coveralls on the driver's seat next to him. He lifted them and noticed the company logo on the back. Perhaps he could pretend to be loading up one of the trucks then slip in at the last moment. At least that way if he was noticed, he could attempt to talk his way out of it. In any case, he'd have a running chance if they decided to try and grab him.

He put on the uniform and waited in the driver's seat of the truck, getting a couple of hour's fitful sleep. He woke before dawn and hid there until he noticed activity. Men were starting to move around the warehouse. A short time later, they began driving the trucks, one by one, to the building to be loaded. Slipping out of the van unobserved, he started walking across the vast packing lot toward the loading docks, which stretched the entire length of the low, brick building, a large beehive of activity.

He spent most of the time walking back and forth between the trucks and the warehouse, all the while observing the loading dock. When he saw the trucks starting to pull out on their routes, he walked toward one he had been watching and started moving cases of milk into the almost full van. He had noticed that just before the trucks departed, the driver entered the cab and most of the dock workers moved to the next vehicle to begin the loading process again. One of them remained, however, to shut and lock the rear doors of the truck before slapping the side panel to signal it was OK to go.

Somehow, through luck and timing, he contrived to carry in the last case. The other men, who hardly gave him a glance, had already moved off to a newly arrived truck. As he was about to shut the door and slip in, the driver walked up. He had gotten out without Zeiggie noticing him.

"Who are you?" he asked, lighting up a cigarette. "Where's Carl? I haven't seen you around here before."

"I'm new," said Zeiggie. "I just started today."

"Well, I know all the guys here. I haven't met you."

Zeiggie smiled and held out his hand. He was about to give the man a fictitious name when the foreman walked up.

"What are you two standing around jawing about?" he said. "We've got milk to deliver. Quit yapping and get that truck out of here."

The driver gave Zeiggie a quick look, threw his butt away, and ran back to the cab.

"Is this truck ready to move out?" the foreman asked, evidently not noticing or caring whether Zeiggie was new or not. The place apparently had a high turnover as far as dockhands were concerned, so a new face here or there didn't attract much attention. That is except for the nosy driver.

"I got to check one more thing," said Zeiggie, opening the door and putting his head in.

"Make it fast and move it out," ordered the foreman, moving hurriedly to the next truck.

Zeiggie looked back and forth as the driver started up the vehicle. It was the last truck in line on the loading dock, just empty field behind him. There was no window in the back of the cab allowing the driver to see into the rear. At the last moment, Zeiggie slapped the side panel, hopped in the truck, and closed the door behind him as it drove off. He hoped it was headed toward the city.

Pushing some cartons aside, he made a small seat for himself on others, holding the door slightly ajar so he could see where he was going, although at this point, it all looked the same - farm fields dotted with small homesteads. Grabbing a quart of milk, he twisted off the top and took a long pull of the liquid, still cold from storage in the plant's large refrigerators. He drank the whole thing in a few gulps then opened another. Soon, as daylight grew, the surroundings began to look more suburban. Not long after that, they were in city neighborhoods.

He couldn't be certain, but he had the impression they were headed toward one of the Burroughs surrounding Manhattan. From there he wasn't sure what he would do. Getting out of the mental hospital was one thing, staying out was another matter. He was pretty sure whoever had put him there wouldn't be happy to find he had escaped, especially now after what had happened at the concert. He wasn't sure what resources they had at their disposal, but was certain it was more than he had.

The first thing he had to figure out was how to get in touch with his lab friend, who had analyzed the broken piece of baton. He had to see if there was any trace of what had caused him to get ill when he used it. Whatever the stuff was, there was a good bet that it was the same thing they used to make David go blind during the concert. Zeiggie was sure of that, despite his uncertainty of many other things. That was the easy part. Getting the results, if indeed there were any, to David, was another matter. He tried to work it out as they drove toward the city.

Peeking out of the back of the truck, he saw they were in an urban neighborhood of close-packed brownstones and low townhouses. The vehicle stopped at the back of a large supermarket located on the top of what appeared to be a high hill, with a view of the Brooklyn Bridge in the background. Zeiggie jumped out unnoticed as the truck slowed to a stop, and disappeared around the corner of the building before the driver was out of the cab. He had discarded the coveralls, and had on a gray sweatshirt and a pair of gray pants, a bit underdressed for the season, but not out of place either. As the driver opened the rear door of the truck he noticed it had not been latched or closed properly, and cursed the new guy back at the depot.

Zeiggie made his way down the hill along streets of similar apartment buildings and single-family, lookalike houses, toward the East River, which was just starting to sparkle in the morning sunlight. He moved quickly but not so fast as to attract attention, and fit right in to the mixed-racial neighborhoods he passed through. By noon he was crossing over the Brooklyn Bridge footpath into the city.

Chapter 13

"Turn that off!" yelled David, hearing the opening phrases of his new symphony. Mark had put on the newly released DVD of the concert hoping to inspire his friend out of his funk, but it had just the opposite effect, causing the composer severe distress. "I can't stand to hear it. It gives me a headache. Turn it off!"

As a matter of fact, David couldn't listen to any music, none of his old favorites, which he used to love playing and conducting. Beethoven, Mahler, Stravinsky, Bartok, they all made him sick. The only music he could tolerate was the early Beatles and old, sad country songs, things he hardly paid heed to before. David had changed. He was no longer the buoyant, happily creative person he had been. He had become old before his time, bearded, bent, and thin, with the listlessness of a starving concentration camp inmate. Only sad or simple music seemed to sooth him.

Mark had given up trying to coax him to health and make him write again. It was no use paying for expensive experts and specialists if the patient refused to cooperate, even if they had been handpicked so as not to expose too much. Mark had to tread a fine line between trying to bring David back to creative health and revealing the true nature of his illness. Bribes and payola could only go so far for so long. Life on the streets of his native Scotland had taught him that.

He had always looked out for David, but it had been more for what David could do for him than for any true fondness for him as a person. He liked fighting anyway, so why not beat up on the bullies who picked fights with the sissy piano player. Although David could handle himself in a pinch, it always helped to have a gang behind you like Mark did. Life was hard in the back alleys of Edinburgh where they grew up.

His father had also been a researcher at the institute, and had worked closely with David's father on a number of projects, of which Mark knew little, but he knew it was important and took both men away for long periods. When David and his family left Edinburgh Mark had been deprived of a means of status and lunch money. It had been a tough, troubled time, so when he got the phone call one day offering him a job and asking him to go to New York, Mark jumped at it, even knowing what it involved. It was only natural that when he presented himself to David, at a critical time in his career - just after his first big success and his first marriage - that David would hire Mark on the spot. He had just the critical skills and talents needed, a friend from the old neighborhood who had looked out for him and whose thick accent reminded him of home.

Since moving in, David had taken to locking himself in his room, a large, high-ceilinged space with a small bath and walk-in closet. He would let no one in, taking food through a hatch he had installed in the door, and only to his strictest specifications. His prodigious mind and intellect was now focused on one thing, keeping the world at bay. Both Ben, the male nurse, and the part-time Hilda had left at David's insistence, as had a string of others, none of who he liked or trusted. Mark was spending more and more time there taking care of his ward. He was the only one David allowed in his room, which he kept dark and shuttered with thick curtains and drapes. The place was a mess, but at least he let Mark have it cleaned once a week, though only with them both present, David barking out orders to the cleaning crew as if he were conducting the orchestra. Mark was at his wits end when he found Colleen.

Colleen had come highly recommended by every reference and contact he could gather. Some called her a miracle worker for her success on rehabilitating many lost causes, cases everyone else had given up on. So Mark had hired her as a last resort

"You can start immediately," he told the young, attractive brunette on meeting her for the first time. She was attentive and bright, and had a nice smile and a perky manner, and eyes so big and round you could fall into them. Her mouth was large as well. Her round face gave her the appearance of being a little heavier than she was, though her body was otherwise slim and athletic. He told her the situation and her duties, which amounted to keeping the patient clean and well-nourished, and if possible trying to rehabilitate him, at least to the point of being able to care for himself. She was to make sure he got his daily dose of eye-medicine. She understood it would be a difficult mission, especially when she confronted the locked doorway.

"Mister Reid, sir, I'm your new nurse, Colleen O'Malley. Can you let me in please?"

There was no answer from the other side of the door, though she thought she heard someone walk across the room, the slight tapping of what sounded like a cane on a hardwood floor.

"I'd like to talk to you and introduce myself," she said again. "I have your supper for you."

"Where are you from?" asked David, noticing her slight accent.

"I was born in Ireland," she replied. "A little town near Dublin, but I've lived in New York near all my life."

"I'm from Edinburgh," he said through the door, almost forgetting his loneliness on hearing a voice, besides Mark's, from the old country.

"I know," said Colleen. "My Aunt has followed your career since your first Young People's concert in Boston. She was a big fan. She said you were the next Leonard Bernstein. I'm Colleen, Colleen O'Malley."

David unlatched the door and let her in, stepping back out of the way.

Colleen kept talking as she carried the tray into the room, looking around with dismay.

"Where can I put this?" she asked, squinting in the darkness.

"Over there on the table," he answered, pointing vaguely to the other side of the room where there was a cluttered card table placed against the wall. She looked him up and down as she walked across the floor talking the whole time.

"I used to go to her house to listen to her record collection when we visited Boston. She had every recording he did and he did a lot of them. She just loved Bernstein. She had tons of classical records, Mozart, Beethoven, Shuman, and Tchaikovsky, everybody. She taught me a lot about music. She told me all about you even before you were famous. She knew you'd be somebody."

"What's your Aunt's name?" he asked, walking across the room to the table, using his cane expertly to avoid the end of the bed. The cane was his one concession to his blindness. Although he knew the contours of the room by heart and didn't really need it, it felt good in his hands, like his baton.

"Mary, Mary Herlihy. She was my mother's sister. She lived in Boston. I'm sorry she's gone now. She passed away last spring. She so much wanted to hear your symphony."

"Oh, I'm sorry to hear that," said David, for once involved in someone else's troubles instead of his own. "Can I ask what happened to her record collection?"

"She left it to me, along with her stereo system and wall-size speakers, but they're much too large for my little apartment."

"Well, maybe we could set them up here," he heard himself saying much to his surprise.

"I may take you up on that," she replied laughing. The sound reminded him of his mother. "I made your favorite soup," she said helping him to the table. "Your friend Mark gave me the recipe. My aunt used to make it too. I hope you like it."

"I'm sure I will," he said sitting down and feeling for his spoon. Leaning his face into the bowl, he slurped the warm, thick contents into his mouth.

"Hmm, that's very good. Just like my mother used to make."

"I'm glad you like it. I put tomatoes and carrots, and onions and potatoes, and pieces of beef in it. There's bread too if you want some."

"Yes, this is great," answered David, feeling relaxed and contented for the first time since his accident.

"Gee, it's so dark in here," she observed as he ate. "Do you mind if I open the curtains and pull back the shades?" She didn't wait for him to answer but moved to the windows and let in the sunlight. "It's a beautiful day, and it's such a nice view from here."

"Doesn't mean much to me," he replied. "I'm blind."

"So what," she said, not letting his self-pity affect her. "The sunlight will do you good whether you can see it or not, and it certainly will make me feel better. Besides, it's important to establish a routine, have a schedule."

"Oh, and why is that, Colleen?" said David, feeling a little of his annoyance returning even though the soup was delicious and the conversation refreshing. For the first time in months he had forgotten about himself and was interested in another person. At the same time, however, he was a little peeved at how she just came in and took over.

She looked at him for a long time instead of answering, tears peeking at the corner of her eyes.

"I feel so bad at what happened to you," she confessed, the anguish audible in her voice. "I love your music and what you can do, not just because my aunt liked you and said you'd be famous. I'm not an expert, but I know enough to understand what you've accomplished, and how you're music has touched millions of people around the world, common people who know nothing about Bartok and Schoenberg. I was there. I saw the whole thing, and when you fell down I thought my heart would stop beating. I want to help you."

"You're helping me just by talking. It's been a long time since I've been able to be with someone like this." He hesitated. "To trust someone."

"Good," she said, touching his shoulder. "That's the first step. The next is to have a routine, put some order in your life."

David liked her voice and her touch, and when he shook her hand goodnight, the feel of her skin. He liked the fragrance of her hair and her lilting accent. Who had sent this angel to soothe his pain and ease his days? He made a note to congratulate Mark on his choice.

He lay up all night thinking about her, wondering what she looked like, actually looking forward to the coming day. When she knocked he was already waiting by the door. He opened it immediately.

"Well, that was quick," she said, walking by him with his breakfast tray. "Did you sleep well last night?"

"Not a wink," he admitted.

"Oh, that's not good. Do you want something to help you sleep?"

"No, I was thinking about you."

"Now, Mister Reid, are you flirting with me?" she laughed, placing the tray on the table, as she began straightening up the room. "This place sure is a mess."

"It's just that you remind me so much of home. I was thinking about my childhood. I miss Edinburgh."

"Are your folks still alive?" she asked, knowing only that he had come to the US when quite young.

"My dad's still living. He's back in Scotland. My mom's dead. They got divorced when we moved to the States. She didn't want to leave her family and friends."

"And you, how did you feel about it?"

"I thought it was great. I couldn't wait to get out of there. I thought the place was old and stale and full of stodgy old men who thought they knew everything. I miss the place now though."

"Why'd you leave?"

"Not sure. I guess my father thought there'd be more opportunities for me here in the States, and he was right."

"How come he moved back?"

"You sure do ask a lot of questions. I thought you knew all about me."

"No, just what my Aunt Mary told me. I'm not one of those crazy fans or groupies, you know. This is strictly professional."

"Oh, you're a professional woman," teased David. He hadn't teased anyone, especially a woman, since his first wife.

"And don't you forget it," she replied, laughing back.

"Do you know that I've been married three times?"

"No, I didn't," she answered, a little taken aback. "I don't read the gossip magazines. You must be hard to live with." She fluffed the pillows, punching them several times, and threw open the curtains. "Another perfect day."

"I wish I could see it."

"What do the doctor's say, about your eyesight I mean?"

"Nothing. They say it's in my mind. What, didn't Mark tell you, I'm a nut case?"

"He said they didn't know what was wrong with you, but that they had eliminated a number of possible diseases, including cancer. That's all very good. Have you been going to anyone?"

"No, what good would that do?"

"They may be able to find out what's wrong, get to the bottom of your illness, help you see again. Sometimes these types of things can be very difficult to diagnose."

"What if I never see again?"

"Is that what you're afraid of, that you'll find out the condition is permanent? So what? What if it is? A lot of people are blind, that doesn't stop them from doing great things. You can learn to live a normal life. You could write again."

"I'll never write again," he yelled, swiping his glass and plate from the table in anger. "I'm sorry," he said immediately. "I didn't mean to make a mess."

"Don't worry," she assured him. "I don't blame you for feeling that way, but you can't give up on life, it's not fair to the One who gave you such a great gift."

"How do you know what's fair? How do you know there's a God? That my gifts, as you say, are not just an accident? I'm nothing but a freak of nature. They should pickle my brain after I die so they can experiment and find out what quirk of nature is responsible for this circus oddity you see before you."

"I know you don't believe that," she said.

"How do you know what I believe? I've never met anyone so presumptuous in my life. Get out of here, get out!" he yelled, moving in her general direction brandishing his cane. She told him to watch himself or blind man or not, she'd knock him on his ass. Then she picked up his glass and cleaned up the mess, saying nothing as she gathered up the breakfast tray and left the room.

"You can get your own second cup of coffee," she said, slamming the door behind her.

If David could have seen, he probably would have wondered at the smile that played on her lips as she left the room, and the happy bounce of her step. For she thought the session had gone very well, very well indeed.

David felt terrible. He hadn't felt this bad since his last failed marriage. Why couldn't he carry on a simple conversation with a woman, let alone a relationship? He had treated his wives like members of the orchestra, with friendly familiarity but otherwise controlling and cold. That is when he had treated them at all, being away most of the time during all three marriages. It was revealing that neglect had been mentioned more than once in his various divorce suits, along with mental cruelty and verbal abuse. He admitted all of it and paid them off with large alimonies, happy to be free, free but alone. Colleen was somehow different. She didn't seem to want anything from him. She only wanted to help him, and look how he had treated her. He hoped that she wouldn't be mad enough to leave, and sat brooding in the sunlight all morning. He was relieved when there was a knock on the door later in the day around lunch time."

"It's open," he yelled.

He heard the door open and someone enter, though it didn't sound like a woman's tread, but the heavy booted foot of a man. David grew stiff with alarm.

"David, are you all right?"

It was his father's voice.

"Is that you, Dad?"

"David, my boy, it's so good to see you. What have they done to you?"

"No one's done anything to me," replied David. "Things happen. Easy come, easy go."

"Whatever is that supposed to mean?"

"Never mind. What are you doing here? How did you get in? Have you talked to Mark?"

"I've come to help you. You're in grave danger."

"What danger? What are you talking about? You're starting to scare me. Why did you leave so abruptly in the first place? And why didn't you answer any of my letters or emails. I never got a chance to say goodbye."

"I left for your own good, but I can't explain all that to you now. I've got to get you out of here."

"Why, what's going on? What are you talking about?"

"They told me they wouldn't hurt you. That they would protect you, but they lied."

"Dad, what the hell are you talking about?" David yelled.

Just then there was a knock on the door, which David's father had closed behind him.

"It's open," yelled David again, much to his father's concern.

"Oh," said Colleen, a little surprised at finding another person in the room. "I didn't know you had a guest."

"Nurse Colleen," David said formally. "This is John Reid, my father. He's just arrived from Scotland. Colleen here's from the old country as well, just across the Irish sea."

"Nice to meet you," replied David's father awkwardly. "I've got to go, but I'll be back. Colleen, I'd appreciate it if you didn't mention my visit to Mark, Mister Burns. I didn't leave on the best terms and want a chance to talk to him before he knows I'm back in town. He may take it wrong."

"I work for Mister Burns," the nurse informed him dutifully.

"Nurse Colleen is the model of discretion, aren't you, Miss O'Malley," said David. "In any case, Miss O'Malley works for me and will do as I tell her. Won't you, Colleen?"

His father looked at his son and smiled. "I see you're already getting some of your old gumption back."

As he was leaving he whispered to his son who stood next to him near the door, while the nurse took the lunch tray to the table across the room.

"Don't trust anyone. You're in danger. Don't trust anyone. I'll be back soon."

With that he was gone, leaving David more in the dark than ever.

Chapter 14

Zeiggie had managed to elude the authorities, who had organized a half-hearted attempt to re-capture him. There were just too many other important and dangerous fugitives on the loose. Thanks to the surreptitious way he was brought there, the hospital in New Jersey knew nothing of the New York police department's desire to question Zeiggie regarding the murder of Tina Fong. Mark Burns was preoccupied with other matters, and missed the call from his man at the facility.

The ex-cello player made his way across town to his old neighborhood, where he found the lock on his door had been changed. There was a 'For Rent' sign hanging in the front window of the apartment building. At least they hadn't let it out yet. Luckily, the old man was downstairs in the liquor store and not his sadistic son.

"Hi, Ben," said Zeiggie, entering the building to the sound of the bells hanging above the door.

"Zeiggie, where have you been?" the owner said loudly, looking up from his paper. "I haven't seen you in ages. I thought you might have given up the bottle or something."

"You know I don't drink anymore," he replied, looking around and noting the place was empty. "How's business?"

"The same. Folks got to have their taste now and then. Hey, someone was just in here looking for you."

"Who, me? Why? What for? When?"

"Just yesterday, a couple of cops. Not from this precinct. No one I've seen around here before."

"What did they want?" asked Zeiggie.

"What do cops usually want? You in trouble?"

"You could say that," said Zeiggie. "I just got out of a mental institution and they want to put me back in. What did they say they wanted me for?"

"Well, they wouldn't say. It was actually Bobby that did all the talking, and he gave them an earful. Told them what a deadbeat you were and how you owed him money."

"I paid him back that money," Zeiggie replied indignantly.

"I know, I know, calm down. He was just trying to act big, like he knew something in front of the cops, but he ended up being more help than he knew. He told them you'd never dare come back here again 'cause you'd be scared of him. He told them you'd be on your way to Florida on a Greyhound bus."

They both cracked up laughing, in spite of Zeiggie's situation.

"Can you help me out, Ben?" he asked. The store owner looked around, then went to the door and locked it, putting up the 'Be back soon' sign.

"Tell me what's going on," said the old man, leading Zeiggie to the back of the room where they would not be seen behind the wine counter.

"You know that big composer, that Reid guy, the conductor of the New York City Philharmonic?" began Zeiggie, feeling good to get the whole thing off his chest. "You know, the one who fell off the stage after his concert and went blind."

"Of course," answered the old man, looking hard at his friend. "It was in all the papers for weeks."

"Why are you looking at me like that?" asked Zeiggie.

"Those men looking for you said you're wanted for questioning about that woman they found hanging in her apartment, your friend's assistant."

"What?" yelled Zeiggie. "Hanging? What are you talking about?"

"That young woman who was working for that Reid fellow. At first they thought she had hung herself, but I guess they found out she was really murdered, someone trying to make it look like suicide. They wanted to ask you some questions."

"Why would they want to question me? I hardly new the woman, why would I want to hurt her? You know me better than that."

"I asked them the same thing. They said you had some kind of confrontation with her and was arrested. Jesus, Zeiggie, what kind of trouble you in? That's what happens when a brother tries to get ahead in the world. These big-time people and their friends only gets you problems."

"Ben, it all makes sense," explained Zeiggie, seeing the truth in a flash. "She's the one who was poisoning David. They were using his baton. That's what I found out that night they arrested me. She lied to them about how I was trying to come on to her and they locked me up. Then when I tried to tell David what they were doing, she had me arrested again. Someone must have killed her to keep her quiet. It was probably a professional hit. The way they just carted me away to some mental institution certainly wasn't normal. They drugged me out. It was in New Jersey someplace. They tried to make me disappear."

"Holy crap," swore his friend. "That's the damndest thing I've ever heard. What are you going to do?"

"I took a piece of Reid's baton when I discovered it had been tampered with. Pretty near burned my eyes out when I touched them after holding that thing. I'm having a friend, kind of a druggist out on Long Island, analyze it for me, seeing if it's coated with some kind of poison or something. He's got his own lab set up in his basement. Can you help me?"

"Sure," said the store owner and landlord scratching his head. "But I may need a drink. I thought it was funny them saying you had something to do with that girl's murder."

"Thanks, Ben. You're a real friend in need."

"Bobby hasn't rented out your room yet, though he's been trying, but he's asking too much money, jacking up the rent."

Someone started banging on the front door. The owner looked over the counter and saw his son standing in the street pounding on the glass.

"It's Bobby. He's going to break the door down if I don't let him in. Come back this evening around eleven when I'm closing up. You can stay in your old place overnight and leave when I open up in the morning. That lazy son of mine will only work the afternoon shift so he can party all night and sleep in all morning, but at least he does something. I couldn't handle this place myself."

He led Zeiggie out the back way and then went to open the front door.

"Where you been, old man?" queried his son, pushing past him to the cash register. "What's the idea of locking the store in the middle of the day?"

"I had to take a dump," responded the old man. "If you spent more time here helping out I wouldn't have to lock the door like that."

"I'm here on schedule," replied his son, opening the register and pocketing some cash. "Don't gripe. Just make sure you're back by 5:30."

Zeiggie met his old friend up the street and walked with him to his apartment where they shared a couple bowls of spaghetti with sauce

Things had been going much better since Mark hired the new girl. She seemed to have a way with David. If things continued as they were

114

going he wouldn't be surprised if the patient started writing again. The only wrinkle in the plan was the alarming news from his employer that David's father had left Scotland for parts unknown, and might have come to New York. He'd have to be especially vigilant.

"How's he doing?" Mark asked Colleen on one of his rare visits to the apartment.

"Very well," answered the nurse. "He's actually learning how to get around, but I was hoping to talk to you about his condition."

"We're doing everything we can, Miss O'Malley. Just keep administering his medicine as instructed."

"But I was wondering, sir, if we might find someone to help him see again. He's awfully depressed and seems to have no hope of getting better."

"Miss O'Malley, it's your job to see that he resigns himself to his condition. He's seen the best experts in the country on the matter. There's nothing more they can do."

"Well, sir, if it's a psychological condition, perhaps we can..."

"Miss O'Malley, you do your job and I'll do mine. I'm working to maintain Mister Reid's substantial business interests so he has something to fall back on in his time of trouble. He's well taken care of for the rest of his life, but it takes a lot of work to keep it all going. I am also seeing to his health and well-being, which is why I hired you. You are more than welcome to go through his medical records and if you have any suggestions, you can talk to Doctor Steele, his chief physician."

"Well, sir, I've tried to contact the doctor, but he never returns my calls."

"I'll talk to him and have him call you. Will that take care of your concerns?"

"Yes, I guess so, but..."

He cut her off.

"Has David had any visitors lately, an older gentleman?" he asked.

David's father had been coming over quite a bit recently. She had fixed them lunch a few times, which they ate in David's room while they talked. The visits seemed to do him good, so she encouraged them. She had long ago learned the benefits of close family contacts at a time like this.

Mark had left explicit orders that there were to be no visitors when he hired her, but she was only half listening at the time. In any case, she didn't think the restrictions applied to family.

She didn't answer one way or another. She was new and had to see how things were before she made up her mind about it.

"No," she said, with her fingers crossed. "I would of told you."

There was something about the short, wiry Scotsman she instinctively disliked, something about him she didn't trust. He reminded her too much of the troublemakers back home, always looking for a fight, walking around with chips on their shoulders. She almost didn't take the job because of it, but when she heard the patient was her dead aunt's idol, she had changed her mind.

"Why are you so against him seeing anyone?" she asked, voicing her concerns.

"It's not that, but you must understand such visits must be carefully controlled."

"But you make it so difficult that no one can see him."

"All they have to do is make an appointment."

"That's the problem, you're too busy and your underlings could care less."

"I prefer you use a less offensive term, Miss O'Malley. Remember, you're one of my underlings, as you say. I don't think having someone call my office to make an appointment to see David is an unreasonable request. That is unless they want to keep their visit a secret, in which case I'll have them arrested for trespassing."

"But human contact is good for him. If you expect him to improve, the more people he sees the better. It should be encouraged. We're making it difficult for his friends to see him."

"David doesn't have friends," replied Mark. "He has business associates, students, old teachers, acquaintances, and collaborators. I'm his only friend."

"It's not enough. He needs human stimulation."

Mark was starting to regret hiring her. She may be a miracle worker but she was becoming a royal pain in the neck. She was also his last hope.

"That's exactly why I hired you. You're the human stimulation that we need to get him on his feet again. Trust me, Miss O'Malley, Colleen, can I call you Colleen?"

"Sure, but..."

"I'm doing all I can to help David, but there's a very good chance he will never see again. We have to try and prepare him for that eventuality the best we can so he can continue to live a productive life. I'm sure you can understand that. All I'm asking is that anyone who wants to see David make an appointment with the office. That's standard procedure with someone of David's stature, especially after all the publicity from his last concert."

Before she could answer, he said what he had come here to inform her about.

"I've hired a private security company. There will be guards in the apartment twenty-four hours a day."

"You know David will never agree to that," objected the nurse.

"Then I'll have them posted outside in the hall and out back, I don't care, but I'm going to make sure David's protected."

Protect the golden-goose, she almost said, but instead said nothing.

"Can you agree to that?" he asked, looking at her sternly. She returned his gaze calmly.

"Sure," she said evenly. "I'm just trying to do my job, that's all."

"And we appreciate that greatly, Miss O'Malley," he assured her, apparently forgetting his wish to call her by her first name. "You've done a wonderful job, and I hope you will continue to help David. You really have done wonders."

"I just wish there was more I could do," she replied.

"You will, just be patient. These things take time," observed Mark, as if he knew all about it.

Later that day after Mark had left, David's father appeared. Again she found him in his son's room talking to David. She hadn't heard him come in. He certainly didn't ring the bell or knock.

John Reid had long since realized that the nurse was the key to the whole thing. If he could convince her that David was in danger and win her over, she might help, that is if she wasn't in on the whole thing.

"Oh, hi, Mister Reid," she said on finding them together. "I didn't realize you had come in. It's too bad you didn't come a little earlier, you could have met Mister Burns."

"Ah, I suppose you're wondering why I haven't announced myself," replied the old man.

"You did say you were going to. It is his apartment you know. He has a right to know who's here."

"And did you tell him I've been here?"

"He didn't ask," she lied.

"And if he did?"

"I'd tell him your visits were good for David. Who should visit him if not his own father, unless you're hurting him in some way."

"And why would I hurt him?"

"I don't know, but fathers have been known to be cruel to their sons."

"Am I being cruel to you, David?" he asked turning to his son.

"I resent being talked about as if I weren't here," answered David. "I've been trying to figure out exactly who to trust in all this. What did Mark say to you, Colleen?"

"He asked if you'd had any visitors recently." She looked at David's father. "He wants everyone to make an appointment with his office before seeing you, which seems reasonable enough."

"Mark always was protective," observed David.

"Yeah, for his own benefit," replied his father. "I thought you said he hadn't asked?"

"I lied," she said with a wry smile. "He told me he was going to hire a guard to watch the apartment."

"I'll never allow that. I'll move out," objected David.

"That's what I've been trying to tell you," said his father. "You'd have just as much trouble trying to get out of here with those guards as someone will have trying to get in, I can assure you. You've got to leave as soon as possible."

"He's going to have them out in the hallway and in back by the doors," the nurse informed them. "You weren't even supposed to know about it."

"Sounds like he's trying to keep me a prisoner," said David, growing indignant. "Since when do I have to consult him to have guests?"

"So you did lie for me. Why?" David's father asked Colleen.

"Like I said, I thought you were good for him, and I don't trust that man for some reason. He reminds me too much of the troublemakers back home."

"Well, now that we've got that settled," said the old man. "Maybe you can help me get him out of here. It's time for David to disappear."

"What are you talking about?" she asked.

"Father here is trying to convince me that I'm in danger. That Mark has somehow caused my blindness and is using it to exploit me for his own purposes, that it's all part of a sinister plot."

"Oh, it is David, you must believe me," his father assured him.

"It's ridiculous," insisted David. "The whole thing's just crazy. I can't believe a word of it."

"I wish it weren't true, David," replied his father, earnestly. "I really do. Now that he's hiring guards, it's going to be even more difficult to come and go, and there's a lot to do. Well you help us, Colleen?"

The nurse was having difficulty taking it all in. Things were happening too fast, the scenarios facing her too far beyond her usual frame of reference to comprehend. She wasn't sure what it all meant. There were too many blank spots to follow to any conclusions. The questions weren't even formed yet.

"I'm having just as much trouble believing it as you, Miss O'Malley," said David again.

"I told you I can't explain it all here," repeated John Reid. "It's too explosive and you will need some time to digest it. I can't tell you everything at once. Suffice it to say that Mark works for someone who made a very substantial investment in your future. Now they're trying to cash in on it. They want to control you."

"I wish you had some kind of proof," replied David, still doubtful. "If there was some sort of conspiracy, the police would have found out about it."

"That's probably why your assistant, that Fong person, was murdered," reasoned his father. "Whoever hired her killed her to keep her quiet. They're that kind of people. We'll have to leave tonight."

"No way!" objected David.

"He can't!" agreed Colleen at the same time.

"Not without some kind of proof or confirmation," said David. "Where would I go?"

"There's no way you can take him out of here tonight," insisted the nurse. "He's not ready for anything like that. He can barely get around the apartment. It's suicidal. I can't let you do it."

He could see that David and his nurse were going to be more difficult to persuade than he had hoped. He somehow had to get beyond their disbelief of his farfetched but true story, and they hadn't heard the half of it yet.

"OK," said John Reid. "You're right. I can see there's nothing we can do tonight, but Miss O'Malley, you have to promise to help us if I can show David is in danger every moment he stays here."

"Not while I'm watching him, he ain't," she declared.

"That's what I'm counting on, but even you can't protect him from these people. If David agrees to go, well you help us?"

119

She thought for a moment still not sure what the truth was but trusting her instincts about human nature and family bonds.

"Yes," she said finally. "If David agrees, I'll do whatever he tells me to. I'm working for him, not Mark Burns, no matter what he says."

"Good," replied the old man. "Then I know he's in good hands. It will be a little more difficult than I hoped, but I think we can pull it off with a little luck. I'll be in touch. I have a few arrangements to make."

With that he bade them goodbye and left the apartment.

John Reid had a lot to think about, so decided to walk the considerable distance to his rented flat despite the damp night. He liked walking in the city at night. He enjoyed the anonymity and the bright lights, and the fact that there was activity no matter what the hour.

He had worked most of it out, all except the actual escape. It would be a little more difficult now that guards had been hired. If the plan he had in mind were executed properly, however, it wouldn't matter. The hard part was going to be convincing David, then keeping him safe and hidden until he could somehow deal with Mark and his employer. With David's notoriety they were bound to be noticed wherever they went. Travel by commercial means was out of the question. That's why he had rented a hunting lodge in the Adirondacks, site unseen. He had also leased a late model Jeep Cherokee under an assumed name, which he kept out of sight in a local garage, another reason he was walking home tonight. He didn't want to use it until the getaway.

John Reid had noticed the short, stocky black man following him since he left his son's apartment, and figured it must be one of Mark's henchmen, who had been watching the place. He waited until he was in a dark, quiet spot a few blocks up the street from his flat before confronting the man. Knowing what was at stake and the true nature of their adversary, he was armed with a 38-automatic. John Reid was not without his own resources.

"Why are you following me?" he demanded, as the man rounded the corner. His hand was in his coat pocket along with his handgun.

"Don't shoot," shouted the startled black man throwing up his hands. "Don't shoot. I ain't following you. This is my neighborhood if you haven't noticed."

"Don't give me that bull," said John narrowing his eyes and looking nothing at all like an ex-biologist. "You've been following me since I left David's apartment. Who are you working for?"

"You know David?" shouted Zeiggie, stepping forward and almost getting shot. "I thought so. I've been trying to find him for weeks. I've got to talk to him. I've…"

"Zeiggie?" John said, recognizing him immediately though they'd never met. John Reid started to relax.

Zeiggie was stunned for a moment with the mention of his name, and instantly on guard.

"How do you know my name?" he asked. "I've never seen you before."

"David told me all about you. He's been worried about you. You're the only one he keeps asking about. I'm his father, John Reid."

"Hello, sir, nice to meet you. David talked a lot about you too. I've got to talk to him. I've got something important I've got to tell him."

"I can't tell you how happy I am to see you."

"I know how they poisoned him. I've got proof."

"Zeiggie, my boy, you're just the fellow I've been looking for," said the old man, taking his hand out of his coat pocket and smiling

"Did you really have a gun?" Zeiggie asked nervously, still not reconciled to following strangers in the dark streets of the city.

"Yes, but don't worry, Zeiggie, I haven't shot anyone yet that didn't truly deserve it. Just to make up for startling you, let me invite you to my flat where we can talk all about it over a glass of ale. There's nothing for it until the morrow." With that, John Reid put his arm around Zeiggie's shoulder.

Chapter 15

Zeiggie and John shared a pizza and washed it down with some dark Scottish ale, while the ex-cello player told the story of his escape from the mental institution, and how he found David.

"I was able to find where David was staying easy enough," he said, settling into his comfort zone. He hadn't forgotten his vow of abstinence, but figured a glass of beer with his new found friend was worth falling off the wagon for.

"Every newspaper in town said he was convalescing in his business manager's New York apartment. Gaining access to David was another matter. He might as well have lived in Fort Knox. The doorman scowled every time I walked by. Forget it when I tried to talk to him. He was downright rude. 'Mister Reid is not seeing any visitors,' is the more polite version of his response, if you know what I mean. I've already been beaten up by one doorman, I'm not about to try it with another."

"I'm sorry, Mister Ziegler," replied John. "David feels awful about it too. All through his own troubles he was most concerned about you."

"I appreciate that. I only wish I could have got to him sooner."

"Well, you tried my boy, you tried."

"How did you manage it?" asked Zeiggie. "I mean how did you get in?"

"Well, it helps that I'm his father. And you know, I hate to say it, but appearances are very important to these people. They go by first impressions. If it's good you can be an ax murderer and get in. I just make a good first impression, that's all. Of course, it helps to have a little cash to throw around. An English accent doesn't hurt either."

"I know what you mean," said Zeiggie, shaking his head. "See how much luck you'd have being a shabbily-dressed, unshaven black man."

"I understand," David's father replied. "So why'd you follow me?"

"I'd been loitering around the place, watching it, you know, trying to figure a way to get inside. I was seeing who went in and out, trying to keep tabs. I saw Mark go in a few times, but that guy hates me. I wouldn't be surprised if he was the one who tried to put me away. I noticed you come and go a couple times, but you obviously weren't a tenant 'cause you never came out in the morning or in at night.

Tonight, when you left and didn't hail a cab or anything, I decided to follow you. As a last resort, I was hoping you'd know something about David."

"You sure picked a dangerous way to find out. I could have shot you."

"Don't remind me," sighed Zeiggie, taking a pull of his drink.

"So where's this proof you were talking about?" asked Reid, seeing it as just the thing he needed to convince his son and Nurse Colleen to go with him.

"I'm having it analyzed by a chemist friend of mine. It's the end of his baton. It was treated with something."

"So that's how he did it," responded Reid.

"Who?" said Zeiggie. They each had a piece of the puzzle and were starting to put things together.

"Why, Mark Burns of course."

"That bastard," swore Zeiggie. "No wonder he wanted to get rid of me."

"You and a few others. I'm sure he's the one who hired that young girl and then had her killed."

"We've got to tell David."

"I already have," Reid informed him. "At least what I could guess at, but I didn't have any proof. Now I do. We have to get those results back. Does anyone else know about this? How about your chemist friend, how reliable is he?"

"If you mean will he go to the authorities or advertise his activities, I doubt it. I don't think he even wants folks to know he's a chemist, if you get my drift."

Reid began explaining what he had in mind.

"What are you going to do that for?" Zeiggie asked after hearing Reid's elaborate plan. "Why don't we just go to the police with the proof?"

"First of all, my well-intentioned friend, they would probably arrest you on the spot as an escaped mental patient. They probably wouldn't believe a word you said despite the evidence. No, they would more than likely turn everything around and pin the whole thing on you, which is what they were trying to do in the first place."

"That's crazy. I didn't have anything to do with this. I was trying to help him."

"I know that and you know that, but our adversaries will do everything they can to make sure no one else knows it. They have a lot going for them. They have many more connections than we do and have the ear of the media. By the time we turned all that around with the little bit of illegally obtained evidence you have, you'd be buried so far in the system we'd never find you, let alone get you out. That is if we could convince anyone to believe our story in the first place. You make a darned good scapegoat."

"I never thought of that," said Zeiggie, not feeling too well. "Crap, what are we going to do?"

"Well, I'll tell you."

John talked late into the night, formulating his plan.

David and Colleen had not heard a word from his father since he left almost a week before. Since then Mark had posted his guards outside the door to the apartment. Colleen didn't like them one bit.

When they first came, they entered the flat whenever they liked and tried to establish themselves in the kitchen, where it was warmer and the fridge always well stocked. After a few tantrums and tirades from David, however, waving his cane in front of him like a fencer, they pulled back to the more peaceful and safer environs of the outer hall between the stairs and the private elevator. David had had no visitors since their arrival, and certainly not his father, who the security guards had been given a picture of and warned about.

Everything had been quiet in what was turning out to be a rather boring Friday morning, when around 8:00 am there was a commotion outside the apartment door.

Colleen was in the kitchen preparing David's breakfast and didn't notice anything. David came in and asked her what was going on out in the front hall. She took a peek and saw a stocky, shabbily-dressed black man confronting the guard.

"If you don't leave I'm going to call the police," threatened the guard, sizing the other brother up. "You will have to make an appointment like everyone else."

"I've got to talk to him," said the intruder loudly.

"You'll have to leave," ordered the guard, trying to decide quickly if he needed backup or not. "How'd you get by the doorman, anyway?"

"Get out of my way," yelled Zeiggie, gently pushing past the guard who was barring the way. He grabbed Zeiggie by the arm and started guiding him toward the elevator.

"Make an appointment," insisted the guard, and reached for his walkie-talkie to call his partner in the back. "Hey Lou, we have trouble up here," he barked into the unit as he tried to keep the intruder away from the apartment door. "You better come up right away."

"I'm not leaving," said Zeiggie.

"You'll have to go," replied the guard, standing in front of him and pushing the button for the elevator. It soon came up, along with the other guard and the doorman. They all escorted Zeiggie back down and out of the building.

"And don't come back unless you have an appointment," the first guard yelled at Zeiggie as he slunk away.

"How'd he get by you?" he asked the doorman, while he and his partner had a smoke.

"He said he had an appointment to see David Reid."

"Why didn't you ask to see it?" the other guard demanded.

"I thought that was your job," said the doorman.

"Well, don't let him back in here again," ordered the first guard.

"You got a light?" asked the doorman, as the hired security men finished their butts and turned to leave.

"Sure," replied the second guard, happy to be outside in the warm, January-thaw day. His partner went back up to guard the penthouse.

"Say, who's this guy I'm supposed to watch out for?" asked the doorman, referring to the photograph he'd been shown of David's father. Of course, he recognized him. The man had been coming here for weeks before the guards showed up and the photograph was released. He thought he was family, so had let him in. He had the same last name. Not to mention, he was loose with his cash and told great stories. Someone certainly would have said something all this time if his visits were unwanted. Since he had already let the guy in several times, he figured he'd better keep his mouth shut. No sense incriminating himself.

"I don't know," answered the guard. "They don't tell us much, just that we're not supposed to let him in, and we're to notify headquarters if we see him. Thanks for the help."

"Sorry about that," said the doorman. He had been paid well for his lack of attention. "He must have been watching me. I didn't leave the door but two minutes to get my hat. He must have slipped in."

"Well don't let it happen again, or you'll answer to Mister Burns," warned the guard, returning to his post at the rear of the building.

In the time it had taken them to hustle Zeiggie down the elevator and out of the building, and then stood jawing, David's father had slipped into the back of the apartment and given David the news.

"What's going on? What was that all about?" asked David when Colleen let his father in.

"Just a little diversion. Can you get me a glass of water?" he asked the nurse. He had been waiting in the stairwell while Zeiggie played his part, and now stood panting from the exertion of climbing the stairs to the eighth floor apartment.

"That was Zeiggie, come to pay his respects," he told them, taking the glass from Colleen and finally catching his breath.

"Zeiggie!" cried David. 'Where is he? Zeiggie's here?"

"There's no time to talk," explained his father. "They'll be back any minute." He told them that Zeiggie had discovered the vital bit of proof that showed how it was being done, and how a type of poison had been found on the baton, albeit not in an entirely legal fashion.

"Now will you believe me?" he asked finally, telling them everything he and Zeiggie knew. "We put it all together over the last few nights. He was here watching the building. He followed me back to my flat. This is the evidence we need to indict that bastard and his associates once and for all."

"Perhaps now that we know what it is, we'll be able to cure your blindness," said Colleen.

"That's just what I was thinking," echoed his father. "But first we have to get you out of here and away from that man and his minions – excluding you of course, Colleen. I have a lot to tell you and we have even more to do. We don't have much time. Here's what I have in mind."

Later that night, some time after the second security shift arrived, just as the new guard had settled into his first cup of coffee and the evening papers, the nurse came rushing out of the apartment in alarm.

"Help me," she begged. "He's having a heart attack. I just called 911. The ambulance will be here any minute. Please help me get him ready. Time is of the essence. Every minute we delay could mean the difference between life and death."

The guard hadn't exactly been trained for this type of situation, despite the assurances of those who leased him out. He was pretty good at intimidating would be intruders and blocking overzealous fans, but wasn't quite sure what to do in a medical emergency. So he followed the nurse's orders like an obedient school boy.

"In here, quickly, help me get him into his clothes," she ordered.

She led him into the bedroom, where David sat in bed fully dressed.

"I've packed some things," she said hurriedly, helping David to his feet. "The suitcases are over there."

"Yes, ma'am, but shouldn't we wait for …?"

He was about to finish his sentence when there was a knock at the door.

"That's the ambulance," she informed him. "Get the suitcases and help me."

The guard grabbed the two heavy bags and went to the front door, opening it. Two men in white uniforms with red crosses on their shoulders stood waiting with a wheel-chair, which they rushed into the room. They soon had the patient sitting in it covered with blankets. David looked pale and in pain, but otherwise sat quietly with his eyes closed.

"Where are you taking him?" asked the guard.

"To Bellevue Hospital Center," answered the short, stocky medic. "It's the closest one."

"I'll follow you," volunteered the guard dutifully.

"That's not necessary," said Colleen. "You stay here and watch the apartment. I'll call Mister Burns from the hospital."

The guard, not sure he should be taking orders from a nurse, hesitated.

"This is a medical emergency," she assured him, looking at him sternly. "I've been trained. I know exactly what to do. I'll be with the patient the whole time. You need to stay here and hold down the fort until I can inform Mister Burns. He'll tell you what to do. You'd better not leave your post until he tells you to."

That sounded like good advice to the guard, who went back inside to wait. The night doorman was nowhere in sight. The man out back had not even been alerted.

Zeiggie drove the rented ambulance north out of the city and over the Tri-borough bridge, where they all transferred to the Jeep Cherokee. Soon they were heading towards upstate New York and the Adirondack Mountains.

"So far so good," said John Reid turning in his seat to look back at Colleen and David. "Are you comfortable back there?" he asked.

"Yeah," replied David, staring straight ahead as the blind are apt to do, looking pale and peaked.

"Well, that went off without a hitch," gloated David's father proudly. "You all did a superb job, especially you Colleen. I really thought David was dying there for a minute, the way you were carrying on."

"It's just play acting," she told him, looking at David with concern. "We used to do it all the time as kids."

"I bet you played nurse too," quipped David.

"How'd you guess?" she responded touching his arm.

"We have a long way to go," observed David's father. "I hope that guard doesn't make any phone calls until morning."

"He was pretty cowed," said Colleen. "I'd say we have a couple hours at least."

"Good," replied John Reid. "We'll be above Albany by then and at the camp by morning. We have enough supplies to last a month. That should be enough time."

"Enough time for what?" asked David.

"To disappear," said his father.

Mark got the phone call from the security company around 4:00 am that morning, saying David Reid had been rushed to Bellevue earlier that evening with an apparent heart attack.

"Why wasn't I informed immediately?" he barked into the phone, expecting the worst. "How is he? Do you have someone at the hospital with him?"

"What? Your man's still at the apartment? Why? Why didn't anyone call me sooner?"

"*Who* said they'd call? The nurse? What the hell's going on there?" Mark yelled, his anxiety rising with each answer from the unit supervisor. "Who's in charge? Well let me talk to your boss, immediately."

The news just got worse. Apparently David had suffered what appeared to be a heart attack shortly before midnight and was rushed to the hospital. Unfortunately, there was no record of his being admitted to Bellevue Medical or any other hospital in the city. David Gordon Reid, famous composer and conductor, the talk of the town, the world's first great twenty-first century composer, had disappeared. Mark assumed it was kidnapping and did his best to persuade the authorities that's what it was as well.

"Have you received any ransom note or instructions?" asked the detective who came to Mark's office to interview him about the case.

"No, but it's only a matter of time," answered Mark. "They must have been planning this for quite awhile. That new nurse was in on it, I'm sure of it. She went with them. For all we know she's the ringleader."

Whatever the kidnappers wanted, he assured the police, he would pay.

"Do you have any idea who could be working with her?" asked the detective.

"I have a lot of ideas. She definitely wasn't working alone. She had to have help getting the ambulance. There were at least two other people with her according to the security guard, an older man and a black man. I have reason to believe the last man was a recent escapee from a mental institution in New Jersey, where he had been placed for harassing the conductor. His named Leonard Zeigler. He's also wanted for questioning in the Tina Fong murder. It all makes sense, they're part of a conspiracy to poison and kidnap David. He's worth millions. That's why I hired the security guards."

He didn't mention that he actually knew the name of the older man. It didn't pay to give the police too much information when he was trying to hide so much himself.

"Well, don't worry, Mister Burns," the detective assured him. "The airports are being watched, along with all the bus and train stations. They can't get far. Mister Reid is a very famous person, and from what you tell me severely handicapped. It won't be easy to avoid detection, what with the internet and media coverage these days. I'm sure we'll find him. In the meantime, the FBI will have an agent on the premises twenty-four hours a day to monitor the phone. We'll have a man here as well. If you have any questions or if anyone contacts you, please call this number." He handed Mark his card.

"They may tell you not to involve the authorities," the detective went on. "But you can tell them we're already involved, and there's nothing you can do about it. Let them know that you want to cooperate. Someone will be here soon."

Mark was beside himself. The worse possible scenario had materialized. He had been concerned when his associates informed him that the elder Reid had left Scotland, but he could have gone anywhere. He certainly acted faster than anyone could have anticipated.

He called his own man immediately after talking to the police. He should have had Frank take care of the security detail in the first place, but he needed to save him for more delicate and covert missions like the current one.

"Hi, Frank, sorry to get you up at this time of day, but we have a little problem. Seems someone has kidnapped David Reid. Yes, kidnapped him. Staged a little medical emergency and drove off with him in an ambulance. I want you to do a little errand for me. No, nothing like that. I want you to look up a few addresses for me. Yeah, John Reid and his family, going back to 1998 or '99 when they first got to the States. Also any address they may have had in town here. Yeah, and any of his son's known addresses while in college, roommates, relatives, you know the drill. We think it might be the old man who took him. Yeah, for the money. I guess they had some sort of row. Thanks, Frank, I knew I could count on you. I know, but I didn't want to get you involved baby-sitting. I only have myself to blame, but we'll work it out. We always do. Thanks."

Before he hung up, he gave his man Leonard Zeigler's name as well, and asked him to check his last known addresses.

He felt better after talking to Frank. Like David had Mark to protect him, Mark had Frank, and heaven help you if Frank was after you.

Mark wondered where they could have gone. They might be hiding out in the city. After all, it was a big place with a lot of nooks and crannies to disappear in, with everything you need close by, including medical assistance. He had covered all the obvious places they might go, including the normal escape routes. As the police said, David Reid was an extremely well-known figure with a very distinctive handicap. Pictures had been provided to the news media, which plastered the air-waves and papers with not only David's photo, but those of Lenny Zeigler and Colleen O'Malley as well. For some reason, known only to Mark Burns, David's father's picture wasn't shown. As a matter of fact, there was no mention of John Reid at all, just an older gentleman with dark-rimmed glasses.

He tried to remember if David had ever mentioned a summer camp or place in the country where they might have gone as a family, but David and his father never took vacations in the summer, or any time for that matter. David was usually busy shunting back and forth from one music program or lesson to another, living in hotels half the time and on the road the other. Mark had covered all the bases. Of course, there was always the possibility they had driven out of town to parts unknown. They could be in a hundred other places in six hours - north, south, east or west. They could be anywhere.

Chapter 16

It was almost dawn. They had driven for five straight hours since ditching the ambulance on east 168th street near Harlem, the last hour and a half in deep woods along steep mountain gorges. Finally, the woods opened out to a large clearing where the trees gave way to an extensive field of long grass that swept down a gentle slope to a wide lake, which glistened in the early morning light. A large log cabin nestled next to the lake, with a screened-in side porch facing the water. It looked inviting after driving all night in the darkness.

"This is it," announced John, rousing Colleen and David who had fallen asleep. "We're here."

Zeiggie looked bleary-eyed and wired as he parked the jeep in a gravel space between the cabin, which was on a slight rise to the left, and the lake, which shimmered below on the right. A small stone path led in both directions.

Colleen helped David out of the car and described the location.

"Quite a place," observed Zeiggie, helping John with the supplies and luggage. "I was expecting something a little more rustic. This isn't like any hunting camp I've been to."

"Nothing but the best for us, Zeiggie. We're going to be hiding out for awhile, might as well do it in comfort."

It took several trips before everything was unpacked. Colleen helped in the kitchen, while David rested on the couch. She had put the TV on to listen to the news. So far there was nothing but farm reports and hillbilly music. Once they were settled, Colleen made a light breakfast for everyone.

"Are you sure no one's going to find us out here?" asked Zeiggie.

Before his father could answer, David asked his own question. "Where are we?"

"We're in the Adirondack Mountains, fifty miles from the nearest civilization," his father informed them. "There's nothing but summer camps and hunting lodges up here, and it's between seasons. I rented the place over the Internet with just a temporary debit card from a local bank after I checked it out. I told the realtor we might do some bird-watching and hiking, and wanted to take advantage of the mild winter. The owner's away, cruising the Caribbean on his yacht. I gave them enough money to ensure our privacy, told them we'd be here a month, and if we liked it we would come back every year. So there's added incentive for them to ensure we're not disturbed. They think I'm a rich foreigner. There's nothing to link our party with the goings on back in the city."

The others were dubious, but much more interested in hearing Zeiggie's story than discussing it further. Zeiggie kept everyone spellbound through the simple breakfast of steak and eggs describing his ordeal and escape, after which everyone crashed in their rooms for much needed rest. They planned on regrouping for a late lunch at three when John would try to explain what was going on. He told them it wouldn't be easy. David wondered what that meant.

There had been a lot going through David Reid's mind these last few hours, as he tried to put the recent events and pieces of information picked up over the last few days into perspective. From hints his father had dropped he assumed that some sinister person or persons was trying to cash in on his success and control him for their own benefit. Tina had been hired to poison him and then murdered. The poison was apparently being administered through his baton. Zeiggie had proven that, bless him, and paid the price.

The most difficult thing of all to accept was that Mark had turned against him, and had only pretended to be his friend all these years. He still couldn't believe it despite the proof.

"All this proves is that someone has blinded me on purpose with some kind of poison," reasoned David when they resumed their discussion after a late lunch of sandwiches and coffee. "It doesn't prove who it was. Why do you think it was Mark? He'd be the last person I'd suspect."

"Not me," said Colleen. "I don't like him. He gave me the creeps from the start." She explained her dislike and how he reminded her of the thugs back home.

"Me neither," agreed Zeiggie. "But that's 'cause he didn't like me."

"Mark's just over-protective," explained David. "None of you saw him do anything but try to help me. Dad, you've got to have more than that."

"I do, but it's not going to be easy to explain."

"Well, then you'd better start talking," said David speaking for them all.

"It all started before you were born," began his father.

* * * * *

The kidnapping and disappearance of David Gordon Reid was the news story of the century, first page in every paper on four continents. Rumor was rampant as everyone waited for the expected contact or ransom note from the kidnappers. The problem was not that a ransom note didn't come, but that there was a tide of letters and emails all claiming to know the whereabouts of the missing composer. Many asked for millions of dollars or made ridiculous demands, as the mentally disturbed came out of the woodwork at the distressing but sensational news. The authorities were stumped.

"What do you mean, you have no idea where they could be?" yelled Mark over the phone, losing his temper once again, as he tried to deal with the crisis and the demands from his employer. "The kidnapper's a bloody foreigner. David's the most famous person on earth. He's blind, for Christ's sake. How the hell can they just disappear?"

He didn't bother waiting for an answer and slammed the phone down, regretting the action as he performed it, but too mad to listen to more lame excuses. He couldn't really blame them. His own sources were coming up empty as well. So far Reid and his son had made no contact or overt moves. What could they be up to and where were they?

The only added piece of information the police and FBI had come up with, was that the mastermind of the kidnapping plot was the estranged stepfather of the composer, who had left the country a few years ago after a sharp altercation with his son over money. This was finally divulged by Mark, who as a last resort claimed only recently to have discovered it. John Reid, according to Mark, was not the biological father of the famous maestro at all, and had taken David from his home in Scotland when he was ten years old against his real mother's wishes, thereby shortening her life by several years. He had been exploiting the young genius ever since. That is until David had finally stood up to him and thrown him out. Now he was back, exacting his revenge. Mark had made a point to stress the old man's greed and vindictiveness when he told the authorities the story, on orders from his employer.

Mark didn't know the whole truth, but had pieced much of it together from what his employer had told him and hints he had picked up over the years, something about a debt and John Reid's firstborn being the payment. In any case, he knew that he had been hired to incapacitate the composer in a very specific manner for the purpose of gaining possession of his fortune.

Although Mark didn't know the name of his employer, nor even how to contact him, he received explicit instructions every week via secret couriers, who left them in prearranged locations like spies in a James Bond novel. Mark didn't mind the melodramatics. The pay, which was accruing with interest in his secret offshore accounts, more than made up for the inconvenience.

Mark had been recruited for this special mission soon after he had gotten out of prison for armed robbery and assault. This was years after David had left Scotland. While David was working his way through college and making a name for himself in shows and concerts in the States, Mark was working his way through a ten year sentence of hard time. If it wasn't for his employer, who apparently had significant pull - at least enough to get him an early release - he would have still been there. Instead, he was sent to the States where he went to work as David's manager.

It hadn't been hard to pull off. After all, he really had been a friend and had watched over David when they were kids. He was a natural salesman with the glib talk of a conman. Before that, he had been headed for a hard career on the street. Now he found himself in the perfect position, with skills made for the job. He was making more money than he had ever dreamed of, even as a thief, but it was all in danger of coming down around his ears.

Because of David's disappearance and the rapidly changing circumstances, his employer had made arrangements for Mark to call him from a specially installed secure landline in a rented office across town, leased under an assumed corporate identity. It was an expensive and time consuming operation for a single phone call, but that's how important the situation had become. Things were unraveling. The golden canary had flown the cage.

"Hello, Mister Smith," said Mark, following the instructions he'd been given. "This is Goldstar."

"Hello, Goldstar," answered his employer with a cultured European accent, using Mark's code name. Mark knew the man only as Mister Smith. "Are you calling from the secure phone as instructed?"

"Yes, sir," said Burns, with military respect, like a good soldier, which was what he felt like.

"Good," said his employer. "There's a lot I want to tell you and it must be kept completely confidential."

"I understand, sir."

"Have the police or FBI found out anything yet? Do they have any leads?"

"No, sir, none from what I can find out. I even have my own men working on it. I've checked all the places they've lived, their old addresses in Boston and New York, any relatives or places they were known to go, you know, vacation spots and the like, but we've come up empty. You'd think someone this famous would be easy to locate, especially a blind person."

"We think he's still in the area and didn't go far," Mark's employer informed him. "Within a two or three hundred mile radius is my guess. It's likely that they've rented something, maybe a hunting lodge or summer camp in the mountains. It's off season and they're looking for privacy, so it should be easy enough to find them. Reid left Scotland around the fifteenth. Look for ads in the New York papers or Want Ads for camp or cottage rentals in the country any time after that until his son's disappearance. They're hiding out somewhere close by, but not in the city, and they're not moving. It would be good if we found them before the authorities do."

"Yes, sir, I'll have my men on it right away."

"Did you disseminate the information about Reid to the police?"

"Yes, sir. I told them he was the stepfather and took the boy against the real mother's wishes, and that he had been demanding money from his son, which resulted in the argument and him leaving the States. I think it had the desired result. They're treating the old man as the number one suspect and ringleader. I've also convinced them that one of the accomplices, Leonard Zeigler, is dangerous and might harm David if things become violent."

"Good, now all you have to do is find them," said his employer. "Focus on vacation areas three or four hours from New York or Boston, which is where he lived while in the US, Upstate New York, maybe Cape Cod, the White Mountains or Southern Maine."

"That's quite a range," replied Mark, who had his own theories where they were, as did everybody. "They could be anywhere. They might be right here in the city for all we know. What's to keep them from going to the media or the authorities themselves? What's to keep David from telling everyone he hasn't been kidnapped?"

"One of the people with him, that Ziegler person, has already been implicated in the murder of the Fong woman, and has a history of mental illness, thanks to your efforts. The world will soon know about the notorious rogue scientist John Reid. How he has broken every criminal and moral law on the books, experimenting with human embryos and cloning. How he was fired from his position at the Roslin Institute and driven out of Edinburgh for his outrageous crimes. How he is wanted by the authorities in Great Britain for his criminal activities, of his malicious influence over his stepson. Who knows what he's been telling the young man. No one is going to believe a word they say. The police would rightly come to the conclusion that David's confused or being manipulated, a poor afflicted young man who has suffered a tremendous shock, first the sudden blindness on the eve of his great success, then the sinister influence of his step-father. He has been taken by force from a comfortable apartment where he had constant medical care to parts unknown and under who knows what conditions. The people around him are criminals. They are up to no good, including that new nurse - who was the beginning of all our problems - all of it for obvious monetary gain. This is the story you are to tell. This is the truth you are to establish."

"You know best," answered Mark, impressed with the web of lies and half-truths his employer had woven about the events, which even he was beginning to believe. Things sure were getting confusing.

Chapter 17

John Reid's revelations that late afternoon were less than edifying, as he didn't relate much more than he had the previous evening about a vague plot to take control of David's assets. His music was revolutionary and threatened to change the art forever. It was only natural that some group or crackpot would try to stop him or take control of everything. He even hinted that it might be the Russian mafia. Whoever they were, he said, Mark Burns, from Edinburgh Scotland, worked for them, but he couldn't prove it, at least not to David's satisfaction. It was only afterward, later that evening as they sat alone by the fire, that his father told him the real truth. And that had been well near impossible to believe.

"I don't believe it," said David hotly. "You really have lost your mind. You're crazy."

"I told you it would be difficult to accept."

"You're out of your mind," David repeated. "That's the most preposterous thing I've ever heard. I can't believe it."

"It's true, every last word of it. I'm sorry to tell you like this, but why would I lie to you about something like that? I'm not your real father, but I created you."

"No!" yelled David, getting up from the couch to run from the room even though he couldn't see his way. His father held him.

"Sssh, don't wake the others. Calm down. It doesn't change anything. You're still the David Reid you always were. You're still my son. All it means is you share the genetic makeup of another person instead of me. Think of it as having a twin brother, only he died 300 years ago."

David was silent, in a state of shock, and let his father lead him back to the couch.

"It was one of the great man's ancestors who first came to us with the DNA samples and asked us to clone them. He offered us huge amounts of money. It was a way to prove our theories on super-cloning, a way to use proteins to augment the process to overcome many of the technical difficulties in creating viable clones. You're the result. We could have cloned Einstein and Michelangelo, Sister Teresa and Gandhi, if they would have only let us, but before they stopped us we created you, the clone of Johann Sebastian Bach. All of this cost a tremendous amount of money. We didn't ask where our donor got it, but whoever killed him has come after you to get it back."

"When were you going to tell me that I'm some kind of freaking clone?" asked David.

"You're not a freak. You're as human as I am and I love you as if you were my own son. You are, in all but blood."

"Haven't you heard?" replied David, bitterly. "Blood is thicker than water."

"I know it's a little hard getting used to."

"Hard getting used to?" shouted David, almost waking up the others sleeping upstairs.

"Once I explain what cloning really is," replied his father. "You'll see it's just like any other form of reproduction, as natural as the good old-fashioned way. It's the way of the future."

"Spare me," said David, trying to stand again, but losing his balance and falling back onto the couch. "I don't want to hear anymore of this."

"At least now do you believe me that Mark is behind your blindness?"

"I don't know what to believe. I believe less now than I did before you started explaining it to me."

"David, why would I make this up?"

"I don't know, to drive me insane and take my ..." He stopped in mid-sentence.

"When have I ever lied to you, or told you anything that would harm you? I've only wanted what was best for you. A child is a responsibility, but you were special. I dedicated my life to making you happy and letting you fulfill your destiny. I never pushed you into anything. I always encouraged you and provided whatever you wanted. When did I ever say no to you except to keep you from harm? I know I should have told you sooner, but you have to agree, this is not something that comes up in the normal course of things and not easy to explain. It is only under the most serious conditions that I could bring myself to confront you with it. I was afraid of the harm it might do, but now I have to take the chance and hope you can handle it if I'm to protect you from an even greater and more immediate danger."

"I have to be alone," said David getting up again with his cane. "I don't want to talk about it anymore. I've got to think."

"OK, David, I understand. I'll be here if you need me or have any questions about things. We have a lot to do, and the longer we take, the more chance of us being found by Mark and his employers. Whoever was backing our donor is ruthless. They killed him and now they want to control you."

David went to his room, which was on the first floor under the stairs, tapping his way around the furniture and corners. His father sat for some time in front of the dying fire, before he too went up to bed. He tried to think how David must feel, being told he's not only a clone - a super-clone at that - but the genetically identical duplicate of the great Johann Sebastian Bach.

David did not emerge the next morning for breakfast.

"Where's David?" asked Colleen noticing his absence at the table.

"Oh, we were up late last night talking," replied his father. "He must have overslept. I'll check on him later. He has a lot on his mind."

"What did you say to him?" she queried, suspiciously.

"Oh, nothing. I'll let David tell you if he wants."

"Keeping secrets from us again," said Zeiggie, coming to the table looking well rested and fed, and healthy for the first time in days. "After all we've done for you."

"No, it's just a rather delicate family matter and I prefer David tell you in his own time and in his own way. You can understand that, Mister Ziegler."

"There's a lot I don't understand, like why David's business manager would want to do something like this. Aren't they childhood friends? The guy did seem to have David's best interests at heart, even though I can't stand him."

"Mark is being used, as I've told you," answered John Reid. "He was hired to keep an eye on David for his employers, like a zookeeper in the circus takes care of the prized cats. It's his job. Anyway, I know Mark better than any of you, and what he's capable of. He has a criminal record, and if you check it closely you'll find he got out early due to some vague figure in the background pulling strings, his employer."

"The Russian Mob?" guessed Zeiggie remembering what Reid had said the night before.

"Something like that," replied Reid.

Later that morning he went to David's room, where his son was lying in the dark staring blindly at the ceiling.

"How are you doing?" asked is father.

"How do you think?" answered his son.

"You want something to eat? You've got to eat you know."

"Why, didn't you clone me a double stomach?"

"Don't dwell on it. Get over it. Move on."

"Easy for you to say, you're not a freaking clone. Leave me alone. I'm not hungry."

"Want to take a walk?" suggested the old man, opening the shades.

"Yeah, sure, I'd like to see the sights."

"It's warm and the sun's out. It's been a very mild January. It will do you good. I'll get you a warm coat and you can sit in the sun by the lake."

David declined.

"OK," said his father finally. As he left he added, "If I were you, I'd be focusing on who did this to me and how to get my life back, before I worried about how I came about. Now you know the truth you have your whole life to reconcile yourself to it or not, but you also have a fate like every man. All you need is the courage to live it and you can conquer anything."

David stayed in his room most of the day, but later in the afternoon, about three, he asked Zeiggie to take him down to the lake so they could talk about music and things. They stayed there the rest of the afternoon, sitting in the sun, until a little after four when it grew dark and chilly. John had a good fire going by the time they came in, and David was feeling noticeably better. Colleen cooked a supper of fried chicken with roasted potatoes, which everyone enjoyed. Zeiggie thought he had died and gone to heaven.

That evening David broke the ice and told the others.

"And so ladies and gentleman," he announced, after finishing his story. "I'm a bona-fide clone of Johann Sebastian Bach."

Colleen stood staring, her mouth open, not knowing what to think. It only made her want to take care of him all the more. He was something special, one in a billion. But at the same time she felt sorry for him, as if he had to be protected like some kind of endangered species.

"Well, that explains a lot," said Zeiggie, chuckling and wanting to keep things light.

"I know," agreed David, laughing.

"That's incredible," said Colleen finally getting her tongue back and looking at David as if she wanted to hug him and cry. "That's just unbelievable."

She looked back and forth between father and son.

"So who is this guy again, the one after David's money?" asked Zeiggie, more interested than ever in the Bach connection, his great hobbyhorse.

"My colleague and I did private research in Scotland," John explained. "I believe the people who were backing our work, people who I only knew of indirectly, killed Mister Felix Mann, a distant relative of Bach's, who had located his ancestor's lost remains and brought us the DNA samples. Whoever they are, they feel they have a right to recover their money by whatever means they can. They're getting back at me by coming after my son."

"It's like a bizarre movie plot," observed Colleen. "Whoever heard of such a thing?"

"Ah, you'd be surprised at what deep secrets reside in the hearts of men," replied John Reid.

"Now that we know what's going on and why," said Zeiggie. "What are we going to do about it?"

"Good question, my friend," answered the old man. "Good question indeed."

"Why all this hiding and secrecy?" asked Colleen. "Why don't we just go to the police and explain everything? David can tell them he hasn't been kidnapped, and that we took him away from the people who were trying to poison him. We have Zeiggie's evidence."

"That's just what they want us to do," explained David's father. "I'm sure that's what they're expecting. Don't underestimate our adversary. He's very powerful and determined, quite ardent in his beliefs and willing to go to any lengths. He's already killed two people. He won't hesitate to do so again. Who knows who he has in his pocket? Look how long it took me to convince David and you folks of the truth. I doubt I'll get a chance to do that much talking with the authorities. None of us would. They'd have us locked up and muzzled so fast your heads would spin. They'd probably put David in a hospital for observation, to keep him incommunicado. Whoever is behind this has the power and means to do all those things."

"So what are we going to do?" This time it was David who asked.

"I was planning on getting us across the border to Canada and to Edinburgh from there," answered John Reid.

"What?" replied David forcibly. "How do you plan on getting us across the border and out of the country? That's crazy."

"Thanks for your vote of confidence," said his father.

"And what do you think they'd do to us once we got to Edinburgh?" asked Colleen.

"I was hoping we could tell our story. There are people there who know about this and are more susceptible to the truth, no matter how unbelievable. They know about the cloning. I'll take my punishment for doing it, but David will be protected. He can continue his work there, away from all the madness and publicity."

"What, like one of your laboratory experiments?" replied David. The room was silent.

"So how you figure to get us across the border?" asked Zeiggie, trying to ignore David's outburst.

"Well, if David continues not to shave as he's doing, I doubt even his mother - God rest her soul - would recognize him. If he somehow gains his sight back, things would be easier, of course, but in the meantime, with disguises and the right timing, we just might pull it off."

"We just might all be caught trying," said David. "You think we'd have a better chance telling our story to a bunch of border guards than the authorities here in the States?"

"Perhaps," replied his father. "If they happen to be Canadians we might have a better chance. Timing is everything."

"What do you mean?" asked Colleen.

"Well, if we wait until the heat's off, try it during an extremely busy time or late at night when there are few staff around, maybe devise some sort of diversion, change our appearance, we might blend in enough to get through. At least there, we'll have a chance to tell our story and find a sympathetic ear."

"Is that your plan?" asked his son. "You jeopardized our lives and futures to drag us out to the middle of nowhere on some harebrained scheme to cross the border like a gang of desperadoes? Let me turn myself in to the nearest state police station and save us all a lot of trouble. You've got us all crazy with your conspiracy theory nonsense."

"I agree," said Zeiggie. "It does sound kind of crazy. If that's your plan, we might as well turn ourselves in now. Border guards, cops, I don't see much difference."

"You all have more confidence in the American justice system than I do," observed the old man, who had been an active anti-American demonstrator in his youth, in the turbulent sixties. "Zeiggie, you seem to forget how easy it was for them to manipulate you into a mental institution without so much as thank you ma'am. Ask David how difficult it was tracing you. You disappeared, my friend. You were swallowed whole by the system. Who do you think did that? Do you think it was an accident? You've been around long enough to know things don't happen like that, not even here, not even to a man of your persuasion."

'You mean a black man?" replied Zeiggie, remembering all too well. "It *was* kind of strange the way they just put me in a van and dumped me off at the hospital, in another state. I never did get to see a judge, not even a phone call that second time. They just took me away and started drugging me. That is until I stopped taking the stuff and broke out."

"That was quite a feat, my friend," John Reid replied. "It shows a lot of ingenuity and gumption, not to say intelligence and courage. The only proof we have of the conspiracy is what you brought us. You're just the type of person we need in our current battle."

"There's got to be a paper trail," reasoned David.

"What?" said his father.

"A paper trail that connects the poison to Mark and Mark to his employer."

"I doubt it's as easy as that. I know them. Any connection to Mark and whoever hired him would be non-existent. If there were, Mark would disappear."

"Hmm," said David, finally focused as his father had advised, on who had done this to him and how to get back at them. For besides inheriting the great Bach's musical genius, he had also inherited his indomitable will and a belligerence that left most of his adversaries bruised and beaten.

"No, our only chance is to get across the border to international ground," insisted John Reid, knowing the power of their enemy and how he worked. Their adversaries would have the city saturated with their own people and those in their employ, who would make sure only the story they wanted would get out, with their slant and their scapegoats. He knew that in the eyes of many his son was an idiot savant, someone with incredible gifts in one thing, but a complete incompetent in all other aspects of life, unable to even do his own laundry. He would be treated with respect, but like a child who didn't know what was good for him, especially with his current handicap.

"But we have to wait," he continued. "It's too soon. That's why I got this place. We can hide out here, far enough away from the city and the border, but close enough to slip across in a few hours through any number of out of the way crossing points when the time's right."

No one said a word. David was beginning to think his father might be right. In his current condition he was in no position to direct events. He'd have to rely on them for everything, so he should be the last to try and conduct things as he had always been inclined to do. Still, he knew they were waiting for him. Their fates rested on his decision.

"OK," he said finally. "It's not much to go on, but you've obviously given this much more thought than we have, and you know these people, whoever they are, a lot better than we do. I just wish I could see."

"You will," replied his father. "They have some of the best eye specialist and toxicologists in the world in Montreal, and they're not in the pay of Mark Burns or his boss. Zeiggie, there are a few things in the back of the jeep, could you please grab them for us."

"Sure, what is it?"

"Just a camera and a few other things. I want to set it up at the entrance to the road we took to get in here, so we can monitor who's approaching. It might give us the time we need to slip out the back if someone comes looking for us."

"Nice precaution," said the ex-cello player. "You really have thought of everything."

"Ah, you couldn't imagine," answered John Reid. "I've been preparing for this moment David's whole life."

Chapter 18

"Yes, sir, they got there just a short time ago," said Mark, again in a leased office space on a secure phone to his mysterious employer. "We followed your instructions and searched through all the ads for rental properties in the areas you mentioned, and followed up on the few that sounded promising. The last one was a hunting camp on a lake in Upstate New York, in the Adirondack Mountains, pretty rough, isolated country. But when the state police got there today the place was deserted, although there were signs of recent habitation. They must have had a warning and taken off before we got there. They found a camera on a side road leading to the camp, and a few wires, but they were cut. There were no other signs of equipment, just some empty cans and dirty dishes."

"Do they know how long before the police arrived they left?" asked his employer, upset they had slipped through their fingers.

"Less than an hour from the looks of it," replied Mark. "We just missed them. They're apparently on the move again. We think they're headed for the Canadian border."

"You've got to stop them," ordered his employer, whose accent he couldn't quite place. "Who knows what will happen if they get out of the country. I'll send some of my people over to help out at the crossing, to help handle things."

"OK, but I've already got my own men up there. That's the first place we figured they'd go."

"Good. They were probably waiting for things to die down. Too bad they didn't wait an hour longer, we could have had them."

"We're close. The border's closed. There's no way they can get across without us knowing. I've been spreading cash around pretty liberally up there. I got the whole place covered, every crossing."

"OK, keep me informed," his employer commanded. "We'll let you know when it's time to talk again."

The line went dead. Mark used the phone to make a few calls of his own, to make sure things were being taken care of up north before he headed there himself to supervise the search. Now that they were closing in on them he wanted to be on the scene when they were apprehended.

There had been an all-points bulletin out since David's disappearance the month before. Then no word as the manhunt intensified throughout the country. Speculation was raging, especially in the media, which had been kept mostly in the dark. Much of the real work of tracking the kidnappers was taking place behind the scenes, kept from the public and press, as well as from the authorities. Except for the heightened state of alert on the US side of the border fueled by Mark Burns and his employer's money, everything was business as usual. The public, although still concerned, had lost the intense interest that characterized the early days of David's disappearance. Still, many wondered about his whereabouts.

Jean St. Pierre, the supervisor of the Canadian border patrol, also wondered what had happened to the famous blind composer, and half expected his body to be found in some river or ditch. He had been a border guard for almost thirty years and was due to retire soon. He had seen it all. He wasn't happy to be here on the graveyard shift, but it was Boxing Day, and most of his men had finagled the night off. Being the supervisor and wanting to keep his team happy, he had volunteered along with a few other diehards who needed the time-and-a-half and had no family or friends. Not that Jean didn't have family or friends, but his boys had grown up and had children of their own, and most of his friends had retired and moved out of the area. His wife, Francine, had died a year ago.

His boys were the thing in life that he was most proud of and he was thinking of them when he saw the car dart out from the line of traffic at the American booths and speed for the Canadian side a few hundred feet away. Jean was in the supervisor's post, a concrete building on the center island separating traffic going into the country from vehicles leaving it.

It had been a busy night, the skeleton crew kept constantly occupied on his side of the crossing by a continuous stream of Canadians coming home from a day of shopping and sightseeing in New York. The warm weather and sunshine had drawn thousands across the border to the States over the long weekend. That crowd had thinned out now, and it was almost time for the next shift to come on. Things had been particularly uneventful all evening until now.

There was a shot, as someone on the US side discharged their weapon in the air and several state police cars immediately gave chase. It was over almost as soon as it began, the driver apparently thinking better of trying to crash the border after hearing the gunshot. The vehicle pulled to a stop before it had gone halfway across the no man's land between the US and Canadian guard posts. It was immediately surrounded by gun-wielding border guards and New York State Police. Jean's walkie-talkie sputtered to life.

"Wilson here. You there, Jean?" It was his counterpart on the other side.

"Oui, Wilson, quel est le probleme, eh?" he answered in French, watching a rather stocky black man being pulled from the vehicle and handcuffed before being placed in the patrol car and driven back to the US side.

"We got somebody trying to crash the border," replied the voice through his walkie-talkie. "The situation's under control."

"Je peux voir, mon ami. Is there anything we can do to assist you?" he said in French.

"No, that's OK," the man in charge on the US side responded. He resented the fact the Frenchman refused to speak English even though he spoke it better than most of his own men. "We'll take care of it."

Vehicles were starting to move back and forth again, as everyone recovered from the excitement. Guns weren't discharged at the border every day. He was about to shut off the radio, when it burped to life again.

"Hold on there, Jean," said his counterpart on the other side. "We got us a celebrity here. Mister Leonard Ziegler, wanted for escaping from a mental institution in New Jersey, and for the kidnapping of one David Gordon Reid."

"Sacrebleu!" replied the Frenchman. Of course, Jean knew about the famous composer and his kidnapping. He had been one of those millions watching the concert, and like everyone, had been shocked at the bizarre ending and the subsequent kidnapping. His team had been put on high-alert to provide any assistance necessary to their compatriots on the other side - hopefully by catching the culprits themselves and showing-up their erstwhile American colleges. Now he had just been informed they had apprehended one of the kidnappers themselves, without his assistance. Ah, c'est la vie.

"That is wonderful, mon ami. Are you sure there is nothing we can do to help?"

"We'd like to have you lockdown your side of the border. There may be more of the kidnappers trying to get across."

148

"You know I can't do that without orders from my superiors. It's four in the morning, but I'll see what I can do."

He instantly hit a switch and got on the phone to his guard posts, three of them side by side, where vehicles were already being waved through.

"Hold up the line," he ordered through the radio, as he pulled on a jacket and stepped outside. It was still balmy, in the mid-forties, unusually warm for this time of year, but he didn't know how long he'd be standing outside and would miss the warmth of his office.

A few cars were just coming to a stop at the border post. An official vehicle could be seen speeding across the intervening distance from the US side, while the increased activity there could be clearly observed by the floodlights that had been turned on. The Americans always did overreact. He preferred to keep things low-keyed.

There were just a few cars and trucks at the crossing, all waiting for the red lights in their lane to turn green, while they answered questions. Soon, though, if he didn't get things moving again, there would be a long line of irate Canadians, way too many to handle with his small skeleton crew.

While he waited for the patrol car to reach him, he stood by the nearest guard post, where his man was questioning the occupants of a vehicle with Canadian plates. When the Americans pulled up next to him his counterpart got out, along with a New York State trooper. The other supervisor handed Jean some photographs, which he held up to the light. One was a recent publicity picture of a clean-shaven David Reid in his tuxedo. The others were a picture of David's father that was quite old, and a high school graduation photo of Colleen, which although not old, did not do her justice. Jean let his counterpart know that he would take care of his end and they could take care of theirs. He didn't want any US personnel telling him or his people what to do, and sent them on their way.

Taking over for the nearest guard, he told him to help search the car in the next lane, ordering them to hold every vehicle for him. He had decided to check them all himself. Hopefully he could determine quickly if someone needed to be interrogated or searched in more length or not. It was simple when you were looking for something specific. He would let a few through with their cheap bottles of liquor or toys to catch his man. Obviously, whoever they apprehended on the other side had been acting as a decoy for the others to slip through. It was an old ploy. People did a lot of stupid things for money. He knew exactly what to look for.

He quickly interrogated the nearest car, and as quickly let them through, then the one behind it, another Canadian plate, with a young family and two small children sleeping in the back. Then he closed the lane and walked to the next one, where a fat man in a Cadillac was arguing with the guard.

"What seems to be the problem here?" he asked his man.

"This gentleman refuses to open his glove compartment," answered the young, efficient guard.

The overweight driver had slicked black hair combed back off his wide forehead, and a thin mustache. There was a big diamond ring on his pinky finger. He was just the kind of person who Jean normally would have hassled simply because of his attitude and general appearance. He had a girl in the car that looked young enough to be his daughter, but obviously wasn't. Though she was probably technically not underage, he checked her ID anyway. Normally he would have kept this loudmouth, arrogant jerk tied up at the border for hours just on principal, but not tonight. He knew they weren't the ones he was looking for, so he told him to drive through. His men were still under the assumption this was business as usual, where you looked for the typical things. Tonight was different. He told them so.

"We are looking for three people," he informed them, showing his men the photographs. "A woman and two men. One of them is the famous conductor and composer David Reid. We believe he's been kidnapped. He may be under duress and in physical danger, so we must proceed with caution. Unless they fit these descriptions, try to keep them moving through until the next shift arrives. And for God's sake, if you have any doubts call me. I'll be right out here with you, checking vehicles. Unless they have passengers, let all the semi's through. If you see anyone that looks suspicious escort them to the side lane and have them step out of the vehicle so it can be searched and their papers checked. You know the drill. Then call me."

There was still one vehicle at the last lane, a pickup truck standing by itself. He went over to talk to the driver, an older man in dirty denims and a baseball cap. He noticed the truck had New York plates as he approached cautiously. He also noticed that there were two other occupants, man and woman.

"Bon Nuit," he said, as the man rolled down his window. "Comment allez-vous?"

"Sorry, I don't speak no French," replied the man, in the familiar accent of a North Country hillbilly.

"I'm sorry for the inconvenience" said Jean in perfect English. "But we are under heightened alert tonight. There's been a breach of the US side and we have to be extra vigilant. I won't keep you long."

"Yeah, I saw some damned fool try to run the line, probably a dope smuggler."

"Can I see your passports or birth certificates please," he asked, liking this person even less than the last one. Why did he have to get all the creeps when he couldn't treat them like they deserved?

"Ain't got no passports. T'aint been anywhere. We got our birth certificates, though. Good thing you told us we'd need 'em," he said looking over at the young woman sitting to his right, presumably his daughter or some such relation.

"Where are you going?" inquired Jean, looking at the three occupants suspiciously. There was a young girl with short cut, black hair and a thin man in his mid-twenties with a full beard of long, black hair and dark glasses. He reminded Jean of the rock band ZZ-Top. He too had on a dirty baseball cap and a pair of coveralls over a T-shirt. "What's your business in Canada?"

"Ain't got no business," answered the driver. "We're going to Montreal. It's our first time out of the country, but since we lived so close all our lives and have heard so much about it, we decided to go. My son and daughter here are taking me for my sixty-eighth birthday, before I get too old."

"Oh, that's a very nice gift," replied the Frenchman, sticking his head into the vehicle to get a better look at the three occupants. None unfortunately, looked like his pictures. Still, they were looking for two men and a woman.

"Pardon-moi," said Jean. "But why are you coming across so early. Most people, they are coming home at this hour if they are not already there, eh. There won't be anything open in the city when you get there, no cafes and no stores. Everyone will still be asleep. This is not the normal time of day, you will agree, oui, to be going on vacation."

"Well, it is for us. We get up around this time anyways. Why spend it waiting around? It's my birthday, been so for over four hours now and I want to celebrate. Thought we'd beat the crowds. How'd I know all these damned fools would be out tonight? What is it, the Canadian New Years or something?"

"No, it's Boxing Day."

"What the hell's that?" said the man.

"It is a holiday where some people have the day off and the others trade places with their bosses. It's an old English custom, not so big here in Quebec, but a lot of people take advantage of the holiday to visit the States and shop. Some of them are just getting home."

"Well, it figures. Just on my birthday there's got to be all this damned traffic."

"So, you are from Chazy, eh?" Jean asked, returning the man's papers. "Nice area. I used to fish out there."

"Is that so?" replied the old man. "Never had much time for fish'n myself. Too busy trying to dig a living out of the ground. Never had time to sit and dip a pole in the water. You going to let us go or what?"

"Hello," said Jean to the other occupants in the car, ignoring the man's question. "How are you this evening?"

"Fine," answered the young lady sitting in the middle between the two men.

"This your first time to Canada?" he asked.

"Yes," replied the girl.

"How about you?" he inquired of the young man with the beard, sitting on the far passenger seat.

"Once, in school. Our band played a concert around here," said the young ZZ-Top lookalike.

"Oh, where was that?"

"At St. Johns. The high school there run by the Brothers of Religious Instruction."

"Ah, I know the school well. I grew up in St. Johns. Was Brother Francis there then?"

"I don't know," replied the young man, looking at him and smiling. "I was just a kid. I only remember the other band director's name was Brother Peter."

"Ah, Brother Peter. He was a great music teacher. He's gone now."

"Yes, I know. That's too bad."

"So what did you play?"

"The trombone," answered the young man.

"Damned waste of time if you ask me," interjected the older man. "His mother's idea, rest her soul. He's a real educated dandy now since he's been to agricultural school."

"Oh, where was that?" asked Jean.

152

"Messina," replied the young man. "I majored in horticulture and fruit trees."

"He's got the damnedest ideas about trees," said the old man. "Wants to turn my whole place into an experimental tree farm."

"There's a lot of money in fruit trees," the young man informed them.

Normally, he would have let these people through. They obviously didn't fit the profile nor look like the photographs. Their stories seemed authentic enough, and one of them even knew the old band teacher in his hometown high school. They must be from the area. They seemed OK. Yet something held him back. They were the same age and sex as the three he was looking for, but something didn't fit. If these were kidnappers, then one of them must be the victim. Yet no one here seemed to be under duress. If anything, they were all working together at whatever it was they were doing, if anything. He took a quick look in the back of the truck, where a tarp had been thrown over some shrubs.

"I'll have to ask you to step out of the vehicle," Jean announced after looking underneath. He opened the cab door. "I'd like to ask you some questions in the office there and take another look at your papers."

"What for?" objected the old man, pulling the door closed again. "We ain't done nothing wrong. You got no right to detain us here. If you don't want us in your country, we'll turn around and go home."

"No you won't," insisted the supervisor, signaling his men to join him and opening the door again. "Those trees you're carrying are illegal. Please, all of you. Come with me."

Mark had finally arrived at the small border town called Champlain, a short distance from the New York and Canadian border, on Route 87. It was a little before 1:00 pm. He had driven all morning up the interstate from the City as soon as he got the word around five that morning, getting stuck in rush hour traffic on his way out of Manhattan.

One of the alleged kidnappers had been apprehended earlier that morning trying to cross the border. Lenny Zeigler had either decided to leave the country on his own, or had been used as a decoy to help the others get away. The latter theory was considered the most likely, since three people, two men and a woman, had been detained on the other side - identities unknown. Apparently, for some reason, the Canadians were being less than cooperative.

Because of a communication snafu he had to wait at the State Police barracks next to town for someone to meet him and take him up to the border. It seemed that a delicate international situation had developed. Mark got as much information as he could, and had some fresh coffee and donuts while he waited. It was almost 2:30 pm before he arrived at the scene.

Although Mark had no official standing, as David's business manager, he represented the interests of the presumed kidnapped victim. Both the FBI and police officials treated him as such, as did the US government, who like everyone else in this affair, were deeply concerned. David Reid, after all, was a figure of national prominence, with an international reputation, famous around the world. Moreover, because of the money Mark had been able to throw around, he had considerable influence with the locals on the ground as well.

"What do you mean you don't know who they are?" Mark asked the FBI man in charge at the US border. The morning crew, who had been there when Zeiggie was arrested, had all left, except for the supervisor and a few of the State Police. Everyone else involved had been interviewed and sent home.

"All we know is the Canadians detained three occupants of a New York vehicle this morning," replied the FBI man. "But we don't know who they are. The truck is registered to a Leon Pickney of Champlain, New York, and was reported stolen this morning around 7:00."

"It's that little French peacock, Jean St. Pierre," the supervisor from the early am shift informed them. "He's making a big stink as usual about their national sovereignty and trying to tell us it's a Canadian matter. Told me to call the US consulate if we want to communicate with the detainees."

Mark was furious but held his temper.

"Can I talk to the prisoner, the man you caught trying to crash the border this morning?" he asked.

"You'd have to take that up with the State Police," replied the border official. "They took him away hours ago."

As much as he wanted to interrogate Zeiggie, Mark realized there was much more at stake here at the border, especially if the people in custody really were David and his father.

"What did Mister Ziegler say? Does he know anything about the others?" Mark asked the FBI man.

"No, he says he was trying to get out of the country on his own. Says he hasn't seen David Reid since before the big concert there. Insisted he didn't know the other people."

"Do you know anything about them?" Mark asked the border guard. "Your people must have seen them go across."

"Yeah, three hillbillies from their description," answered the supervisor. Didn't look at all like the pictures. Everything seemed in order. Rude old coot by the sound of it, nothing like the description of the people we were looking for. Anyway, we had a border-jumper on our hands so things got a bit hectic."

"Kind of convenient wouldn't you say?" observed Mark.

"What, are you saying this Zeigler character and them hillbillies are together?" asked the FBI man.

"These are very clever people we're after. No telling what they might do. Any way we can get over there and talk to them ourselves?"

"Well, sir, that's the problem," replied the border supervisor. "That damned Jean St. Pierre is making a big stink about the whole thing. He says he's detaining them for some illegal plants they were taking across. Says they have nothing to do with who we're looking for and when he's done with them for smuggling banned fruit trees into Canada, we can have them."

"Let me talk to him," requested Mark.

"I don't know," said the overworked and tired supervisor, who had been on the job since ten the previous evening. As far as he was concerned, as long as they had been caught and were being dealt with, who cared what side of the border they were on. "We have to follow procedure and go through proper channels, just like they do. It's not as simple as just going over for a chat."

"I could make it worth their while."

"I wouldn't try that, sir, not with an official of a foreign government, especially Jean St. Pierre," counseled the border guard.

Mark was about to object, when an expensive looking car drove up. The driver got out and opened the rear door for an elderly but well dressed, light-skinned black man. Mark had been expecting him.

"Hi, inspector," said the newcomer, approaching the FBI man and extending his hand. "I am Doctor Henry Fitzroy of Interpol. Now that David Reid's kidnappers have left the US they are in our jurisdiction. We have a warrant from the ERU for John Reid for other crimes, including criminal use of cloning and industrial espionage. We're dealing with an international criminal organization here, gentlemen, and John Reid is the ringleader."

"You'll have to deal with the Canadian authorities," the US border supervisor informed him, introducing himself and bringing the international lawman up to speed on the situation. He knew better than anyone who they were dealing with on the Canadian side.

"That's why I'm here," replied the cultured black man from Brussels with the impeccable credentials and manners.

A short time later a cavalcade of vehicles was on its way across the border. It included two State Police cars and two SUVs containing several US officials and border personnel, along with Mark and Dr. Henry Fitzroy of the European Criminal Investigative branch of Interpol.

Chapter 19

For Jean St. Pierre, the morning had turned out quite different than he had expected when he started his shift exactly twelve hours earlier. Things had gotten exciting enough with the failed attempt to crash the border and the subsequent lockdown. They got decidedly more interesting when he detained a few dirt-farmers with a truck full of illegal plants. It was serious enough that kidnappers or no, he had to detain them. What happened next was downright Kafkian.

"You've got to help us," whispered John Reid as Jean brought them into his office. He pretended not to hear and told them to sit in chairs along the wall, while he questioned them at his desk one by one, the older man first.

Jean St. Pierre was startled and didn't know if he had heard the man correctly. He went on as if nothing had happened.

"You've got to help us," pleaded John Reid again as Jean continued to question him. His hillbilly accent was gone.

"Pardon moi?" he asked, as if he no longer understood English.

"We need your help. David hasn't been kidnapped," John answered in perfect rapid French. The following brief, partly whispered exchange took place in that language, although John spoke a Parisian style, while Jean St. Pierre spoke a local Quebec dialect.

Losing Zeiggie had been heartrending. Neither David nor his father had wanted him to do it. After some persuasive arguments on Zeiggie's part, however, he convinced them it was the only way for them to get across. They reluctantly went along, hoping somehow they would be able to get him out later, once they told their story.

The first part had worked well enough. They might have made it all the way, but the guard at the Canadian side decided to search their vehicle. Unfortunately, it was something they had not considered doing themselves. As luck would have it, the truck they chanced to borrow happened to contain some plants that were illegal to transport into the country.

Jean St. Pierre stopped them out of instinct, feeling something was not right but couldn't put his finger on it. Whatever it was, combined with the recent incident on the US side, it was enough to make him wary. When he found the plants, all thoughts of kidnappers vanished, as he was filled with indignant anger that these rubes had tried to put one over on him and the Canadian government. Who did these hillbillies think they were coming in here with their illegal fruit plants! Now, however, the conversation was making him distinctly uneasy.

"What does this all mean?" he exclaimed in English, after listening to John's story.

"It's true," insisted David, who had been following their conversation. "I haven't been kidnapped. I was blinded and held against my will by my business manager."

"This is the only way we could get away," continued John. "He, or whoever he's working for, has a great deal of influence in the US, especially in New York. They control the local authorities there. We had to get on neutral ground."

It was only then that Jean noticed that the young man was actually blind, and had been looking off slightly as he spoke to him, as though he didn't know exactly where Jean was sitting. He was actually talking to David Reid, the famous composer. It took him a moment to recover from the double shift in reality - from hillbilly to famous kidnapped victim to asylum seeker.

He made them repeat their story again then again, and on one pretense or another kept everyone out of the office, as the shift changed and the phone began to ring with urgent calls from the US side. First John, then David, then Colleen, then all of them together, he interrogated them for an hour, and each time got the same story.

It was easy for him to believe that whoever they were fleeing from had bought off the authorities. He saw it every day in the news. The rich with their big cars and flashy jewelry - enough sitting on a woman's finger to feed his family for a year - got away with murder, while the poor were locked up for stealing a loaf of bread. His mind worked fast as he strove to take it all in and understand the implications, seeking a way to make it work for him and his country.

They had been at it several hours. Jean St. Pierre ordered breakfast with coffee for himself and his prisoners, while he held the outside world at bay. His dictated response to the requests of the US authorities had resulted in a barrage of angry counter demands and threats, all of which he ignored. When he could question the prisoners no longer, he let them rest in the small detention cells at the back of the office area. Then he made some phone calls to his superiors and a few colleagues. There was no rest for the weary. He had just gotten off the phone after explaining the situation to his boss and was resting his eyes at his desk when there was a rap on the door.

"You've got company," announced the current shift supervisor, resenting the way St. Pierre was always trying to take control and grab the limelight for himself. Just because he had stumbled onto something didn't mean he owned it.

Getting up from his desk, Jean peeked out the blinds, which were keeping out the dull, grey morning light. A caravan of official vehicles was on its way over from the US side. He slipped on his coat and cap and went to meet them, smiling at the other supervisor who held the door for him. Jean St. Pierre had seniority and didn't let anyone forget it. Despite his lack of sleep, he was ready for them.

"Bonjour mes amis," he said in French, as the visitors got out of the vehicles and gathered in front of him. "To what do I owe this visit?"

"We'd like to talk to your prisoners," replied the FBI man in charge.

"I already told you," answered Jean in English. "These people are being detained for trying to bring in a truck full of illegal plants. It has nothing to do with your problem."

"Now, Jean Pierre..." began the US supervisor.

"Why don't you let us determine that," interrupted the FBI man.

"It's Jean St. Pierre," he answered, correcting his counterpart and ignoring the FBI man, being intentionally rude to both of them at once. "I speak the English, at least you can do is pronounce my name correctly."

"Pardon moi," said Doctor Henri Fitzroy, pronouncing the words in a perfect French Parisian dialect, with which he continued speaking in a rapid fashion.

"I'm with the European Bureau of Criminal Investigation. We believe you have a John David Reid in your custody. We have outstanding warrants for his arrest and an extradition treaty with your government giving us jurisdiction in these matters. I'm sure you will find everything in order." As he spoke, he tried to hand Jean St. Pierre some papers, which the border man ignored.

"That is all well and good," replied Jean, switching to French again. "But as I have been trying to tell my friend here, you will have to follow protocol. I just can't hand these people over to you. They have broken Canadian law and that takes precedence over whatever other crimes they may be suspected of. You will need to talk to the judge, as they say."

159

"Hello, Mister Jean St. Pierre. My name is Mark Burns," announced Mark stepping forward. "I represent Mister David Gordon Reid. We believe he is under duress and has been kidnapped by his stepfather and these other people. No matter how it may appear, he could be in grave danger the longer he is in their hands. He may be lying to save himself and those around him."

"I'm sure wherever these people you are talking about actually are, this may be so," insisted the tired but determined supervisor in English. "But I assure you, these people are not who you say. They are three farmers who are trying to smuggle plants across the border. This is a very common but serious crime, because these plants are ruining our environment. Still, they ignore our laws and flaunt our customs. Now they must be processed through our system. If they are wanted for more serious crimes elsewhere, I'm sure that will all be sorted out in due time. Your consulate can keep you informed. Now what more can I do for you gentlemen?"

"Can you at least let us talk to them?" asked Mark. "Let us determine for ourselves if these are the ones we're looking for?"

"And what purpose will that serve?" replied the Frenchman, "other than to bypass our legal system. I'm afraid we can't allow that to happen. I have my orders, gentlemen. It would be the same way if the shoe was on the other foot, no?"

"We have a kidnapping here," said Mark, raising his voice. "My friend is in danger. Please let us see him and take him home. You can have the others."

Jean St. Pierre saw no further reason for subterfuge. On the contrary, telling them the truth - at least the way he saw it - would further his agenda perfectly.

"And what if this David Reid, as you say, what if it is him and he refuses to go?"

"What?" they all asked in unison.

"These people are seeking asylum in Canada," explained Jean, letting down all pretense. "They are asking for protection from you, Mister Burns, and your employers, who have a great deal of influence over the government and the police. Just another example of the ongoing dominance of the English speaking people..."

"That's preposterous!" exploded Mark.

"What are you trying to pull here?" said the FBI man. "Who do you think you are? These people are federal fugitives. You're aiding and abetting kidnappers and terrorists. Not even your government would be foolish enough to try and protect these people. I demand you let us see them. Release them at once."

"I'm afraid I can't do that," responded Jean St. Pierre. "I don't take orders from you or from your boss's boss. You can go all the way to the top of your bosses and I don't take orders from them. I only take orders from my superiors, who are telling me not to let anyone see the detainees until they have had a chance to talk to them themselves, which I was trying to arrange when I was informed I had visitors. Now if there is nothing else I can help you with, I must ask you to leave, as you are disrupting the busy morning crossing."

The FBI man was fuming, while the US border officials just frowned, knowing well the histrionics Jean St. Pierre could be capable of. Mark was looking at Doctor Fitzroy who was looking at the Canadian customs man with an amused expression, half between admiration for his chutzpa and surprise at the turn of events. John Reid and his son had asked the Canadian government for political asylum from the United States of America. How would that play on the evening news?

With no recourse, the American team got back in their vehicles and returned to the US side.

"What's this," raged the FBI man, "the Berlin Wall or something? For crying out loud..."

"I told you," replied the border man. "Jean St. Pierre can be a real prick when he wants to."

"He can't get away with this," fumed Mark. "Isn't there anything you can do?" He looked at the Interpol man, the person his employer had sent to take care of things.

"I'll have to make a few calls when I get to a secure phone," said Doctor Fitzroy.

It didn't take long for the events at the border to hit the news-waves and when it did, all pandemonium broke loose. By five that evening every newspaper, radio station, and television network in both countries had a reporter on the scene. Jean St. Pierre had gone home for a brief nap but was back at his post, guarding his charges, while every politician from the New York Governor to the US Attorney General had gotten involved, as did their counterparts on the Canadian side.

The pressure on Jean to give the trio over to the US authorities was tremendous, but the crafty Frenchman refused to give in. He held out even against his own government, who like the Americans didn't know quite what to make of the alleged amnesty request and wanted to keep the whole thing quiet. Well, it was too late for that. The cat was out of the proverbial bag. More importantly, David Reid and his friends now had a spokesman.

Jean St. Pierre had been giving interviews to all the French newspapers and media, who hurriedly printed and reported everything he said verbatim. His message was getting out. Now maybe people would listen to him when he tried to warn them about the big, corrupt, multi-national industrial complex and the results of their overriding greed. Another one of their greatest citizens has had to leave their country. Maybe now folks in Quebec would realize it was time to succeed from the Commonwealth and start their own French Republic.

"Are you saying that David Gordon Reid wasn't kidnapped?" asked one of the first US reporters to get an interview with him.

"He is with his father and his nurse. That hardly sounds like kidnapping to me," he replied. "David is in good health. He was being kept against his will since his blindness by his business manager, a Mister Mark Burns."

"Those are very serious accusations, Mister St. Pierre. Why didn't they just go to the authorities in the US with these allegations in the first place? Why pull this kidnapping trick and alarm everyone?"

"They were going to as soon as they got David to safety, but then the kidnapping alert went out. They were afraid they wouldn't be given a chance to tell their side of the story before David was in the custody of his manager again. Mr. Burns works for a very powerful syndicate with tentacles that reach deep into the government and police. That's why they have come to Canada for sanctuary."

"Can we talk to them?" asked another newsman.

"No, not at this time," answered Jean St. Pierre.

"Do they have any proof of these accusations?" asked another. "Who is this syndicate you're talking about? How do we know these aren't just the ravings of a couple of con men?"

"One of the reasons they left the US is to gain time to gather the necessary evidence, which spans several continents. You must realize the amount of money involved. The publishing rights alone for Mister Reid's last work are worth millions. Anyone who controls that business controls all of that money."

Many found the story hard to believe. The more that came out, the more difficult it was to swallow. The real truth, of course, was still a secret known only to the four refugees. Jean was surprised that many, even on his own side of the border, were still skeptical. That there could exist a sinister underworld syndicate that could control the police and elected officials, was a given as far as the cynical Frenchman was concerned. Why did people find it so hard to believe? David Reid was a revolutionary musician. Everything he touched turned to gold. Little wonder someone wanted to get in on the action. It was the same old story of corruption and greed in high places. Now all he had to do was convince the world.

Mark's worst nightmare had materialized like a sudden storm, which now raged around him. His name had become a household word for betrayal and infamy. He and the person who hired him were being blasted out of the shadows by the bright light of publicity.

The simple task of intercepting the quartet at the border had been his responsibility after it was known where they were headed. The job had been assigned to him, a job he had been handsomely paid for - well beyond most people's dreams - and he had failed. Now he was doing his best to control the situation with his own net of lies and accusations.

"David Reid has been a very confused and sick man since his breakdown," he told the reporter for the New York Times. After the incident, he had tried to protect David, his boyhood friend, from the public. He had attempted to keep him safe and hide his secret. There was nothing wrong with David Reid's eyes. He had suffered a complete nervous collapse and mental breakdown from the severe pressure and stress of first composing the revolutionary symphony, and then rehearsing and performing it in such a short time. The hectic pace broke him. Even with all the doctors and experts, he was unable to take care of himself. David Gordon Reid was totally helpless. Mark was the only person who had stood by him and taken care of him. Now others were trying to take advantage of the situation for their own benefit and destroying Mark's good name, after all he had done for his friend.

Mark could be very persuasive. And the things he said about David's father, being a greedy and base man, who had been taking advantage of his son all his life, rang true. When David had tried to stand up to the old man and stop him from abusing their relationship, his father had threatened him and left the country, hatching the kidnapping plot. He then came back secretly to carry it out. David is so vulnerable and susceptible he'd do or say anything his father told him to. The allegations against Mark were absolutely absurd with not a shred of truth, told by the old con artist and rogue, John Reid.

The papers were having a field day, each one taking one side or the other in the standoff. Not surprisingly, the majority of the Canadian papers supported Jean St. Pierre's version, not a few of these with great glee at the embarrassment it was causing the US government. Many of the American papers still viewed the detainees, all except David Reid, as kidnappers and criminals. The American president wanted to know if the stories were true, thus the involvement of the State Department. Was it a kidnapping or not? State told the top man in the FBI to find out, no matter what resources he had to tap to do it.

Mark's employer, however, had resources and contacts of his own, throughout Europe and the US, not to mention Canada. Those strings were being pulled that needed pulling. A great deal of pressure was being asserted by the European side for the extradition of John Reid for other crimes, and the return of David Reid to the US where he could get the treatment he needed. Jean St. Pierre, however, and the local Quebec officials, on the grounds of the requested political asylum, refused to be budged. Backed up by their superiors, they stuck to the letter of the law and the slow, halting process of the overcrowded Canadian legal system.

Chapter 20

Things had become decidedly strange for David Reid since he had put his life in his father's hands. He still had trouble reconciling himself to the whole thing, especially the part where he was the clone of Johann Sebastian Bach. The idea didn't really mesh with the way he thought of himself. Now he didn't know who he was.

David and his father, along with Colleen, were being kept under house arrest in an undisclosed location just outside Montreal, under constant surveillance. The three of them stayed together in a suite of several rooms with all the amenities due to someone of David's stature. An army of doctors and specialists had been to see him, but only under the utmost secrecy, and no one from the press was being allowed to talk to any of them.

The Canadians were treating the whole thing as a political asylum case, although they were taking their sweet time and still under immense pressure from the US government. Even if many Canadian politicians and editors felt that the claim was a bit farfetched and looked at the whole affair as a farce, they all saw it as leverage in those matters of more import where it could be used to good effect. So despite the American protests Jean St. Pierre had the backing of his government as he continued to speak out on behalf of David and his father, becoming the perfect conduit for their story. David, however, was not so sure he liked the idea of being under house arrest no matter what the circumstances. He certainly didn't like the interrogations he was undergoing, as if he were some kind of public enemy.

"I don't like it," David repeated to his father for the tenth time that evening. "How long are they going to keep us here? Do you know the penalty for claiming political asylum under false pretenses?"

"These aren't false pretenses, David," replied his father, repeating himself as well. "You know full well what Mark and his employer are capable of."

"Mark and his employer, that's all you talk about."

"That's all there is to talk about. They won't be happy until you're in their complete power or dead. What more proof do you want than what's happened to you already? That was no accident you know."

Since the day two weeks ago when they had been hiding out in the Adirondacks of New York state, David had been slowly but surely recovering his eyesight. It was around that time that his father discovered Colleen was still administering the eye-drops Mark had given her and threw it out after taking a small sampling to test. David was just now able to see different shades of light, where before it had all been total blackness. Soon he hoped he would be able to see shapes again. And then? He wouldn't let himself think beyond the present moment. That was troubling enough.

"Well, they're treating me as if I was a criminal," he said. "I don't like it. Why don't they let us go? I don't like being cooped-up here."

"You call this being cooped-up?" replied his father, motioning to the expensive room where they sat at a rich mahogany dinner table beneath a crystal chandelier. "We've got all the comforts of life here. We're being treated like royalty."

"Yeah, royal prisoners, next it will be off with our heads. Why are they keeping us here? Why won't they let us talk to anybody?"

"Supposedly for our own good," answered John Reid. "Remember, we're seeking the protection of the Canadian government. We must be running from something. We need their protection so we're being protected. You've got to understand the pressure they must be under from the US to have us returned. This is a highly embarrassing situation for them, and the longer it lasts the worse it is."

"Well, I don't like being locked up in here like this. I need to be back where I can work."

"Well, David, that *is* a good sign. That's the first you've mentioned working again since your, um, your accident."

"It wasn't an accident, remember."

"Yes, and it's good that you don't forget it either. You're still in danger, and that's well to keep in mind. This is just what we needed. It couldn't have worked out better if I planned it myself, which you have to admit, I did, sort of. That little Jean St. Pierre is a veritable pit-bull. We could not have found a better advocate and spokesman. He has an international audience, and enough political and local backing to pull it off. The worst thing for Burns and his employer is publicity. We've tied Mark's name to a sinister international plot. Now all we have to do is wait and let them self-destruct. That is if they don't get us first."

"Who am I?" David said forcibly, changing the subject to what was really on his mind.

"I told you, David. We've been through all that."

"Tell me again. Who am I?"

"You're David Reid. You're my ..."

166

"I am not your son," David interrupted. "I'm a bastard clone. I have no father."

"That's not true."

"I was bred in a freaking test tube!" David shouted, looking angrily at the man he could no longer call his father. The empty void it left made him feel hollow inside, like half a man, as if he were hardly human. He wasn't sure he could live with the knowledge.

"You were bred in your mother's womb. It just so happens you're the genetic twin of Bach. So what of it? You are a hundred percent human. I brought you up as my son. Your DNA is only incidental. Hell, 98.9% of our DNA comes from apes anyway. You're as natural as the next man. What's the big deal? Get over it. It's only a few chromosomes, which if I hadn't told you would not have affected you at all."

"What about my musical gifts? Are those natural?"

Before his father could respond, he asked another question in partial answer to his first.

"If all this is so natural, how come you haven't told anyone?"

"I don't think that's relevant. It's a private matter. We have enough publicity on our hands without adding to it. You know how people are. The less they know of your private life the better."

"Exactly," said David, knowing full well why his father hadn't mentioned it. "No one would believe you and if they did, they'd think I was some kind of freak. And they'd be right. I am a bloody freak."

"That's not true, David. Your gifts are natural. They have nothing to do with being cloned from Bach."

Of course, his father knew that wasn't entirely true. David's talent had everything to do with being a clone of the great musician, and the intense program of musical training David underwent modeled after that of Bach's. Long ago, however, John had resolved to only tell his son what he needed to know, and then only what he thought he could handle safely. There was a great deal yet to tell, but the time was not right.

"Obviously, you have some inherited talent," admitted the elder Reid. "Call it a predisposition, an aptitude if you well, but nothing more. The rest is natural talent and hard work, and a good environment."

David wanted to believe his father, but was filled with doubts. He didn't know what to believe.

"In any case, it's your secret," said his father. "You well have to learn to live with it."

"Easy for you to say."

"No it isn't. I have to live with it every day just like you do."

"It's not the same."

"No, it's worse. I feel responsible. I want only what's good for you."

"Why did you do it? Why did you clone me? Isn't that illegal?"

"In some places," answered his father half-joking.

"Everywhere!" yelled David, exasperated at the level of denial. "We were doing something men had only dreamed since the beginning of time."

"You were playing God."

"Yes, we were pushing science to the brink of the infinite, realizing man's full potential, achieving the impossible. You are the future, David, a race of supermen with powers beyond reckoning."

"You're mad. I've finally got proof, you're crazy. You always have been."

"Maybe, David, but you can't deny the good you've done, the gift you've given the world with your music."

"That explains a lot," said David, as if the previous discussion had never occurred.

"What, what explains a lot?"

"Why I'm not tall and distinguished like you. Even mom was tall and thin. I always wondered why I'm so heavy-set and you and mom are so slim. I look like Bach, not you or mom."

"Yes, you have his physique. As far as I can tell he was a bit on the stocky side like you, although he did love his ale."

"And his sex, didn't he have a dozen kids or so?"

"More than that. You have a lot of catching up to do on that score, but there's plenty of time for that. He was sort of combative like you as well. As a matter of fact, as you can imagine, you have quite a lot of the traits of your twin brother. That's the whole idea. But you're completely your own person. What you've accomplished, you've accomplished on your own."

David didn't answer. He couldn't. He had no answers, only questions and doubts.

Mark was back in New York, the whole matter taken out of his hands by the FBI and State Department. There was absolutely no evidence in support of the accusations against him. It was starting to look just as Mark had told the press, like the ravings of a very sick individual and his sleazy, con-artist stepfather. It was the worse kind of cheap, gossip magazine scandal, and the press was eating it up.

The Canadians were looking increasingly as if they'd been duped. In spite of the lack of hard evidence, and due to David's stature and position, grand jury investigations were being undertaken by both the state of New York and the province of Quebec.

After the debacle at the border, Mark had not heard from his employer, not one order, not one word. He did not think that was a good thing, although he hadn't actually gotten fired yet. From what little he knew of the person he worked for, getting fired would be a very unpleasant experience.

He had put a lot together since first accepting the offer to escape a long prison sentence and ride herd on an old friend. He figured some mobster wanted to break into show business, so what. When he was asked to poison and otherwise incapacitate the subject, however, he decided to learn everything he could about his employer, just in case.

He was obviously very wealthy and most likely lived in Germany or Austria. Whoever it was had powerful political connections throughout Europe and was extremely secretive. To be able to summon a member of Interpol to the Canadian border and kill Tina Fong, indicated they were not only well connected but very dangerous.

He had been able to trace the phone calls from London to Vienna and from there to several other cities in Germany, France, and Italy using the fictitious company name given to lease the office space, but all his leads came to the same dead end. While Mark had his own resources and was not unintelligent, he was stymied by the maze of trails and tangled paths that led nowhere.

Mark assumed that he had been hired to keep an eye on David and insinuate himself into his old friend's confidence for financial gain. As David's business manager he was in position to steal millions. That no orders to do so had yet been issued just convinced him the payoff was even more substantial, much more than the money he would be able to embezzle in the normal way.

He thought they would work through the publishing companies and recording contracts he had started on David's behalf, to siphon off what they wanted. David paid no attention to these things, leaving all the details to his trusted partner. The orders to poison his friend were an unexpected twist, and met with some resistance on Mark's part. It's not that he was squeamish about such things. He just didn't think it was necessary There were other ways to gain control of the maestro's assets, but his employer wasn't about to listen to him. Maybe there was more to it.

It was then that he realized they were after more than money. They wanted to control the composer like a puppet on a string. He began to wonder just what their agenda really was. He thought back to what Doctor Henry Fitzroy had said during their brief discussions with the Canadian authorities, something about John Reid being wanted for illegal biological experiments. Cloning was what he thought the European agent had said. Cloning what?

He knew that their fathers had worked together doing private research, but that was before he was born, and he hadn't paid much attention later when he was old enough to understand such things. It had something or other to do with bio-engineering. Mark had always thought it involved plants more than anything else. It was only after his father and John Reid had left the institute under a dark cloud, discredited and disgraced, that cloning was ever mentioned. It was during the announcement of Dolly the Sheep, the first cloned mammal. The broadcast had driven his father to distraction at the time.

His dad had gone on for days, raving how they had stolen his work and forced him out so they could take all the credit. He became obsessed with regaining his standing, only to die a few years later a broken man. It was soon after this that Mark took up his life of crime, graduating from petty larceny to armed robbery to grand theft auto. Now he wondered if their work had something to do with cloning.

All the research and experiments they had done together was before they joined the institute. Perhaps it was that very work that got them hired by Roslin in the first place. For the short time they were there they were much in demand and had considerable authority. Then it all went sour, but that's how things always were where his old-man was concerned.

He spent many hours mulling over the connection. What was it their fathers were doing that involved so much money they had to go into debt to his ruthless employer? What did he have on Reid and his son? As important as getting David back, finding out who had hired him and why became even more critical. So important in fact, that in the midst of all his troubles Mark took the red-eye to Scotland to see if he could find out something that would help explain what was going on.

He hadn't been home to Edinburgh since he'd gone to prison, almost ten years before. His father had died shortly after, hit by a bus when he stepped off a curb without looking near Piccadilly in London. Mark had been devastated, especially since he knew how disappointed his father had been with him before he died. His death left him angrier and more bitter than ever.

He and his father hardly ever spoke and when they did it was usually in a yelling match. His mother died early from a heart attack, probably from all the yelling and secondhand smoke. It didn't help that she was grossly overweight and drank too much. He really hadn't had much reason to go home, but now he was on a mission.

He arrived at Edinburgh Airport late in the evening, around 10:00, and made his way through the rain-splattered streets to his family home, where his father had died in 1999, shortly after David and John Reid had gone to the US. His father had left the Roslin Institute along with John Reid four years earlier. 'In disgrace' the papers had said. His dad spent the rest of his days toiling away by himself in a makeshift lab he built in the basement, where he worked broken and alone. His old-man always had been kind of combative. Mark figured he had burnt one bridge too many. It certainly hadn't helped his ten year old son's prospects.

His old boyhood home was still in the family, owned by an aged aunt in her late eighties, who spent most of the year in Brittany across the Channel, but who still used the house in the summer. He hadn't bothered telling her he would be visiting.

It was silent and deserted when he got there well after midnight. He didn't know quite what he was looking for, but vaguely wanted to find out what his father had been working on, or anything that might shed light on what his employer could want. If they had stolen money from him, they certainly didn't spend any of it on themselves or their family.

It only took him a few moments to jimmy open the rear door to the house, which entered the kitchen area. He could still smell the lemon fragrance of the cleaner his mother used to wax the hard wood floors. He wasn't there to reminisce, however, and was not sentimental. He had long ago shut out the memories of his unhappy childhood.

He was interested in his father's papers, if any of them were still around, which he rather doubted, but he had nothing else to go on. He made his way down to the basement room at the bottom of the stairs, which used to be his father's office and lab. It was now unused and gathering dust. He quickly noticed that his aunt had kept his dad's thick wood desk, which stood against the wall just like it had when he was a kid.

He had never been allowed down to the room, and had only been in it once as a boy. He was expressly forbidden to enter it without his father's presence, and his father never invited him in. But he remembered sneaking down one day, and regretting it for the rest of his life. As an adult, while in prison and pondering his fate, he had blamed all his trouble on that one foolish act of disobedience.

They say curiosity killed the cat. Well it almost killed young Mark Burns - of fright. One rainy afternoon he took advantage of his parent's absence to steal down to the room, jimmy open the door – he had learned how to do this at a very young age - and take a look around. There were books and papers strewn all about the place, on the tables and chairs, and even on the floor. A long blackboard stood at the front of the space, covered with lines of indecipherable numbers and symbols written across it in chalk. Cases of books lined the wall.

On a long table in the middle of the room were the typical accoutrements of biologists everywhere, beakers and Petri dishes, test tubes and burners. But what drew Mark's attention was a stand in the middle of the floor on which stood some sort of object covered with a thick, green cloth. It reminded him of the kind of thing you'd see on a magician's table, where when the cloth was removed something wondrous and magical would appear. And like at the magic show, Mark just had to see what was underneath the veil.

Approaching cautiously, he carefully removed the cloth, not sure what he'd find, but certainly not expecting the small, pickled fetus that stared back at him with its little baby eyes. It had a well formed, small head connected to a miniature body, with tiny fingers and toes all waving at him from within the jar of formaldehyde.

The hair on the back of his neck had stood up. Yelling and throwing the cloth back over the jar to hide the monstrous thing from his sight, he ran screaming from the room, but he could not hide the image from his mind. It haunted him all that evening, long after his parents had returned, and for many days and nights afterward. His school work suffered and his anti-social behavior increased. Unfortunately, his father was too involved with his own troubles by then, and his mother with her chocolates and alcohol, to notice.

Mark shook off an involuntary shudder at the memory, and searched through the desk, which was unlocked, but found little except receipts for old bills and letters from various family members. Most of it was from the last few years of his father's life, and none of it was applicable to his quest.

He kept looking and shortly found a shoebox full of family mementos from his childhood, cards he had given his parents, early school awards for his achievements, his Scout medals. Someone had cared enough about him to keep his things. He was touched, and felt that perhaps he had been loved after all, at least once. It was just that no one knew how to express it other than yelling. Of course, it was always for his own good, so he would grow up to be a man, but he never really did grow up.

He searched the desk completely, but there was nothing of relevance, no letters from John Reid, no evidence of whoever hired them. He spent the remainder of the night and most of the next morning going through the rest of the room's contents, much of which he suspected hadn't been looked at in thirty years, but none of it was pertinent. Then he found it, tucked in a corner behind an old cabinet and discarded piles of paper, a small metal container about the size of a shoe box. It was locked, but that didn't stop Mark, the artful-dodger, though it had probably kept everyone else out.

Much of what he found was over his head, pages full of complex equations and formulas only a chemist or biologist could decipher, but there were many things he could understand. Much of it had to do, as he suspected, with cloning. He also found letters from John Reid to his father, and a journal with a notebook of his father's that was at the very bottom of the box. Again, much of it was in the unintelligible language of genetic engineering, but some was in plain English, and what it intimated was almost as shocking as the fetus in the bottle he had come upon in his father's lab those many years ago.

Chapter 21

Count Ernst Hohner was a man with an ax to grind. It was one he had carried all his life, ever since his ninth birthday. It was then that his dying grandfather left him his title and his fortune, and had made him take an oath that was to change his life forever.

They were alone in the old man's room where he lay on his deathbed. Little Ernst was terrified, but his grandfather had asked for him personally, and his mother, the old man's daughter, had told him it was a great honor and that he must go in, alone. He had gone in as told and knelt by the old man's bedside.

His Grandfather told him he was the last male in a very distinguished and old family line, but before he could give him all that was his to give - an immense fortune beyond the boy's wildest dreams, and his titles - he would have to swear an oath before God. Before Ernst could say a word the old man grabbed his wrist and held it firmly between them. Then he spoke the words and told young Ernst to repeat them after him.

"For three hundred years and ten generations..." intoned the old man, the last of his line with the Ernesti name.

Ernst didn't understand most of what was spoken, a long harangue of half-intelligible statements with strange sounding names and long-winded utterances, but he said them anyway. And over the years, as he began to grasp the true import of the words and what he had promised, they became the guiding light of his life, his sole reason for being.

He surveyed the night skyline of his native Vienna from the opposite bank of the Wien, where his schloss nestled on a slight promontory along the Danube Canal. It was time to cut his losses.

Ernst was the last living male descendent of Johann August Ernesti, the famous rector of St. Thomas's School in Leipzig during Bach's time there. He was immensely proud of his heritage and the long line of academics and churchmen who came before him, and he had sworn to protect that birthright against all that would stain its honor. Johann Sebastian Bach was such a one.

Not only had this beer-hall musician, this mere organ-grinder, this upstart Latin School teacher, belittled and dishonored his famous ancestor, he had polluted the holy precincts of the sacred church with his monstrous noise, his dissonant and unholy cacophony of sound. He had strutted about like he was God's gift to music, when all the while he was really the devil's bequest. Count Ernst Hohner knew the truth and had dedicated his life to upholding it.

The owner of many authentic Bach manuscripts long thought lost, he would not be happy until all the so-called master's work was hidden in a vault beneath the earth so deep no one would ever hear it again. If he had his way - and his immense wealth ensured that in many places he did - Bach's name would be expunged from the annals of music never to be heard again. He would be made as obscure as Ernst's great ancestor's, known only to a handful of scholars regulated to the basements and backrooms of antiquated libraries and archives.

It was a daunting and overwhelming task, for the man's name and music were everywhere, even now after 300 years and all he and his ancestors had tried to do to stop it. Imagine Ernst's horror on hearing his great forebear's nemesis, his family's sworn enemy, was again among the living, strutting about in the form of a clone!

His ancestor and those who followed him did much to make sure the great Bach's remains were hidden and lost to the world, as they did much to make sure his family ended their days in poverty. That is all except Philip Emmanuel. Bach's wife and other son, Frederick, sold some of his best work to the rector who then hid them away. Then, despite all their efforts, the unthinkable had happened. One of Bach's distant ancestors, a Felix Mann, found the remains, some of which had been well preserved at the time of burial, and brought them to a couple of rogue biologists in Scotland.

The story he told Mark Burns, who he had hired to carry out his scheme, about them owing him money, was just a ruse to get him on board. Felix Mann, Bach's ancestor, supplied the funds and the DNA for the work, and he had died horribly for it when Ernst found out, but not soon enough.

At first he had wanted the clone-bastard destroyed, but by then, ten years after the fact, it was too late, the damage had already been done. He decided instead to make the clone his own, but one of the biologists took it and fled to America, where it was harder for Ernst to get to him. The other rogue scientist, however, paid the ultimate price for his foolishness.

It hadn't been hard to find them, for the clone-bastard stood out like the abomination it was, becoming an overnight sensation with his debut Broadway Musical. Ernst knew how one becomes an overnight sensation. One makes a pact with the devil. Now he had lost him again, after having him in his grasp, and the publicity being stirred up around it threatened to destroy everything he and his forebears had worked for these past hundreds of years.

Not only had Reid and his partner created a genetic duplicate of the beer hall player Bach, they had a living, breathing twenty-first century replica of the man in the flesh. The biologist who fostered the clone-child, John Reid, was also a historian and music lover, and knew just about everything there was to know about J.S. Bach. He exposed David to the same type of environment and learning, teaching him music at a young age and providing the best training possible as he grew older. It paid off. The young clone-child had turned out to be the greatest composer-conductor in history, not to mention a virtuoso on the keyboard. It was a true copy of Bach, a super-clone.

Ernst had exalted at the thought of having complete control over him. He would own Bach and exploit him for his own personal gains and the name of his ancestor. Controlling the asset was essential, but when the foster father stole the clone and left Scotland, something drastic had to be done. Thus Mark Burns, the perfect solution, a friend from David's youth, smart and cultured, yet a street tough opportunist who wanted to get rich quick and didn't care how he did it.

John Reid had broken several international and ethical laws, even if he wasn't a kidnapper, and there were countless European and North American agencies working overtime to make him pay. He was totally discredited. There was not a single piece of evidence to back up his accusations against Mark Burns. Still, why hadn't Reid disclosed the whole story to the public? Perhaps he had not even told the clone. Maybe John Reid knew like Ernst did, that this information must never get out, or maybe he was only biding his time. Not even Mark, his man on the scene, knew the truth, but how long could the secret be kept? He would have to put an end to it once and for all.

Of course, it would be an accident. It always was. A slight nudge off a curb in front of an oncoming bus, a rape and suicide, even if the latter hit had been botched. It was all impossible to trace even when someone knew it wasn't accidental. He only dealt with professionals of the highest caliber. He would make the necessary phone calls, give the required orders, and they would be carried out. All of them would be eliminated - Mark, John Reid, and his son, the great David Gordon Reid, the great clone bastard.

He had just received intelligence that Burns was in Scotland. That would make things easier, since he already had people on the ground there. Although there was nothing in Mark's contract that made it against orders for him to travel, under the circumstances, the unannounced trip was highly troubling. What could he be up to wondered Hohner, not that it would matter where Mark Burns was going.

The rector's ancestors had nearly single-handedly stamped out Bach's music in the early eighteen hundreds, when his popularity had been at its lowest. Despite their efforts to steal and hide his work and discredit it, however, Bach had emerged one of the greatest and most famous composers of all time. His fame and popularity only grew with the passing of the years. While Ernst's great forebear, the admirable Rector Ernesti, had gone down through history as a joke, a foil for the great Johann Sebastian. Those days were about to end. Bach's glory and that of his clone would be destroyed once and for all.

Zeiggie was starting to regret his heroics at the border that warm January night two weeks ago. Since then his life had been full of nerve-tingling fear alternating with mind-numbing boredom. He had been taken to a maximum security prison for the criminally insane in Upstate New York, where he had been held in solitary confinement in a sixteen by twelve padded cell. He had talked to no one, been interrogated by nobody, and was fed through a slat in the door. Sometimes they kept the harsh lights on in his cell all night to make it difficult for him to sleep. Sometimes they'd walk by in the wee hours of the morning and bang on his door with their clubs to rouse him from his slumber. He had seen no judge, spoken to no attorney, felt the warmth of no human contact, not even the face of a guard after that first night. Yes, he was starting to feel sorry for his decision to sacrifice himself, but what other alternative did they have? They had been cornered at the border like rats in a dead end alley.

He wasn't sorry he had gotten involved with David Reid and tried to help him. After all, the guy had given him a job. But Zeiggie had his own problems now. He was not likely to break out of this facility like he had the last one. In any case, he had nowhere to go. He could only hope that whatever plan David and his father had contrived would work and work soon. He didn't know how much more of this he could take without becoming truly insane. He didn't even know if his friends had made it across the border or not, and if so, what succor they would be able to obtain.

He was still having problems, even in his solitude, getting his mind around the fact that David was a clone of Bach, and he had plenty of time to contemplate it. The fact that someone was doing the same thing to David that he had theorized Bach's enemies were doing to him in the past, was even more difficult to contend with, and Zeiggie was right in the middle of it. Maybe his mother was right after all. There wasn't any such thing as coincidence. Everything happened for a reason. In his confinement his imagination ran rampant.

It was too much to be just coincidence. If Leonard's theory was correct, Bach's arch enemy the Rector Ernesti had tried and succeeded in killing him. Was someone doing the same thing to his clone?

The concert music business is a mean, cut-throat world, despite its polite cultured veneer. The competition for a seat in an orchestra like the Philharmonic was worth several hundred thousand a year. Bullet holes have been known to show up in the door of more than one would be competitor for such a seat. Commissions for musical works are scarce and hard to come by, and requests to conduct the great orchestras were even rarer and offered to only a chosen few. David and his protégés had monopolized these positions for years. David was a phenomena and not a bad person at heart, but he had hurt more than a few swollen egos and ruined more than a few careers with just a careless word. No wonder there were people who wanted to harm him, just like they did old Bach. Or was there more to it? Zeiggie didn't know, but as he sat alone in his cell in the darkness, he could imagine anything as possible. He never felt so confused and alone in his entire life.

Despite the words of his father, David was having difficulty dealing with his new-found identity. Now he had clammed up completely, refusing to talk to anyone, including the authorities who continued to try and interview him. His father was beginning to worry. Perhaps he had been wrong to tell him as much as he did.

The international standoff continued, although both countries were eager to reduce the publicity and the embarrassment of their respective positions, both feeling foolish as things played out. The Reids couldn't prove their accusations, but they couldn't be disproved either, as the grand jury investigations continued. The US agreed to drop all kidnapping charges, as it was obvious no one had been abducted. It had all been a misunderstanding.

David and his father were now under house 'protection' in a five star hotel in Montreal, still claiming asylum. With the help of Jean St. Pierre and the considerable assistance of a cadre of French lawyers, the Reids continued to fight deportation to the United States, insisting their false papers and disguises were necessary to escape with their lives.

Since the various investigative committees in the States could not talk to the principals in person, it was impossible to substantiate any of the claims and statements coming out of Canada, so there was no move to arrest Mark Burns, although he was scheduled for questioning later in the month by the Grand Jury. Mark's story had more or less been adapted by the press. Great concern was felt for David Reid by all involved, and not a few were starting to wonder about his state of mind. There were many questions to be answered, and more were being asked each day, as the proceedings continued and got no nearer the truth.

With the stopping of the eye-drops that Colleen had innocently been giving him - which turned out to be a combination of certain experimental drugs and toxins not yet fully analyzed - David's eyesight was slowly returning. He could see vague shapes and outlines of things, but it was far from normal vision and the light still caused him pain. For all intents and purposes he was still clinically blind, but improving. That should have given him some comfort, but it didn't. He didn't seem to care whether he could see or not.

They were now confined in a suite at the Bonaventure Hotel, where David had stayed many times during his visits to the city. His father and Colleen were with him. No one had been granted an interview with the refugees despite tremendous pressure. The only thing coming out was the official story as first told by Jean St. Pierre, and everyone was getting pretty tired of that. Though the surroundings were luxurious and they were afforded every comfort and convenience, there were two armed police guards outside their door.

"Can you talk to him?" David's father asked Colleen.

"Why, what's the matter?" she replied. She too had noticed the change in David's behavior over the last few days.

"Well, for one thing he's not eating."

"No, I mean why is he so depressed? He hardly says a word. He won't even look at me."

"He's worried about Zeiggie," said the elder Reid. "He feels bad that he allowed Zeiggie to talk us into letting him get captured like that. David's not going to forgive himself. All his attempts to help his friend have been in vain."

"It's not his fault. Zeiggie practically forced his idea on us. We wouldn't have made it otherwise. We'd be right where we started. Who knows what would have happened."

"I know, but he's having a hard time about it. Maybe if you talked to him. Once we get this whole thing straightened out, we can take care of his friend."

"I'll see what I can do," she said reluctantly, not sure what she could say to help when his own father couldn't. She felt it might have more to do with his being a clone than concern about Zeiggie, which they all felt. She still hadn't come to terms with it, and suspected David hadn't either. How could he when he couldn't even talk about it.

A short while later she knocked on David's door carrying a tray of food.

"Hi, David. Your dad ordered something from room service. You've got to eat."

"I'm not hungry," he answered through the door. It reminded her of when she first met him, only a few months before. It seemed like so long ago.

"I don't care," she replied. "I'm staying right here until you open the door. You've got to eat whether you're hungry or not. It's your favorite, beef stroganoff. I had them make it special for you. It'll be easy to eat. Come on, open up. I want to talk to you. We haven't talked in days. Please, David."

He relented and opened the door, but turned and walked away before she entered, purposely ignoring the tray of food she placed on the table.

"Doesn't this remind you of something?" she asked.

He didn't answer.

"Remember when we first met. You didn't want to open the door then either. I'm glad you did. I'm glad you're getting better. Now you can get your life back."

"I can never get my life back," he said dejectedly. "I never had a life in the first place. It was nothing but a lie."

"Don't say that. You've still got so much to live for."

"I have nothing, nothing to live for."

"Why do you say that? What's wrong?" she asked, troubled by the hopelessness in his voice.

He didn't answer.

"Please leave," he said finally.

"I know you want to be alone, but the doctor says no. You've got to talk to me, doctor's orders. What's wrong?"

"Everything, my whole life is wrong," he answered, finally turning toward her. "Everything I did, everything I wrote is wrong. It's all a damned lie, a damned fabricated lie."

"David, what on earth are you talking about? Everything you're saying is wrong. Your music is wonderful. Everyone says so, the whole world."

"What do they know?"

"You're just feeling sorry for yourself, but you'll get over it, I know you will. Just don't dwell on things so much. Maybe you should go home, back to New York. Get together with your friends and acquaintances, back to your work. Staying alone like this isn't good for you."

"I'll never work again. I'll never write a single note as long as I live. I'll never conduct. I'll never play the piano. I'm done with music. I'm not going back to New York. I don't know where I'll go, but when this is settled, I'm going away, somewhere far away."

"You just feel like that now, but things will change."

"Don't patronize me!" he yelled, surprising himself. "I'm sorry, please leave. I promise I'll eat something. Just leave."

"OK," she said. "But you promised. I better see most of that food gone or it won't be so easy to get rid of me next time."

When she left, he locked the door and went to try and force down some food, but he could only eat a few bites without gagging. He was so disgusted with himself that even eating repulsed him. He could barely stand his own thoughts, thoughts that seemed foreign to him now that he knew the ugly truth about himself. It was as if someone else were talking in his head, Bach maybe. He felt he would go mad. It was only the memories of his childhood in Scotland that gave him some comfort, and then only those that had nothing to do with music, rare memories indeed.

Chapter 22

Mark wasn't sure, but from all that he had been able to gather from his father's notes, as unbelievable as it sounded, he and John Reid had actually cloned a human being. No wonder people were after him. It appeared someone had paid them to do it, under the utmost secrecy, presumably his employer.

Putting two and two together, the child they cloned had to be David Reid. All of it had taken place the year David was born. That's why his employer said John was only David's stepfather. David was a clone. It took some time for the thought and it's implications to sink in. Someone had done the unthinkable and created an actual human test-tube baby.

From the evidence in the notebooks, they had cloned Bach. The thought hit him as absurd, as if it had been Peter Pan and Tinker Bell. His imagination was getting carried away. Perhaps the stress of the past few weeks was getting to him.

But there it was in black and white in the notebooks, plain for all to see. Obviously, they had planned to publish someday, when the time was right and the world was ready. Perhaps John Reid still intended to make his great achievement public. No, Mark decided, there was no mistaking what was written there. They had cloned Johann Sebastian Bach and that clone was David Reid.

He took another sip of Scotch and wrote down a few more notes. There was a knock on his hotel room door. He was scheduled to fly home in the morning and wasn't expecting any visitors. He hadn't ordered room service.

"Who is it?" he asked, looking through the peephole and seeing an older gentleman with horned-rimmed glasses in an expensive suit.

"Mister Burns?"

"Yes, who is it?"

"I'm with the US State Department, sir," the man announced through the door. "I've been asked to escort you back to the States for Grand Jury testimony."

"I'm not due to testify until next week. I'm leaving for New York tomorrow morning. I don't need an escort."

"Sir, you've been indicted by the Grand Jury."

"What? That's preposterous," said Mark, loudly through the door.

"I have the papers here, sir. I thought we'd avoid an international incident and prevent you being arrested in public at the airport tomorrow. It's your choice, sir."

"Do you have some identification? I'd like to see the papers."

"Certainly, sir," said the man, showing his ID through the peephole. "You'll have to open the door to read the papers, sir."

Mark looked closely at the man's credentials, which seemed valid enough, though he was still wary. He couldn't believe they had actually swallowed John Reid's story. Had something happened since he had been in Scotland to convince them? He looked hard at the man, trying to determine what kind of threat he posed. He was about fifty and looked a little overweight, with droopy eyes behind thick lenses, just another overworked, tired official doing his job far from home. Where do they find these people he wondered, as he opened the door.

"Sorry to disturb you like this, sir," said the man, handing Mark the papers from the Grand Jury ordering his arrest and return to the US. "It'll be a lot more pleasant than being picked up by the local boys. You'd spend a few unnecessary days in one of their crummy jails being questioned by a bunch of inbred nitwits. They'd probably throw in a full body search just for good measure, if you know what I mean. We'll have you back in the States by morning. I'm sure with your lawyers you won't be detained long. My personal opinion, sir, is this whole thing's a bunch of hogwash. Though you probably never should have left the country like that with the investigation going on. It made everyone nervous. So they issued this subpoena."

"Thank you for your support, but I'm really not ready to leave this evening. Can't you escort me on the plane tomorrow?"

"Sorry, sir, but I wouldn't be doing my job if I did that. I have to take you back tonight. You have a couple minutes. I'll wait out in the hall if you like."

"No, that won't be necessary. I'll just be a few. Make yourself comfortable."

Mark's mind was working at light speed as he stuffed his clothing and belongings in his suitcase. He made a mental list of people to call on the flight, the first one being his lawyer. He was putting his father's notebooks in his briefcase along with his own notes, when he noticed a blur out of the corner of his eye. Instinctively, he reached out and grabbed a man's arm just as it tried to jab a hypodermic needle into his neck. Before his attacker had time to react, Mark hit him in the head with a hard right hook, knocking him to the ground.

Trying to capitalize on his advantage, Mark ran toward his opponent to hit him again while he was down, but the man swung his leg around and kicked Mark in the knee almost taking him off his feet. Then without stopping, he stiffened his leg and kicked Mark, who was leaning toward him, in the face, knocking him sprawling on his rear.

His attacker got to his feet, the needle still in his hand, and came toward Mark, who scurried backwards trying to get away, kicking his legs wildly, as he attempted to knock the hypodermic out of the man's hand.

Just when his assailant was upon him, the needle only inches from Mark's nose, he reached up and grabbed his briefcase from the bed. Swinging it hard at the man's outstretched arm he knocked the syringe out of his grasp and across the carpeted floor where it came to rest next to the bed stand.

Springing to his feet, he tackled the man as he ran for the needle, knocking down a lamp and telephone in the process. Tumbling over the nightstand onto the floor, they rolled back and forth, first one on top, then the other, trading punches.

It was obvious now that Mark was in a life and death struggle with an opponent who was no soft, overweight desk clerk. The fat was muscle and there was nothing flabby or weak about him. His moves were expert, but Mark was getting the upper hand as they struggled. Muscling himself on top of his opponent, he hit him with hard rights. Pulling back to deliver another, he was yanked into a straight hard jab, then flung over his opponent's head face first.

The man was on his back before Mark could rise. Sitting on top of him, he pinned Mark down and grabbed the cord from the broken lamp lying next to the bed where they struggled. Wrapping it around Mark's neck, he pulled back with all his strength arching Mark's body backward. He was in total agony, his face beet red, as he was being strangled and choked to death. As his eyes began to flutter shut, he noticed the hypodermic lying just out of reach against the wall, half hidden behind the nightstand where it had fallen.

Using his last bit of strength and breath, he clenched his teeth and bent his head forward, straining against the cord. With the man on his back pulling on it like a rider on a runaway horse, he crawled toward the needle, straining for each inch. Just as he was about to black out, he reached out his hand and after a brief, frantic search, found it. Without even knowing what end he had, he jabbed it blindly into the first body part he could find. He didn't remain conscious long enough to know if it hit its mark or not.

John Reid was in a heap of trouble. No matter what side of the story you supposed to be true, he had a lot of explaining to do. If you believed Mark, then he was a manipulative and greedy old man who was exploiting his stepson for personal gain. To believe his side of the story stretched most peoples' credibility, especially since it was only half the truth, the critical piece needed to convince anyone being kept from them. Without David's testimony no one knew what to believe. Because of the great musician's prestige, however, pressure had been enormous in Canada to grant him asylum and make him an honorary citizen. His father, however, was another matter.

Disturbing accusations had emerged, still vague and not fully understood, charges stemming from experiments he and a Doctor Burns conducted in Edinburgh related to human cloning before they had both joined the Roslin institute in the early nineties. He was wanted there for this and other questionable practices he had been involved in over the years, having nothing to do with his son. In spite of these troubles, the Canadian authorities had told them they would be free to go in a few days. While the others were elated, finally relieved to be set free, David didn't seem to care. He didn't know where he would go in any case. There was nothing but the empty present in his mind, no future, and a past he couldn't look at. If he tried to think of a place to go, all he could summon was a black, endless void.

He woke up from that void one evening and listened in the darkness. There was not a sound. He had no idea what time it was, although he assumed it must be close to midnight. When he had gone to bed a few hours earlier around nine, he could hear the others talking and the TV playing quietly in the next room. Now all was silence. His hearing had grown especially acute with these past few months of sight deprivation. Being accustomed to the darkness, he got out of bed and made his way across the room without turning on the lights. Opening the bedroom door, he called out.

"Dad, Colleen, is anyone there? Dad?"

No one answered. He went to Colleen's door and knocked quietly.

"Colleen, are you up? Can I talk to you? Colleen?"

There was no answer, so he tried the door. It was unlocked. He opened it quietly and walked in.

"Colleen, it's David. I want to ask you something. I'm sorry to barge in on you like this. I hope you don't mind. It's not like I'm going to see anything. Colleen?"

He wanted to ask her if she would stay with him until he was fully recovered. He was thinking of renting a cottage someplace where he wouldn't be bothered, but he'd need help. He reached for the bed and felt for her feet.

"Colleen, are you here?"

To his surprise the bed was empty, but he had sensed that even before he felt for her. All concern about waking somebody dispelled, he called out in alarm.

"Colleen, Dad? Are you here? Where is everybody?"

There was no answer. The place was completely quiet. He moved through the suite, calling their names, but there was no one there. His father's bed had not been slept in either. He hadn't heard them leave.

Going to the front door, he unlatched it and opened it slightly.

"Hello," he called out to the hallway. "Is anyone there?"

No one answered. The guards had left, either on a coffee break or for good. Maybe the house arrest had ended. Where could everyone be he wondered, closing the door again. He thought he sensed someone in the room, or was it just his overwrought imagination?

"Hello," he said. "Is anyone here? Are you guys playing a joke on me? This isn't funny, you know."

He felt helpless. Even though still half blind, he was uncomfortable in the dark and went to turn on the lights. As soon as he did, someone hit him in the stomach, knocking the wind out of him. He fell to the floor in a heap, gasping for air.

Barely having time to register the surprise and pain, he was dragged by the collar roughly across the room, knocking his head into something hard that momentarily blocked his way. Punched several times, he was pulled to his feet at the sliding balcony door. He tried to protect himself by holding his hands in front of his face, but his assailant punched him in the stomach and groin, forcing his hands down. Then he'd hit him in the face again. David collapsed, leaning against the glass-paneled door dazed, while his attacker fumbled with the latch to unlock and open it.

He tried to crawl away, but was grabbed by the shoulders and thrown back against the glass panel so hard he thought it would break, hitting his head hard. He heard the door slide open and felt the cold night air. It was then that he realized what was happening. Someone was going to throw him off the balcony, thirty stories above the pavement.

Grabbed again, he was pulled to the opening. He held his arms out wide and caught the edges of the window resisting, but his attacker punched him in the stomach and threw him through the door out onto the balcony. As he fell onto the concrete floor, his attacker took hold of his collar and lifted him to his feet again. Spun around by the arm several times, David was thrown up and away like a shot-putt. For an instant, he thought he was being thrown over the balcony to the street below, but instead, his opponent, who was toying with him sadistically, threw him back against the glass-paneled door. He crashed through it heavily, shattering the glass and cutting his head severely before he fell to the floor half senseless. Then he felt himself being lifted to his feet again. He tried to open his eyes to discover who it was, but the blood oozing down his forehead made it impossible to see.

As he was lifted to his feet, David, who had taken about all the punishment he could stand, and who had a deep fund of strength and determination in his makeup, braced his strong legs against the floor and shoved off with all his might. Holding his arms straight out in front of him, he clawed his opponent's eyes as he rushed forward pushing the other man backward, screaming loudly as he did so, until they hit the waist-high railing. Without stopping, with a ferocity born of desperation and fear, David continued to push as the man bent backward then flipped silently over the balcony.

He caught himself just in time, before he too tumbled over, and slumped back against the wall, collapsing on the floor and panting hard for breath, his body shaking uncontrollably. He didn't know how long he had lain there when he felt himself being gently shaken awake by Colleen.

"David, David!" she said in concern. His father stood behind her. "What happened? Are you all right?"

He could vaguely sense others in the room as well, but couldn't speak at first, his mind racing over the events of a short time ago.

"Are you all right?" she asked again. "What happened?"

"There's been an accident, David," he heard his father say. "Someone has fallen from the building. Was it here? David, did he fall from here? What happened?"

"Yes," David answered slowly, as if speaking from far away. "Someone attacked me. I was all alone. Where did everyone go?"

"The police took us down to their headquarters for questioning," replied his father. "Interpol was trying to extradite me to Brussels and the New York Grand Jury is trying to subpoena Colleen back to the States. The guards went too. You were the only one who stayed. There was supposed to be someone with you. It must have been a set up."

"Lie still," said Colleen, as David tried to rise. "You have a bad gash on your forehead. The medics will be here in a minute. Hold this over the cut in the meantime." She handed him a damp towel and pressed it to his head. "Just lie still now. It look's like you had quite a fight."

"I did. He was trying to throw me over the balcony," replied David. "Why would anyone want to do that?" he asked.

"I guess they're playing for keeps," said his father.

"Who's playing for keeps, Mister Reid?" inquired Inspector Philippe Beaudro of the Royal Mounted Police, in charge of the Montreal area.

"Suppose you tell us, Inspector," David's father shot back. "You were the ones who were supposed to be protecting him. Who ordered us to be questioned this evening?"

"That sir," said the Mounty, "is what I intend to find out."

Chapter 23

Mark was back in the US and scheduled to testify before the New York Grand Jury to answer the allegations, however farfetched, against him. As reluctant as he was to divulge his theory – even with the evidence of the notebooks – the magnitude of what he had uncovered, coupled with the recent attempt on his life, left him little choice. He knew it was his employer who had tried to kill him, and Mark knew he wouldn't stop until he succeeded. He also knew that his only hope was to expose whoever it was, but he needed some sort of collaboration, some independent bit of evidence that would tip the balance in his favor.

Who else knew about this besides John Reid and perhaps David himself? How much did Reid tell the others, everything? David and his companions were still in Canada, but he could still get to one of them. Leonard Zeigler was currently incarcerated in Upstate New York where he had been kept since his capture over a month ago. Mark had intended for everyone to forget about Mister Zeigler, but now he wanted him to tell his story to the world, and saw him as his one chance to convince people that what he had to say was the truth.

Although bereft of the support of his employer, Mark still had resources of his own, most important of them in the office of the New York FBI chief. He was able to get a State Police escort to the high-security mental facility where Zeiggie was being held.

They arrived late one evening to accompany the prisoner back to the City for questioning by the Grand Jury. Zeiggie was surprised and alarmed when Mark Burns turned up at his solitary cell. It took some talking on Mark's part to get him to go with him.

"I know everything, Zeiggie. I'm here to help," announced Mark when they were alone in his cell.

"The hell you are," replied Zeiggie, standing up from his cot. "You're the one who put me here. You're trying to poison David and take all his money."

"The people I was working for tried to kill me," he whispered to Zeiggie. The warden and his escort stood at the far end of the cell block, giving him some privacy as requested. Mark's presence there was unusual, but they had orders to give him their full support, and the state police had written instructions from the FBI chief giving Mark complete authority over the prisoner, who they were to take back to New York City.

"That kind of changes things, don't you think?" continued Mark. "I know the whole story. I know why they wanted me to do those things. I didn't sign up for anything like that, but well, they're hard people to say no to. I want to help. I want you to come with me and tell your story to the Grand Jury. Together we may be able to put a stop to this whole thing."

"Why should I believe you?" Zeiggie said resentfully. "How do I know you won't just kill me as soon as you have me alone?"

"Because I need you. I know I haven't exactly been your friend, but things are different now. Anyway, what choice do you have? Look, I'm sorry for what I did, but John Reid isn't exactly Mister Clean in all this either. I know the truth about David."

"What truth, what do you mean?" said Zeiggie, wondering how much Mark really knew or if he was just on a fishing expedition.

"I can't say now. Just come back to New York with me and testify to what you know. I'll explain everything."

"And what am I supposed to know?" asked Zeiggie, still not convinced.

"What did David's stepfather tell you?"

"Not much. Just that you and the people you worked for were trying to poison David and take over his business."

"Did he tell you who my employer was and why he wanted to control David?"

"No, not exactly. I thought it must be the Costa Nostra or the Russian Mafia or somebody. He was always kind of vague about it. It wasn't until David told us...." He paused without finishing

"What, what did David tell you?"

"I don't know," replied Zeiggie, not wanting to say more. "Like you said, who knows what to believe."

"They never told you what they talked about?"

"No, not a word," lied Zeiggie, not trusting Mark after what he had done to him. "That was strictly between David and his father."

"Well, I think I know what it was, but I can't talk more about it here. Will you come with me?"

"And what if I don't?"

"I'll see you get out of here by tomorrow and I'll compensate you for all the trouble I've caused, but I may not be able to convince them of what I know by myself, and David may suffer for it. You've done so much for your friend. This may be the most important thing you can do."

After a few more assurances from Mark, Zeiggie, against his better judgment, agreed to go back with him to New York. As Mark had reminded him, what choice did he have. One more night in that cell and he really would have needed shock-treatment.

Zeiggie felt a little better once he was out of the prison for the criminally insane and on his way back to the City in a luxury SUV with a police escort, after his first hot meal in weeks.

Once in Manhattan Mark proceeded to get his testimony ready for the Grand Jury. Despite his fear of assassination, he was determined to tell the world what he knew. He was still in the dark as to who was pulling the strings or why, but he hoped his appearance would make things too hot for any more attempts on his life, or David's for that matter.

News had leaked out that Mark's testimony promised to be dramatic and controversial. After all, he was the main person in the case about which so much had been alleged. It was his turn to speak and the crowd at the hearing was the largest yet, filling the courtroom and its galleries to overflowing. Security was at a high state of alert.

Mark sat at a bank of microphones before a panel of distinguished jurists and judges, who would be interrogating him this afternoon. Next to him sat Zeiggie in a new suit and tie. After they had been sworn in, the presiding judge on the panel began the proceedings.

"Mister Burns, you have been summoned here today to testify before this grand jury on allegations brought forth in regards to the David Reid affair by his father, John Reid. Leonard Ziegler has agreed to testify with you on your behalf and this jury has consented to this highly unusual proceeding. Some very serious charges have been brought against you involving the poisoning and subsequent keeping of Mister David Gordon Reid, the noted composer and conductor of the New York Philharmonic Orchestra, against his will."

"You have countered by stating for the public record that these accusations are false and the fabrications of one John Reid, the purported stepfather of the conductor. You have further stated that David Reid is mentally unstable and in the power of his stepfather who is taking advantage of his sickness to manipulate and exploit him. These claims and counterclaims concerning someone so prestigious and prominent have caused grave concern. Kidnapping has even been claimed on both sides. As you know we have not been able to question the Reids concerning this matter, but that has not stopped the speculation and adverse publicity for both the United States and Canada."

"We would like to get to the truth in the matter and have asked you here, under oath, to explain your part. Mister Burns, how do you respond to the accusations made against you that you poisoned and held David Reid against his will, and that you did these things in the employ of some person or persons whose service you are in?"

"Guilty as charged, your honor. It's all true," he replied.

The matter-of-fact admission to the charges, thought by most to be preposterous slander, caused a commotion that nearly cleared the courtroom. The presiding judge had to bang his gavel repeatedly before order was restored.

"Mister Burns, are you aware of the serious nature of the charges you have just admitted to?" asked the judge after restoring order somewhat.

"Yes, your honor," replied Mark loud and clear. "It's all true, every word of it. I was hired four years ago to insinuate myself into Mister Reid's business affairs and gain his confidence. I was recruited out of prison in Britain, an early release you could say, and hired because of my previous connection with David. Our fathers worked together doing private bio-engineering research before they were hired at the Roslin Institute in Edinburgh to head up the cloning efforts there. We were friends as kids. I became David's business manager at my employer's urging. He ordered me to poison David just enough to make him ill and susceptible to being controlled. The goal was to take over all the publishing rights for his music and records. They are worth millions, your honor."

The crowded courtroom remained stunned to silence, a quiet so deep you could hear the ruffle of a dress. People held their breath from word to word.

"We put a substance on his baton to make him blind," continued Mark.

"We? You had an accomplice?" asked the judge, still finding the whole thing incredible.

"Yes, sir, Miss Tina Fong."

"The woman who was murdered, David Reid's assistant?" asked another panelist.

"Yes, sir, the one who was found hanging. They thought she had committed suicide at first, but later discovered that she had been murdered. She was killed by someone hired by my employer, although I had nothing to do with it and have no direct knowledge or proof."

"Who is this mysterious employer you're speaking of?" inquired the first judge.

"I do not know, sir. He hired me through intermediaries and only contacted me by special means, never directly. I was paid through an offshore account. None of it's traceable. It's very old and secret money, perhaps the mafia. That's why there's extra security here today. There has been an attempt on my life."

"Hmm," grunted the judge, not sure what or who to believe.

"Did you order the Fong girl's murder?" asked another panelist on the jury.

"No, sir," answered Mark. "That was done without my knowledge. Like I said, they also tried to have me killed as well. I'm afraid they will try to kill David and his father too."

"There was already an attempt on Mister David Reid a few days ago," the presiding judge informed him, causing another stir in the courtroom at the news. "They failed. Mister Reid and his father are safe."

Mark was relieved to hear this, as much because it supported his story as it meant David was OK.

"Mister Ziegler, I understand you have something to add to this," said the judge

Zeiggie hesitated before speaking. He had rehearsed what he was going to say with Mark and alone in front of the mirror, but now he was here before all these people he was having trouble trying to speak. Then he thought of David and what was happening to him.

"Yes, sir," he replied finally, clenching his jaw in determination. "I discovered someone was tampering with Mister Reid's baton. I was fooling around with it one night after rehearsal, and got sick after I touched my eyes. Tina Fong was there. She told security I had verbally assaulted her and had me arrested. When I tried to tell David about it the next night, she went hysterical and had me arrested again."

"It's all on the record, your honor," Mark added. "Mister Ziegler kept a piece of the baton he had broken off when he discovered the poison. He had it analyzed. Here's the results."

He handed a piece of paper to the court secretary who gave it to the judge.

"Have someone tell me what this is," the judge ordered one of his assistants, who scurried away to get the necessary expert opinions.

"Was David Reid kidnapped?" another jurist asked Zeiggie.

"No, sir. David went with us on his own. His father convinced him Mark was trying to hurt him, though he didn't believe it at first."

"Oh, and what convinced him to leave the comforts of his friend's apartment?"

"I don't know," answered Zeiggie, sticking to his story. "Something his father told him."

"And what was that?"

"I'm not sure, sir, but he mentioned Mark was hired by someone who John Reid owed money to. I thought it was the mob or something."

"That's OK, Mister Ziegler," said the judge. "You don't need to speculate. Just tell us what you know."

"Sir," interrupted Mark standing up again. "The powder on the baton was a combination of other toxins and Formoguanamine, an experimental drug for inducing blindness in fish. I believe my employer was somehow connected with the work my father and John Reid were doing twenty-five years ago. He may have provided the funds for their research and now he wants to own the results."

"And what results are those, Mister Burns?" asked the judge, not sure where the witness was going with all this.

"The result of their research is David Gordon Reid himself," announced Mark, "a human clone and an exact genetic copy of Johann Sebastian Bach."

For a moment the courtroom was stunned by the revelation, many not sure they had heard Mark correctly.

"What? What did you say?" asked many on the panel. The question was echoed by the crowd.

"What did he say?

Cloned what?

Who's a clone?"

Mark waited for the judge to regain control of the room. It didn't help that he had just admitted to lying for the last four years. The courtroom erupted in a chorus of disbelief.

"He's lying," cried a spectator.

"That's preposterous," yelled another.

"Absurd," uttered a panelist.

To some his words were so shocking that they had trouble understanding them.

Mark strove to make himself heard over the din.

"John Reid and my father were working on human cloning," he shouted when the crowd grew quiet enough to hear what he was saying. "They extended the technology to achieve viable clones of mammals and humans. Their work led to the cloning of Dolly the sheep in 1996, but because of their radical ideas and experiments on humans, they were forced to leave the institute. I have his notebooks and journals. In early 1987, almost ten years before they came to Roslin, a distant ancestor of Bach's, who had located his final resting place, came to John Reid and my father with his remains and paid them to clone them. David Reid is the result."

These statements were the last words of testimony heard that day, as the courtroom burst into chaos. People yelled insults at the speaker and tried to lunge at him, while others called him a liar and spat at him from across the room. It was only the added security that saved Mark from being mauled by the crowd, so incensed some of them had become at his words. Fighting broke out among bystanders as others tried to come to Mark's defense or wanted to hear more of his fascinating testimony. Eventually the judge had to clear the courtroom and postpone any further testimony until the next day. Scant hours after it had happened in court it was all over the evening news.

'Composer and Conductor, David Gordon Reid, a Clone of Johann Sebastian Bach!'

David and his father were sitting in the kitchen with Colleen when the news broke. They had known Mark was testifying that day, but otherwise had tried to avoid the whole thing. Hearing it on the news would have been bad enough, but the way they heard about it made it even more disturbing.

It was a program where one newscaster interviewed another about the day's events and their impact on society and the world. After talking about the presidential hopefuls in the upcoming elections and the state of the economy, one of them mentioned Mark's Grand Jury testimony and its implication.

"If this is true," said the second newsman, commenting on his colleague's remark, "it could be a world changing event. This would be the first time in history a human being has been cloned."

Both David and his father looked up at each other and then at the TV.

"Of course, if it's found true John Reid and his partner would be guilty of grave crimes. It's illegal to clone another human. They will have to conduct a costly and lengthy series of tests and examinations to determine the truth of the matter. DNA samples would have to be taken from both David Reid and the purported donor."

"I understand Bach's remains have been destroyed or lost."

"That's what they say, but a lot remains to be determined. They're only beginning to investigate all the details."

"What about the legal ramifications?"

"Well, other than the possible prosecution of John Reid - his partner's dead - there's the question of David Reid's legal status. For instance, does a clone have legal rights to property?"

"You mean does David Reid, the clone, have rights over his own music?"

"That's correct, Frank. Until his legal status can be determined, the copyrights and publishing rights to this music, which are worth millions, may be in limbo. It could take years for something like this to be sorted out in the courts."

David's father quickly got up and shut off the TV. Both David and Colleen sat in shocked silence, their dinners unfinished. David could hardly believe what he had heard.

"They were talking about me like I was something from outer space, as if I didn't have any rights, as if I was some sort of Frankenstein."

For once his father was unable to respond.

"My God," the elder Reid said finally. "Burns kept a bloody notebook. We swore we wouldn't keep any journals. That bastard was going to publish. Now the whole thing's out."

"I thought you said no one would ever find out." David turned to Colleen. "Meet my creator, Mister Frankenstein."

"You're being melodramatic, David," said his father. "We've been through all this. You're just as human as the next guy. Don't let these idiots bother you."

"There's a whole world of idiots out there. They'll want to probe me and study me and analyze me. I'll be like a bug under a microscope. They're already talking about me like I'm some kind of specimen."

"Don't let it bother you, David," counseled Colleen. "It doesn't bother me. Why should it bother you?"

"Because you're not the freaking clone, I am!" yelled David angrily. "Not just any clone, but the clone of the great J. S. Bach."

Before she had time to reply, there was a knock at the door. David's father answered it.

"Hello, Mister Reid," said the short, mustached official. He had four uniformed officers with him. "I've been asked by the Ministry of State to escort you all to other quarters where you can be better protected."

"By whose orders?" asked John Reid suspiciously. "Who are you? Show me some credentials."

"My orders come from the Minister himself. I am Monsieur Francois Fountain." He showed John Reid his id and papers. "You are all to come with me. The Canadian government is responsible for your safety and under the circumstances we can no longer ensure that safety here."

"Since when?" asked David, not wanting to leave.

"I am sorry, Mister Reid, but the situation has changed. You must realize that some people are very superstitious and don't understand science. They might try to hurt you now that they know who you are, now that they know the truth."

"Nothing's been proved yet," shouted David's father. "You can't believe everything you hear on the television, gentlemen."

"This has nothing to do with the news, Mister Reid. Our information comes from impeccable sources. Now will you all please gather your things and come with me."

After his testimony and confession Mark Burns had been taken into custody, while the notebooks and journals he discovered in his father's old study were turned over to the court for further analysis. None of this mattered to Mark. His confession had been a matter of survival, the only way he knew to protect himself and maybe disrupt his employer's activities enough for him to get some breathing space. Who knew, perhaps he had gotten rid of him for good, but he doubted it.

His first bit of business would be to secure his release from custody, while the truth of his testimony was being ascertained. His lawyers assured him that it would only be a matter of a few days. The authorities had their own hands full handling the fallout and publicity from his sensational testimony.

Zeiggie's situation was a little more uncertain. No one knew quite what to do with the ex-cello player. Now that Mark was in custody and had his own worries, Zeiggie had been left to his own devices with nowhere to go and no advocate. Again, he found himself in a minimal security mental facility undergoing psychiatric evaluation. At least this time it wasn't under the supervision of doctors paid to keep him out of the way.

He had found out quite a lot during his conversations with Mark in preparation for their testimony, and now felt stronger than ever that there was a connection with his theory of Bach's murder and what was happening to David. In his current situation he had plenty of time to think about it. At least they weren't pumping him full of drugs, and when Mark gained his freedom, which Zeiggie had no doubt he would, he would hopefully be able to help him. After all, Mark may not have known it, but he needed Leonard Zeigler now more than ever. Zeiggie knew something about their adversary that perhaps no one else on earth knew.

That small, almost disintegrated scrap of paper with the initial evidence that had sent him on his search for Bach's real killers back in the early 1980s, found between the pages of an old manuscript at the University of Leipzig where he had done his research, was the smoking gun. Now here, 262 years later the same thing was happing to the same person – or at least his twin brother! Zeiggie could hardly contain himself with the realization and paced back and forth in his small room. As he did, he played back all the information in his head trying to disprove his theory, but he couldn't. Try as he may, he kept coming to the same conclusion. Someone was attempting to kill Bach's clone just like they had killed Bach himself back in 1750.

Of course he could tell no one, not even Mark, for they would surely lock him in a padded cell and throw away the key. Why give them the evidence to declare him insane, for insane it was. The whole story was too much to believe, even for Zeiggie, who had the evidence to prove it.

Everyone thought he was crazy when he told them his theory. 'Why would someone want to kill a person for something as trivial as a petty argument about teaching prerogatives and musical style? The whole idea is crazy.' And at times Zeiggie was apt to agree, but now here it was happening again in front of the whole world. Perhaps there would be fewer voices telling him he was crazy now, after Mark's dramatic testimony.

He knew there was more to Ernesti's hatred than arguments about Bach's insistence on skipping his teaching duties and picking his own stand-ins. It was deep and abiding, and from the lost letter Zeiggie had found in which the rector bared his soul, it was obvious it was Bach's music for the church that most offended and angered him. Of course, he would never have admitted as much, not wanting to appear old-fashioned and out of step with the majority, that's why the letter was never sent. But religion has been known to generate fierce hatreds, and Zeiggie was convinced that Bach's church music had affected the rector in this way. To Ernesti it seemed to fly in the face of religious sentiment, which for him meant the music of the past, with simple harmonies and peaceful melodies. Bach's music was full of dissonance and complicated counterpoint, with everyone playing at once, vying for attention, just like Bach himself. Instead of glorifying God, the arrogant, beer hall musician glorified himself, bringing agitation to the mind instead of peace and tranquility like good church music should. At least that's what the rector believed and Zeiggie knew it. It had been enough to make him want to kill the old Master, who had been there before he arrived, and who had the backing of very powerful protectors that made him impossible to touch. The rector had to swallow his pride and eat crow more than once. This and his deep religious animosity to the apostate Bach had been all the motive he needed to murder the great capellmeister. Were the same motives driving someone to try and kill David now?

Could Ernesti's deep hatred of the great composer have somehow persisted and followed Bach's very genes into the twenty-first century? Was such a thing possible? Did they clone the rector as well? Zeiggie's mind raced to all sorts of wild conclusions. It was all a bit too much for him to keep to himself. He had to tell somebody, but who? How could he divulge what he had to say without seeming mad?

Chapter 24

"I'm sorry David, but there's nothing I can do," said Jean St. Pierre, obviously distressed. "He has to go with them."

They were in an undisclosed location in the Laurentian Mountains north of Montreal, actually a hunting camp owned by their benefactor. David had regained his eyesight somewhat, although he still got tired easily. The blackness in his soul was another matter.

If it hadn't been for the intrepid Jean St. Pierre, David would have probably been strapped to a medical bed to be probed and tested by scientist sent from the International World Court at the Hague to determine whether or not Mark's statements to the New York Grand Jury were true or not. Was David Reid a clone?

While the Canadian government in Toronto may have kowtowed to pressure from the international court, Jean St. Pierre and the immigration department did not. Despite a zealous regard for the sovereign rights of his country's French citizens, he did not always agree with the policies of the government in the English-speaking capital. Jean knew something about human nature, and understood that everyone would want to prod and study David, and then want a piece of him. He knew the phenomenal value David now represented to the world. Above all, he wanted to preserve the honor and glory of his country.

The International Court at the Hague may have pull in the courts and government offices in Toronto, but they didn't pull the strings in the immigration offices of Quebec, and there were obscure rules of sanctuary that could make things very difficult for anyone, even his own government, who tried to take him away once his department had control of him. The World Court may have had a few agents at the scene, but Jean could summon dozens of armed men and vehicles. He controlled the situation on the ground. Since he had been the one who thought to move first, the initiative was his, so they were now hidden away in this hunting camp, which few knew about.

"But I thought you said they couldn't touch us, that you had jurisdiction," said David.

"Yes, but that doesn't apply to your father, who has been indicted for crimes against humanity. We cannot keep him here. He has to stand trial, don't you see. It's for the best."

"Best for who?" said David, not at all reconciled to his predicament or his father's.

Although Jean sympathized with David and understood his attachment to the old man, who was the last vestige of his past, Jean's real sympathies lay with those who wanted to prosecute John Reid for his irresponsible act. Though Jean thought the best of David, he felt sorry for him too and understood some of the feelings he was undergoing. He wanted to help him if he could, but most of all he wanted to protect him from the inevitable fear and greed his presence in society would gender. He was not only the first human clone, but a clone of the famous Johann Sebastian Bach, with more of the old master than one could hope to expect hidden in his borrowed genes.

"For you, my friend," replied Jean St. Pierre. "You are not responsible for John Reid. He has to face the consequences of his actions like everyone else. You are only responsible for yourself."

"But don't you see, once they have him they'll want me as well. They'll need me to verify his innocence or guilt. They need my blood to know if he's guilty or not."

"That's not going to happen. They will have to prove it some other way, without you or your blood, as you say. If we try to keep him we may lose you. If you insist on tying your fate to his, you will end up exactly as you fear, being tested like a guinea pig."

"What will they do to him?" asked David.

"I don't know. Probably put him on trial."

"God, it will be a freaking circus."

"I'm afraid you're right, mon ami. That is why it is important we keep you shielded from all of it."

"It's just going to make the pressure to turn me over that much greater."

"That's why I want to plan a number of statements from you that we can release in a timely fashion over the coming weeks to state your case. There are a lot of people who support you and don't care who your real parents are. Many like me who just want to see you back making that incredibly wonderful music of yours."

"I'll never write music again!" David shouted, all the pent up fury of the past few months coming out unexpectedly. "Never! I hate music. I hate it!"

"I know how you feel," said Jean St. Pierre, slightly stunned at the outburst. "This is all a bit much, all this nonsense about someone wanting to poison you and kill you, and this cloning foolishness. You must feel like your head is spinning, but it is all just noise, my friend. Life is a gift. Wherever it can occur, however it can come about, life well bubble up like an irresistible pool of lava, a force from the Infinite. That's what you have to realize and keep in mind all through this. See the big picture."

David didn't know what Jean was talking about, but it shut him up and made him think. He didn't know why he felt responsible for the old man. It certainly wasn't because he had been that great of a father. David could count the times on one hand they had done things together like father and son. But he had nurtured David's talents, taught him music and made sure he had all the opportunities possible so he could realize his gifts. He had provided for David and his mother, but there had been something missing – love? Now he knew why. Then he thought of his mother, who he hadn't thought of in years.

He had never really appreciated her quiet wisdom and simple piety, until now. The only glimpse he ever had of a religious or spiritual life was through her. As far as he knew his father was a devout atheist and never once went to the Anglican services with them. He stopped going himself at an early age, to practice his music with his father's support, shortly before leaving for the US, much against his mother's wishes. His parents never discussed religion or God in the house, but she never stopped being a pious, God-fearing person. He tried to remember what it was like in the early years, before music became such an overriding passion and took over his life.

Something Jean St. Pierre said struck a chord. Now he remembered. His mother used to say that life was a gift. She would tell him a lot of things in the early years when it was just them together, mother and son, sitting in the back garden in the sun. She would talk about all sorts of things, not caring much if he understood or not. His first memories of her were warm and filled with love. Why had he forgotten? If she wasn't his true mother, she was as real as any mother could be. Why hadn't he thought about her in all these years? And what about his own children, why had he never had any? He certainly wasn't careful and never practiced safe sex. Although he hadn't actively tried to have children with any of his three ex-wives there were certainly enough chances for an accident to occur. Was it because he was a clone?

All he had to show for his three failed marriages were huge monthly alimony bills. The thought made him feel empty inside and just added to his sense of guilt. He had sacrificed it all for the music, for the fame and glory, and what did he have to show for it? Now he couldn't even call his creations his own. They belonged to someone else - the father of his genes.

"It's not fair," he said finally. "Why can't they just leave us alone?"

"Ah, that is not the way of the world, is it, my friend. No one, it seems, is just left alone. You have to fight for your way in the world. Life might be a gift, but it is a terrible gift demanding much from the recipient. Each moment is precious. One must only realize it to grab it."

"I know you mean well, Jean St. Pierre, but I think you're full of it," said David rudely.

"You are full of it too, my friend," laughed Jean St. Pierre. "But I like you anyway."

"And I you," said David. "I'm sorry. I really do appreciate all you've done. If you hadn't come along when you did I don't know what would have happened to us. I understand you're doing all you can. Do whatever you must. I just wish things were different."

"Yes, David, I wish so too, but we must take things as they are, one day at a time. It is important to see things as they really are, eh? For then you can do what must be done rather than blunder through life."

"Can I see him? Where is he?"

"He is in his cabin getting ready. I'm going to drive him back to Montreal tonight. You and Colleen will be here alone. I have my men outside and on the road coming in. You will be safe here. No one knows about this place except a few of my most trusted men."

David followed Jean to the adjoining cabin where his father was finishing his packing, a few socks and underclothes, shirts and slacks, most of which would soon be replaced with standard prison garb.

"I'm sorry, Dad," he said on entering the cabin. "Jean told me. There's nothing he can do."

"None of that matters as long as you're OK. I didn't want it to happen this way. No one was ever to know."

"Not even me? Didn't I have a right to know?"

"What does it matter? It's irrelevant, an accident of circumstances. It means nothing in the scheme of things. Remember what I've told you, David. You're as human as any man or woman on this earth. You are the very essence of what it means to be human. The feelings you have, the love and beauty, the hope and yearning that comes out in your music, it's all human, as human as anything that can be found. Your talent is your own. It wasn't cloned or given to you by some magic formula. It wasn't grafted onto you. It's your own innate ability. You've worked hard for it. You were born from your mother's womb like every other baby on this earth. You were a real, struggling, crying, infant human baby. You grew up like every other boy, albeit one with tremendous talent. Don't let them get to you, David. You're not alone. Jean here will take care of things. The best thing I ever did was get us arrested by Canadian immigration."

David tried to laugh but burst out in tears instead.

"Don't worry, David," said his father, embracing him. "Everything will be fine. I'm not sorry for what we did. You were the best thing that ever happened to me, and I didn't need God to make it happen."

Jean and John Reid left a short time after that, leaving David to ponder his father's last words, which jumbled around in his head with all the other half-formed thoughts and images residing there. Was his father playing God, a God he never believed in?

Then he heard the music, the beginning of a new piece that came into his head unbidden. It was a choral introduction in English to a solemn mass, with solo voices soaring over a quiet contrapuntal refrain to join in a dazzling, heavenly harmony. It was the last thing he wanted to hear. Not only had he never written church music, he had no desire to write again. He drowned out the sound in his head with intense physical activity, rushing around the camp, cleaning the cabins and picking up debris. Then he raked the leaves off the dirt road leading to the site and ended the day chopping wood.

"You're going to build too many muscles if you're not careful," yelled Colleen from the porch. "Want a cup of coffee? I just put some on."

Jean St. Pierre was happy at the opportunity to get David's father out of the way. Not only was he glad to be rid of him and see him get his just deserts, he wanted David and Colleen to spend more time together. With his father there to hog the conversations and monopolize the time, David and Colleen were hardly ever alone. Jean hoped that this might be just what David needed.

Jean had noticed the way she looked at David, as well as her devotion to him, and knew David relied on her as well. Besides that, he thought they looked good together and would make a great couple, just what a man needed to get his life back together. He was hoping that time alone with each other might allow nature to take its course.

"OK," replied David, relieved the music in his head was gone. Although he thought Colleen attractive, he wasn't interested in her sexually. Despite their time together he still thought of her as his nurse, an employee, although no one had paid her in some time. In any case, she wasn't really his type, built a little too big-boned like him. She didn't have those long, shapely legs he had always been attracted to, or the stunning, glamorous look all of his ex-wives were known for. Colleen was more cute than beautiful, with a strong athletic body built more for hiking than modeling. She had sky-blue eyes, and a fresh complexion that looked better the closer you got, plump and pleasing rather than the look-to-die-for figure you see in the lingerie magazines. But it was a look that would last and she had a heart that would last even longer. Besides that, she had a good sense of humor, which David desperately needed at this time in his life. Despite himself, she could sometimes make him laugh. At least she never stopped trying.

"I'm bored as a donkey in the desert," she said, as they sat and drank their coffee. "If I read one more sportsmen's magazine I'll go absolutely bonkers. Do they have anything but *Outdoor Life* and *Hunt to Kill* around here? Even an old *National Geographic* would be better."

"I saw a couple *Seventeen* magazines and a *Vogue* back there," suggested David trying to be helpful.

"Yeah, probably with the *Playboys*. I wonder what the good old boys do with those? What I wouldn't give for a good romance novel right now."

"You sound like my first wife."

He heard himself mention an ex before he knew he was doing it, the kiss of death when talking to another woman.

"How many times have you been married?" Colleen asked. Despite their time together she still didn't know much about him. Now, after all the sensational news, she thought she knew even less. This was one of the few times they'd been completely alone together and she wanted to get to know him better.

"Three, I've been married three times, got the final papers from the last one just before all this happened. I told you, remember? Besides being a clone, I'm a three time loser."

"I'm making something special for us tonight," she replied, ignoring his remark and changing the subject.

"I'm not hungry," he said, getting up and going to his room without another word, putting a damper on the evening and any thought Colleen had of getting closer to him.

205

John Reid enjoyed his ride back to Montreal in the van with Jean St. Pierre, even though they were accompanied by two armed guards and he was handcuffed. The conversation with the Frenchman was interesting and they shared many of the same ideas, especially when it came to David. John felt fortunate they had found him. A better advocate could not have been fabricated.

Things turned sour, however, once he was handed over to the Canadian Bureau of Criminal Justice, who quickly gave him to Interpol. His dual citizenships and ambiguous nationality gave them jurisdiction in the end. He was told by a man with a distinct German accent that he would be tried as a war criminal. That was bad enough, but the men who took him into custody from his jail cell looked like they'd just as soon hang him as look at him.

"Where are you taking me?" he demanded, when it appeared they weren't heading toward the airport.

"We have a jet waiting at the edge of the city, at a private airport," replied one of his escorts.

"I thought we were taking an international flight out of Montreal. At least, that's what Jean St. Pierre told me."

"Well, your Jean St. Pierre isn't here now, Mister Reid. There is only us, and we will take you wherever we want. You'd better get used to it."

John decided to shut his mouth and bide his time. He knew it wouldn't be pleasant, but as long as David was safe, he knew he'd somehow make it through.

The car pulled up to a vacant warehouse near the river, under one of the many bridges that span the wide St. Lawrence.

Before he could object, he was taken from the car and ushered into the huge, empty storehouse, then into a tiny office where a card table was set up with a couple of chairs placed opposite each other. A rather large, intimidating looking man stood next to the table. He didn't look like he wanted to play cards.

As soon as John Reid was through the door, the man came toward him. Taking him firmly by the shoulders, he walked him to the table, forcibly sitting him in one of the chairs. Then he stood over him. When Reid tried to rise, the man put both hands firmly on his shoulders and forced him back down again. A moment later the door to the office opened and a rather austere looking man in a gray flannel suit, with graying hair and close-trimmed beard, entered the room and sat in the chair opposite him. He had sharp features and dark piercing eyes, and carried a briefcase. He reminded John Reid of some of the more rabid district attorneys he'd known.

"Good evening, Herr Reid," the man began in a thick German accent. "I apologize for these rather odd arrangements, but you see, the Canadian government has gone back on their agreement and only delivered half of the package. So we have had to make a change in plans."

"I don't know what you're talking about," answered John Reid.

"Where is David Reid?" the man demanded.

"I don't know," replied his father. "We were taken someplace in a closed van. I don't know where it was."

"You are lying," said the man. "But it doesn't matter. You will tell us soon enough. Where is the clone bastard?"

"Who are you?" yelled David's father. "You're not with Interpol."

"You are correct, Herr Reid, and there are no laws or codes that can protect you now."

He tried to stand, but was immediately held down by strong arms in an iron grip.

"Where is David Reid?" asked the man again.

For the next several hours the only sounds coming from the small office to echo off the walls of the empty warehouse were the screams of John Reid in reply to his tormenter's quiet questions. It was only a matter of time before Count Ernst Hohner got what he needed to know.

Chapter 25

News of John Reid's death caused an international sensation. His body had been found in the Seaway and looked as if it had been run over by an oil tanker. The Canadian government was being widely criticized for allowing it to occur on their watch, but they had followed all the rules and procedures. Someone had infiltrated Europe's crack intelligence agency to pull off the abduction and murder, for that's what it was being termed.

The news still hadn't reached David and Colleen in their isolated cabin, where they passed the time without the convenience of TV or newspapers, although there was a small radio that was seldom on. If Jean St. Pierre had his way they would remain ignorant of events, isolated and cut-off, as long as possible.

He drove to the crime scene in a state of shock to identify the body. Even though the prisoner had been in the custody of the Criminal Investigation Bureau when abducted, Jean still felt responsible. His own prejudices and feelings toward the old biologist had made him blind to the possible dangers. He should have seen the risk and reacted to avoid it rather than blindly go along, not caring one way or the other what happened to the man. How was he going to tell David he wondered, as he made the long, lonely drive up to the mountains.

Whoever had killed David's father must have been the same ones that tried to kill the composer earlier. The ease with which they had infiltrated Interpol made him uneasy about his own security detail, even though they were made up of handpicked men, men who he had known for years. Anyone could be bought with enough money. Every group had at least one disgruntled individual who thought they should be treated better or appreciated more, or who felt they should have been promoted over the other guy. It only took one.

In spite of his precautions, there still might be ways to discover where David was being kept, even though that too was known to only three or four others, and those, the most highly trusted people in long time positions of authority. There was always the question of what John Reid had told his abductors. It looked like he had been tortured severely. It was doubtful he could have held out, but then what did he really know? They were driven to the hiding place in a van with no windows in the back, though someone observant could have figured out the direction they were headed and the terrain. David would have to be moved.

He had turned off the main highway an hour ago and had been threading his way deeper into the mountains along a narrow tarmac road, when he made a sharp right and followed a dirt track that snaked its way deeper into the woods. During the season it was prime hunting ground for black bear and deer, not to mention moose and elk, but that wouldn't come for another nine months yet. He drove for twenty more minutes until a fork in the road led him to an even narrower dirt path, with a large tuft of grass between the tracks. He soon spotted the first guard post.

"How are things going?" he asked in French.

"All right," answered his man. "Things are pretty quiet. We've got everybody on full alert as you ordered."

"Bien. I just viewed the body. It was pretty bad. They busted him up terribly, looked like a train hit him."

"That's too bad. You think they'll try anything up here?"

"I don't know. I hope not, but one can never tell. Hopefully, we're the only ones who know he's here except for the chief and the head of the Bureau. The roads are being watched to make sure I'm not being followed. We should be OK, but we need to be alert. Have you got men working the perimeter?"

"Oui, sir, Francois and Pierre."

"Good, I want people walking it 24/7, got that?"

"Oui, sir. I've also got Jacque and Henri stationed at the house. We rotate the team with four others, twelve hours on and twelve off. They're at the next camp."

"Good."

"Anything else, sir?"

"If I think of anything, I'll let you know. Just keep your eyes open. Anybody that can infiltrate Interpol and pull off what they did with John Reid shouldn't be underestimated. Let's assume the worst. And get that truck out of sight. I don't want to attract attention if someone passes by. There's not supposed to be anyone up here. Let's make sure it looks that way."

As Jean drove down the rutted track to the camp, he saw his man pull the jeep behind some trees and begin covering it with brush. He had a good team, men he could depend on. If anything went wrong they were ready, as ready as they'd ever be. Now for the hard part.

As he drove up to the house he saw David out in the yard chopping wood. Colleen was sitting on the porch sipping a tall glass of iced tea. It was a warm spring day. David stood in the sun. He had his shirt off."

"Look's like you've been working out since I've been away."

"It feels good, keeps the music out of my head."

"Oh, and what music is that, Monsieur Reid?"

"The music I don't want to hear."

The remark disturbed Jean as did the expression on David's face.

"Well, be careful not to hurt yourself with that axe."

"Don't worry," said Colleen getting up from her chair. "He's becoming pretty good at chopping wood. We have a whole stack out back, enough for two winters."

"Yes, David is getting quite a physique. He's become a real mountain man."

Everyone laughed but David.

"How's my father?" he asked.

"Not well, I'm afraid. Why don't we go inside."

"Why, what's wrong?" said David, not moving.

"David, I'm afraid your father has been killed," Jean informed him without more ado.

David looked at Jean in shock.

"What did you say?" he rasped.

Colleen came quickly down the stairs and ran to his side.

"The people who took him were not who they said they were. They murdered him. We found him this morning."

"Nooo!" David wailed, more a cry of a wounded animal than a word. He dropped the axe and slumped down on the large stump of wood he had been using as a chopping block. Colleen held his shaking shoulders.

For a moment he couldn't speak, overwhelmed with grief. He looked at Jean St. Pierre with an accusing, half-disbelieving stare, shaking his head back and forth in denial. Tears welled up in his eyes.

"You promised it would be OK," he said.

The look and words pierced Jean like a blade. His eyes watered as well.

"Je suis si desole," he said, his voice quivering. "We had no way of knowing. They were professionals. They infiltrated Interpol. We underestimated the hatred that your father's crimes would engender in some circles."

"Are you saying he was killed for what he did, for creating me? He was killed because of me?"

Jean was sorry he had said anything. Despite his training he couldn't have handled the situation any worse. He felt like a man hanging on a ledge who had just let his best friend slip from his grasp. David began laughing hysterically.

Colleen looked terrified.

It was a hollow laugh, devoid of mirth or humor, inhuman in the depth of its despair, as if he had suddenly wakened to the total absurdity of his existence. It was a sound that left the soul of the hearer empty of all hope.

"I am a monster," he cried through the laughter. "A hideous monster that deserves to die."

His laughter grew more frantic, his eyes wild and darting, his mouth wide in a hideous grin. Now it was Jean St. Pierre's turn to be afraid. He had already started moving toward David instinctively, when he saw him reach for the axe. Colleen was trying to stop him.

"A monster, a monster!" screamed David, straining for the axe handle.

Jean St. Pierre grabbed him in a bear-hug and held him down, while David struggled to get free.

"The cabin, the cabin!" Jean yelled into his walkie-talkie, hoping someone would get there in time.

Mark Burns was as shocked as most people to hear about the brutal death of John Reid, but he was not surprised, and rightly guessed it was the work of his ex-employer. He may have lost a couple of his hired killers, but he had not lost his fangs.

The first thing Mark did on being released from custody was head for his penthouse apartment and a good stiff drink. The second thing he did was look up Zeiggie and get him released from the mental facility where he was being kept for observation. He set the ex-cello player up in his own apartment not far from where he used to live and made sure they kept in touch.

When news of the murder in Montreal broke, Mark was one of the first people picked up for questioning. He had been under constant surveillance by the FBI since his release, so they ended up being his best alibi, but there were many who wanted to lock him up just on principle. The odds were good, given his past history and his recent testimony, that he was somehow involved in the ex-biologist's death.

So it didn't hurt that Mark's good friend, the Bureau's director of New York operations, vouched for his whereabouts.

"It was the same person who tried to have me killed," Mark insisted when he was finally alone with the Bureau chief in his office. "The person who hired me has infiltrated Interpol. One of his men, an Interpol agent named Dr. Henry Fitzroy, was at the border that day the Reids tried to cross. We were both working for the same person."

"I don't know," said the Bureau chief. "There are plenty of reasons someone might want to kill John Reid. There're all sorts crackpots out there. You accused the man of what some would call crimes against humanity."

"That may be, but none of them could pull off swiping him right under the nose of the Canadian police. The Mounties always get their man."

"So do we, so don't try to con me, Mark," said the FBI man.

"I'm not. I came to you with the whole thing. I turned myself in, remember. I want to work with you to get this bastard. I'll do my time, but I want to get him first. Anyway, I'm a dead man in prison. If I'm going to go, I want to take this creep with me."

"You're just giving me more reason to lock you up. I can't have you running around hunting some phantom menace. You said yourself the man's untraceable. How do you expect to catch him if you don't know anything about him? That is if he really exists."

"Oh, he exists all right," said Mark, remembering his recent conversation with Zeiggie. "John Reid really did create a human clone. My father's notebooks and journals prove it. They also show that the donor of the DNA used in the cloning was Johann Sebastian Bach. There was no reason for my father to lie. The notes tell the truth in an objective, scientific manner so that the experiment could be reproduced. The donor was mentioned only in passing. As the journals describe it, the DNA samples came from hair and tissue specimens from Bach's scalp encased in a glass amulet. The techniques used to take still living cells from tissue and hair samples are now well known. Extract the genetic contents of the donor cell's nucleus and inject them into a human egg to be implanted and incubated in the womb of a living woman, in this case Reid's unknowing wife while she slept one night after intercourse. Reid and my father developed techniques to increase the viability of the cloned cell a hundredfold. It was still a secret when they left the Roslin Institute, all taken with them. This is all described in the most tedious detail in my father's notebooks. It's also in the letters my father kept between him and John Reid, hidden these many years in the basement of my old family home. This is no fantasy, Larry, this is the real thing. And that's not the strange part."

"It all sounds pretty damned strange to me," replied the bureau chief. "Was there any mention of another partner, someone who might have funded their work and now wants his payoff?"

"No, but that's what I was looking into before I stumbled onto all this. The only name mentioned in the journals was this Felix Mann, a distant descendent of Bach's, who had learned the true location of his lost burial place. It's possible Mann funded the whole thing himself and my employer only told me that story to throw me off the track. David's friend Zeiggie, the one who tried to warn him he was being poisoned, has a theory about how Bach was murdered that could be relevant."

The FBI chief was about to interrupt.

"No, wait Larry, let me finish," insisted Mark not giving him the chance. "I know it sounds crazy, but he's done years of research and unearthed some pretty incriminating letters. Zeiggie has found evidence that implicates the rector of Leipzig University of killing Bach by putting toxins in his eye medicine after his operation. He thinks someone may have gotten the same idea, someone who knew about the original crime, perhaps a descendent or distant relative, who knows."

"That's ridiculous. No wonder they locked your friend up in a mental institution. What possible motive would they have?"

"Greed for one," answered Mark. "Remember, I was ordered to incapacitate David and then take control of his business, not kill him. Whoever hired me wanted to own him like a trained dog. Zeiggie seems to think the motive may have something to do with David being Bach's clone, which means whoever is doing this knew about it all along. He thinks this Ernesti hated Bach enough to kill him. Bach snubbed him and got the better of him, but the rector had the last laugh, at least Zeiggie thinks so. He has some compelling arguments, especially the religious angle. Ernesti saw Bach as the epitome of a Godless approach to church music. As you know, religion has caused more wars in history than almost any other motive, so it's not that farfetched to see it at work here."

"And you think it's some descendent or ardent admirer of Bach's old nemesis, what did you call him?"

"Ernesti, the Rector Johann August Ernesti."

"You think they're doing the same thing now, some 250 years later?"

"Yes, it's possible," said Mark, still not fully believing it himself, but then everything that had happened these past few weeks was equally unbelievable. "For all we know they could have cloned Ernesti too."

"You think they'll go after David in Montreal?"

"I'm sure of it. It's only a matter of time. They've already tried once. They killed John Reid and sure as we're sitting here talking, he'll try to kill David again too."

"Well, there's not much we can do about that. He's under Canadian jurisdiction and they're not about to hand him over to us, not after what just happened."

"I know, but Zieggie has an idea, a way to find whoever it is," said Mark. "We'll need help from your counterparts in Europe, hopefully not those in the employ of our killer. Zieggie thinks we should start by tracing any known living descendents of the rector. He's composed a list. Like I said," continued Mark, handing the FBI man a typewritten directory. "He's been doing his homework."

"OK, Mark," replied the FBI chief, rubbing his forehead where a throbbing headache was beginning to declare itself. "I'm having a hard time swallowing all this, but I'll see if I can get the boys at the NSA to lend a hand. If they can't find a link, no one can."

Chapter 26

David's breakdown had given everyone a scare, and he had been put on a suicide watch under a doctor's care. He had recovered quickly, however, and was ready to go home. Exactly where that was, he wasn't quite sure. His whereabouts was still a secret, but no one was sure for how long.

"If I stay here another day, Jean, I'll go absolutely insane. I need to get out of this place."

"Well, if the doctor says you are ready, and Colleen can go with you, then we can talk about it, but where would you go?"

"Where no one will find me," replied David.

Jean was about to say something, when a somewhat familiar face appeared on the TV screen in David's room. It was his discredited business manager, Mark Burns, talking to a top anchor for NBC Morning News.

"Yes, Bill, David is well," announced Mark looking into the camera.

"How come they haven't thrown you in jail?" Jean said, glaring at the image on the large color screen. "What are you up to?"

"He's fully recovered and anxious to get on with his life," said Mark continuing his interview.

"What about the accusations that you tried to poison Mister Reid and take over his business?"

"I admitted all that to the Grand Jury. John Reid was in league with some very bad people, the same ones who hired and duped me. He's the one who persuaded David to leave my care to run off to Canada to seek asylum. He did this so he could take advantage of David at a very critical time in his life when he was at his most vulnerable. I was able to discover the truth and expose John Reid's crime, as well as my father's, but David is innocent. He is a very special person."

"How can we believe a word you say after what you've already admitted doing?"

"I have pleaded guilty to everything. I've disclosed the truth to try and save David. I feel my guilt or innocence is secondary to David's safety."

"How is David taking the death of his father, the man you accuse of creating a human clone?" asked the newsman, relishing the rating numbers he was piling up with this interview.

"Despite John Reid's crime, David is taking his death very hard," Mark responded, as if he knew firsthand. "John Reid, although exploitive and self-serving, was the only father figure David ever had. He misses him very much. As a matter of fact, he's dedicating a new work to him."

"You say David Gorder Reid is working on a new piece, can you tell us about that?" asked the newscaster.

"No, except to say he's trying to get his life back together after what's happened to him. He needs privacy, however. That's why he's keeping a low profile. He does not want to be disturbed. That's why his whereabouts is being kept secret and he's not giving any interviews."

Jean St. Pierre switched off the TV. What could be going on he wondered. Why was this despicable man acting as a spokesman for the very person he was trying to destroy? Was it some kind of publicity stunt to help his upcoming trial? Colleen was sorry she had changed the channel, trying to find something more stimulating than Mister Ed reruns. She had no idea David would be the topic of conversation, let alone that his onetime friend and current nemesis would be sprouting lies about him on national TV. She saw the look of helpless desperation on David's face and feared the worse, but he remained calm, and only asked Jean what this could mean.

"It means your old friend is up to his old tricks. But don't worry, mon ami, I will get to the bottom of this or my name is not Jean St. Pierre."

He called his superior from the hospital, who reminded him he was no longer on the case, and told him to keep his mouth shut and mind his own business. Next Jean called his superior's boss, who said if he so much as breathed anything about David Reid, he would be arrested and sent to prison in the Yukon. When he called the head of the Immigration and Culture Bureau himself, an old hunting buddy, he was finally told the truth.

"Yes, Jean, we are working with the American FBI. They think they may have a lead on whoever killed John Reid. You were taken off the case to throw them off the track. Apparently you're being watched."

"Pas du tout!" protested Jean.

216

"Don't worry, they still don't know where he is yet and we want to keep it that way. That's why we're going along with the Americans. You are not to visit David Reid again."

"I am here with him now. Do you think I was followed?"

"We know you were, but it was taken care of before they could relay the information. It was a close call. We can't afford another."

"Oui, Minister, thank you for explaining everything."

"You are a persistent little prick, Jean St. Pierre."

"Merci, Minister. I come from a long line of persistent little pricks."

Agents from the Federal Bureau of Investigation had been searching the genealogies of the Ernesti family for weeks following Zeiggie's lead, while they pursued possible sources of the exotic toxins used to blind David Reid, all of which seemed to lead them to Central Europe. Even if they identified a suspect, however, there was little to arrest him on. For that matter, they didn't even have enough to hold anyone for questioning, since the evidence they had was not only flimsy but downright bizarre.

Several at the Bureau believed the whole thing was ludicrous, but they were overruled by the chief. Larry Talbot had seen a lot in his twenty-five years in the service, but this whole David Reid thing took the prize. He had never dealt with anything remotely resembling it. If he could believe Reid was the clone of Bach, he could believe anything, including that Reid was being chased by Bach's old enemy. At least if they had an idea of who it might be, they'd know where to look and who to look for.

While all this was going on, Mark was trying to solve his own problems, like how to stay out of jail, which he was one step away from. He had no idea where David was or what was happening to him. In any case, he knew he'd be the last one the Canadians would tell. He only hoped David was safe. He was sorry for what he had done, but even more upset that he had been lied to and used. He didn't like being another man's punk any more than he liked having someone try to kill him. He was going to find the SOB even if it was the last thing he did. First, he had to solve the immediate problem and concentrate on his upcoming trial, but that was the farthest thing from his mind.

Zeiggie had not totally accepted the fact that he was now working with Mark, the one who had caused all the trouble in the first place, although he knew Mark was attempting to make up for his sins. Still, he didn't trust him.

"Don't leave town," Mark had said when he dropped Zeiggie off at his new place. "I may need you."

"Don't worry. You know where to find me," replied Zeiggie. "I ain't going anywhere."

"Well, thanks for all your help, Len. I think you may have stumbled on to something with your theory. It's the only thing we have to go on."

"No big thing," said Zeiggie, shaking Mark's outstretched hand. "I appreciate your help. Once I get on my feet, I'll pay you back for everything."

"Don't worry about it. It's the least I can do for what I did to you. I owe you."

That was days ago. They hadn't spoken since.

Mark took a sip of his Scotch and looked out his penthouse window at the New York skyline, contemplating his misspent life. Now he finally had a chance to make up for all that if only they could stop his ex-employer. His phone sprang to life. It was Larry Talbot, his friend at the FBI.

"Does the name Count Ernst Hohner mean anything to you?"

"No," said Mark, trying to place the name. "Who's he?"

"The last living male relative of Rector Johann August Ernesti of Leipzig University," replied the agent. "His mother's father was Frederick Gustav Ernesti."

"I'll be damned," said Mark. "There actually is a bleeding descendent. Zeiggie was right after all."

"He's a very wealthy recluse. Lives in Vienna, Austria, which is where the drugs found on the baton are from, as far as we can tell."

"What are you going to do?" asked Mark.

"There's not much we can do, even if we could locate him. He's done nothing wrong. There's no way we could get the European authorities to cooperate with the flimsy evidence we've got. This is, after all, a pretty preposterous theory."

"Preposterous or not, it's true," insisted Mark, really believing it for the first time. "Wait until I tell Zeiggie. Why can't you locate this guy?"

"For one thing, like I said, we don't exactly have the cooperation of the local authorities over there. We've sent a couple of our own people over, but the guy doesn't appear to be at his currently known address, some castle in Vienna. They were told he travels frequently, but no one knows where he went. He could be anywhere."

"Do you have a photograph?" asked Mark.

"Yes, I'll show it to you when you come by the office. I want to see you. We need to talk about your upcoming court appearance."

"Do you know where David is?" asked Mark, more worried about his old friend than his trial.

"The Canadians are being pretty tight-lipped. Some people in our government may know, but they're not about to tell us. If I were them I'd be planning on putting him under some sort of witness protection program."

"That might be easier said then done. For one thing David's probably one of the best known people in history, and who's ever after him is no ordinary individual. Who knows what kind of resources he has at his disposal. You've got two guys on me and I still don't feel safe. The only thing I've got going for me is the madman is too interested in David to waste his time with me."

"You think he'll go after Reid?"

"Like I said, you can count on it."

Count Ernst Hohner had eliminated the creator of the clone-bastard, John Reid. Unfortunately, his man in Interpol had been compromised in the process and had to be removed as well. It was a delicate task and one only Franz could do. Franz was family, and family was only used for such matters as a last resort. Short of doing it himself, Franz was the only one he could trust for such an assignment. It was he who made Donna Douglas, the first woman they had hired to poison the conductor, disappear when she got cold feet. It was Franz who killed the Fong woman when she was compromised. Now he would kill the clone-bastard in front of the world.

Franz was his younger cousin by fifteen years. Not only was he arrogant and rude, he was downright spooky. Not too many people made Ernst uncomfortable, but Franz was an exception. His father had been a sadistic butcher for the East German Stasi, known for his brutal though effective interrogation methods. Franz was even worse and seemed to enjoy inflicting pain. He had been expelled from more than one school when young for torturing animals and bullying other children. Though arrested while in collage for allegedly attacking and raping a girl in a church confessional, he was never prosecuted for any crime because of the Family's influence and money,.

Franz had not only made Fitzroy disappear, he had located the missing David Reid himself. The local thug he hired to shadow the Canadian official in charge of the conductor was arrested while following his man. The unfortunate fool knew Franz only by a cell phone number, which was untraceable. He had watched unobserved when the man was apprehended by plainclothes Mounties and carted off. It took only a simple process of elimination to identify the small hospital where Reid was being cared for. He had used a drone to follow the cavalcade taking Reid from the medical facility into the foothills of the Laurentian Mountains, to a collection of hunting lodges where he was being kept. He had reported to his uncle shortly afterward.

"That is good news, Franz," said Count Hohner on hearing the information in his hide-away in Europe. "You think you know where they are? Ya, that is good, You must be careful. Do you think you can get to him without being caught? Are you sure? Good. Ya, do what you must do, but be careful. I don't have to tell you how important this is. The clone must die."

The words were music to Franz's ears. He had killed many things in his young life, but never a human clone. This job was special. Franz had many gifts, some natural, some learned, all developed with a single-minded zeal bordering on excessiveness. He was a master of disguises as well as an expert marksman from his years in the Austrian alpine Special Forces. He could change his appearance without even using make-up, just by tousling his hair and assuming a different expression, changing his features as if his face was made of plastic. He could alter his voice with equal fluidity, and spoke several languages fluently. He had nerves of steel and catlike reflexes, and strength built up from hours in the gym. He did 200 pushups every night before going to bed and could jump in the air, spin around 180 degrees, and kick out a light bulb hanging from the ceiling.

From one of his many moles in the Canadian police, Ernst knew they were taking the clone out of the country to put him in protective custody.

"You have no time to lose, Franz," he told his young cousin. "We have to move quickly."

Jean St. Pierre had followed orders and stayed away from the location David was being kept. After the arrest of the suspect caught following him to the small, isolated hospital, they had moved David back to the camp further up in the mountains. Jean stayed behind and verified the convoy was not pursued. He failed to notice the small drone flying high overhead, shadowing the vehicles up the highway. Communicating with his security team stationed around the hideaway by radio, he had warned them about the breach, notifying them they would be moving their man back to the hunting camp prior to getting him out of the country under an assumed name. Now he sat in the small cafeteria at the medical center a half hour away contemplating the situation.

Looking at his watch, he spoke into his radio, "Jean, calling Jacque, come in, Jacque. How is it going up there?" Jacque was his man at the head of the road leading to the site. "Jacque, are you there?"

He wondered where his man was. Jacque usually answered promptly. The men had been ordered to monitor their radios at all time. Where the hell could he be wondered Jean.

He called his team lead stationed at the camp. "Jean, calling Henri. Come in Henri ."

"Henri here," came the prompt reply. Jean sighed in relief.

"Hi, Henri , this is Jean. I'm having trouble getting hold of Jacque up at the road. Do you know what's up?"

"I just talked to him fifteen minutes ago. Things were quiet."

"Well, see if you can raise him on your end. I'll try to get one of the guys walking the perimeter to check in on him. Keep me posted."

"Yes, sir," answered the man at the cabins.

Jean felt relieved as he checked the schedule to see who was on the line moving around the edge of the property, and dialed their call-sign. He became frantic when no one answered.

What was going on? He had been ordered not go to the camp unless instructed, but all his instincts told him that's where he should be. Thinking he might still be under observation, he put on a hunting jacket that was hanging near the door and surreptitiously left the building. There was a set of keys in the pocket of the jacket, which belonged to one of his men on guard at the campsite. Quietly checking the vehicles in the small employee's parking lot, he soon found the pickup truck they fit. He opened the door and jumped in. Before he left the medical facility, he had tried contacting the team at the neighboring site. No one answered. He was full of concern, but didn't want to call headquarters in Montreal. He knew what they would say, stay where he was and wait for backup. However, he was certain he had to move, and quickly.

Jean did not carry a gun, but was happy to see that the man whose truck he had borrowed was an avid hunter and had his high-powered hunting rifle, a 30-30, on a gun-rack in the back of the cab.

Starting off slowly so not to attract attention, he sped up and drove as fast as he could as soon as he was out of sight of the facility, checking his rear view mirror frequently to make sure he wasn't being followed. His anxiety increased with each tick of the clock. He swore to himself as the vehicle seemed to crawl along the road to the camp.

Fifteen minutes later he approached the head of the dirt entryway and slowed to a crawl as he came to the first guard station. Getting our, he looked around. The guard vehicle was there, but the post was deserted. He beeped the horn three times, the signal to anyone within hearing, but no one responded. As he was getting back in the truck he spotted a patch of blood on the ground. He did a quick search of the area, but turned up nothing. Then he called headquarters and asked for backup now that he was sure something bad had happened.

"Jean, here. Reid is in danger. Send men to the camp, as many as you can. Several of my men are missing and may be hurt." He didn't bother answering their demands to know what he was doing there

Going to the pickup, he checked the rifle, loading it with shells he found in the glove compartment. Then he slung it over his shoulder and started walking down the road to the camp. If he had looked a little more carefully, he might have found the body of his man, stuffed in a narrow ditch, his throat cut from ear to ear.

As Jean approached the campsite, he noticed how quiet it was. Normally there would be some activity, someone talking or a radio or David chopping wood, but the place was as silent as a church.

Walking around the cabins cautiously with his gun pointed forward, he searched for signs of life. He was tempted to call out, but thought better of it. Not knowing the situation, he decided it would be unwise to announce his presence.

Did they decide to move David somewhere else without consulting him? He had just talked to his team lead twenty-minutes ago and nothing was mentioned. Are they hiding in one of the cabins? He squatted behind a barrel and scanned the area. Nothing was out of place. Has David been taken? He heard someone moaning behind him. There in the bushes bordering the clearing was his man, Henri .

"Henri ," Jean whispered crawling to him. "Are you OK?"

He appeared to be hurt and was trying to tell him something.

"I've been shot. We've been compromised."

Jean examined him and determined he had been hit in the shoulder. It was hard to tell with all the blood, but it looked like the bullet had just missed his heart. Jean applied firm pressure to the wound, and bandaged it up with a strip of his shirt as well as he could, working quickly. As he did so, he talked to his man.

"Lie still. Help's coming. What happened? Where is David?"

"He came up on us before we knew what was happening. I couldn't contact anyone else on the radio."

"It looks like they got the others, even the backup team. How many of them are there?"

"Just one, but he's good. He's got an automatic with a silencer. We never heard him. I heard Phil shout and ran toward the cabin. He shot me from there. I went down and was out of it for a minute or two. Then I crawled back into the bushes here. He must have thought I was dead. I think they're still in there."

"OK, Henri . You did well. Just lie still now and try to rest. I've got a team coming. I'll deal with the guy in the cabin."

Jean ran the short distance across the clearing toward David's cabin, keeping low. He was not a military man and had minimal training, but he knew enough to keep his head down and hold his rifle in front of him. Not sure what to do, he edged up to the cabin and listened. He thought he could hear talking and strained to interpret it. What was happening? What was he to do?

Maybe if he waited they would come out. Perhaps he could get the assassin as they were leaving? But something told him David would never leave the building alive. Could he get a shot in through a window or would he be seen before he got it off? Could he take that chance? That would more than likely get David and Colleen killed. Jean wasn't that good of a marksman, though he could hit a target if not far off and given enough time to line up his shot. From what Henri had told him, it didn't sound like he'd get the chance with this opponent, obviously a professional hit man.

It appeared they were in the small living area in the front of the building. It sounded like someone was giving a lecture, punctuated with slaps and punches. Edging his way to the front porch, he quietly opened the screen door and crawled to the main entrance. Then he stood against the wall, steeling himself for action.

Flinging open the door, Jean rushed into the cabin with a yell, brandishing his gun around the room,

"You are surrounded," he shouted. "Give yourself up."

David and Colleen stared at him, their eyes wide in shock. They were sitting on chairs side to side, with their hands tied behind them, gags on their mouths. They were bloodied and bruised, both naked and showing signs of being tortured. They were alone.

Checking the small kitchenette, Jean walked toward the rear bedroom cautiously. David's and Colleen's pleading eyes made him freeze. Only the hair on the back of his neck moved as it stood in fear. He heard a voice behind him.

"Halt! Drop the gun or I will blow your head off," said the man coming from behind the door.

Jean, who was already frozen, stood as still as an ice castle.

"Drop the gun, now!" yelled the assassin.

Slowly lowering the gun to the floor, he wondered what he could have been thinking to rush into the cabin like that. He was no commando, but he knew he had to do something fast. His instincts were telling him David was about to be murdered right before his eyes.

"You are just in time to see the clone-bastard die, the abomination."

Jean turned around and faced the speaker, who was a tall young man with short, blond hair. He wore tight-fitting, green camouflaged combat gear and held a muffled Uzi.

"You can't protect him," the blond man continued, looking at Jean with a sadistic smile. "You can't save him from the hand of God."

He pointed the weapon in David's direction.

Without thinking, Jean charged across the intervening distance and knocked David and his chair over, just as a burst erupted from the automatic. They all tumbled onto the floor, Colleen included, as high-velocity bullets tore into the cabin's pine siding. Suddenly, Jean felt a searing pain in his right calf. He looked up to see the assassin standing over them.

"You will all die," he intoned, his gun pointed at Jean's head. "You can die with the clone-bastard."

Two more shots rang out. Jean flinched and closed his eyes, waiting for the bullets to hit him, but none came. When he opened his eyes again, the killer was lying on his side, staring wide, blood oozing from a large hole in his temple. Jean looked up to see his man Henri at the window with his finger still on the trigger of his 45-special, the barrel resting on the windowsill.

Chapter 27

Jean woke up in the medical facility surrounded by doctors and police. His right leg hung over the foot of the bed in a sling, a cast up to his thigh. He had been shot multiple times in the calf with high-velocity bullets and had lost a lot of blood, but he'd live to suffer another day, albeit with a limp.

The assassin, who had been killed instantly with a shot to the head, was id'd as Franz Bernhard, a descendent of Johan August Ernesti and on the FBI's list. The fact that David had been saved and the assassin killed should have given Jean a great sense of satisfaction, but nine of his men had been butchered. Even his new status as a national hero did not help mitigate the disappointment and pain. He felt the loss of his men deeply, but he was thankful that the conductor and his nurse were safe.

David and Colleen, although bruised and battered, were recovering rapidly. Colleen had been burned with cigarettes and David had a broken nose and three fractured ribs. They had been taken to an undisclosed location outside of the country.

The authorities were no closer to apprehending the mastermind of the plot, but the killer's DNA was the same as that found at the site of Tina Fong's murder, which did much to confirm Mark Burns' story and support his case, not that Jean cared much either way. Burns was the least of his concerns.

Jean was out of the picture now, as the US and the FBI had taken over the protection of the famous composer, but he was still in the immigration man's thoughts. What was to become of David Gordon Read?

"Are you sure it wasn't Hohner?" asked Mark, hearing about the attempt on his old friends life.

"No, it's not him," replied the FBI chief, Larry Talbot, "although he appears to be a relative living here in the States. Hohner doesn't sound like the kind of person who would do something like this himself."

"I wouldn't be too sure of that," said Mark. "He's probably running out of accomplices."

"I hope so. I'm getting too old for this," observed Talbot.

Mark was concerned that the FBI and Interpol - who had finally been convinced to help with the investigation - still hadn't located Count Hohner. Although they now knew who he was, he had apparently left Europe for parts unknown and disappeared.

Mark's own predicament had improved. His trial had begun and it was going well. With the identity of the assassin established and Mark's story verified, his case looked good. However, his ex-employer was still out there, for all he knew sitting in the gallery watching his trial. Every FBI man in the state was on the lookout for him.

"I wish I could see David," said Mark, voicing his desire.

"He's in the witness protection program," Larry Talbot informed him. "They aren't going to let you talk to him."

"I don't want to talk to him," replied Mark. "I want his DNA. People are starting to doubt what I'm saying and what's in my father's notebooks. They think the whole thing is one big fabrication. They're painting me like I'm some kind of pathological liar. No one believes me, but it's important they know the truth."

"I believe you, Mark, and I think you're right about this all being tied to the fact Reid may be a clone of J.S. Bach. It sure fits. I'm just worried Hohner might come after you."

"That would be all the proof we need, wouldn't it?" said Mark.

"Yeah, but I hope you don't get killed in the process of vindicating yourself."

"So do I," replied Mark. "But I wouldn't mind so much if I could take the bloody bastard with me."

David was on the other side of the world, 6000 miles away, as far from New York as he could be and still be in the United States. Everyone agreed that while the person or persons trying to kill him were at large, he would be in constant danger. So the United States and Canadian governments cooperated to put him under the witness protection program.

He had been thinking of where to go for quite some time, even before his father's death. So when he was asked, without much soul searching, he answered Hana, on the island of Maui, taking a page out of Charles Lindbergh's playbook. He and Colleen, who went with him as nurse and companion, were given assumed names and identities and whisked away in a private jetliner to the Hawaiian Islands twenty-four hours later.

David sat alone on a black sand beach watching the Pacific surf crash against the rocky shoreline. The looming presence of the 10,000 foot extinct volcano, Haleakala, towered behind him, while the large Island of Hawaii was visible across the channel in the distance. It was a heart-aching, lonely scene, and he loved it. He spent most of his time in solitude on the far side of the island wandering the wide, flat plain between the mountain and the ocean. He was bitter and angry at the world, at how people looked at him, at what they thought of him, at how they treated him. He was nothing more than a zoological specimen, a curious oddity to be talked about and gawked at by those who had once praised and esteemed him. He wanted to hide from the world.

Even the small, quaint cottage on the edge of Hana - where they were lucky if a car drove by all day - wasn't quiet or isolated enough for David. After three sleepless nights and as many fitful days, he found a deserted shack beyond the Seven Sacred Pools, and convinced the son of the old folks who had once owned it to let him squat there for a hefty fee. He didn't even bother putting in electricity or running water, but lived like the natives who left their petro-graphs on the rocks a thousand years before, with only fire to light his evenings and water from a nearby stream.

Colleen, who was not happy with the situation, brought him food and supplies everyday, but after one night with the spiders and mice she'd had enough. It was uncomfortable enough to be there in the day with the cobwebs and things scurrying around on the cabinet tops, but at night, when the candles made the walls and floors move as if covered with vermin, it was downright uninhabitable. David, despite his previous life of comfort and luxury, didn't seem to mind.

Colleen had been worried about him ever since his father - or the closest thing David had to one – had been killed. That, the revelations of his origins, and the most recent attempt on their lives, had been a lot to deal with and had almost led to another breakdown. She wondered if the time alone here was therapeutic or bad for him. She hoped it was the former, since it was such a beautiful and peaceful spot, but the landscape between the back of the mountain and desolate, rocky shore had a gloomy, prehistoric character. She was worried that it might lead someone in David's state of mind to dark thoughts. There were times, sitting with him alone on the beach, that she half expected a dinosaur to come loping around the corner instead of a stray cow. At least they were safe here, or so she hoped.

David still had a full beard and long hair, and with his open shirt and cut-offs jeans, looked like a down and out beach bum. It was a hot sunny day, but he would have hiked back toward the mountain, which he gazed at now, if he hadn't worn his flip-flops. He spent most of his time exploring the far side of Haleakala or sitting on the beach, always thinking, always brooding. What would it be like to be normal? He would have given anything to know.

He could no longer relate to anyone, not even Colleen, who he loved. Despite his wish to be alone, his constant fear was that she would leave him. Even so, he could hardly bring himself to say two words to her. He had far too much to say, none of it things she would have wanted to hear. So instead, he kept it all bottled up inside and said nothing.

After sitting a while he got back in his jeep and drove the short distance to his shack. Colleen's station wagon was in the dirt drive. He found her in the kitchen trying to clean things up enough to have lunch.

"Where you been?" she asked when he entered.

"Oh, nowhere, just up the coast a bit."

"It's quiet in town today," she observed. "No tourists. You want to come up to the house tonight for dinner? I thought you could stay over. I hate being alone there at night. It's so quiet and isolated."

"Stay here," David offered, forgetting the last time she tried staying.

"No. It's a little too primitive for me. I don't like sleeping with the wildlife."

"Well, I can't stay in town," said David. "I may be recognized."

"Is that what you're worried about?"

"Among other things."

"Like what, spending time with me?"

"We spend time together. We're together now."

"You know what I mean. It's always on your terms."

"Well, that's the way it has to be for now. I don't want to socialize."

"We don't have to socialize. We don't even have to go out. Look where we are. There's no place to go even if we wanted."

"We were told to keep a low profile."

"How low do you have to go? What, do you want to disappear?"

"That's the general idea," said David. "I'd just as soon disappear. Who cares?"

228

"I care," replied Colleen.

"Well, don't. I don't."

"That's the problem," observed Colleen. "You can't just give up on life."

"Oh, and why the hell not? Do you know the life expectancy of a clone? I've already outlived it by three years. My clock's running out anyway."

"You don't know that. You don't know when you're going to die, just like the rest of us. It could be tomorrow, it could be fifty years from now. All it means is that you've got to make the most of the time you've got."

"That's easy for you to say, you're not some damned experiment."

"Are you still crying about that?" she replied, in her tough Dublin brogue. "Get over it, David. Get on with your life. Don't let that stand in your way. You've got too much to offer and you've worked too hard to give it all up. I won't let you."

He didn't reply, but went out the kitchen door to the back of the house. While the place itself was no more than a shack, it was situated in a stunning setting, on a high bluff overlooking the ocean behind it, with the mountain in front, across the road. Surrounded by a high hedge, it was hidden from the road, while in back a broad, green field swept unobstructed down a wide hillside to the rocks and water below. It was a dramatic scene, and on a clear day like today, you could see for miles down the desolate Maui shoreline. Very few travelers made their way this far out, just a few local ranchers and cowboys - no tourists.

Colleen followed him out to the windswept field.

Handing him a sandwich, she said. "Maybe we'll be able to go home soon."

"What makes you think I want to go home?"

"I don't know. I thought you might like to get back to civilization, back to work."

"Are you crazy?" he yelled. "Where the hell have you been the last few months? Have you been listening to anything I've said? I can't stand the human race. I want nothing to do with it. You got that? Comprendre?"

"You don't have to shout, David," pleaded Colleen, upset at his outburst.

"I'm sorry," he replied. "I just need to be alone."

"OK, if that's the way you feel," she said, stalking off.

David felt terrible the moment she left, driving off in a cloud of dust, but he made no move to stop her. Instead, he threw away his sandwich and started walking toward the mountain in his flip-flops.

Zeiggie had read the accounts in the newspapers of the attempt on David's life and the killing of the would-be assassin. He wondered what David thought of Mark's disclosure. As a matter of fact, all Zeiggie could think about was David. Maybe it was because he didn't have much else going on in his life. Maybe it was because he had no one to talk to or confide in. Or maybe it was because David was the clone of his favorite classical composer. Whatever the reason, Zeiggie was obsessed with David and his whereabouts.

He had tried several times to get in touch with the composer, but to no avail. Even the Canadian government claimed not to know of his whereabouts. No one knew where David was or what had happened to him, although several newspapers conjectured he may have gone into hiding or voluntary exile after yet another attempt on his life. Whoever it was that was after David was still out there.

Zeiggie had tried everything. He called anyone and everyone he could think of and searched the net ceaselessly for cues. He left coded messages in the personal ads of newspapers that only David would recognize. But he was no further along than when he started several weeks before. Then he remembered his sister's boy, Freddy.

Unfortunately, Zeiggie wasn't that close to his older sister. She had always been a prima donna and treated him with typical big-sister scorn. However, he had driven down to Virginia with her one time to see her son, who was doing some soft-time in a prison there, and they had gotten a little closer. Her boy was there for some white-collar computer crime he committed while working for a big, high-tech company in Boston.

His sister was divorced with three kids. She was quite upset that Freddy had landed in prison, his promising career all but finished before it started. Being the oldest and most promising of the lot, she had expected so much from him. Zeiggie was playing in Reid's musical at the time and at the height of his career. He was something of a family role model, and it was hoped his visit would have a positive influence on his nephew's future. Freddy, however, didn't seem to care much for his Uncle Zeiggie's kind of music, and did nothing but brag about his exploits the whole time, saying how he could hack into any computer there was.

Zeiggie hadn't kept in touch with his sister, especially since his own divorce. Now he wondered if his nephew, Freddy, still worked with computers. His first impulse was to call his sister who he hadn't spoken to in over two years, but that would have been awkward at best, especially asking her son's whereabouts for some job he couldn't really explain. No, that wouldn't work at all. Instead, he called his cousin Shirley, who had kept in touch with him over the years, and who he had always liked.

"Hi, Shirl," he said when she answered the phone. "It's Lenny."

"Lenny, how have you been?" answered his first and favorite cousin. "I haven't heard from you in ages, although I must say, I've been hearing plenty about you. I've been meaning to call you. How did you get mixed up in all this David Reid business?"

"I'll have to tell you about it sometime," said Zeiggie, not wanting to talk about it even though it was the reason for his call, "maybe over some of your fried chicken and gravy."

"You know you're invited over any time," replied his cousin. "We'd love to see you. You still playing?"

"No, not recently, not even the bass, been kind of preoccupied."

"I'll say," she observed. "How you doing? Everything OK?"

"More or less, I'm keeping busy," he lied. "I'm getting by. No great shakes, but I'm doing OK. Listen, Shirl, I need to get hold of Freddy, Leona's boy. You know how I can get in touch with him?"

"Oh, poor Leona. That girl's life has been one disappointment after another, especially Freddy. He had such promise that one, with his skill with computers and all. Too bad he turned out bad. He had to go back to jail for computer theft again, hard time cause it was his second offense. He didn't have a chance after that, couldn't get a job programming computers to save his life. He's been doing odd jobs here and there. Still lives with Leona, but he's more of a burden than a help. What do you want with him?"

"I may have a job for him."

"Not with computers I hope," said his cousin.

"No, with my friend David Reid," he lied again.

"The composer who's always in the news? Didn't he disappear or something? I figure they got him stashed away somewhere for his own protection. Boy, isn't life funny. In the limelight one minute, at the top of the world, and the next, disappeared as if you never existed."

"Yes. Can you help, Shirl?"

"Sure, Lenny, anything to help poor Leona. Why don't you go over or give her a call."

"Hmm, I don't know," replied Zeiggie. "Leona and I aren't on the best of terms, and I'd just as soon she not know I'm talking to Freddy. She might get the wrong idea."

"Just what are you up to, Leonard?"

"Nothing, I just want to talk to my Nephew, if that's OK with you."

"It's OK with me, but you better talk to his mother first. Here, I'll give you the number. I think Freddy's working repairing cars down at McGuffey's Garage on the boulevard."

Zeiggie wrote it down, promised to call his cousin more often, and clicked off the phone. Instead of calling his sister, he took a bus down to Columbus Ave in the upper west side.

He showed up at the garage around lunch time and asked one of the guys standing by the lunch truck if Freddy White was there.

"He's out back working on the Ford," answered one of the men.

Zeiggie walked to the rear of the garage and found a pair of denim-covered legs sticking out from beneath an old, gray Ford station wagon, which sat propped up on a couple of jacks.

"Do you still think you can hack any computer on earth?" said Zeiggie.

A body materialized suddenly, as Freddy slid himself out from beneath the car in one fluid motion.

"Uncle Leonard!" said Zeiggie's nephew. "You're just about the last person I expected to see. What are you doing here? Have you seen mom?"

"Hi, Freddy. How you doin'? It's been awhile. Good to see you. No, I haven't seen your mom. It's you I been meaning to talk to."

"You still fiddling?" asked Freddy, wiping his hands on an oily rag and extending the right one to shake his uncle's.

"No, not lately. I guess you could say I'm retired."

"I heard about your trouble there. I flipped out hearing your name on the news. I told everybody, that's my Uncle Leonard."

"Well, I wouldn't go around braggin' that you know me, might not be too good for your reputation."

"I don't know if you're aware, but I don't have much of a reputation. If I had, I wouldn't be fixing junk heaps for these jerks, for the scraps they pay me. Mom got me this job. She said if I didn't keep this one she'd throw me out on the streets."

"Times tough?" asked Zeiggie.

"That ain't the beginning of it. The cops are on my ass all the time. I can't spit without being hassled. Every time some smart-assed punk hacks a computer they haul me in for questioning."

"Hmm, that's too bad. You want to get a cup of coffee? I want to talk to you about something."

"Sure, OK," replied Zeiggie's nephew. "I could use a break."

Fifteen minutes later they were sitting in a diner a few blocks down the boulevard, Zeiggie telling his story.

"So you think he's in Witness Protection?"

"It makes sense, don't it?" said Zeiggie. "Mark, that's the guy who was trying to poison David, he's confessed and is trying to help now. He told me David was being protected by the FBI until the person trying to kill him is apprehended."

"What do you want to find this David Reid dude for?"

"I want to help him. After what happened to him he needs someone to watch his back."

"What, you don't trust the FBI to do their job?" his nephew said sarcastically.

"Whoever's trying to kill David infiltrated Interpol in Europe. If they did that, they could do the same with the FBI. Besides, David has a lot to deal with, things the FBI can't help him with. He needs a friend."

"I don't know why you'd want to help this white boy after all that's happened to you on his account."

"He helped me get back on my feet. He helped me, now I want to help him."

"Is he all alone?"

"I don't know. Maybe Colleen's with him."

"Who's Colleen?" asked Zeiggie's nephew.

"She was the nurse who was taking care of him when we took off. They were getting pretty close. She may be with him, I'm not sure."

"So you want me to hack into the FBI mainframe and find your missing David Reid?"

"Yep, that's about it. I can't exactly pay you, but I may be able to get Mark to help. Of course, he can't know what we're up to."

"It might be fun, but it will be expensive, even if I do it for free. I'll need a good fast computer and a high-speed, secure wireless internet connection and modem. I can't use a free WIFI service for this, so you'll have to get me a private service provider. All of this, of course, will have to be under an assumed name. Best thing would be to buy it outright with cash. I'll give you a list of everything we'll need. With all the software it will cost you a couple thousand bucks."

"Whoa," said Zeiggie. "I didn't think it would be so expensive. Geez, I could buy a new cello with that. Why can't we just go to a computer café and use a free one?"

"Cause we're not going to just surf the web. We're going to break into the FBI mainframe, one of the most highly secure systems in the world. That takes time and finesse, and the right kind of equipment, especially if you don't want to get caught. I can't afford to leave any traces behind, not even one byte of information that can lead them to me. They're just waiting for me to mess up again."

"OK," said Zeiggie, mopping his brow. "I'll see what I can do about getting a backer."

A short time later Zeiggie was in his apartment reviewing his nephew's list of equipment and computer software. Working up his story, he decided to give Mark a call.

"Hi, Zeiggie, to what do I owe this unexpected pleasure?" said Mark on answering the phone and hearing Zeiggie's voice.

"How are things going?" asked Zeiggie. "How's the trial progressing?"

"OK, I guess. My friend Larry Talbot from the FBI is testifying. My lawyer thinks that will help our case. It all hinges on proving David is a clone and connecting the person who hired me to that fact. It's a long shot, but all we've got to go on."

"I just wish it would have turned out better. I'm concerned about David."

"He's safe. My lawyer said he's in the Federal Witness Protection program."

"Good. Look, Mark, I know this is a bad time, but you, well you said if I needed anything to ask."

"Sure, Zeiggie, what can I do for you? What do you need, buddy?"

"Well, I was thinking of getting my instruments back, buying a new cello and trying to get back playing. Maybe pick up a gig. I'll need two or three thousand dollars. I know it's a lot, but…"

"Don't worry about it, that's nothing. I can give you five grand for now and more later if you need it."

"Thanks, Mark, that's great. That's more than enough. That will keep me going until I can get a job. I'll pay you back as soon as I can."

"Don't worry, Zeiggie. I'm glad to help. I can't wait to hear you play again. Just do me a favor, stick around town for awhile. I may need you."

"Don't worry, I'm not going anywhere," Zeiggie assured him.

Chapter 28

Colleen was at her wits end. She had tried everything to help and support David and he had only drifted farther away. They hardly spoke, that is when he was even around. The shack was deserted again today. She wondered if he stayed there any longer, although the food she had brought the day before was gone, and the person who owned the land said he had seen David recently. So she knew he must still be about, somewhere.

Of course, he wasn't known as David Gordon Reid to the locals. They were Mister Michael Williams and his sister Betty. Mister Williams was a wealthy American industrialist recovering from the loss of his wife and only child in a car accident. His sister Betty was doing her best to take care of him in his time of grief, but he had become a recluse. At least that part was true. The only good thing to come of it all was that if there was anybody still trying to kill David, they would have a very hard time finding him.

She was starting to regret her decision to come to Hana with him. She had never been so lonely or felt so far away from home in her life. The days of solitude and boredom were bad enough, stuck in a place where nothing happened and it rained almost every day. But the nights alone with the silence and the numberless stars was almost too much to bear. If it wasn't for the kind, elderly Japanese couple who lived in the cottage next door, and who invited her over to dinner from time to time, she would have gone absolutely bonkers.

Having nothing better to do, she drove a few miles further down the coast to the black sand beach, knowing David sometimes went there and hoping to find him, but the place was deserted.

Hana was isolated enough, but at least there was always a tourist or a local fisherman about. Out here, you could sit all day and not see another living soul, and the scene was so desolate it seemed like a place before time. Or better yet, a place that time forgot, where the dry bones of driftwood strewn across the beach and the stunted trees dotting the rock-covered plain looked just as they had thousands of years before. Again, she could easily imagine a prehistoric creature appearing around the next rocky outcropping.

She stood on the edge of the beach, where it dropped steeply several feet to the surf below as if scooped out by a steam shovel, looking out at the Big Island across the channel. Suddenly, the water, which had been low, began to rise, and kept rising until it was level with the ground she stood on. It didn't come rushing to shore as a normal wave, but seemed to climb in place like the earth itself was sinking before it. Soon it towered above her, a massive wall of water ten feet high. She stood transfixed, unable to move as the mound of water continued to rise before her eyes.

"Run!" a voice shouted behind her, as someone grabbed her around the waist. Before she knew what was happening, she was being carried backwards rapidly away from the shore. A moment later the wave crashed onto the beach in an avalanche of water and rock, right where she had been standing, obliterating the sand like a water cannon.

The wave surged over the beach, piling up bolder-size rocks as if they were pebbles. Then just as quickly, the giant wave rolled back out to sea, sucking sand and driftwood with it. Now she knew why the beach looked like it had been scooped out by machines. She had no doubt that if she had stayed where she was she would have been swept to her death. Looking around to see who had saved her, she saw David's bearded face staring back.

"That was close," he said, not letting her go. "You've got to be careful out here. You could have been killed and no one would have ever found you. The waves and undertow are really bad. They come thundering through the channel like mountains. See how steep and rutted the beach is. Lucky I saw you and decided to come over. I got here just in time. Never turn your back on the sea. Things can happen so fast, turn your head and you'll miss it, and off you go."

"Is that why you come to this place?" she asked, still reeling from her near accident. She clung to him like seaweed.

"No, I come here because it's so wild and beautiful. This was a holy place, you know."

"Oh, and how do you know that?" she asked, starting to relax. David took his arms from around her waist.

"There are petro-graphs nearby, ancient rock paintings, and right down the beach here is a field of stone cairns. It was a sacred place to the natives. Still is."

"So that's why there's nothing but cactus and sagebrush out here?" said Colleen unimpressed.

"You can walk miles and not see a soul. I love it."

She had to admit, despite his unkempt appearance, David looked in good shape, tanned and well-muscled, his eyes clear and bright.

"Well, I miss civilization," she replied. "I'm going stir crazy. I want to go home."

"Who's stopping you," said David, not liking her complaining.

"Are you going to live your whole life out here?"

"Maybe. What's wrong with that?"

"You can't waste your life like this, squander the great talent God gave you."

"Oh yeah, watch me," he replied, turning and walking off toward Haleakala and the setting sun.

Zeiggie had set up the computer equipment in his apartment where his nephew, Freddy, came each day at noon to work until four or five, when they took turns cooking supper. They found they enjoyed each other's company much to their mutual surprise.

He had long ago given up asking for status updates every half hour. Now he left his nephew alone and didn't ask any questions. It was all beyond him anyway. His sister's boy had to hack his way into a half dozen systems and services before he could access the FBI mainframe, stealing the encryption keys and documentation he needed on the way. With the money left over from what Mark had given him, he was able to pay Freddy for his time as well, which greatly eased things with his mother, who thought her wayward son was working as Zieggie's assistant helping to manage David Reid's affairs in his absence.

To help him bide his time waiting for his nephew to perform his magic, Zeiggie bought a used cello with the left over cash. He practiced daily, re-conditioning his fingers to press the strings firmly, slowly getting his intonation and bowing back. It would take a lot of practice to regain his chops, but it felt good to play again.

"What's that you're playing?" Freddy asked one day, after almost a week of trying to hack the FBI computers and find his uncle's friend.

"A Bach work, one of his cantata melodies," said Zeiggie, stopping and starting the piece from the beginning again. "I don't do it justice, but this is the basic idea."

"Nice melody. Sounds like you're getting back into it, Uncle Leonard."

"Oh, I got a long way to go yet, but it feels good to have a fiddle in my hands again."

"I think I've got something here for you," announced Freddy after Zeiggie played a few more bars of Bach's Cantata.

"Does the name Michael Williams mean anything to you?"

"Nope," answered Zeiggie. "Can't say that it does, why?"

"I had to hack right down to the database level. They have an Oracle system and store the data in an encrypted format. Even once you've decrypted it, you'll never see the person's real name or where they're located stored with the alias. This information is kept in other files. There's no way to cross reference these separate files unless you have the key, which is not maintained on the network. The only way to hack it is to be at the place itself, and there's no way I'm going in there. The only good thing is there aren't many people going into the system at any one time. If you have an idea of the timeframe and know something about the person like we do, you can use a process of elimination and can get a pretty good bead on things. There're only two people in the database with entry dates in the period we're looking for, a Mister and Misses James Reynolds, and this Michael Williams and his sister Betty. From the ages and descriptions, I'd say Michael Williams is your David Reid. The sister must be this Colleen you mentioned."

"You said the location is kept somewhere else, how do you figure that out?"

"Same process of elimination. There are dozens of locations listed, but knowing your friend, who according to the Net has become a recluse, shunning the world, and his stature and notoriety, I looked for the most remote and desolate spots. There are several of these, mostly in quiet rural areas. I made a list of the most remote addresses, then hacked the airline systems to find flights leaving Montreal, where he was staying, to any of these places within our timeframe."

"Freddy, my boy, you're a genius. Where are they?"

"Hana in Maui," said his nephew smiling. "And if you go, I want to go with you."

A few hours later Zeiggie was sitting alone in front of his TV. He had no intention of taking his nephew to Maui. He didn't even know how he was going to get there, but he had all intentions of trying.

He had thought of calling Mark again and asking for more money, but balked at the idea. Mark would certainly want to know why he needed that much money so soon, and might even figure out what he was up to. He didn't have many other options, however, and was about to pick up the phone and call David's ex-manager, when it rang of its own accord. He flipped it open and said hello.

239

"Hello, Mister Ziegler," said the caller. "You don't know me, but I'm an old teacher of David Reid's. I talked to him awhile ago, just before the debut of his masterpiece, before all this nonsense started. He mentioned your name. He was my protégé you know, and I care very much about him. He said you were helping him. I was wondering if you knew how to get in touch with him. I am concerned about his well-being and have been trying to locate him for some time. I didn't know who to turn to, who I could trust with all that's going on, but he said you were a friend and from your actions I know you have his best interests at heart, like me. I suggest we pool our resources and work together to find him. I will pay you well for your time and any expenses."

"Who did you say you were again?" asked Zeiggie, excited that his prayers were being answered by a stranger calling out of the blue.

"Alexander Shaffer from Boston," answered the man, with a slight although indistinguishable accent. "I was David's piano teacher while he was going to school here in Boston."

"Yes, Mister Shaffer," said Zeiggie, feeling a bit relieved. "David has mentioned you often. He speaks very highly of you."

"Ah, he is such a wonderful talent, but all these terrible things that have happened, and the worse things they are saying about him has upset me terribly. I want to try and help him if I can. He needs the support of his friends, and he has many, but until now we have been unable to do anything but stand by helplessly."

"I understand, Mister Shaffer," said Zeiggie. "What can I do to help?"

Larry Talbot's testimony, given behind closed doors to the judge and chief prosecutor, did much to help Mark Burn's case. He was still under indictment for the poisoning of David Reid, but because of his cooperation and the important nature of the documents he had uncovered and handed over, he had been able to stay out of jail. The fact that David was in the Federal Witness Protection program and still in danger, made any attempt to have him testify, or even ascertain the truth of Mark's earthshaking disclosure, impossible, at least for the time being. Still, Mark was concerned. He knew the resources and the cunning of his ex-employer and that he was utterly ruthless. The knowledge that this person had disappeared and was still out there after David made him distinctly uncomfortable. There was nothing he could do, however. They had to find Hohner.

240

"If the NSA can't find him," said the FBI chief. "Then no one can."

"He can't just disappear like that, can he?" asked Mark, knowing perfectly well anything was possible with enough money and cunning.

"If he doesn't use a bank card, or cell phone, or call any one of a dozen numbers, or mention any one of a few hundred words and phrases; if he keeps a low profile and knows what he's doing, then yeah. A person can drop off the face of the earth for awhile. It's a big place, but sooner or later he's got to pop up, and when he does, no matter where he is, we'll spot him."

"It may be too late by then," said Mark. "David could be dead."

"You didn't seem to care about that when you tried to poison him," replied the FBI man, not forgetting how his friend had lied to him and had used their friendship to screen his true activities. It had almost ruined his faith in human nature, not to mention their friendship. Despite his occupation, his belief that people were basically good was still strong, probably a result of his strict Roman Catholic upbringing. It was something they had in common, and there was something about the feisty Scotsman he liked. The big, soft heart behind all the tough bluster would only take him so far, however. He didn't like being lied to. They had never talked about it.

Mark didn't answer immediately, but put his head down and looked up sadly.

"I'm sorry for that, Larry. I really am. I would have done almost anything to get out of prison. The job seemed harmless enough in the beginning. Just work myself into David's confidence, into a position of trust."

"You were hired to steal from him," said Talbot angrily.

"But I didn't. I didn't steal a dime."

"You followed orders and you got paid for it."

Again Mark didn't answer.

"The fact is," he said finally. "I didn't steal anything from David or his business, but I did follow orders like you said. I did attempt to blind him, but only temporarily, only enough to incapacitate him. They assured me no real harm would come to him."

"So the plan to was take over his businesses, keep him working so you and your employer could reap the huge benefits."

"Something like that," admitted Mark, shamefully. "I said as much in court."

"You should be serving time you know."

241

"I know, Larry, but right now I can do much more for you out of jail than I can in. You need me."

"Oh, and why is that? Except for a good story now and then, I'm not sure what for."

"Because I've talked to this guy, I know his voice. I've been doing business with him for over two years. I know how he thinks. He's after more than David's money. He wanted to control him, to own him. Zeiggie thinks it's because David is a clone of Bach and Hohner hates Bach. It's a hate crime. It sounds crazy I know, but you have to admit, it's the only crazy thing that makes sense in this whole insane mess."

"I'm more apt to think it's because, like you said at the grand jury, he probably funded all John Reid's and your father's research, and now he wants to cash in."

"Yeah, I thought so at first, but my father's notes don't mention it. They imply Mann put up the money, Bach's ancestor. He was rich enough. There was no need for him to get funding elsewhere. From the sound of it, Felix Mann wanted to keep all the glory for himself. He wasn't about to share it with anyone else. No, I think Hohner just wanted me to think it was the money to throw me off the track."

"My investigators told me the same thing, that there was no evidence of Hohner funding Reid's research in human cloning. Just because there's no paper trail, though, doesn't necessarily mean there's no connection. Felix Mann was murdered you know."

"Yeah, and probably by Hohner," speculated Mark. "No, it's more than money. Zeiggie mentioned this religious angle, and you know how much hatred and animosity religion can stir up."

"Amen," said Talbot.

"What if Hohner somehow finds out where David's hiding?" asked Mark, thinking out loud. "Do you have anyone there watching him?"

"Having a team of FBI bodyguards would defeat the whole purpose of the witness protection program, which is to make people disappear by making them blend in. We can't jeopardize that by stakeouts and armed patrols, but we have a good presence on the island. I think the closest agent is in Wailua on the northeast coast, just a few miles from Hana."

"One agent, forty miles from Hana? It'll take him all of three hours to get there along that single coast road through the mountains, and that's on a good day. David might as well be alone in the middle of nowhere."

"That's the idea. They don't have a cell phone, a credit card, or an ATM. He gets paid from Social Security checks made out to an assumed name."

"What if someone hacks your system?"

"That's impossible."

"Humor me, Larry, what if someone hacks the mainframe?"

"It doesn't matter," said Talbot, with confidence. "There's no way to track their old name to their assumed name in the system."

That didn't seem to make Mark feel any better.

Talbot looked over at his computer as an email flashed on his screen.

"Hmm, this is interesting," he said. "I just got a dispatch from Boston. Seems one of David's old piano teachers was killed yesterday. They think he was pushed in front of a subway train. Seems there's been a lot of that going on up there lately. Three such incidents have occurred in as many months; a grandmother standing on the platform with her groceries, a BU student from Bangladesh, and this Mister Alexander Shaffer."

"Any connection?" asked Mark, vaguely recognizing the name.

"I don't know. We have an agent investigating. It looks like a string of related murders. Maybe they have a serial subway killer out there, but no one wants to be the first to say it. I don't think there's a connection, although someone could be using current events to hide a more purposeful homicide. I don't see how it could jeopardize David Reid's situation. Has David ever mentioned this guy? Did he know him?"

Mark thought for a few minutes.

"Yes, I remember David mentioning him once or twice," he replied, finally putting an occupation to the name. "He was David's piano teacher when he first got to the States. Even though David soon outgrew him, they stayed in touch. David was thoughtful that way. He had me make sure there was a seat available for him and his wife at his last concert. But they weren't that close. They never spent time together if that's what you mean, not like a father and son thing. Shaffer would have had no knowledge of David or his whereabouts, though he might have tried to contact him like many of his old acquaintances have."

In spite of their inability to see a connection, the piano teacher's murder in Boston made them both uneasy.

Chapter 29

It was another rainy day in Hana, the sixth in a row. Here she was in a tropical paradise and Colleen was stuck on the part of the island that got more rain than her home in Ireland. She hadn't seen David in days, and had stopped bringing him food. She wasn't going to make his obstinacy easy for him. Besides, he was hardly ever at the shack and seldom ate the food she brought. Who knew, maybe he was hunting for his supper or fishing off the rocks with a harpoon. He certainly looked enough like a wild man, with his long, unkempt hair and thick, straggly beard.

She tried to fight off the depression by working on her garden when the sun was out, which was rarely, or visiting the elderly Japanese couple next door. It was lonely being in such a beautiful place with no one to share it with. Today she was sitting on her porch watching the rain bounce off the tarmac lane. The percussion of it pounding on her porch roof sounded like a hundred steel drums.

A lone car drove by and surprisingly stopped in front of the house. Cars seldom came by and never stopped. At first she was curious, but this feeling quickly gave way to alarm. She was about to go inside and lock the door when a thickset black man stepped out of the vehicle, who she instantly recognized.

"Zeiggie!" she yelled, beside herself with joy. "Zeiggie, ain't you a sight for sore eyes."

She ran over to him and hugged him in the middle of the yard in the pouring rain. She hardly noticed the older man stepping out of the passenger's seat and unfurling a large umbrella.

"Zeiggie, I can't believe it's you," she said stepping back and looking at him. "What are you doing here? How did you find us?"

"It's a long story. I was worried about David. Come on, let's get out of the rain. This is a friend of David's from Boston," he added, as they made a dash for the porch. "David's piano teacher, Mister Shaffer."

"Hi, nice to meet you," she said, extending her hand as they reached the shelter of the porch.

Zeiggie'd had qualms about leading the stranger to David, but when he met the piano teacher in his Boston apartment and got to know him, all doubts vanished. Shaffer knew things about David only

244

someone who knew him intimately during his youth would know. And when they sat down and played a piece from David's musical together, Zeiggie was convinced that the stranger was heaven sent to help him. The fact that he offered Zeiggie a job playing cello after their return made him dispense with any critical judgment he had left.

Already the rain had begun to slacken and the sun was peaking out from behind a cloud, a typical Hana day.

"Zeiggie," Collen said. "How the heck did you find us? Nobody's supposed to know we're here."

"Don't worry. We weren't followed. You couldn't have found a more out of the way place. Do you know what we had to do to get here? I have my ways though."

"What, an insider in the FBI?" she asked.

"Something like that," replied Zeiggie, not wanting to give away his nephew's secret.

"I'm sorry, but David's not here," Colleen informed them, happy to talk about David now that she had someone to confide in. She wasn't especially concerned that Zeiggie had found her, although she realized that if he could, so could others. "He doesn't live in town with me. Oh, Zeiggie, I'm so glad you're here. I've been so worried about him."

"I figured he'd have some heavy soul searching to do," said Zeiggie. "I knew he'd need more than police protection."

"Oh, Zeiggie, you're a darling. I can't tell you how happy I am to see you. How did you get here?"

"Mister Shaffer helped out. He booked our tickets and the hotel, rented the car. I couldn't have done it without him."

"Oh, it was nothing," said the piano teacher. "I was glad to help."

"Can I get either of you anything?" asked Colleen. "Something to drink? I have ice tea and some fruit."

"Anything cold and wet would be nice," said the piano teacher.

"Yes," agreed Zeiggie, seconding the request. "It was a long drive."

As Colleen prepared some ice tea with lemon, she told them about David.

"He lives like a mountain man," she said. "Traipses about all day on the side of the volcano or along the coast looking for petro-graphs and secret grottos. You'd hardly recognize him he's let himself go so."

"I can't believe this has happened to that dear boy," said the stranger. "He has such a talent. To be shut away like this, like a wild man, is terrible."

"At least he's safe," replied Zeiggie. "That's the main thing."

"Where is David?" asked the old man. "Can we see him?"

"He was staying at a shack out past Koki Park, up the Pistani highway."

"It looks like it's clearing up," observed Zeiggie's new found friend. "Why don't we take a drive out that way and see if we can't find him. Seeing some friendly faces from his past may help. Maybe we can persuade him to come back with us."

That sounded like a good plan to everyone. They finished their drinks and headed up the coastal road in Colleen's station wagon. As they drove, the sun burned away the clouds hugging the rugged coastline.

They reached David's shack late in the day. It was deserted, but there was evidence he had been there recently.

"Look's like we just missed him," said Zeiggie, looking around and finding a note tacked to the wall near the door. "It's for you."

He handed the note to Colleen.

"He wanted me to wait here for him if I came by," she told them reading it. "Says he'll be back around supper time. It's about that time now."

She stepped out the back door and peered down the sloping field to the sea, putting her hand over her eyes to shield them from the bright reflection off the water. "He's not out here," she observed.

They strolled by the side of the old cabin and out through the tall front hedge to the road. The volcano loomed in front of them like a giant wave of earth, 10,000 feet high and three times as long, covered with pale-green grass and stunted trees. Between it and the ocean stretched a broad, windswept plain dotted with short shrubs and low bushes. Not far away in the distance they could see a lone figure walking toward them along the road.

"Who's that?" asked Zeiggie, noticing the man. "Is that David?"

"I think so," said Colleen. "Only cowboys on horses or locals in their pickups out here, nobody fool enough to hike in the middle of nowhere all alone but my David."

They both looked back at Mister Shaffer smiling. The smiles froze on their faces. The friendly piano teacher was standing there pointing a Luger at them.

"OK, you two," he said. "Hold it. Back into the cabin, quickly. Now, move!"

He spoke with a distinctive German accent, which he no longer attempted to disguise, and looked at them with such unmasked hatred that they jumped to obey his commands, clutching each other as they hurried back toward David's shack.

Colleen could hardly breathe. The unimaginable had occurred. The vague danger lurking in the distant shadows had finally materialized in the flesh and was now leering at her, holding a semi-automatic pistol at her head.

Zeiggie broke out in a cold sweat when he realized the danger he had put them in, his heart beating like a tympani. He couldn't believe he had been tricked, that he had brought David's killer right to his doorstep. As he neared the door, he glanced back to see David only a few hundred yards away. He could have kicked himself for his stupidity. Was his careless obsession to find his friend going to get them all killed? No, not if there was a breath left in his body, he wasn't going to let that happen.

As they were about to enter the house, he caught their captor glancing back at the approaching figure. As he did, Zeiggie did a quick back-step and threw a thrusting kick at him.

He had studied karate in the service, nothing serious, but enough to learn a few kicks. Even a cello player had to know how to defend himself if he was a black man in the hood. His kick was not well aimed and didn't have much power, but it was enough to knock the man back and off balance, almost making him drop the gun. Zeiggie made a grab for it. It went off with a loud bang.

David Reid had been doing a lot of thinking these past few weeks, wandering alone on the far side of Haleakala, between the volcano and the jagged eastern coast of Maui. The words of his father, John Reid, and his mother, Mary, and his many teachers and mentors, echoed in his mind. His life flashed before him in a hundred small vignettes, scenes of great success and stunning failures, disastrous marriages and fulfilled dreams. Was he human or something else, some experimental parody of a man spawned in the demented womb of science? He didn't know, but walking among the ancient hand-paintings of a race that had vanished long ago and seeing their stone monuments on the windswept, desolate shore, the insignificance of his life struck him like a slap in the face, and woke him to the truth that it didn't matter. Life

247

was life, a bubbling urge of creation that would sprout and reach toward the light in any way it could. It made no difference if he came from a test tube or a mother's womb. He had feelings and a mind. He could think and reach for the infinite. That was the measure of all things he realized, the reason for his mind, the purpose of his self-conscious being, to know the inestimable 'I Am' and to express that knowledge in his music. Nothing else mattered.

He cried and he laughed. He yelled it a thousands times into the solitude, "Thank you! Thank you! Thank you!" He was healed of his pain and suffering, to suffer again until he was no more, just like every other sentient being in the universe, just like every other human since the beginning of time.

He saw the moon and the starlit sky behind the shadow shrouded mountain, and in his insignificance became part of it, one with the immensity of the universe and its meaning. He moved as if he walked on air. All sensation left him except the awareness of his unity with the vast expanse of creation, a design he was as much a part of as any other breathing, feeling, thinking, self-reflecting living thing, and he felt whole again. He couldn't wait to get back to Colleen.

He saw her station wagon parked by the road, and thanked his lucky stars she had come. Maybe this time it would be different. Perhaps a clone could have children after all, he'd have to see, but he knew this was the woman he wanted to spend the rest of his life with, if she would have him. Then he saw the others. Who were they? Moments later, as he was almost at the shack, he heard the gun shot.

He stopped abruptly, for there could be no mistaking the loud pop of a high-powered handgun. Who had been there with her? There had been two of them. A dark looking man about his own size, and a second man standing further off the road. The first one reminded him of Zeiggie, and he had started walking faster at the thought, until they disappeared behind the hedge and he heard the shot.

He waited, but there was no other sound except the distant crashing of the waves along the rocks below. His mind was working in allegro time, mincing all the information his brain and senses could gather. Had he been found? Had the person who had been trying to kill him all this time finally found him? Was that Zeiggie? Had Colleen been shot? With these thoughts bombarding his brain, he began running toward the house. Before he got far, a man emerged from the high hedge surrounding the shack, and began running up the road after him. He was tall and slim and ran well, and he was carrying a gun.

David turned and ran back up the Pistani road as fast as he could, thinking of his options, of where he could best elude his pursuer. A shot rang out and he instinctively ducked, but if the bullet came close to him he never knew. The sound gave wings to his feet.

He found himself headed down the road, hugging the coast, toward the black sand beach. There were cut-offs and switchbacks between the many sandstone outcroppings and rocks along the highway and below that gave him hope of a hiding place. Anything was better than the wide open spaces between the volcano and the sea.

He was at a point where the road swept around a high embankment with gullies running through it down to the sea. As he rounded a bend in the highway, he glanced behind him. Seeing no one, he made a sharp turn behind a tree to the left and onto a partly hidden grassy path between the rocks. Stopping to catch his breath, he took a peek around the sandstone outcropping. Seeing no one, he continued running a short way down the grassy slope to where the path turned sharply to the left again, to run further down the cliff side and out of sight. He stopped, trying to decide what to do.

It would be dark soon. That would help. With any luck, whoever was pursuing him would run past the opening and he could double back to help Colleen. But that risked keeping an eye on the road and being seen himself. The path he was on led down to the black sand beach in a roundabout way. He decided to continue to the beach, hoping he could hide there until dark and then cut back. Once it was dark, he reasoned, he would have a better chance of eluding whoever was after him. The thought that Colleen could be hurt, drove him to distraction and made it hard to stick resolutely to any plan.

Soon he found himself at the black sand beach. Looking around for a hiding place, he saw only piles of driftwood and small boulders thrown up by the waves, not much to conceal himself. Once it was darker perhaps he could hide among the many crevices in the rocky cliff side and sandstone hills, but in the light of the waning day he would be spotted easily, even if he had been wearing camouflage instead of a loud Hawaiian shirt and white cut-offs.

He waited, crouching behind a large boulder that had been there since the beach was formed, watching the path behind and the main entrance a few yards in front of him, approached down a narrow dirt track just large enough for a jeep.

Looking up after having glanced behind him, he was startled to see a man coming around a large bush near the entrance to the beach. The man noticed him at the same time.

With nowhere to go, David made a mad dash toward the water. His pursuer caught him halfway across the beach, where the hard-packed black sand swept steeply down to the churning sea only a dozen feet below.

"Stop where you are," ordered the man with a German accent. Stopping dead in his tracks, David turned around to face his pursuer, putting his hands up. He was standing with shoulder to the sea, which he could just make out below them. The man facing him and pointing a large 9mm Luger in his direction was a complete stranger.

"Who are you? What do you want?" yelled David, in a rather high-pitched voice, edged with terror, which he hardly recognized and didn't much like.

"I have been waiting a long time for this, Herr Bach," said the stranger with the gun.

"What, what are you talking about?" asked David Reid.

"Oh, don't try to deny it, Mister Reid," replied the man. "You are the clone of J.S. Bach, as the whole world knows. Don't try to deny it. Do you think the likes of you was going be suffered to live among us?"

"Who are you? What in God's name are you talking about?"

"Do not dare to utter His name you spawn of the devil. But let me introduce myself, Herr Bach. I am Count Ernst Hohner, son of Margaret Hohner, youngest daughter of the late Count Frederick William Ernesti. Does that name ring a bell, Herr Bach?"

"You're crazy," said David, recognizing the name from his music history, Bach's great arch-nemesis, the one Zeiggie had been raving about. Here was one of his distant ancestors coming out of the mists of time to haunt him. He could hardly believe what he was hearing, except that the barrel of the gun pointing at his head looked all too real. It consumed his every thought.

"Quit calling me by that name," he said. "I'm Michael Williams."

"Yes, I'm sure you are to somebody, but we both know you are David Gordon Reid, and that you are a human clone created from the DNA of Bach."

David tried to edge away, stepping to his right, but the man with the gun moved with him as they circled around each other. Hohner now stood holding the Luger at him with his back to the sea.

"Don't move or I will kill you where you stand," he said firmly. "I have sworn a sacred oath in the name of my great ancestor to stamp out your fame for all time. We've stolen and hidden your music. We hid your body for generations until that turncoat, Felix Mann, betrayed us and brought Bach's DNA to John Reid and his partner. We have denigrated your music every chance we had. Now you have the effrontery to turn up again 300 years later to stand in our very midst? Well, we have been waiting for you, Herr Bach, waiting to drive you back into the pits of hell where you belong for your blasphemous ways and sacrilegious music. You are an abomination, an apostate, who brings nothing but lies and sin into the world with your self-glorification and vain pride."

"You're crazy," repeated David. They stood close to the steep drop off where the sand ran precipitously down to the churning surf below. "You're out of your mind."

"Oh am I?" replied the man holding the gun steadily on him.

"Are you going to kill me?" David asked finally, having enough of the cat and mouse. "If so, get it over with. I'm tired of playing your games."

"No," said Hohner. "I have much bigger plans than for you to die alone where no one would ever know. No, you are going to kill yourself in front of the world and denounce your clone twin brother, you spawn of hell."

"And how do you intend to make me do that, you coward?" replied David taking a step toward the man and making him move backward and closer to the drop off. "You better kill me now."

"Before you get any ideas, Mister Reid, consider this. I have your girl and your friend, Mister Ziegler, back at the shack. I have no compunction about killing them, one by one and slowly if I have to, to get you to do what I want. Are you so eager to die that you would see your only two friends in the world die too?"

"Don't hurt them," pleaded David in resignation. "I'll do anything you say. What does it matter, I was going to kill myself anyway. That's why I left that note for Colleen."

David was lying, trying to stall for time. Maybe if this person thought he wanted to die anyway, he might get overconfident and careless, and make a mistake. It was the only chance he had.

"Good, I'm glad you came to that realization. Now let's go."

It had grown dark while they stood there, the water no longer visible against the dark, gray-black, cloud-covered sky. The man with the gun motioned in the direction he wanted David to go."

"How do I know you won't kill them anyway?" asked David, standing where he was. "Just what do you have in mind?"

"You will tell the world how you hate who you have become, what this monster John Reid has made you, the clone of an irreligious beer hall musician. How you can no longer live with the infamy of knowing who you really are. Since you seem to love publicity and to flaunt yourself on TV, we will televise the whole event."

David could not see the ocean below them, but he sensed it boiling and churning as the wind blowing up the channel from the earlier storm picked up in intensity. Some subtle shift in the atmosphere spoke of a change in the level of the water even though he could not see it, as the silent wave built into a wall of water, ten feet high and growing. Still he stood there, listening to the madman drone on about his intended suicide.

Suddenly, the water raced to shore in a foaming, rushing roar, as the unseen wave rose in front of him. The man with the gun looked back just in time to see the giant mound of water come crashing down on him from out of the darkness, a fifteen-foot wave full of driftwood and rock. David had already turned and was running as fast as he could up the beach to higher ground, where the rock outcroppings and trees at the edge of the sand offered something solid to cling to when everything was sucked back out to sea.

The water swept up around him, first to his ankles, then to his knees, then sweeping him off his feet as it swirled around his hips and waist. He fought to stay above the foaming liquid as it carried him into the rocks. He had made it far enough up the shore, however, that he was able to grab the base of a sturdy little tree and hold on as the tide washed back out, carrying everything it had deposited with it.

David clung to the tree for some time, and got up slowly, looking back across the beach to the retreating water. Another wave crashed against the steep-graded beach, throwing more rocks and driftwood on the shore. There was no sign of Count Hohner.

David made his way tentatively back toward the highway, looking across the sand as he went. The beach was empty. Nothing moved except the violent, shaking sea.

* * * * *

It had been almost a week since Mark had talked to his friend Larry Talbot of the FBI. He hadn't heard from Zeiggie since before that, and was thinking about him as he checked his phone messages that morning. To his surprise, he found a message waiting for him from the ex-cello player.

"Hi Mark," said the familiar voice. "This is Zeiggie. I have to go out of town for a few days. Thanks again for the loan. It really came in handy. I bought a new Cello and am starting to play again. Even better, I have a gig in Boston. You'll never guess who called me the other day, David's old piano teacher. David had mentioned my name and told him I played cello. He asked me to play in his orchestra. Mister Shaffer's giving me a chance to get my life back together. Talk to you soon, bye."

Mark's ears had perked up when he heard Zeiggie mention a piano teacher in Boston. He was wondering how this had come about out of the blue, when he heard the name Shaffer and almost fell out of his chair.

Since then he had been frantically trying to track Zeiggie down, but his tracks proved elusive even with the FBI's assistance. Of course, there was no gig in Boston, and Shaffer had been murdered as Mark well knew, although a man of that name bought two tickets to LA from Logan, with the one and only Leonard Zeigler.

Mark was on the next plane to Los Angeles with his FBI friend, Larry Talbot. From there they would follow the trail and take a connecting flight to Hawaii.

"I've called ahead to Honolulu," said the FBI chief, as they sat waiting for their flight to take off. "One of my men will meet us at the airport. We can charter a flight from there directly to Hana on Maui. There's a small airport close to the town. It will cut hours off our travel time. We can rent a car there. We'll be in Hana a half hour after we land. There's no doubt they're headed there."

"Great," replied Mark, buckling in for the six hour flight. "I just hope we get there in time."

The flight to Hawaii was excruciatingly slow, even on a supersonic jumbo jet, as the plane bucked a fierce headwind the whole distance. Mark was wired with too much coffee, his nerves frazzled from lack of sleep and too many worries.

"Relax," suggested Talbot, used to this type of stress, where hours of tedious waiting were interrupted by brief spurts of adrenalin-pumping excitement. "We have a long ride yet. Why don't you try to relax and get some rest."

"How can I relax when I know Zeiggie is on his way to see David with a killer as his traveling companion?"

"My man in Weilua is in Hana by now," Talbot assured him. "He can keep an eye on things until we get there. He's been warned. He has a description and a picture of Hohner. Reid will be OK."

"I hope so," replied Mark, who still wasn't able to relax, until Talbot gave him a small pill that knocked him out like a first time mixed-martial arts fighter for the rest of the flight.

He was groggy as he boarded the small plane to Maui, after a short stopover in Honolulu, where they grabbed a quick breakfast. He managed to stay awake for the brief, half-hour inter-island flight by drinking cups of black coffee the whole way. The Hana airport was deserted, although it was a nice, bright sunny morning, the first in days.

Talbot's man, who had been watching David's house all evening, met them at the airport with his all-terrain vehicle, and reported no one had been at the cottage all night.

"There's a strange car parked in front of the place," the agent informed them as they drove to David's dwelling in Hana. "It's a rental, leased to Alexander Shaffer."

"That's the murdered guy in Boston!" shouted Mark. "He's here!"

"That doesn't mean he's found David yet," said Talbot. "They could be anywhere."

After talking to the old Japanese couple next door and learning of his hideaway down the coastal highway, they jumped in the agent's vehicle and hurried up the road.

They passed Kiki Point, where tourists gathered at the Seven Sacred Pools, taking advantage of the rare sunshine despite the early hour. As Mark and Talbot traveled further south along the east coast of the island, they were struck by the rugged shoreline, populated with exotic rock formations and empty black sand beaches. The volcano towered on their right, filling their sight at all times, its desolate plain of cactus and sage brush sweeping down to the sea.

"This must be the place," observed the agent as they passed a low abandoned-looking shack with a white Ford station wagon parked in front.

They pulled to a stop and got out, the FBI men with their service revolvers drawn and at the ready. Entering the house, they soon found

David and Colleen tending to a wounded Zeiggie, who had been shot in the arm.

"Help him," cried Colleen as soon as she saw the FBI men. "He's been shot."

They helped Colleen patch up Zeiggie and called for a medevac helicopter to fly him out and to a hospital in Honolulu.

"What happened?" asked Talbot, after Zeiggie was safely on his way. David and Mark stared at each other silently, neither having seen the other since David's supposed kidnapping, neither knowing what to say.

Colleen jumped in, describing events.

"Zieggie showed up with another person who he said he was a friend of David's. When the man saw David coming he pulled a gun on us and put us in the shack. Zeiggie tried to grab the gun and he shot him. Then he tied us up and ran after David. I don't know what happened after that."

"I was coming back from a long hike," explained David. "I saw Colleen's car and the two strangers. I was wondering who they were and was only a few hundred feet away when I heard a shot. I stopped and waited, not knowing what to make of it. Then this guy came out with a gun. I was terribly worried about Colleen, but there was nothing I could do. I ran back down the road to the cliffs and tried to hide in there. He cornered me at the black sand beach, the place I found you that time," he said, turning to Colleen.

"He was crazy," continued David, looking back at the FBI man, "some descendent of one of Bach's enemies, I guess, sworn to avenge his ancestor. He thought I was some sort of anti-Christ or something. He was nuts. He was going to make me commit suicide in front of millions of people on TV. He threatened to kill Colleen and Zeiggie if I didn't do what he said. We were standing on the beach."

He turned to Colleen again.

"It was dark and I couldn't see, but I sensed a big wave forming out in the channel. He was holding his gun on me with his back to the ocean. By the time he heard the wave behind him it was too late. I just managed to get far enough up the shore to survive, but when I looked back he was gone. I'm afraid he was swept to sea."

"Thank God," said Colleen, relieved.

"That's a good thing," agreed Talbot. "But it's a shame we couldn't have questioned him. He's responsible for several murders that we know of and I wonder how many more."

"I doubt you would have gotten much information out of him," observed Mark. "Like David said, he was crazy."

"Will Zeiggie be all right?" asked David, sorry the one person who had tried so much to help him had been hurt because of it once again.

"Yeah, he'll be OK," Talbot assured him. "It was a clean wound, went right through. No bone shattered or arteries hit or anything. He should have pretty near normal use of the arm. He was lucky."

David and Mark looked at each other.

"What are you doing here?" David demanded finally. "Haven't you caused enough trouble?"

"I'm sorry for all that, David, I really am," replied Mark. "You have to believe me."

"You're the one who tried to poison David," observed Colleen, giving him a piece of her mind as well. "You were trying to take all his money. You worked for this guy."

"I know," admitted Mark again, dejected, even though David was now safe. "There's nothing I can say to atone for what I've done. The main thing is you're safe."

"Mister Burns here has been cooperating with us on the apprehension of this Count Hohner, the man who was trying to kill you," Talbot informed them. "Without his and your friend Mister Zeigler's help, we never would have found out who this guy was. Mister Burns came forward and jeopardized his own future to help you."

"Oh, yeah, and how's that?" replied David with some bitterness. "By telling the world I'm a freaking clone? What the hell's that about, Mark? Where do you get off? You did it to save your own skin, which is the only thing you care about. You don't give a crap about anybody else."

"That's not true, or at least not the last part," answered Mark. "I did testify to save my own skin, at least at first, but after I found out the truth I knew what I had to do. I had to expose him, lay open his dark, deep secrets, which have been kept concealed all these years. The only way I could save you was to smoke Hohner out and throw the light of day on the maggot. It worked. It's all true, I am a self-serving bastard. Even when I was pretending to be your friend, I was just taking care of myself. I admit it and am deeply sorry, though it may take me a lifetime to make it up to you."

"You should be in prison," said David. "And I'm going to do everything I can to make sure you end up there."

"I'm sorry you feel that way," Mark replied. "I can't say I blame you, but I care about you more deeply than you could possibly know."

"Oh and why is that?" asked David, not knowing what to believe. He only knew he didn't like this person very much, and resolved not to have anything more to do with him.

"I found something else in our fathers' notebooks, something I didn't disclose to anyone until now. There were many samples of Bach's DNA in the tissues brought to them by Felix Mann, enough for several clones. A second modified cell from the samples was inserted into the womb of another local woman who gave birth to a child a few weeks before you were born. Unfortunately, the child was premature and almost died, weighing less than seven pounds at birth. The host mother was Missus Margaret Burns, my mother. I'm your twin brother." David stood looking at Mark, shaking his head, still not knowing what to believe.

He thanked the FBI agents for all their help, cautioning them not to trust a word Mark Burns said.

"Now if you'll excuse me," he announced. "I have a life I want to start living again."

Talbot told him they would soon be in touch to discuss any need for continuing under the witness protection program.

"Of course, you'll have to testify at some point," said the FBI chief. "But we can arrange to conduct that interview at your convenience, wherever you decide to go. I think you're safe now."

David thanked them again, and walked over to Colleen who was standing by the car. The others soon left and they were alone.

"What do you think about what Mark said?" she asked as he walked up.

"I don't know. I can't believe a word that guy says after what he did."

"He tried to help you," she said. "And you know I'm no fan of Mark Burns, but he had tears in his eyes when he saw you were OK. I don't think he's that good of an actor to fool me."

"I wouldn't put anything past him," replied David. "I don't want to talk about him. I want to talk about us. I'm sorry for the way I've been acting. I've been like a spoiled brat."

"You had a lot to contend with," said Colleen. "I understand, really, you don't have to say anything."

"Yes I do. I have to say I love you, Colleen. And I'm not just saying that because of post-stress trauma. I came to a realization while

I've been walking around on the side of the mountain. Even though the world is filled with people, it can seem a huge, lonely place if you have no one to share it with. Life may be a gift, but having someone to share it with is a prize beyond compare. That's how I feel about you. I know I've been terribly selfish these past few months, and yet you've stayed by my side. You have a heart like a lion. The closer one gets to you, the more beautiful you become. It's a beauty that will last, just like your love. You're the one I want to see every morning when I awake and every night when I go to sleep, for the rest of my life."

"Please, be my wife, Colleen. Please let me take care of you and watch over you and share my life with you. It can be in New York or Europe or anywhere. I will work and make love to you. I will make the most wonderful music for you, but as much as I love my work, I love you more. No fame, no acclaim, nothing can compare with you. And if a clone can have children, then we will have them by the dozens, and if not, we will adopt them, if that is your wish. I will be the best husband and father a woman could ever know."

Colleen looked at him, tears welling in her eyes, her heart breaking with overflowing happiness. Then she screamed.

Out of the hedge burst Count Ernst Hohner. His hair and what was left of his clothing was plastered to his face and body. He was limping and had a gash on his forehead, where he had been smashed against the rocks as the giant wave engulfed him and swept him out to sea. Only his determination and strength had saved him, that and his intense hatred of the clone, David Gordon Reid. He had somehow made it to land and managed to drag himself along the rocky shore with only one thought in mind, his anger fueling him beyond the realm of normal human stamina. In his hands he had a large, thick piece of sun-hardened driftwood, which he wielded like a two-handed sword, smashing it down on the hood of the car where only moments before David had been leaning.

Colleen screamed again and put her hands to her face in shock as Hohner swung the impromptu club at David's head a second time. He ducked and darted away to the right keeping low to avoid the blow, which whizzed by his ear. But he lost his balance and went sprawling on his face in the dirt. His attacker raised the club to strike again, when Colleen sprang on his back. Whirling around in a rage, Honner flung her against the station wagon, which she banged into, losing her hold and falling to the ground stunned. Ignoring her, the mad count turned back to the real target of his wrath.

"Die, abomination, die!" he yelled, bringing the heavy driftwood bat down at David's head as he struggled to get up.

Twisting his body at the last minute, David managed to avoid the blow, which thudded into the ground just inches from his ear. Before he had time to move, the heavy object banged down again, just missing his other ear, as he snapped his head away at the last moment. The next blow hit and broke his arm as he tried to raise it in defense. The one after that came down on his hip with a crack that sent him doubling over in pain. Colleen sat against the car still dazed, but not enough to block the horrible scene before her eyes, as Hohner raised the hard, heavy piece of driftwood over his head for a killing blow.

He yelled and with all his might brought the club down at David's head, but before the arc of the blow reached its target, a shot rang out. The heavy stick flew out of the mad count's hand as he hit the ground - dead.

Larry Talbot kept his revolver on the killer while Mark ran to David's side. The other FBI man tended to Colleen. Soon another medevac was on its way to bring David, who had a fractured arm and a broken hip, to the hospital. As they waited, David asked Mark, who never left his side, a question.

"What made you decide to come back?"

"Oh, just a hunch, a feeling I had, you know, instinct. You and me, we're bound together by something stronger than brotherly love. I knew you were in danger and I had to help you. You'd of done the same for me. We're connected whether you like it or not. I'm afraid you're stuck with me, bro. Now try to lie back and rest until the medevac gets her or Colleen will never let me hear the end of it."

"That's right," she said, coming over and putting a cold cloth on David's head. "I think you really do have a friend here."

David wasn't sure and was in too much pain to worry about it, but Colleen's warm, firm hand in his gave him peace and assurance. With her by his side he could face anything the future might bring. Then he heard the music, the sublime choral introduction to his ode to creation, his mass to life, and he knew it would be the greatest thing he would ever write.

The End

To my mother, Marie Gioiosa Bebo, who always encouraged us to follow our dream and taught us life was a gift. It is to her I owe my imagination and to her I dedicate this book.

www.ingramcontent.com/pod-product-compliance
Lightning Source LLC
Chambersburg PA
CBHW060414180626
46817CB00007B/2581